INVERCLYDE LIBRARIES

D0241290

# THE WRONG MAN

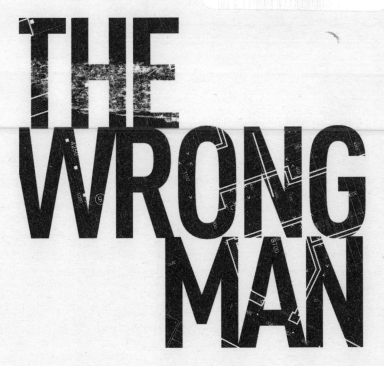

Inverclyde Libraries

34106     002938665

# THE WRONG MAN

## JASON DEAN

INVERCLYDE LIBRARIES

headline

Copyright © 2012 Jason Dean

The right of Jason Dean to be identified as the Author of
the Work has been asserted by him in accordance with the
Copyright, Designs and Patents Act 1988.

First published in 2012 by
HEADLINE PUBLISHING GROUP

1

Apart from any use permitted under UK copyright law, this publication may
only be reproduced, stored, or transmitted, in any form, or by any means,
with prior permission in writing of the publishers or, in the case of reprographic
production, in accordance with the terms of licences issued by the Copyright Licensing Agency.

This is a work of fiction. The lives of now deceased historical figures have been used
as the starting point for events within the plot, however such events are derived entirely and
absolutely from the author's imagination and bear no resemblance to real life. All characters in
this publication, with the exception of said historical figures, are fictitious and any resemblance
to real persons, living or dead, is purely coincidental.

Cataloguing in Publication Data is available from the British Library

Hardback ISBN 978 0 7553 8268 2
Trade paperback ISBN 978 0 7553 8269 9

Typeset in Adobe Garamond by Palimpsest Book Production Limited,
Falkirk, Stirlingshire

Printed and bound in Great Britain by
Clays Ltd, St Ives plc

Headline's policy is to use papers that are natural, renewable and recyclable products and made
from wood grown in sustainable forests. The logging and manufacturing processes are expected
to conform to the environmental regulations of the country of origin.

HEADLINE PUBLISHING GROUP
An Hachette UK Company
338 Euston Road
London NW1 3BH

www.headline.co.uk
www.hachette.co.uk

To my agent, Camilla Wray, and my editor, Vicki Mellor.

For their ceaseless enthusiasm, invaluable guidance, and their tireless efforts in getting this novel onto the shelves. But mostly for giving me a chance, for which I'll always be grateful.

# ONE

When James Bishop regained consciousness, he raised his head from the floor to look at the wall clock and calculated he'd been out for thirteen minutes. His next thought was that almost anything could have happened to the Brennans in that time.

Maybe everything.

Using the kitchen island to pull himself up, Bishop picked up his Glock from where it had fallen next to the refrigerator and pushed the catch on the side that released the magazine. It was still full, with a round still in the chamber. Frowning, he checked the rubble for his knife. No sign. Which made no sense at all. If anything, he figured it should have been the other way round. You don't leave your enemy with his gun unless it's for a good reason. The thought weighed on his mind, but he didn't have time to dwell on it. Not now.

He made an effort to control his breathing. Whatever he'd inhaled had left a sharp, metallic taste in the back of his throat. His head was throbbing and he still felt woozy. The attacker had come from behind, just as the rear door had blown inwards, and he'd forced the damp cloth over Bishop's mouth before he could react. Before the drug had completely invaded his system, Bishop had managed to use his knife to stab at his assailant's arm around his neck, but he hadn't had the strength to drive the blade in further before he'd blacked out.

The October light was fading now. Bishop moved to the blown-out doorframe and saw Thorpe's legs and boots sticking out of the small gazebo in the distance. *One man down, at least*, he thought. But what about Neary at the gatehouse? Chaney? Tennison? Oates? Bishop couldn't believe his whole protection team was down. Fourteen minutes had passed since he pressed the panic button, which meant the Long Island estate should have been swarming with cops by now. But everything was quiet. All he could hear was the beat of his own heart.

I

For now, he had to assume he was on his own. But he still needed to find his clients.

He turned towards the hallway, his gun leading the way. As he advanced, his rubber-soled shoes squeaked on the polished floor and he shifted his weight to his toes. At the front of the three-storey house was a large entrance foyer with a grand staircase leading up to the second floor in two graceful semicircular sweeps. When Bishop reached the end of the corridor he jammed a heel hard into the floor and waited for a moment. When no shots came he moved into the open space.

A figure dressed in black lay at the base of the left staircase, head covered by a ski mask, a stubby Heckler & Koch MP5K inches from his hand. Surrounding him was a congealing pool of blood. Bishop checked his pulse and found no sign of life. Fifteen feet away, leaning against the front doors with his legs splayed out and his chin touching his chest, was Tennison. *That makes two then*, he thought. The man was bloody but alive and Bishop could hear a faint whistling sound as he breathed.

Bishop moved quickly up the white-carpeted stairs. At the top, two passageways ran off the landing. He turned down the left-hand one and pushed open the third door on the left. Inside, an unused bedroom led to another smaller room: the safe room – a small space surrounded by seven inches of concrete. No windows. Only one entrance. No way to break in. Once the interior button was pressed, a reinforced steel fire door slammed down over the doorway. Randall and Natalie Brennan should have been inside, but the steel door had not been engaged. The room was empty.

He clenched his jaw tight. *Not possible.*

At the first sign of trouble, the *first* sign, get the principals to the safe room. It had been drilled into his team enough times. He couldn't believe both father and daughter had been left exposed during the assault. Oates had been using the room to grab some shuteye, but he would have woken immediately at the sound of gunfire. Then he should have grabbed them both, brought them back here and sealed them in in less than a minute. Just like he'd been trained. Which meant he'd either screwed up big time or the hostiles had top intel. Neither option made Bishop feel any better.

He heard a faint thump from the floor above. Then a familiar creak on the metal staircase at the end of the other passageway. He ran back towards the landing, stopped and raised his Glock with both hands, his light blue eyes fixed on the exit from the right-hand corridor.

A second later, a heavy-set man dressed identically to the dead man downstairs emerged. Over his right shoulder was a large black holdall, in his right hand an MP5K. With his left he was pulling a cotton ski mask down over the bottom half of his face. On his right sleeve was a blood-smeared rip.

Bishop stepped out. 'Halt,' he said.

Instead, the man turned quickly and Bishop's reflexes and training took over. He fired three shots straight at his chest. They all hit home. The man grunted and fell backwards down the curving staircase, bouncing off the banister and landing on the floor, sprawled on his back. Almost a mirror image of his friend on the other side.

Bishop looked over the railing and waited until blood seeped through the man's clothing where the rounds had hit. He then ran down the right-hand passageway and leapt three steps at a time up the small spiral staircase. At the top, he pushed through the double doors to Brennan's office.

He almost tripped over Oates's body. The young ex-soldier lay on his back just inside the double doors, three dark stains on his unprotected chest, his light brown eyes staring sightlessly at the ceiling. His gun lay a few inches from his outstretched hand. Although he'd only been in the team eight months, Oates had been a good protection officer, the soldier in him ever alert. Yet somehow the enemy had managed to take him totally by surprise.

Bishop saw the large antique desk in front of the window was undisturbed. On it was a state-of-the-art laptop and a small silver-framed photograph of the smiling family. Directly in front of the desk, Natalie had been stripped to her waist and tied to a chair. Her body was drenched in blood from the neck down and the carpet underneath was soaked. Bishop could see straight away she was dead.

On Bishop's right the selection of photos on what Brennan smugly called his Wall of Fame watched him. At his left were two floor-to-ceiling bookcases. One had been pushed aside to reveal a thick steel door, partly open. That was when Bishop knew the attackers were professionals. Until that moment he himself had had no knowledge of any secret vault.

Close to the door, the silver-haired Randall Brennan lay stretched out on his side, his eyes open under a creased brow, his mouth slack. He looked like he was contemplating the crimson pattern on the carpet in front of him, except that his throat had been cut.

Bishop turned and stepped over to Natalie. Her throat had also been cut and her head had rolled to the side, her long black hair obscuring her features. Countless lacerations haphazardly criss-crossed her torso and breasts above a deep stab wound in her flat stomach.

Crouching at her side, Bishop looked up at her open blue eyes for a long time and gently touched her cheek. The pale, blemish-free skin still felt faintly warm against his palm.

'Jesus.' Seventeen years old and her life already over.

He studied the cuts on her chest. They looked frantic, as if the killer had gone at her in a frenzy. Like you'd find in a lover's murder, not a professional hit. *What the hell was going on?* Bishop turned to check Randall Brennan for similar cuts and saw his missing knife lying next to the body.

Then a voice said, 'What you doing in here, boss?'

Bishop rose and slowly turned round, his gun at his side. Sam Chaney stared at him. He was standing with his back against the doorframe, his left arm lying useless against his side and a steady flow of blood dripping onto the carpet from a wound in his right thigh. His Glock was aimed at Bishop, the barrel steady. Resting his head against the frame he glanced at the knife next to Brennan's body and said, 'The one who took me out was carrying a big black bag that was kinda hard to miss. So where is he?'

'Christ, Chaney. Stand down. He's at the bottom of the stairs with three in his chest.'

A head shake. 'There's only one dead perp down there and there sure as hell ain't any bag with him. Where were you? You know, while the rest of us were getting our asses shot off?' He nodded at the bodies on the floor and coughed once. 'While all this was going on?'

Bishop studied him as sirens sounded in the distance. Watched as Chaney's blood began to pool on the carpet and his thigh muscles started to contract. And it dawned on him why he'd been left unharmed. An inside man. A nice scapegoat for the cops.

'Maybe you should put your gun down,' Chaney said, his right hand beginning to waver slightly. 'Like right now. I don't wanna have to shoot you.'

4

'Lower your weapon, Chaney. Somebody's setting me up. Maybe you. Or have you already forgotten who's in charge?'

'The piece, Bishop. I won't tell you again.'

'You seem real quick to—' Bishop was beginning when Chaney pulled the trigger.

# TWO

### Thirty-two Months Later

Bishop opened his eyes and stared at the fluorescent light behind its steel grid in the ceiling. Then he studied the spot-welded railing of the bunk directly above him. Then back to the ceiling. Not that it made much difference. The eight-by-nine cell was hardly brimming over with visual stimulation.

There was a combo washbasin and john in one corner. A small, barred window with a brick wall for a view. Three shelves weighed down with toiletries and books. A desk built into the same wall. And a plastic stool.

Stretched out on the bunk in the prison-issue grey shirt and pants, Bishop absently scratched at his goatee before reaching down to knead the muscles around his collarbone. The facial hair was only one example of how he'd changed in the last two years and eight months. In addition, the professional Harvard haircut of his old life had grown into a shoulder-length brown mane. His naturally tanned complexion had become a distant memory too, and his six-foot-one-inch frame had filled out a little thanks to the starchy food. No prison tattoos, though, which was something.

The room's other occupant was Jorge, an overweight Latin American forty-something whose last armed robbery meant he might see daylight again in fifteen years. He sat on the stool, carefully rolling a 'Grand Central Special' from leftover butts in his improvised ashtray. He was humming to himself as he waited for his call to the visiting room, a part of the prison Bishop had only seen once in the nine hundred and seventy-three days he'd been there. At his request, his older sister, Amy, hadn't come a second time. Although he'd appreciated the thought, he didn't like her seeing him in this place. He was fairly sure she hadn't enjoyed the experience much, either. Further visits would only make things harder for both of them.

Bishop just hoped his cellmate wouldn't start talking. He usually did at some point and then Bishop had to try to block him out. But

6

humming he could live with. He'd heard it so many times it had become a sad soundtrack to his life in here. In truth, it actually helped him think, although he'd never admit that to Jorge.

The so-called evidence that had led to Bishop's arrest for the murders of Randall Brennan, Natalie Brennan and Ryan Oates had been expertly planned. Whoever set him up had spent a lot of time and effort making sure the cops didn't need to look anywhere other than at him.

In Bishop's rented Queens apartment, they found blueprints of the Brennan house on his hard drive with convenient notations marking the secret vault's location in the third-floor office. They also found over a hundred pornographic shots of Natalie Brennan that appeared to have been taken in his bedroom. Career-ending 'evidence' that had simply added further motive for Bishop's actions that night. And at the house, there'd been nothing to back up Bishop's story of his fight with the missing fourth raider or his claim that his comms and pager had been jammed. But it was the knife that really did him in.

Covered in the Brennans' blood and with Bishop's prints all over the handle, it must have seemed like a winning lottery ticket to the homicide detectives when they got the results back. Especially when forensics found enough similarities between the 9mm hollow-points in Oates and Bishop's piece to add Oates's murder to the charge sheet, too. He was just surprised they hadn't tried to pin Neary's death on him as well.

Add the three dead raiders and you were left with a body count of seven. The newspapers had loved that, of course. As far as they were concerned, seven bodies constituted a *massacre*. It might have been nine had Brennan's wife and son not been holidaying in Malibu with friends at the time. That was something to be grateful for, at least.

The timing had been perfect, too. Bishop's team, having completed their four-month rotation, had been expecting their replacement squad that very evening. The impostors had merely turned up an hour earlier with the right identification and the correct authorization codes. Everything seemed to check out. Until the shooting started.

And as for motive, a little digging into his email account brought up a cryptic message leading the cops to an offshore account in Bermuda. One opened in Bishop's name two months before which suddenly became two million dollars healthier on October 18, three days after the attack.

Tucking his free hand under his head, Bishop could see how plausible it must have all sounded to a cop unwilling to think outside the box. But most of it was just lazy. For instance, if he'd been smart enough to pull the rest off, how could he be dumb enough to leave the knife without wiping his prints off first?

His thoughts went back to the questions of 'who' and 'why'. Two little words, but the only ones that counted. And Bishop knew that without figuring out one, he would never get the other to reveal itself. He also had a feeling the 'why' was going to be easier to solve than the 'who', since everything usually came down to money and Randall Brennan had plenty of the stuff.

In this case two million had been set aside just to make Bishop look bad, an amount that would tempt any number of heist men just on its own. Which meant the vault must have held something more than that. A *lot* more. After all, Brennan must have had the vault built for a good reason. As a highly successful international arms negotiator, he must have had plenty of income lying around he couldn't afford to declare.

But Bishop wasn't about to rule out revenge as a motive, either. His team hadn't been hired as a status symbol to impress the neighbours. The family had been receiving threats. Serious threats. Brennan hadn't reached the top of his game by playing by the rules and it was entirely possible he'd made a dangerous enemy somewhere along the way. Someone who'd do anything to achieve satisfaction and was more than willing to corrupt one of RoyseCorp's men to get the job done. But that was always when Bishop hit the wall. Because why involve him?

Even if he was just a diversion, why not somebody else? There had to be a reason good enough to want him locked up for life. It would have been a lot simpler just to add him to the night's victims. And this was the part that really got him. Not everyone could set up an attack against New York's top protection firm and bank on Bishop's getting life for a triple murder charge. Which meant it came down to one of the three survivors from his team. Sam Chaney, Chris Tennison or Martin Thorpe. To influence the night's events and arrange all the evidence against him, the man needed to be there. On the spot. Without a doubt.

Along with Neary, all three had been a regular part of his team for years. Private security and close protection attracted more than its fair share of disreputable characters, so you tended to keep the ones you could trust close. Which was why Bishop insisted on handpicking his own crew when he was promoted to team leader less than a year into his RoyseCorp service. His immediate supervisor, perhaps sensing he would have walked otherwise, had consented to his wishes. Thorpe was the first to be picked, with Chaney and Neary following close behind. Tennison had just two and a half years on the team, with Oates the most recent addition.

And although he had to sometimes reproach one of them for the occasional lapse, it was never for anything serious or they'd have been out. If anything, he'd gone out of his way to understand their idiosyncrasies. Like red-headed Tennison's attitude, or Thorpe's claustrophobia, or Chaney's wandering eye when it came to little ladies in distress. So after spending his first week inside going through everything he knew about each of his men and getting nowhere, Bishop had decided that maybe he needed to look at it from their point of view.

It was possible a mild rebuke from Bishop had stuck in one of the men's craws, and grown until the idea of setting him up for murder seemed a fair revenge. Although Bishop hadn't believed this angle he'd still evaluated every job they'd done together over the past six years. Another week later he was back to square one. Nothing flagged up. And the one thing he could rely on was his power of recall.

Bishop never forgot anything. Never had. Not since school. Photographic or eidetic memory, they called it. Found in less than ten per cent of children and usually gone by the time they reach their teens. Usually, but not always. Bishop was living proof of that.

So, by day fifteen of his sentence, he'd concluded he wasn't going to find answers by concentrating on Chaney, Tennison or Thorpe. Which just left the guy he'd shot on the landing. The one who'd drugged him. Since the doctors who worked on Bishop had found no trace of any drug in his system, the cops claimed he and the raider had been working together. Which only fuelled Bishop's anger and made him even more determined to find the guy. And he knew once he found him, he'd be able to trace everything back to the source. To the Judas on his team.

And that was where Bishop had got his first small break. Just before he'd shot the man he'd caught a momentary glimpse of his lower facial features as he'd pulled down the ski mask. Cleft chin, lipless mouth, slightly sunken cheeks and long, almost patrician nose with a ridge along its centre. The image had buzzed around Bishop's brain like a mosquito and he became certain he'd seen it before. Somewhere. And not too long before the attack.

Unfortunately, a photographic memory wasn't like accessing a hard drive with everything filed neatly by category or date. The mind didn't work like that. Everything he'd seen was stored in there, but sometimes it took a while to find the right folder. In this case, it took longer than usual. Much longer. The mental torment of not being able to place the guy had actually been worse than the physical confinement. For months he'd chased the memory through his tour in the Marines, the two years spent in LA, and then the six years with RoyseCorp. But he hadn't been able to pinpoint that face. It had almost driven him crazy, until finally, six months and two days after he'd been admitted into Greenacres Medium Security Prison in the picturesque south-westerly region of Ulster County, the answer flashed before him at an unexpected moment. He'd just stood there at the urinal, mid-flow, with a dumbstruck expression on his face.

Randall Brennan's Wall of Fame. *That's* where he'd seen him.

Slotted in amongst photographs of Brennan shaking hands with politicians, heads of state, and the odd sports celebrity had been a colour shot taken at a private aircraft hangar showing Brennan with King Saleh of Yajir. On the right-hand side the tail of a small jet just made it into the frame, while a smiling Brennan and the king shook hands in the foreground, surrounded by assorted flunkies. And in the background, partly obscured by the king's bodyguards, had been a Caucasian face. Brown, wavy hair over a high forehead. Light-coloured eyes. Dark complexion. Small ears set flat against the skull. And the exact same long nose. The same sunken cheeks. Same cleft chin.

It was the man who had chloroformed him at the house. He was certain of it. The killer was someone Brennan had known or worked with before Bishop's team even entered the picture. He was the link to the traitor who set him up. All Bishop had to do was find him.

Trouble was, his next parole hearing wasn't for another twenty-seven years.

Bishop glanced over at Jorge, who was reading an old letter and blowing smoke towards the ceiling, stinking the place out even more. Amidst the constant clamour of prison life, he heard the sound of approaching footsteps and knew it was a guard without looking. They were the only ones in here with leather soles.

The footsteps came to a halt a few feet away and a voice said, 'Visitor.'

Harris, by the sound of it. One of the real mouth-breathers. Continuing to massage the spot on his clavicle where the 9mm Parabellum from Chaney's Glock had passed through, Bishop watched Jorge put down the letter and crush the cigarette remains in a cup as he prepared to rise.

'But not for you, Jorgey boy,' Harris said.

Jorge sank back onto the stool and threw a questioning look at Bishop, who frowned and swung his legs off the bunk. The short, burly guard stood outside the cell, looking down at him with his usual bored expression as he noisily chewed gum.

'Yeah, you, Bishop,' he said. 'On your feet, let's go.'

# THREE

'The courier company they're using is Bearer Logistics,' Miles Pascombe said, facing Bishop across the table in the visitors' area. 'They'll be making the delivery on September eighth. Three Sundays from now.'

Bishop sat with his arms crossed and studied the overweight, badly dressed lawyer. He was surprised at the news. And seventeen days didn't give him much time.

He leaned back in his seat and cast his eyes around the visitors' room. Most of the tables were occupied by inmates and their wives, girlfriends, relatives, kids or lawyers. Thanks to the high ceiling, the noise level almost equalled that of his cellblock.

'They give a time?' he asked.

Pascombe dipped his head briefly to look at the legal papers in front of him, his chin instantly disappearing into his neck. Bishop studied his slightly shabby grey suit and wondered if he was the guy's only client. It would explain why he was here when a simple phone call would have been sufficient. Or maybe he just felt news like this should be delivered in person.

'Says here it'll be between midnight and six a.m.,' Pascombe said, looking back up. He tilted his head slightly at Bishop's neutral expression. 'I thought you'd be pleased. We won the suit.'

'Believe me, I'm smiling on the inside,' Bishop said. 'Anything else?'

Pascombe rubbed his upper lip with a forefinger. 'Well, you're under a gag order like I guessed, but that's usual in these early settlement cases.' He frowned and said, 'What isn't usual is how quickly we got a verdict. I still can't quite believe it. I mean, in my experience these things usually go on for *years*. I was thinking five or six, maybe. Not *two*.'

Bishop stroked his beard. He'd been wondering the same thing.

Just two years since he found that weak spot in the system he'd been searching for. Followed by three weeks in the prison library going through the pitiful selection of law books to find the precedents he needed. Finding a lawyer hadn't been a problem, with Pascombe more than willing to actually file the suit and wait for his fees at the back end. He'd said he knew he was onto a winner, and he'd been proved right yesterday when the judge handed down his verdict. More important to Bishop, however, was the tiny clause he'd insisted on. The one that legally bound the defendants to notify the plaintiff immediately of the exact time and date of delivery.

'What's your take on it?' he asked as Pascombe began putting his papers back in his briefcase.

'Not sure,' the lawyer said, pausing. 'All I can think is maybe our suit caused a few ripples within the system and they wanted it wrapped up quietly.'

'Before inmates in other prisons started getting ideas.'

'Could be.'

Bishop nodded. It made as much sense as anything. He rose from his seat and said, 'Good job, anyway, counsellor. Thanks.'

Pascombe stood up as well and shook the hand Bishop held out with a grin. 'You're welcome,' he said.

Bishop gave him a final nod, then began walking towards the door. The lawyer had done his part and Bishop hoped the success gave him better paid jobs from now on. Enough to buy a new suit anyway. His thoughts then shifted to his preparations and the two weeks he had to work with. It really wasn't much time. But not impossible. It was just a challenge, that's all. Probably the first real one since he'd been in here.

# FOUR

The warden might call it a library for official purposes, but in reality it was a small, low-ceilinged room with a scant selection of books and old magazines, and few genuine visitors. Nestled in the north-east corner of the main building like a forgotten relative, the area wasn't even patrolled by the guards very much. Twice a day, they accompanied the state-appointed library supervisor to and from his private office, which took up one side of the room behind its wall of bars. The lights were on and Bishop could hear the amplified sounds of a game coming from inside. Sounded like football highlights on ESPN again. The guy was really earning his pay in there.

Four reading tables filled the space between the bookshelves and the entrance. Two were currently in use as a couple of inmates pretended to read magazines as they listened to the commentary. At the rear, in the alcove nearest the windows, Bishop stood facing a man with dreadlocks. He was an inch taller than Bishop and, at a hundred and sixty, about fifteen pounds lighter. He was slowly going through the stamp books for a second time.

'Don't talk much, do you?' Owen Falstaff said.

'What's there to talk about?' Bishop said, watching as Falstaff flicked through the prison currency. 'I told you what I need. There's the money.'

Falstaff finished counting and looked at him. 'That ain't what I meant. You got the whole population scratching their heads, you know. Folks here like to know everything 'bout everybody, but you're still a closed book even after three years. Like, this is the first time you ever called on me, and I supply *every*one in here. Even the odd Aryan, believe it or not.'

Bishop shrugged. He should have known Falstaff would be the curious type. 'So?'

'So, most of the fools in here I class as bad boys who were just itchin' for the law to slap cuffs on them. But you don't fit the profile, man. You don't be*long*.' He started tapping the stamp books against his lips.

'I had to guess, I'd say somebody screwed you over, big time. Probably someone you trusted, too.'

Bishop hid his surprise. Falstaff was a lot sharper than he looked. But then, to be a successful hustler he probably had to be. 'All right,' Bishop said, 'let's get it over with.'

'Get what over with?'

'You're building up to a question. I can feel it.'

After a few moments chewing his inner cheek, Falstaff said, 'Okay, I admit I got curious. A while back one of my sources got me a copy of the trial transcript and the thing kept me up all night. Man, all that evidence they used on you . . .' Placing the books in his shirt pocket, he leaned forward and used his fingers to count off all the points Bishop knew by heart. The knife. The blueprints. The offshore account. Natalie Brennan. The bullets in Oates.

Bishop only half listened. In his defence, he could have told Falstaff how ballistic fingerprinting was hardly an exact science, especially when it came to the problematic polygonal rifling of a Glock. Or how hard it was to convince a jury you'd been unconscious for the entire duration of the assault when doctors had failed to find any trace of a drug in your system. But he just waited for Falstaff to finish and said, 'So?'

'A hell of a lot of work just to get you sent up the river, ain't it? Expensive, too.'

Bishop sighed. This wasn't exactly news to him. Although it *was* the first time he'd heard it come from somebody else's mouth. 'That your question?'

'Uh, uh. My question is, just what did Brennan *keep* in that vault in the first place? The Ark of the Covenant?'

Bishop shrugged, 'Hey, your guess is as good as mine.' The only thing he did know for sure was it had to be more than two million. He arched both eyebrows at Falstaff and said, 'Anything else I can help you with, or can we get back to business?'

Falstaff grinned and tapped his shirt pocket. 'I believe we're good to go.'

'All right. How long?'

'Three, three and a half weeks. Maybe more. Depends on availability, you know?'

That meant another twenty-four days. At least. 'No good. That's too long.'

Falstaff shrugged. 'Hey, the Buddha's a breeze, but the other thing ain't gonna be easy, even for me. Gonna take a lot of arranging I hadn't planned on.'

And at that moment, a big, shaven-headed Aryan with a face full of hate pushed open the entrance doors and stared straight at Falstaff.

# FIVE

Out the corner of his eye, Bishop watched the two cons at the tables silently get up and walk out. He kept watching as the thug came forward and leaned against the table nearest them, his thick arms folded across his chest, sleeves rolled up to show off the tats. Up close he wasn't pretty. He had a mass of acne scars that went right down to his neck and a nose too big for his face.

Falstaff followed Bishop's stare and frowned when he saw the large man.

'I told you about my refund policy, Alvin,' he said. 'And you got what you wanted in the end.'

'I'm here about something else,' said Alvin, smiling. It wasn't a friendly smile. He finally turned to Bishop and tilted his head to indicate the rest was a private matter.

Bishop got the message. He shrugged at Falstaff and sauntered past him towards the gap between the reading tables. In Alvin's right-hand pocket he saw the irregular shape jutting out. *Shiv*, he thought, which meant the back-up would be just outside. As he passed between the reading tables he casually picked up the thick, well-thumbed copy of *GQ* left there by its previous owner and began leafing through it as he walked.

As he approached the door, Bishop raised his eyes to the two cams located in each corner ahead of him. The one covering the right half of the room still had its green indicator light on, but the other had nothing. Not even a red one. Bishop guessed Alvin had known about the camera being out of service before he'd even entered the library. For the moment, Big Brother was definitely *not* watching. At least, not where it mattered.

He pushed through the door and in the halogen light saw the pale sheen of the back-up's shaved head. His squat body was leaning against the corridor wall, and he was picking at scabs on his scalp like a chimp.

As the door swung shut behind him Bishop took several more steps, stopped and glanced at the empty hallway ahead. He remained stationary as though trying to remember something, casually rolling the magazine up in a tight tube with the squarebound spine facing outwards.

'Ya waitin' for, asswipe?' the back-up said.

Bishop turned back to the Neanderthal. His pig eyes were dull and his mouth hung open as he glared back.

'Inspiration,' Bishop said and swung the improvised bat at the man's face with his full weight behind it.

The spine smashed against the bridge of the man's nose, and as he slammed back against the wall red spray spattered onto the polished tile at his feet. He dropped to his knees with one hand on the floor for support, the other at his face as he tried to contain the blood and mucus.

Bishop looked down at his clothes to make sure nothing had sprayed on him and saw the thug placing a foot on the floor in an attempt to rise. He rolled the magazine up even tighter and took another swing, catching the guy just above the right ear. His head hit the wall with a satisfying thud. By the time his body collapsed to the floor he was unconscious, breathing noisily through his mouth.

Bishop scanned the immediate area. The short corridor leading to the refectory ahead remained empty. Monkey boy's presence must have warned off any witnesses – ironically, most inmates generally didn't want to be around when blood got spilled; it wasn't worth the grief. Bishop stood motionless for a few moments, breathing slowly. He knew he should just keep walking. Down the hallway, through the mess hall and back to his cell. He'd halved the odds for the guy; the rest was up to Falstaff. Whatever the problem was – business dispute, personality clash – it wasn't *his* problem.

Except it wasn't that clear cut. Nothing ever was. And then Bishop realized this might actually work in his favour. At least, that's the reason he gave himself as he turned and pushed back through the library door.

# SIX

Both men were still in the same alcove. Falstaff was pinned against the wall by Alvin, who had his back to Bishop. With the sounds coming from the unseen TV Bishop could make out harsh whispers, but couldn't hear the words.

Keeping to the right, he spotted a pencil under a table. He put the bloody magazine down next to an ancient crime paperback and knelt down to pick the pencil up, keeping it in his left hand.

When Bishop was about twenty feet away, Falstaff noticed him and his eyes got wider. Without turning, Alvin said, 'You don't want to be here.'

'Is that a fact?' said Bishop.

Alvin had his left hand in Falstaff's dreadlocks, forcing his head against the wall. His right held the homemade blade against Falstaff's Adam's apple. The young hustler made no noise as blood dripped steadily onto his grey shirt. Bishop could see the whites of his eyes and smell the acrid stench of sweat.

Without releasing the pressure, Alvin turned to look at Bishop. 'Need some time with your dark meat before he takes the express? If it's your roll you're worried about I'll send it to you when I'm done.' He grinned. 'If I remember.'

Bishop said, 'You're already done.' He briefly considered telling him to drop the weapon, but why waste valuable breath?

'Tough baby,' Alvin said and moved his hand down from Falstaff's hair to cover his mouth before kneeing him in the groin. As Falstaff silently collapsed to the floor, Alvin turned with his right arm extended to display two inches of jagged mirror.

He reduced the space between them and began circling Bishop. 'Just stay right there, black boy,' he said over his shoulder. 'We're still gonna have our fun once I've finished with blue-eyes here.'

In response, Bishop crouched with his empty right hand raised towards

19

Alvin and mirrored the man's movements so only his right side was exposed at any time. Alvin suddenly ducked forward and gave a playful jab to test his reactions and Bishop jerked back with a look of fake surprise on his face.

The Aryan's smile became broad r as he continued to circle, pleased with his own swiftness. That was fine. Bishop had been in enough knife fights to know that overconfidence in an enemy should always be encouraged.

As they shuffled around each other, Bishop studied Alvin's right shoulder muscle. He took three or four steps to match his opponent's and saw the deltoid tense. He jerked back at the exact instant Alvin's arm shot out and almost smiled. Then he saw the shoulder begin to twitch again and took another step back as Alvin lunged forward and missed his face again by inches.

The Aryan's grin faltered. 'Bad baby,' he said. 'No dessert for you.'

Bishop remained silent as he awaited his cue. This was already taking too long.

Ten more seconds passed as they circled, each waiting for the other to make his play. With every movement their rubber soles squeaked on the polished tile. Twenty seconds. *Come on*, urged Bishop. *Come on.* Thirty seconds. Then he saw the deltoid tighten for the third and last time.

A millisecond before Alvin thrust his arm forward Bishop dropped his left shoulder, moving his head out of the danger area. He aimed a side kick straight at Alvin's armpit. Alvin saw it coming and began to swerve his body and Bishop's right foot struck the edge of his ribcage instead. The Aryan staggered back two steps and Bishop immediately darted forward. He dodged the outstretched arm and gripped Alvin's shirt, using his right foot to connect with Alvin's left ankle and sweep his leg out from under him. As Alvin lost his balance, Bishop used the power in his hips and threw the bigger man to the floor in one fluid movement.

Bishop came down with him, used his right hand to grab hold of the man's throat and crunched his knee painfully into Alvin's knife arm, trapping it. Tightening his grip on the pencil in his left, Bishop was about to thrust it towards Alvin's shoulder when Alvin's free hand slammed into his throat with the force of a sledgehammer. As Bishop gagged, he felt Alvin's fingers clasp the wrist and start to turn it inwards.

Instead of increasing the pressure, Bishop let the arm go slack. When the pencil tip was pointing towards his face, he relaxed his grip slightly and the shaft came out the other end instead, the blunt end now protruding from his clenched fist like a dagger. He then ground his knee further into Alvin's wounded arm until he heard something snap and the man's grip on him eased. Bishop shook his hand free and immediately plunged the blunt end of the pencil down into Alvin's face. Towards the area where Alvin's cheek would have been if he hadn't turned his head towards the snapping sound.

It pierced Alvin's left eye instead.

The eyeball immediately collapsed in on itself and blood and dark tissue spurted from the wound. Bishop clamped his other hand over Alvin's mouth to stifle the man's animal cries and adjusted his position to avoid the blood. Alvin's movements became frenzied and Bishop took his hands away, grabbed the man's head by the ears and slammed it against the floor. The struggling immediately stopped as the Aryan lost consciousness, blood pooling around his head like a red halo.

Bishop placed his fingers against Alvin's artery to check for a pulse. Still alive. He was trying to decide whether that was good or bad when a shaky voice from behind him said, 'Whoa.'

Bishop got to his feet and looked down at Alvin, frowning as he thought through the pros and cons of leaving him and the one outside alive. After a moment, he decided to go with the lesser of two evils.

'What now, man?' asked Falstaff.

Bishop turned to see him raising himself up against the wall, still in pain. 'You say, "Two weeks, maybe less," and then you leave,' he said.

'Two weeks it is.' The younger man tried to smile and failed. 'Hey, maybe less.'

Bishop nodded. 'So get going.' After a few seconds Falstaff still had not moved. 'I didn't do it for you,' he said, 'so don't bother. Get moving. Keep to the left.'

Falstaff let out a long breath. 'Sure. Sure, man. I'm on it.' He stepped over the body and ran towards the door. When he pushed it open he stopped by the second man on the floor outside and looked back at Bishop briefly. Then he was gone.

Bishop studied the pencil shaft in Alvin's eye. It was shiny with blood now, obscuring any prints it might have held. He jogged over to the door and checked outside. Still nobody, but that could change at any time. Grabbing monkey boy's wrists, he dragged him back into the room and dropped him next to his partner. Then he wiped the mirror piece clean and dropped it in the pool of blood near Alvin's head.

He walked back towards the door and stopped by the magazine he'd used earlier. And people complained *GQ* had too many ads. He tore the covers off and put them in his pocket. He'd flush them in the cell later.

Glancing across at the closed librarian's door behind its barred wall of steel, he could still hear the TV through the frosted glass pane. The state employee was either asleep or still wrapped up in the football. Either option was fine with Bishop. With a final look around the room, he pushed through the door and walked back to his cellblock.

Fifteen days. He just needed to steer clear of any further trouble for the next fifteen days.

# SEVEN

Facing the exercise yard with his back to the wall of F Block, Bishop shook his head at the scene in front of him. A small guy was attempting to drive a long shot from thirty yards, only to crumple under an intercept from a huge point guard. He obviously hadn't yet worked out that pace could only get you so far. To beat them you had to be crafty.

Standing there was about as much exercise as Bishop could hope for since the library incident a fortnight before. With the contract out on him, it was too dangerous. Even a trip to the shower room had to be carefully planned in advance.

The official investigation had been a joke, as he knew it would be. As long as the status quo wasn't disrupted too much, nobody really gave a damn who got hurt. Alvin was currently on a morphine drip in the prison infirmary, but those who mattered knew what had gone down once his partner spilled his guts to the current chief of the Aryan Brotherhood. And of course, Bishop had immediately been labelled a 'target of opportunity'. Within days, he had successfully fended off two separate attacks. Nothing since then, but it was only a matter of time.

A smart man would have closed the book on the two Aryans when he had the chance, but cold-blooded executions had never really been his style. Besides, he figured two unnecessary killings here would have brought down additional security he could do without.

Raising his head to the guard turrets atop the sixty-foot-high concrete walls on this west side, Bishop saw six – no, seven – equally spaced armed guards looking down. He knew behind those walls, surrounding the entire prison, lay a concrete no-man's-land filled with cameras, motion detectors and highly trained dogs. And if, by some miracle, you made it that far you had an impenetrable twenty-foot-high barrier of razor wire to look forward to.

There was always a way, though. Always.

He took a deep breath. The effect of the sun on his face was calming and he closed his eyes, relishing the feeling. It would be so easy to let go for a few moments. Just a few. Since being sent down, Bishop's sleep patterns had been erratic at best. And it wasn't because of the noise. Eight years in the Marine Corps and you learn to sleep anywhere, under any conditions. This was different. In here, any time he began to drift off at night, his mind began working and reworking the same questions that consumed his waking hours. Keeping him awake and further feeding the anger that bubbled away at a steady boil just beneath the surface. But Bishop liked that anger. It kept him sharp and motivated. It had been a constant companion for the last two years and eight months, and he'd be taking it with him when he left. That was for damn sure.

Still, at least Falstaff had come through like he promised. Bishop reached under his collar, letting his fingers brush across the thick black band around his neck until they found the smooth, polished surface of the onyx totem hanging underneath.

He let the insults being thrown across the court wash over him as he rubbed the Buddha icon, visualizing a beer in one hand and two hours to waste at the Giants Stadium watching the Red Bulls slaughter the visitors. Yeah, the small pleasures definitely took on greater significance when they were taken away from you.

But now wasn't the time to let his guard down. Especially not with the all-important delivery tomorrow.

Exercise time was almost over. Pushing away from the wall, he moved back inside F Block before everyone else got called in, his senses on high alert as he began the long trek back to the cell. He passed small groups of cons of varying ethnic denominations, most of whom avoided him like the plague, and managed to keep a minimum of three feet between himself and the rest of the human race as he moved amongst them.

He entered the main section and looked up at the three tiers of cells. The incessant din of two hundred prisoners packed closely together filled the air like smoke. More would join once they blew the whistle in the yard. Cons walked in and out of cells, playing cards, boiling noodles, making deals and avoiding eyes. Some would be in the TV room on the second tier, catching up on the soaps. Most faces turned from him as he passed. Word had gotten around he wasn't long for this world and nobody wanted to be seen talking to a dead man.

Bishop climbed the stairs and at the top tier turned left on the catwalk with his hand on the rail. As he walked towards his two-man cell, he noticed all the other cells between the stairs and his were empty. And he didn't see any movement in the ones beyond, either.

He came to a stop outside the cubicle he'd called home for the last three years and stared at the two large men waiting for him inside.

# EIGHT

For whatever reason, a con involved in a conflict with a fellow inmate might find himself unable or unwilling to tackle the problem on his own, and that's usually where the Three Bears came in. Big Bear, Bigger Bear and Biggest Bear. For a price, they would transfer any load onto their large shoulders and bring a natural end to the conflict.

Once the Three Bears were hired, the client received three guarantees. One: the job would be completed exactly to his specifications. Two: only hands would be used. And three: it would be expensive. In a climate where few could be trusted, the Three Bears prided themselves on their professionalism, their success rate and the almost surgical precision with which they could inflict injury on a person's body. Sometimes to within an inch of that person's life. Occasionally beyond, if the rumours were true.

Two of them were currently occupying Bishop's cell.

'Meatloaf day today,' said Bigger Bear, the more effusive brother. His black hair was cropped close to the skull and he had intricate tattoos from the neck down. He lay on Bishop's lower bunk reading one of Jorge's long letters from his ex-wife. 'How was it?'

Bishop leaned against the cell door, his expression neutral, his mind refusing to let his body respond to the danger the brothers represented. First rule in here: never let anyone know what you're really thinking or feeling. But then, that had never been much of a problem for Bishop. 'How was what?' he asked.

Big Bear turned from Bishop's small, barred window and said, 'You know . . .' He raised an imaginary spoon to his mouth and made chewing motions before turning back to the window.

Bishop shrugged. 'Not hungry.'

'Wise man,' Bigger Bear said and continued reading the letter. After a few seconds Bishop saw the shadow of Biggest Bear hit the cell wall in front of him. It was substantially taller and wider than his. That made three, then. Bears always came in threes.

After a while, Bigger shook his head, put the letter down and rose from the bunk. He had three inches on Bishop and looked down at him with a puzzled frown. 'Your cellmate's seriously weird, man. Still writing puppy dog letters to a bitch who left him for another fool five years ago. What's with that?'

Bishop shrugged again. 'I don't ask.'

'Maybe you should.' Bigger Bear started tapping his forefinger repeatedly against his upper lip and looked past Bishop to Biggest Bear. Bishop felt a large hand urge him into the centre of the room.

'Me, I'm curious about everything and everyone,' Bigger said. 'Like you, man.'

'What you see is what you get.'

'What I see, I don't get. For instance, why'd you turn that white boy into a cyclops?'

'We had a slight disagreement.'

'Yeah? Over what?'

'Whose turn it was to borrow the library's only copy of *Little Women*.'

Bishop heard a throaty chuckle from behind him, but Bigger's frown remained. Big Bear had turned from the window and was watching his brother closely.

Bigger sighed. 'A comedian. Still, a contract's a contract.' He looked at a point above Bishop's head and said, 'Okay.'

A large, bronze, hairless arm encircled Bishop's neck and pulled him back like an anaconda with its prey. Instinctively, Bishop brought both hands up to the man's arm, but the other two brothers took Bishop's wrists and yanked them behind his body. Somehow Biggest Bear managed to grip both in his one massive hand. Bishop could still use his legs, but all other avenues had been closed in three quick actions.

Bigger Bear left his line of sight, presumably to act as lookout, while the smallest brother flexed his fingers several times. His face grew solemn as he let his eyes roam over Bishop's anatomy. The lower torso seemed to get the most attention. After a few moments he pursed his lips, clenched both fists into hard balls and pulled his right arm back.

Bishop felt a sudden, flaring agony in his midriff. It was unlike any pain he'd known, despite his experiences in the Corps. *Jesus Christ, that was one punch*. His stomach felt like someone had set fire to it. When he finally finished hacking, he raised his eyes to see Big Bear in the same boxer's crouch as before. This time Bishop saw the strike coming and clenched his muscles just before it made contact.

It didn't help.

He dry-heaved and the pain only intensified. He tasted blood at the back of his throat and coughed repeatedly.

When his breathing eventually returned to normal, Big Bear approached him and lifted his head up by the hair, studied his face for a few seconds. He then looked at Bigger by the doorway, still flexing his right hand. A silent exchange was taking place but Bishop had no clue as to what was being said.

Big turned back and released Bishop's hair. Then he drew back his right arm once more.

# NINE

Unlocking the door to C-1, Brendan Cook entered the room reserved for the more volatile patients. It was a smallish room. Two beds bolted to the floor, separated by a wide aisle and a barred window. He looked over at the unconscious man on the left-hand bed. A real mess this one, inside and out, with bandages covering much of his face and an IV drip protruding from each arm.

'How's it hanging, doc?'

Cook jumped at the muffled, tinny sound coming from the pocket of his white coat. He checked his diver's watch. 02.03 already and he'd forgotten to check in. Pulling the walkie-talkie out, he pressed the transmit button.

'Sore, but satisfied,' he said. 'Hey, remind me to tell you about it sometime.'

Bill Carmody's Texas twang became more pronounced. 'You got me curious now, son. We got ourselves some stuff to catch up on.'

Cook grinned down at the comatose form on the bed. 'Give you something to look forward to an hour from now.'

'Juicy, huh?'

'Maybe more than you can handle.'

Carmody chuckled. 'Okay, son. Don't let me down now.'

'Wouldn't dream of it,' Cook said and put the radio back in his pocket.

Man, he was shattered. He'd picked up a babe called Leona at a bar in Elmshire and finally managed to break free of her a couple of hours before his shift. That girl had definitely shown him a trick or two. Although she hadn't been as enthusiastic about the facial hair. Maybe he'd shave off the goatee and surprise her next time he saw her.

He bent down to check the sleeping figure's pulse and then raised the man's sole eyelid, flashing his penlight at the pupil. Still dilated. Still no reaction. Too bad, Alvin Farrell.

Alvin had been brought in two weeks before with a cracked skull and a hole where his left eye used to be. As usual, Cook hadn't bothered to check his med sheet and put him straight on morphine. It was only when the patient failed to wake up after three days that he noticed the hand-written notation at the bottom of the allergies section: *Possibility of relapse if opium-based sedatives introduced into patient's system.* He figured a coma qualified as a relapse.

Leona might have been troubled to learn of two similar incidents involving her new lover over the past year. Alvin could make it three if he didn't wake soon.

Cook shrugged. Shit happened. At least in the prison system the repercussions were minimal. Almost non-existent, in fact. The outside world forgot these dregs existed as soon as they arrived, so why lose sleep over the one or two who got lost along the way? Still smiling, he patted the patient on the shoulder and moved towards the man in the other bed.

James Bishop was still in the same position as when he'd checked an hour before. Not that he would have been able to move much even if he wanted. His right wrist was cuffed to the bed railing on Cook's orders. Guy was some kind of badass ex-bodyguard in for life on a triple murder charge, and Cook thought it best to take precautions. 'Better safe than sorry' was a good rule to live by in here.

Somebody had really gone to town on Bishop. The guards had brought him in last night, bloody and unconscious with severe bruising to the body. His stomach resembled a slab of week-old raw meat. There was probably internal haemorrhaging but Cook wasn't ready to cut him open and investigate just yet. Past experience had made him a little nervous about that sort of thing. He'd given the guy some painkillers and was content to let nature take its course for the time being. Bishop would either regain consciousness or he wouldn't. Then he'd decide.

Cook studied the man's features. He seemed about the same age as himself. Thirty-three, maybe a couple of years older, but his face had developed lines and character that Cook's lacked. His gaze travelled down to Bishop's throat. That was odd. He could swear Bishop had come in with a fat, polished Buddha around his neck. Previously, patients would only be admitted to the infirmary building once they'd been relieved of all personal items. But thanks to pressure from the prison's Muslim population, non-metallic religious totems were now permitted.

Still, maybe one of the guards had liked the look of it and taken it for himself. It wouldn't be the first time. *Spend enough time with thieves,* he thought.

Cook started to feel uncomfortable. He couldn't shake the feeling Bishop was watching him through closed eyelids. The physical similarities were beginning to unsettle him, too. As he turned for the door, he decided that maybe he *would* shave his goatee off when he got home.

He'd only taken three steps when he heard the sound of metal on metal and then an arm clamped itself around his neck and pulled him to the floor.

# TEN

'Be still, doc,' Bishop said as he gripped the man's throat and took the key chain from his hand. 'All I want to know is when the truck's arriving.'

'Truck?'

Bishop tightened his grip against Cook's weak struggles, ignoring the dull pain in his stomach. It seemed the good doctor here had been lax with the painkillers. 'Brendan, you see Alvin over there?'

Cook nodded, unable to speak.

'I hear all it took was a pencil.' He put the keys down, pulled a pen from Cook's top pocket and waved it in front of the doctor's bulging eyes. 'Get the idea? Now the truck bringing new medical equipment. Tell me what time it's due.'

Cook's left eyelid began to twitch. 'Three o'clock. Please don't.'

'Good.' He replaced the pen and searched the man's pockets, pulling out a sleek Cobra walkie-talkie from the coat and placing it on the floor along with the man's Motorola cell phone.

He felt a flare in his side and silently thanked the Three Bears. He knew the warden didn't like to take chances and had figured he'd lock this whole section down in readiness for the delivery truck's arrival. Which meant anything less than severe internal trauma would have gotten Bishop ejected back to his cell along with all the other patients who could walk. And for this to work he needed to be right here in the hospital ward. At least he'd gotten his money's worth, even if they'd thought him crazy when he'd hired them a fortnight ago. Maybe he'd send them a bonus if he ever got out of here; the Aryans' counter-offer must have been hard to resist.

Picking the lock on the cuffs hadn't taken him long. Embedded inside the stone Buddha icon had been a small metal shaft, and after some serious jiggling he'd finally popped the cuff open. He'd practised a few times and then relocked them so Cook wouldn't get suspicious. When the doctor was checking on Alvin, Bishop simply freed himself again and waited.

'You got an itemized invoice to check against the delivery, Brendan?' he asked.

'In my office upstairs.'

'Yeah? Which one?'

'Room 1–12.'

Still clutching Cook's neck, Bishop went through the man's wallet. Inside he found a driver's licence, two credit cards, an ID card from Alexford Medical, an expired Blockbuster membership card and some cash. Three twenties, four tens, and six singles. And a strip of unused rubbers in the zipped section.

He released the medic and stood up. Cook stayed where he was and massaged his neck.

'Up and at 'em, Brendan,' Bishop said. 'It's my turn to play doctor. Start with the coat and shoes.'

Still rubbing his throat, Cook pushed himself up. He struggled out of the white coat and slowly started to untie his shoelaces. Took them off and threw them to Bishop. Then he shakily unzipped his pants and slipped them off.

Bishop pulled his white hospital gown over his head, picked up the pants Cook slid over and put them on. They were short in the leg and baggy at the waist so he tightened the leather belt. Then he reached down for the bills and stuffed them in one of the pockets. He felt as though he'd earned it. Once Cook finished taking off his shirt and tie, he just stood there shivering in his briefs until Bishop threw him the gown.

As Bishop finished dressing he nodded at the walkie-talkie. 'How often do you have to check in on that thing?'

'Every hour on the hour.'

Bishop pulled on Cook's white coat and said, 'I'll need that shiny watch, too, then.' Cook huffed and undid the strap and tossed it over. 'You know what I'll do to you if you're lying,' Bishop said, attaching it to his wrist.

'I'm not stupid.'

'No, just incompetent,' Bishop said. 'So it's Carmody on duty tonight?' He'd recognized the Texas drawl coming through the walkie-talkie earlier.

'Right.'

'And he likes to hear about your lady friends, huh?'

'He'll realize you're not me.'

'He won't be able to tell the difference,' Bishop said in a pretty good imitation of Cook's whine. Pleased with the result, he added in his own voice, 'Want me to bring out the pen again?'

Cook shook his head and sighed. 'Yeah, he likes to know about my latest pick-ups.'

'So where'd you go last night?'

'707, on Elmshire.'

'Yeah, I know it,' Bishop lied. 'And what was the young lady's name at the 707?'

Cook stood there and considered his options. Then he said, 'Girl called Leona. She's got a thing for doctors.'

'I bet she has. See what you can remember when—' Bishop glanced over Cook's shoulder at the doorway. 'You hear something?'

As Cook turned to look, Bishop slammed his elbow into the side of his head. The doctor grunted once as he tripped over his own feet and slumped to the floor in a heap.

Bishop looked down at the unconscious man. 'Guess I was mistaken.'

# ELEVEN

Bishop withdrew the empty syringe from Cook's arm and dropped it in his side pocket. As he checked the man's pulse, he felt a glimmer of satisfaction. Something he hadn't felt in a long time. So far, everything was progressing as planned.

With the high propofol dosage he'd just been given, Cook would be out for the next four hours, at least. Bishop checked the time on his fancy new Citizen ProMaster. 02.43. Quarter of an hour.

He raised Cook's head from the pillow and pulled free the rubber band that held his hair in place. As he entwined it in his own, he double-checked the cuffs that held one hand to the railings. He'd attached Cook's other wrist to the bed with duct tape he'd found in the supply room, pulling the stiff white hospital sheet over the arm in case anyone glanced at the bed. He made sure it was still good and tight.

He looked briefly at the still unconscious Alvin, then left the room and locked the door with the third key he tried.

Two rows of twelve beds lay stretched out before him. Only three held patients and they weren't moving much. To his left he could see the barred gate and the electronically monitored corridor. Beyond that, another barred gate and another corridor. And then another. Every time a gate opened an electronic signal was transmitted to the surveillance room in the main building and a short, sharp alarm would go off. Like an over-sized rat maze, until you reached the front entrance to the building.

The night duty guard, Carmody, would now be sitting in his cubbyhole just outside the final corridor watching video feeds as Cook made his rounds. Bishop could only hope his likeness to Cook was good enough for closed-circuit TV. Even so, he still made sure his head was down as he passed through the ward.

To the left of the exit was another barred gate in front of a short hallway. It held no surprises as Bishop had already unlocked it to get the propofol. He'd also taken a minute to check the medical equipment room and the large storeroom in back. In the opposite corner of the ward, a steel door led to the stairs to the offices above. Bishop kept his walk casual and his head down as he approached it in full view of the three cameras covering the room. He was grateful for the minimal lighting.

Playing the role of Cook was a refreshing change after three years of monotony. All that planning and waiting was beginning to pay off. If the stakes weren't so high, he'd probably be enjoying this. But he held himself in check. There was still plenty more to do.

This was only his second visit to the infirmary but he remembered everything perfectly. The first was less than a year into his term when he and seven others had been admitted for acute food poisoning. As he lay in the drab ward, Bishop had noted the substandard conditions and the lack of proper medical equipment. And an idea had hit him. As his body recovered, his mind went into overdrive. It memorized every detail, like kids do before their SATs, and he'd returned to his cell the next day with a new kind of hunger. One that, after three weeks of poring through law books, resulted in his filing a class action suit against Greenacres for inadequate hospital conditions and supplies. At the same time, Bishop also began growing his hair long, so he'd be able to match it to Cook's when the time came. So far, it seemed to be working.

Bishop took the key chain from his pocket as he drew near the steel door. It held fourteen keys, seven of which he had yet to identify: five Yales that looked like office keys and two larger ones. Aware of the cameras watching him, he inserted one of the larger ones into the lock and turned it clockwise. Fifty–fifty chance of success. To allow himself room for error he pretended to check the soles on his shoes as he turned it.

The lock clicked and the door opened.

Ahead of him a thin hallway led to some concrete steps with a camera at the turn. As he climbed the stairs he pretended to wipe dust off his trousers, keeping his face down and his pace slow. At the top was a corridor lined with doors and lit by two dull fluorescent tubes.

The door opposite said 1-7. Bishop stepped out and turned right with his head lowered, stroking his beard. He stopped at the door which read 1-12 and tried one of the Yale keys in the lock. Nothing happened. He picked another key and tried again. The tumblers moved.

Inside the room Bishop pressed the light switch and took in Cook's small office area. One long barred window overlooked a poky room with three large file cabinets along the opposite wall. On the desk was a PC long past its sell-by date, a printer and two trays full of paperwork. He sat down and pressed the on switch for the PC.

As it warmed up he opened each of the drawers and found a flathead screwdriver tucked away at the back of the last one. *Thanks, Brendan.* In Bishop's situation you didn't ignore gifts like that and he placed it in his coat pocket. In the same drawer, he then hid the used syringe, the propofol ampule, and Cook's deactivated cell phone.

Bishop riffled through the papers in the first tray. Halfway down the second tray he found invoice sheets from Medax Medical Supplies in New Jersey. The covering letter was on the company letterhead, but the other nine stapled sheets weren't. Bishop allowed himself a small smile. He'd gotten this far through planning. But planning, no matter how intricate, often relied on gifts of opportunity. Finding the itemized invoice on plain paper was going to make things that much easier.

The screen lit up without a password prompt and Bishop found the Word icon and opened it up. He detached the staple from the corner of the sheets and read through each one. Page nine was the one he wanted and he placed it on top.

Turning back to the monitor, he opened up a new document and started typing.

# TWELVE

'Still sore, doc?'

The voice snapped Bishop's mind back into focus. He checked the diver's watch before picking up the walkie-talkie. 03.05. He took a breath and closed his eyes. The voice was William Carmody's. No, not William. Bill. But Bishop didn't know what Cook was sore about. *Expect the unexpected, like always. And then deal with it.*

He opened his eyes and pressed the transmit button. 'Hey, Bill,' he said in his new whiny voice. 'Sore?' he prompted.

'Right.'

That was a big help. So two possible meanings. But thinking about it, only one, really. 'What can I say?' he said. 'She was a wolverine.'

Carmody laughed. 'Must have been if she's got you frazzled. That's twice I've had to call first. So what was her name, son? Come on, give up some details.'

What had Cook said? 'Leona. About five-three. Ninety, ninety-five pounds. Short, dark hair and the cutest ass you ever saw.'

'Nice. From that place you like on Elmshire? What's it called?'

'Right. The 707. You not been yet, old man?'

'You're forgetting we ain't all young, free and single, doc. Hey, you sound funny.'

*If only you knew*, Bishop thought. 'That would be the sleep deprivation. I'm about dead on my feet after last night's activities.' Bishop paused. 'Hey, what about the delivery truck? Is it still on schedule?'

Carmody gave a chuckle. 'I'll let you know when it arrives, and don't change the subject. Keep going.'

Bishop sighed and pressed transmit again. Carmody was buying it but he wasn't clear yet. 'Well, she had two friends with her and any one of them would have made you seriously question your marriage vows.' Laughter at the other end. 'But I knew which one I—' He stopped when he heard the distant sound of a phone ringing.

'Pause button, doc,' Carmody said.

Bishop waited. Just looked at the cursor flashing on the screen for two minutes. Then three. He scanned the previous few lines of text onscreen then continued typing for several more minutes.

The radio squawked. 'Game on, doc. Truck's coming through the front gates now with Richards riding shotgun to direct him to the rear entrance. You coming down?'

That definitely wouldn't be a good idea. Not yet, anyway. He thought for a second and picked up the radio. 'He'll be here for at least an hour unloading, won't he? Can you escort him to the storeroom for the first couple of trips, Bill? After that, he'll know the way and you can just let him in and out. There are only three inmates left on the main floor and they're harmless.'

Carmody's voice hardened. 'You lose the use of your legs all of a sudden?'

'You should always listen to your doctor, Bill. Seriously, Alexford Medical are on my ass to get a month's worth of paperwork finished by tomorrow, but I'll be down in thirty to check on what he's brought in so far. Make sure everything's kosher.'

Silence from the radio. 'Tell you what,' Bishop continued, 'I've got a little movie of Leona on my cell that'll make you blush. It was going to be just for me, but I'd be glad to share it when I clock off at six. Interested?'

After a five second gap, Carmody said, 'What's on it?'

Hooked and cooked. 'Not much,' he said. 'Just a solo performance from Leona as she readied herself for me while she thought I was in the bathroom.'

'Oh, you dirty, dirty dog,' the guard said. 'Okay, son. Later.'

Bishop put down the walkie-talkie and looked over what he'd written. Then he turned the printer on.

# THIRTEEN

Bishop entered the storeroom. Last time he'd checked, it had been empty except for a forty-watt bulb, three decrepit wheelchairs and a small stepladder. Now different-sized boxes and crates littered the room. The biggest were four flat corrugated cartons about six foot in length stacked together against the left-hand wall. The next biggest were three square wooden crates about four foot by four, placed in the centre of the room. Smaller boxes were spread around them like cubist satellites. He reckoned about forty in all so far. Each one had a sender's shipping label affixed to its side and another from the courier company, Bearer Logistics, with an address in an industrial area of the Bronx.

Bishop took the revised inventory sheets from his coat pocket and began checking off the items with a pen. He started with the flat cartons that held new examination tables and had got as far as a batch of rollaway beds when there was a distant sound of a key in a lock. Not wanting to be surprised by Carmody, he stood behind the tall boxes against the wall. The distant squeak of trolley wheels got louder as they made their way across the ward, and when they entered the enclosed space of the hallway Bishop peered round. He saw a diminutive silhouette pushing a stacked hand truck. Just one silhouette, which meant Carmody was probably waiting at the gate leading to the hallway. Perfect.

Bishop coughed lightly just before the man entered to make his presence known.

'Somebody here?' the man said in a deep Bronx accent.

Bishop emerged from his cover and looked up from the checklist. 'Hey. Dr Brendan Cook. You the courier from Bearer?'

The man stood about five-six, heavy-built with short, curly black hair thinning at the front. The four large boxes stacked on his hand truck were almost as tall as he was. 'Cal,' he said. 'How ya doin'?'

Bishop nodded at him. 'Nearly done, Cal?'

'Already did the really big stuff first. Yeah, one more trip'll do it, I guess.' He squared the trolley fork and slid it out from under the boxes. 'Everything cool so far?'

'So far. I'm about halfway through.' Bishop turned to the three crates in the middle of the room and pulled Cook's screwdriver from his pocket. 'Think I better check inside those big boys while you're still around, though. Make sure it's all okay.'

'Good thinking, doc,' Cal said and mock saluted before turning the cart around and wheeling it back the way he came.

When he was gone, Bishop used the screwdriver to pry the nails from one of the crates. He pulled the lid off and saw, amongst the pink foam peanuts inside, another corrugated box. Inside this was a brand new blood specimen freezer sheathed in cellophane and bubble wrap. Bishop leaned down and lifted the machine, testing the weight. His stomach area pulsated with fresh pain. For a short journey he'd probably be okay, but for where he wanted to go it was too heavy to carry with his injuries. But not too heavy to push.

Of the three wheelchairs in the corner of the room, only one had all four wheels. It didn't have a seat but that was fine. He lifted the freezer and placed it on the wheelchair arms, then slowly pushed his load until he reached the amusingly named equipment room. More a cupboard, really. Unlocking the door, Bishop squeezed the chair past the racks of rusted rollaway beds and deposited it in the corner. Locking the door again, he took the wheelchair back and replaced all the foam that had dropped on the floor.

Then he began ticking off more items on his list while he waited for Cal.


'You're screwing with me, right?' Cal said.

Bishop shrugged. 'Wish I was, Cal. I kind of knew when I read the dispatch labels on the side, but I needed to make sure.'

Cal glared at the three crates. He pulled his own delivery sheets from his back pocket and unfolded them with a frown. 'But it *says* three specimen freezers right here.' He found the last page and showed it to Bishop. 'Right *there*, doc.'

Bishop's right hand pulled at his ponytail and he said, 'Sure, but that order was changed two months ago. Look.' He handed Cal his altered copy as proof. 'This is a small prison hospital. What would we do with three specimen freezers? We've already got one and that's only five years old. What we need are sterilizers and defibrillators. That's what I was expecting, not these things. Somebody must have screwed up at head office. They'll have to go back with you.'

Cal looked up and shook his head. 'Shit on toast. I don't be*lieve* this.'

'Me either. Sorry, man.'

'Sure.' Cal smacked his lips. 'Everybody's sorry. Ain't the first time this has happened and it won't be the last. I tell ya, doc, the more people order stuff online, the more screw-ups I have to deal with. And it'll only get worse, too.'

Bishop nodded. 'It's a brave new world, that's for sure.'

'What can I do?' Cal sighed and shrugged with his shoulders and eyebrows. 'They gotta go back, they gotta go back.'

Bishop pointed at the one opened crate and said, 'Better bring a hammer back with you to close this one up again. I was careful when I opened it, so all the nails are still in place. I didn't bother with the other two.'

'That's something, I guess.' Cal inserted the trolley fork underneath one of the unopened crates and levered it up.

'I guess that's it,' Bishop said. 'Well, I've still got a mountain of paperwork to get back to upstairs, so if I don't see you again, you drive careful, okay?'

'Yeah, sure.' And Cal pushed his load down the hallway without looking back.

Bishop took the radio from his pocket and said, 'Bill? Cal's coming out now with the first of three crates he's taking back to the depot with him.'

'What?'

'There are three specimen freezers here we didn't order. And we're missing some sterilizers and defibrillators that we did. Lines must have got crossed somewhere along the line.'

There was a pause. Twenty seconds passed. Bishop heard the distant sound of the gate opening and closing. *Had Carmody let Cal out or was he coming in?*

'Maybe I should check,' Carmody said. 'Warden'll be pissed if he has to lock down this place again so soon.'

Bishop heard the last few words in stereo. Carmody had let himself in. He had about fifteen seconds. Probably less. He looked around the room and on the floor next to the opened freezer crate he saw one of the smaller boxes that supposedly contained some forceps. He brought the radio to his lips. 'Won't be a problem, Bill. The missing stuff is smaller.'

'So?'

'Small enough to mail.'

Another pause. 'You sure?'

'Yeah. Don't worry about it.'

Bishop listened for the echo of footsteps in the hallway ahead. Another ten seconds and he heard the gate opening once more.

'Whatever you say, doc.'

Bishop exhaled and looked at Cook's watch. 04.09. 'How about we skip the next check-in, Bill? Once I've finished up my paperwork I'm gonna try and get an hour's sleep; I'm about done in. You cool with that?'

'Baby needs his rest, huh?' Carmody said. 'Okay. Just don't forget our movie at six.'

'I'll bring popcorn,' Bishop said.

# FOURTEEN

Bishop opened his eyes as the engine caught. His mind had been so focused on counting he hadn't even heard the rear door close. The vehicle moved off and was in motion for a couple of minutes before it geared down and came to a halt. Bishop guessed they'd reached the inner perimeter gates, which meant they were close to the outside. He heard and felt a door slam shut – Richards exiting the truck? – then one hundred and fifteen seconds later another slam and they began moving again. The truck then jerked to a stop and Bishop waited for the outer perimeter gates to open.

For a while, nothing happened. The only sound was the idling engine.

Then there were voices. Lots of voices. Bishop breathed in.

Through the insulation of crate and packaging, Bishop counted four guards. Maybe five. The engine stopped, the driver's door opened and closed and Bishop heard random banging against the trailer. Then he heard metallic sounds under the truck.

He breathed out. The guards checking for stowaways.

He'd more or less expected this and knew whatever happened next was out of his hands. No point in worrying himself more than necessary. Especially over things he couldn't control. He'd learned that little lesson on his tenth birthday and had never forgotten it.

Then he heard the rear door roll up. Somebody coughing. Footsteps approaching. Then more footsteps. Finally the muffled, creaking sound of wood as it was forced apart.

They were checking the crates too. The final inspection.

He heard Cal's heavy Bronx accent. 'You gonna check each one?' But whatever the response was, it wasn't verbal.

Bishop just sat and listened to the creaks. Slowly breathing in, and then out. He began to count again.

After two minutes, both sets of footsteps finally moved away. Bishop heard the rear door crash down, followed by the sound of a key in a lock. A random check. That's all. He breathed out.

The truck was put into gear and they began moving again. When he heard the faint clunk of a steel gate closing behind them, he smiled in the darkness. They were out.

He pressed a button on the watch and when its light showed him it was 04.33 his smile became a grin. No one had made it out of Greenacres for over a decade, which made Bishop's achievement that much sweeter. That was the kind of record he liked to beat.

As the truck bounced along the road, he manoeuvred himself until he could reach back into his coat pocket and pull out the screwdriver. As he pushed open the box flaps and worked the screwdriver into a corner crack between lid and crate, he actually chuckled. Been a while since that happened, and it felt pretty good. He wasn't out of the woods yet, but he could sure taste new scents in the air. A freshness that had been lacking on the inside.

When he emerged from the crate, Bishop pressed the watch light again. The steel trailer was about twenty-five feet long and empty apart from the three crates and him. Steadying himself against the motion of the truck, he shone the watch face towards the rear rolling door.

It was the only way in. Which meant it was the only way out. There were no release mechanisms on this side and although the door moved in its bracket, it only lifted half an inch. Not enough for a child to get through, let alone a grown man. Bishop kneeled down, got his fingers under it and lifted. Through the small gap he saw a thick padlock. It was attached to a chain that disappeared towards the truck's undercarriage.

Good thing he'd come prepared.

Leaning against the back of the rolling door, he took the choker from his coat pocket and placed it on the floor. He removed the ruined Buddha and put it in his pants pocket, telling himself it couldn't affect his luck as he didn't believe in it. Not unless it was the kind you made yourself. He then took the screwdriver and used the sharp flathead to pierce the choker's soft, black rubber skin. When he'd made an incision along the length of the cord, he pulled it apart.

Inside were two lengths of thin, rough-looking metallic strands. Falstaff hadn't let Bishop down. Somehow he'd gotten his hands on the stuff they used for commercial wire saws: two foot-long pieces of

.025-inch diamond-impregnated 'angel wire' that, given enough time, could cut through just about anything.

Like chains.

Ignoring the pain now pounding in his abdomen like a jack rabbit, Bishop went over to his box, ripped off two flaps of thick cardboard and folded them roughly. Then, using his right hand, he lifted the rolling door up again and pushed the folded pieces into the gap to make a wedge.

He picked up a length of wire and poked one end through the gap. It took several attempts before it reappeared on the other side of the chain. He reached under the door and grabbed it with his other hand.

He checked the watch again. 04.42.

Keeping the wire ends in place with his right knee, he shrugged off the white coat and ripped off the arms. Then he wrapped the cloth firmly around each hand and picked up the angel wire.

As he pulled hard with his left hand he heard the satisfying grinding sound of sawn steel. He got the same sound when he pulled with his right. He blanked his body's pain from his mind and focused on the steady routine. Left. Right. Left. Right. One second per movement.

Bishop cut through the chain thirty-six minutes later. He was getting close to real freedom now. But it was when you were close to the finish line that you needed to stay the most focused.

He dropped the wire, got his fingers under the shutter and raised it up a foot. The crisp night air felt great against his skin. It was still pitch black outside. They were travelling on a six-lane highway, Bishop guessed the I-87, and heading south amongst the sparse, early morning Sunday traffic. The closest headlights were about half a mile back. Two minutes later he saw a sign above the northbound lanes: exit 16, Harriman.

Bishop calculated the time he had left. By 06.05 they'd know something was wrong, if Carmody hadn't figured it out already. Then there would be a search of the hospital and they'd find Cook. Next, a call to the warden. Another one to alert the local law and the state troopers. By 6.30, the US Marshals would have entered the fray. He figured Cal would have reached the Bronx by seven, but Bishop had no intention of still being on the truck by then.

# FIFTEEN

At 08.12, the Staten Island bus dawdled along Richmond Avenue like it had all the time in the world. It paused briefly for traffic at the Katan Avenue intersection before moving forward again. Bishop sat staring out the window. He studied the five-year-old grey Plymouth parked on Katan, two houses down from No. 88. No white stripes on the radials, which kind of gave the game away if you knew what that signified, and he could make out two figures inside. The one in the passenger seat gesticulated while the other sipped from a thermos cup. For undercover cops, they could have been subtler.

Bishop sat back, enjoying the gentle vibration of the engine and the musty, high school smell of the seats. The bus continued down Richmond before stopping briefly to deposit a mother and child, but Bishop had decided to wait for the next stop. Five blocks was only a short walk and he'd be coming in from behind the Plymouth.

Cal had eventually pulled into a service area at 05.35. Bishop had waited for him to park up in the truck section and enter the twenty-four-hour McDonald's next to the forecourt before climbing out. Leaving behind Brendan's coat, screwdriver and walkie-talkie he'd secured the rear door as best he could and then casually strolled over to the gas station itself. A few minutes later he reappeared, carrying a bag containing a tan baseball cap, a pair of cheap, lightly tinted sunglasses, a box of Advil, a can of shaving foam, a disposable razor and a copy of yesterday's *New York Times*. The young clerk hadn't looked at his face the entire time he was in there.

After cleaning himself up in the restrooms out back, he waited in the grey cubicle for twenty minutes and when he glanced outside Cal's truck was gone.

Fresh-shaven and bespectacled with his long hair hidden under the cap, Bishop entered the fast food franchise and came out at 06.07 alongside a long-distance trucker named Ed Chambers. Ed was a bluff,

47

easygoing guy who after listening to Bishop's story of a marital bust-up that ended with him minus a vehicle had patted him on the back and said he'd take him as far as Brooklyn for fifty bucks.

He'd belly-laughed for most of the journey, telling tales of bad women he'd known from a life spent on the road. He finally let Bishop off a couple of blocks from a bus stop at 07.24, where Bishop made use of Cook's change and took the number seventy-nine over the Verrazano Bridge into Staten Island, and from there to Annadale.

Turning from the window, he checked the watch again. 08.13. Right now, Marshals would be contacting every person with whom he'd had contact, all the way back to his time in the Corps. Building up a complete dossier on him. Where he hung out before prison, who he socialized with, his habits, his tastes, right down to his favourite food and music. Anything that could be used to predict his next move. They'd find the lease on his old apartment in Queens expired long ago, so that was a dead end. But Amy's place in Manhattan was guaranteed to be under heavy surveillance, although he had no plans to contact his sister or her family any time soon.

Or anybody else from his past, for that matter. He knew two men on the east coast who'd put up their old sergeant if asked, but as tempting as it was to contact them, he also knew it would be the worst move he could make. He might as well leave breadcrumbs for the cops to follow. To last any length of time after a prison escape you had to be unpredictable and the first rule, the *prime* rule, was to stay clear of known associates. But that was okay. It wouldn't be the first time he'd had to operate in the cold. Back in the day, he'd occasionally been forced to work solo in places like Somalia, Kuwait and Haiti, and this wasn't much different. At least he could speak the language fluently this time. Besides, he still had one lead up his sleeve.

The next stop came into view and Bishop got up and pressed the red buzzer. When the doors opened, he got out and began making his way back towards Katan. Traffic was minimal. The sun had already begun to heat the city and a faint September breeze blew against his face as he walked. Today would be a hot one.

He crossed over Richmond and turned right into Figurea, the street before Katan. He stopped at the corner to tie his shoelaces and checked for more suspicious vehicles, but the traffic was almost non-existent. The only parked vehicles were empty ones. He spotted the bright red tracksuit of a jogger in his late fifties approaching and lowered his head so the visor of his baseball cap hid his face. Another man walked his dog on the opposite side of the street, totally uninterested in the world around him.

Bishop walked on. This area was still fairly affluent, mostly populated by young or middle-aged couples seeking a little greenery and easy access to the city. Coming up on his left was the Robinsons' place. It looked like all the other detached houses on the street. Two floors. Redbrick. Veranda out front. The empty driveway told him they were still making regular weekend visits to their place on Long Island.

Bishop strolled across their front lawn and down the driveway at the side, opened the latch on the wooden gate at the end and passed through. He guessed the crime rate around here was still low, which made people careless. He figured that of all the houses on the street about seventy-five per cent would have their side gates unlocked. The Robinsons were no doubt happily unaware of this ratio.

Aside from a recently built patio, their backyard hadn't changed much. Still the same plot of grass with the same seven-foot-tall wooden fencing all around, separated by concrete posts at six-foot intervals. And the same apple tree in the far right-hand corner. It had provided enough cover when he was a kid, it should be good enough now. The houses on either side partly overlooked the garden and the one backing onto it, but unless somebody was actually looking out a second-floor window right now he would be safe.

He walked over to the small tree and placed both hands atop the fence and pulled himself up. Grimacing in pain, he brought his right leg over, then his left, and dropped to the ground on the other side with a soft grunt.

The backyard of No. 88 was in bad shape. The grass had grown knee-high and turned brown under the summer sun. A shovel, a rake and his old bicycle all lay rusting against the fence.

How much of a mistake he'd made in coming here depended on how much Amy had told the cops about this place. Knowing his sister, probably as close to nothing as she could get away with. But then Amy always took his side, no matter what. She'd never even asked if he was innocent three years ago. She just knew.

After their parents' deaths twenty-six years ago, this house had passed down to both of them, the deeds held in trust until they both reached twenty-one. Tom and Annabel, grandparents on their father's side, had moved in to act as legal guardians and had stayed on even after Bishop left for the Marines at seventeen. But once they too passed away – Annabel nine years ago and Tom a year after – Amy told him she had no emotional attachment to the place and would sign it over to him if he wanted. Instead, Bishop asked her to place it in her name for as long as he remained in a high risk profession, if only for simplicity's sake. He'd take sole ownership himself once he felt the time was right. After much debate, Amy finally agreed.

Today was where it might pay off in his favour. Had his name been on the paperwork the cops would have assigned an army to watch over it. The fact that two locals were deemed enough suggested they were merely covering bases. That's what he was hoping, anyway.

# SIXTEEN

Bishop walked to the paved patio at the rear of the house. Each concrete slab measured twenty inches by twenty. He counted them off from where they met the east fence. Seven to the right, four down. And stopped at the one with the small chip in the top right corner.

He went over to pick up the shovel and inserted it between the cracks. The metal bent a little under the strain but held tight. It took four goes before he got enough leverage to pry the stone block out. Embedded in the earth underneath was a rectangular object about the size of a hardback book, wrapped in a layer of protective plastic sheeting.

Removing the sheeting, Bishop opened the blank DVD case. Seeing it again felt odd. He'd always had it there, just in case, but had hoped he'd never have to use what it held. The feeling hardened into a familiar anger. Followed by the same resolve: to find the person who had taken his old life away from him.

He pulled out the bundle of bank notes held together by an elastic band and added it to the remains of Brendan's money in his pocket. He didn't need to count it. There would be five thousand dollars, just like there had been six years ago. Taped to the inside of the case were two keys. He replaced the stone slab.

Unlocking the rear door, he entered the bare kitchen and walked through the equally spartan dining room. The downstairs smelled faintly of old carpet cleaner with a hint of bleach. He didn't stop to check anything, instead climbing the stairs near the front of the house.

Bishop never expected to feel anything when he came back here. Memories of his parents had faded to the point where he had to concentrate to bring up their faces, although he still remembered the day he learned of their deaths in a road accident. It had been the evening of his tenth birthday, the last one he ever celebrated. From that point on, he'd reasoned that if he couldn't control the fates of those he loved, he'd just have to be more discerning about who he let inside. Amy excepted, of course.

The following years spent under the care of Tom and Annabel had only enforced that belief. At least Amy, six years older, only had to put up with them for a year before taking off for college. Bishop had been glad for her. He knew she'd stay in close contact and make regular visits, and that was enough for him. But he'd have to wait another six years before he could escape, too.

He guessed the fact that they seemed to show more affection for this house than for their own blood explained his mixed feelings for the place. And Amy's negative ones. Thing was, he knew this would make a perfect family home for somebody. Just not him. Not after his experiences here. And although he'd always enjoyed visiting Amy and her family whenever he got the chance, he wasn't sure he could handle one of his own. He wasn't the fatherly type. It occurred to him that maybe this was also partly due to Tom and Annabel's influence. Their general aloofness could have rubbed off on him more than he cared to admit. For most of his adult life, he'd avoided letting anybody get too close and he couldn't blame it all on his reaction to his parents' deaths. It was no wonder Amy wanted nothing to do with the place.

But right now, it had its uses.

At the second-floor landing, Bishop entered the first door on the left. The drapes in his old bedroom were drawn, but the light fabric let in enough daylight. His bed was still against the wall. He walked over to the window and checked through a gap in the drapes. The two cops were still in their Plymouth, still looking everywhere but up.

He turned, took off the baseball cap and dropped his full length onto the bed. A cloud of dust glittered in the soft light of the room. He closed his eyes and relief washed over him like a wave. He was out. He'd made it. He didn't know for how long, or even if he'd still be alive this time tomorrow, but he was here now. On the outside. He'd forgotten how much he missed having empty space around him. And he knew at that moment he wouldn't go back inside. Not for anything. They'd have to kill him first.

The thought forced him off the bed. He needed to concentrate. It wouldn't be easy finding who'd set him up, he knew that, but he'd look at everything with the same commitment and focus he'd always had.

Inside the built-in closet next to the bed were five deep shelves that held his few remaining possessions. He'd never been particularly materialistic, but some things were hard to get rid of. Or maybe just easier to hold onto, he'd never figured out which. He took hair clippers from behind the books and CDs on the second shelf down and tossed them on the bed, along with a number four blade and a spare set of batteries.

On the carpeted floor lay his old equipment bag and he knelt down and unzipped it. Feeling under his Corps fatigues and dress uniform he pulled out his old M9 service Beretta with the serial numbers filed off. Another holdover from Staff Sergeant Hill's school of life: *You never know when you might need an untraceable gun.* Or at least, *most* people never know. Funny thing was, many of his fellow NCOs back in the day had looked down on the M9. Bishop had never understood why. In his experience, it was more than up to the task it had been designed for. He also pulled out a box of ammunition and his cleaning kit and placed them on the bed with the gun.

The second shelf from the bottom held his last surviving clothes and he inserted his hand under the pile until his fingers touched something hard. He removed the black 9¼-inch USMC Ka-Bar combat knife and ankle holster. These joined his Beretta on the bed.

After giving the street below another glance, Bishop picked up the clippers, the number four blade and the batteries and walked to the bathroom.

Bishop cocked a round into the chamber, flicked the safety on and tucked the 9mm in the back of his pants as though it were the most natural thing in the world. Which, to him, it kind of was. A little oil and TLC and the action felt as smooth now as when he'd last used it eleven years ago, back when he was in uniform.

Bishop picked up the folded bed sheet containing his prison hair and unhooked his leather jacket from the back of the door and slipped it on. As he descended the stairs, he brushed his hand across his new buzzcut. He felt like a new man again. Looked like one, too. Amy always said Mom had passed on her youthful good looks to both her kids, but while that might have been true in his sister's case, Bishop now looked every one of his thirty-six years. In the mirror, he'd noticed a few extra lines around the mouth and forehead that hadn't been there before and his hair had receded a little above the temples since the last time he'd paid it any attention. Hopefully, the changes would work in his favour.

At the bottom, Bishop passed the door to the living room and opened the one to the garage. He walked over to the pile of old newspapers in the corner and inserted the folded bed sheet in between some damp, ancient copies of the *Times*.

Retracing his steps, Bishop locked the kitchen door and reburied the DVD case under the stone slab in the patio. It only held the two keys now, but he didn't want to carry any connection to this house on his person. Plus he might need to use the place again.

Staring at the fence, he took the Advil from his pocket and downed three. They were helping, but not much. As good as he could hope for over the counter; anything heavier would need a prescription. But then, climbing over fences probably wasn't helping much either.

Sighing, he pulled himself up to the top again and eventually landed on the other side. He got up, took the sunglasses from his jacket pocket and put them on. As he walked back through his neighbours' property to Katan, he thought of a magazine article he'd read a few years back. A profile of a retired Marshal named Sandy Lennox. According to Sandy, ninety-five per cent of all fugitives were caught within three days or three miles of the institution they'd escaped from. The 'rule of three', he called it. Bishop found the figure hard to believe, just like he found all statistical data suspect – *who* exactly came up with these numbers? – but it stayed on his mind. If true, did the other five per cent have as much incentive to remain at liberty as he did? Less? More?

Probably less, he decided.

As Bishop got onto Richmond to wait for the next bus to St George Ferry Terminal, he thought the very least he could do was make his pursuers work for their money.

# SEVENTEEN

Bishop half watched the game coming to an end from a bench under some maple trees. He sat twenty yards in front of the wire fence that separated the basketball courts from the kids' section of the playground.

Only nine thirty and the park in Brooklyn was already filling up. He watched moms walk close behind their kids. Sometimes with hungover boyfriends or husbands in tow, eyes half shut against the late summer daylight. A few teenage males congregated around the courts, strutting and shuffling to an imaginary female audience and the hip-hop coming from their bass-heavy stereo.

At six-four, the big white guy on the court should have been a natural but he lacked grace and pace. The two opposing players were running rings around him while keeping their distance. But his partner was another matter. He had some moves in him, but the finishing touch just wasn't there.

Bishop turned his face up to the sky and closed his eyes as he leaned back against the bench, whistling softly through his teeth, enjoying the heat. Even the stereo didn't annoy him.

'Who's winning?'

He opened an eye to look at the profile of the attractive woman who'd just sat down at the other end of the bench.

Mid to late twenties, hardly any make-up, dark green combats and a faded red T-shirt bearing a screen-print of fifties-era Elvis. She looked ahead at the game and pecked at a Danish out of a paper bag. She wore a black baseball cap, and a small, black ponytail protruded from the vent at the back. Her nose was straight and he noticed a slight overbite when she took another nibble of her breakfast. The fingers holding the pastry were long and elegant and ended in clipped, clear nails.

He took off his sunglasses and said, 'No idea.'

'You were watching before I sat down,' she said.

Bishop nodded in the direction of the court and she glanced at him. 'It might matter to them,' he said. 'Doesn't much matter to me.'

'So you're waiting for someone.'

Bishop turned, curious. Her eyes were slightly darker than her brown skin, and the whites around the irises made them seem doe-like. He liked the way they watched him. Then again, he hadn't been around women for a while. Even when he had, it was never for very long.

'Is that what I'm doing?'

She smiled and took another bite. 'Put money on it.'

'Why pick on me?'

'I'm just talking.' She turned as a shadow blotted out the sun on her face.

The pale guy with no pace grinned down at her and said, 'Hey, beautiful,' out of one side of his mouth. 'Stranger bothering you?'

He had a small towel in his hand and he wiped sweat from his muscular arms. His dirty-blond hair was the kind loved by some women and the hazel eyes looked intelligent. Insightful, even. He purposely didn't look at Bishop.

'Oh, Lucas,' she said, still smiling, her tone lowering on the second word. Bishop looked past Lucas and watched the other three players strolling towards the bench. The two larger men were laughing at something the smallest was saying as he gesticulated wildly with his hands.

Bishop turned to the woman and said, 'I preferred his late sixties stuff, myself.'

She shook her head and smiled. 'The fifties and Sun Records is where it's at.' Another sip. 'But "In The Ghetto" was pretty great, I admit.'

Lucas finally looked at Bishop and said, 'Maybe you'd like to play.'

'You wouldn't like me any more than you do now.' Bishop shrugged. 'Less, probably.' Then he said, 'Don't forget "Suspicious Minds".'

He usually avoided alpha-male bullshit, but couldn't help himself on this occasion. Something about the guy grated and it had been a long time since he could say something without having to deal with the threat of being stabbed.

The woman started humming the familiar tune and Bishop listened for five seconds, enjoying the sound. When Lucas sat down between them he rose and walked towards the three men. The conversation stopped as soon as he was within five yards. Like Lucas, all wore sleeveless sweatshirts or vests, shorts, and sneakers that probably cost more than Bishop's entire get-up, leather jacket included. Bishop put them all in the same age bracket as the woman.

'Help you?' asked the smallest guy.

'Only if your name's Aleron.'

The speaker turned to the biggest man. 'Know him?'

The man was about six-two and Bishop guessed about twenty pounds heavier than him. His hair had been shaved close to the skull and from a distance he looked pretty intimidating. But he had friendly eyes and he wore a genuine half-smile. He tilted his head slightly, looking Bishop over. 'That's the question. Do I?'

Bishop nodded at him and said, 'Owen.'

The man raised his eyebrows and took a few steps away from his friends. Bishop followed. 'That's the magic word,' Aleron Falstaff said. 'You seen my brother recently?'

'Three or four days ago. He gave me your name as someone to see. Told me you played here on Sundays.' He put his sunglasses back on and said, 'My name's Bishop.'

Aleron showed a flicker of recognition and frowned as he looked over at his friends gathered around the woman on the bench. 'I heard the last time anyone broke out of Greenacres was twelve years ago. How'd you end that run?'

'They carried me out in a box.' Aleron smiled. 'Was he on the level or am I wasting my time?'

Aleron flashed some teeth. 'Wasting time's what Sunday mornings are for. Relax. I heard what you did for him. Give me a second and we'll walk back to my place. It's not far.'

Aleron left Bishop standing in the bright sun and walked over to talk briefly with his three co-players. They each knocked fists with him and he leaned down in front of the girl. She placed an affectionate hand on his shoulder as she listened to whatever he was saying.

Then she stopped smiling and kept her eyes on Bishop as he followed Aleron towards the park exit.

# EIGHTEEN

'One more for luck,' Aleron said.

Bishop looked straight at a reflex camera that was attached to a tripod in Aleron's basement. He kept his expression neutral. Not happy, not angry, just eyes open, mouth closed.

After the shutter clicked, Aleron opened the side of the camera and extracted a small memory card. He went over and reached under the desk to turn something on before inserting the card into his Power Mac. Laid-back music started playing and Bishop immediately recognized Joe Zawinul on keyboards and John McLaughlin's delicate guitar. It was one of his favourite pieces of music and it felt good hearing it out loud again. He couldn't see any speakers and figured they must have been hidden somewhere. Maybe in the walls. Three years out of the world and the miracles of technology had already left him behind.

They were in Aleron's subterranean workshop in a modest house in downtown Brooklyn, five minutes' walk from the park. A few people they'd passed on the way had greeted Aleron warmly and looked right through Bishop like he didn't exist. Which suited Bishop just fine. If it kept happening he might end up finding his prey sooner than he'd anticipated.

The room was filled with a wide variety of industrial printers, as well as an impressive stockpile of printer toner, fuse boxes, paper samples of every weight and colour, and assorted accessories that only a specialist would recognize. Bishop guessed Aleron needed them for his extra-curricular work and was impressed by the man's dedication to his skill.

On the wall facing him, a large plasma TV with muted sound was tuned to a twenty-four-hour news channel. He recognized the US Attorney General being interviewed about something or other. There weren't any accompanying mugshots of Bishop, so he could only assume that whatever they were talking about was unrealated to him. Although that might change very soon.

'Always put this on when I'm down here,' Aleron said. 'Helps me work.'

Bishop turned and saw Aleron's head swaying to the sparse sounds coming from the speakers.

Bishop nodded. 'It helped me sleep inside, too.'

Aleron stopped typing and looked at him.

'*In a Silent Way,*' Bishop said. 'Miles Davis. This second side, in particular.'

'They let you have iPods in there, man?'

'Never needed one,' Bishop said and tapped a finger against his temple. 'Shorter's soprano comes in in about four seconds.'

It was actually five seconds before the sax laid its sound over the other instruments like a spoonful of syrup, and Bishop could have listened to it for ever. Aleron smiled and turned back to his work. Bishop moved beside him, watching. It was always interesting to see a professional at work and Aleron clearly knew what he was doing.

Aleron said, 'Working on your new Social Security card at the moment. You got to realize I can supply you with all the essentials, but none of it will stand up to thorough investigation. You won't be on any database under the name I'm giving you. This is just a cosmetic fix, like a toupee for a leukaemia patient.'

'Most toupees I've seen looked like toupees,' Bishop said, 'and I've worked in California.'

Aleron laughed. 'Okay. Bad example, but you know what I mean.'

'So what's my new name?'

'Eric Allbright. You like?' He passed a pen over his shoulder. 'Here, I'll need a signature sample. Two L's in Allbright, by the way.'

Bishop used a pad at Aleron's side to sign the new alias in his own handwriting. Then he pointed at the circular colour spectrum currently taking up most of Falstaff's screen. 'Last time I saw something like that was at grade school,' he said.

'You never hear of CMYK values?' Aleron asked and Bishop shrugged. 'Printing in any magazine or newspaper is made up of just four colours mixed together. It's all about illusion. All the colours you see on a page are made up of cyan, magenta, yellow or black. Say you mix a hundred per cent of yellow with fifty per cent magenta. That gives you bright orange. Whack the magenta up to a hundred and you got warm red, you follow? That's CMYK, man. All roads lead from those four bad boys.'

Bishop nodded. The concept made sense and he knew better than most that very little is as it seems on the surface. 'So what's the K stand for?' he asked.

'Key plate. Been that way longer than you or I been on this earth. See here?' On the computer, Aleron zoomed in on the lettering at the top of Bishop's new ID card. 'I managed to get the government templates but only in keyline black and white. They're real protective about their colour values, so I've recreated them so they'll come out my printer looking like the real deal. The navy blue in the lettering here' – he pressed the cursor and brought up a window listing the four colours with an empty box next to each – 'I make up by using twenty-seven per cent black, hundred per cent cyan, fifty per cent magenta and three per cent yellow.'

Bishop leaned over Aleron's shoulder and watched, fascinated, as the colours changed according to the percentage of the CMYK colours.

'Hey, man, have a heart,' Aleron said.

'What?'

'The air conditioning in here's good, but not *that* good. Know what I'm saying?'

'I can take a hint, if that's what you mean,' Bishop said, smiling as he scratched the back of his head. 'Just tell me where.'

Falstaff turned back to the monitor. 'Top floor. Last on the right.'

# NINETEEN

Towelling himself off from the shower, Bishop studied the ugly kaleidoscope of purple, red, brown and grey that covered his midsection. *Christ, what a mess.* And if it looked that bad on the outside, he could only imagine what his insides resembled. But bruising came before healing, and besides, there wasn't much he could do about it.

The Three Bears' visit already felt distant to him, despite its being only seventeen hours ago. He checked Cook's watch and was surprised to see it was 10.40 already. He needed to get moving. The longer he stayed still, the easier it would be to find him. Plus he had leads he wanted to follow. Places to revisit. Certain people to see.

In the basement, Aleron was standing in front of the TV with the sound up and his arms crossed. 'Eric Allbright, you're a star,' he said.

Bishop went to stand next to him. An artificially pretty brunette reporter was standing outside Greenacres' main entrance. The yellow strip at the bottom of the screen said she was Melanie Murray, followed by the word *live*. Behind her, Bishop could see a police barricade.

'A source inside Greenacres has told us it was actually the infirmary physician, Dr Brendan Cook, whom the guards found in James Bishop's bed, heavily sedated and handcuffed to the railing. It appears this was the man we caught on film earlier as he was being transported to police headquarters for a statement.'

The screen suddenly changed to jerky, hand-held footage and showed two uniforms and a long-haired man approaching a black-and-white. All three noticed the camera at the same time and the scene froze, zooming in on Cook's startled face. Bishop smiled at the image. The doc looked as though he'd been caught flashing.

'We also expect to bring you an interview with Deputy Marshal Angela Delaney, who's been assigned the task of recapturing Bishop and is currently inside the prison with her team taking statements.' As Melanie spoke, the picture changed to Bishop's three-year-old mugshot, with his hair longer and five days' worth of stubble on his face. That was something. At least he looked a little different now.

Melanie continued, 'To recap, we can confirm Bishop escaped from Greenacres Prison here in Ulster County some time before dawn in the rear of a delivery truck headed for the Bronx. As yet, we don't know exactly where he exited the vehicle but we should be able to give you more soon. We've also been informed that in addition to the US Marshals Department, every law enforcement agency in the country is now on high alert and it is only a matter of time before . . .'

The picture switched to two men and two women in the distance walking towards a plain, unmarked Chevrolet. Melanie called out, 'Deputy Delaney. Deputy. Can you give a statement regarding the escape and your estimation of Bishop's chances?'

Bishop saw one of the women say something to one of the men, who nodded and got behind the wheel. The camera quickly zoomed in on the woman as she looked up briefly before opening the front passenger door. He figured this must be Delaney. Attractive in a stern way, she looked to be a couple of years either side of forty with blond hair hidden under a black cap. Clearly, she wasn't about to grant Melanie any interviews right now. She slid in while the other two got in the back. Then the vehicle moved towards the police barriers to the left of the picture. A uniform let them through and the camera tracked the vehicle until it was gone.

Bishop let Melanie's babble wash over him and thought hard. He'd stayed here too long already, and now that his picture was out there he needed to consider his next move carefully. He had two immediate tasks in mind. Both held their share of risks, so it was just a matter of prioritizing one over the other.

'This stuff won't be ready until early evening,' Aleron said, interrupting his calculations.

Bishop took the hint and rose to leave. 'Just give me a time and a price.'

Aleron thought for a moment. 'Come back around five. A grand should do it.'

'A grand?' asked Bishop as he began climbing the basement stairs. He'd expected it to be a lot more.

'Miles fans get a special discount,' Aleron said, following close behind. 'I don't meet many these days.'

At the front door, Bishop paused on the outer step and turned round. 'You know, I expected a bunch of questions about the murders.'

Aleron shrugged. 'In my line, I've learned it's best not to pry.'

'Thanks. For the shower.' Bishop turned and began walking away.

'No, thank *you*,' Aleron said and shut the door.

# TWENTY

Sitting in a cubicle facing the exit of the inappropriately named Cyber Paradise, Bishop sipped lukewarm tea and casually rechecked his dozen or so fellow surfers. Whoever named the place had only got it half right. There was no arguing the 'cyber' part, but 'paradise' was probably taking things a little too far.

The internet café was located eight blocks from Aleron's place and took up part of the second floor of a Laundromat. Only one way in, so Bishop was sitting at a workstation to the side of the door, next to the room's only window. Just in case he needed an alternative exit. Everyone there was totally absorbed in his or her own world, and for the past thirty minutes no one else had come in.

Bishop checked his screen and finished filling in his fake details for a new email account. He then visited the *Post* website and browsed until he found a grainy snapshot of Sam Chaney. He still had the same angular features, but his face had filled out and his brown hair was longer and brushed forward. The photo had been taken as he was leaving a controversial lap-dancing club called Heroines in Lower Manhattan, which had opened two years before and specialized in pretty young things dressed in skimpy, spandex superhero costumes. If only briefly. According to the *Post*, Chaney was the majority owner of the club and his own best customer. He had resigned from RoyseCorp a couple of months after Bishop's trial and used an insurance payout to launch a major business in the heart of Manhattan.

Sam Chaney. Living the dream. But then, women had always been his obsession.

A month or so after Chaney, Chris Tennison had also decided to leave RoyseCorp to start up his own web-based business, along with a cute name to go with it. Eyetech Associates. He now specialized in the supply of state-of-the-art surveillance equipment to international clients. Business had been good enough after the first year to move his operation from his house in Guttenberg, New Jersey to an office suite on West 20th Street, currently employing a staff of nine.

Martin Thorpe was still at RoyseCorp, although he was no longer a close protecti n officer. One of the injuries sustained in the Brennan raid had resulted in a destroyed nerve in his right elbow and he could no longer fully extend the arm. It didn't keep him down for long, though. He currently held a senior position in Foreign Operations at head office. Which was pretty much as Bishop expected. Thorpe had made no secret of his desire to move on to the corporate side of things whenever a good opportunity came up.

Researching the three men felt weird. Like looking at what Bishop's life might have been in an alternate universe. One where he hadn't been locked away for somebody else's crime. It also felt like turning his back on his own, but he'd been over the choices. Someone on his team had to have been involved for the attack to have been pulled off. And that same man had to have been involved in setting Bishop up.

The internet didn't really give him much. None of their actions following the murders were really out of character. All three still lived in New York and none of them seemed unexpectedly rich. But one of them had to be responsible for aiding the assault team. And *some*body had jammed his comms and pager.

Bishop sighed. At the moment he was left with his main lead: the photo in Brennan's office of the guy he'd shot on the stairs. Find him, find some answers.

Alicia or Philip Brennan would probably know who he was, but Bishop couldn't see them talking to the man they believed responsible for the destruction of their family. So all he really had going for him was the memory of a photo he'd seen once.

Bishop did a search on both King Saleh and Randall Brennan, which scored a big fat zero. The two men were never mentioned in conjunction with each other. He did an individual search on each man, but the links he got numbered in the thousands and would take forever to check. Probably with the same result. He stretched and studied the young guy on the computer next to him. He was waving at someone through a camera affixed to the top of the screen. Bishop watched, curious, as the man then pretended to kiss the camera. He guessed the girl, or guy, at the other end appreciated the light-hearted gesture. Bishop couldn't think of anyone he'd blow kisses at via the World Wide Web, especially in a public place. He'd never been that carefree, even in his youth. But then, maybe he just hadn't allowed himself to meet the right woman.

Watching the young guy, Bishop wondered whether he was approaching his search from the wrong angle. Instead of coming at it from Brennan's side, maybe he should focus on the basics and go back to the photo on the Wall of Fame. And think about what was actually in the picture.

He closed his eyes. It had been taken in an aircraft hangar. Possibly on a private airfield in Yajir, as it seemed unlikely that the king would ever set foot in the main airport. Bishop focused on the plane. Only a portion of the jet was visible. It was white, with the turbofan mounted on the rear fuselage. Above that was the T-tail with a logo and some lettering reversed out of dark blue. One word. Not Arabic. Something western. The logo above it was an arrow in the shape of an S, so the name must have begun with the same letter. *But what was it?*

It took a couple of minutes as his consciousness focused on the detail, but the name gradually became sharp enough in his memory to make out.

*Supreme.*

# TWENTY-ONE

Bishop opened his eyes and smiled. The mind's capacity for storing and accessing information was truly fascinating. He'd read in *New Scientist* once that it was just like any other muscle. That the more you exercised it, the better it worked. Bishop was strangely reassured by that thought. It meant genes and DNA didn't decide everything. That it was partly down to the individual's strength of character in the end.

He leaned forward, typed *Supreme Jets* into the search box and hit Enter. And there it was. Right at the top of the page. He clicked on the link and was taken to their home page where the company promised to supply luxury jet charters for his personal and corporate needs. The logo was exactly as he remembered.

From there, he clicked on *Company History* and the page that came up, although heavy with text, featured an assortment of photos. Some were of the jets, either airborne or in readiness for take-off. Some focused on the corporate headquarters in Washington. But the real prize was the shot of the King of Yajir and a businessman shaking hands in a hangar with a company jet in the background. Along with a man partly in shadow, but with a cleft chin, a long nose and slightly sunken cheeks. *Bingo*.

It wasn't exactly the same photo as the one in Brennan's office. It looked to have been taken a second before or after, as Brennan's face was turned away slightly, his features obscured. If Bishop hadn't already seen the other shot, he would never have been able to place him from this one. The picture was also uncropped to allow the full glory of the aircraft to be seen. A Lear 60 six-seater, it looked like. Or possibly the 55. Both popular models amongst executives, in Bishop's experience. He guessed the presence of royalty had merited the photo worthy of inclusion on the company website. There were no captions under any of the pictures, but on the contact page there was a media representative by the name of Joanne Walsh, along with an email address and phone number.

Bishop deleted the browser's history before logging off, then paid for his time with a twenty, got change from a five and went downstairs. There were two payphones attached to the rear wall of the Laundromat, next to a table bearing three White Pages directories and a pile of old magazines. Bishop picked up the nearest phone, inserted some coins and dialled the number, scanning the shop as he waited. Three of the twelve washing machines were in use, and two female customers were sitting on the chairs by the entrance. Neither one paid him any attention.

A female voice said, 'Joanne Walsh. Can I help you?'

'Yeah, I sure hope so, Ms Walsh,' Bishop said, turning to the wall. 'My name's Rhinehart. I'm a researcher over at the *Post* and one of our writers is planning a weekend society piece on luxury air travel, and the role of private air charter companies as an alternative to scheduled airlines.'

'Sounds intriguing,' Joanne said.

'Well, we're hoping our readers feel the same way. Anyway, I noticed that cool photo on your site with King Saleh of Yajir.'

'You're not the first person to comment on it, Mr Rhinehart. It *is* a cool picture, isn't it?'

'Very. And Rhinehart's my first name, actually. It's German. And on that subject, I was wondering if you had the names of the two westerners in the shot. The businessman and his associate. Looks like one of his security men, maybe.'

Joanne Walsh paused. 'Um, possibly. May I ask the reason?'

'Well, it's nothing important really, but if we can get a nice quote from somebody who's actually met royalty, it might add some pizzazz to the article. You know, something to end the piece with. It would get your company a mention, too, of course.'

'I see. Well, I think I might be able to find their names for you. Do you want me to call you back, um, Rhinehart?'

*Not really*, thought Bishop. 'Probably best if I stay on the line, Ms Walsh. As soon as I'm done with this I'm out of the country on another assignment.'

'Oh. Okay. Can you hold for a few minutes then?'

'No problem.' Bishop leaned his shoulder against the wall and studied the nearest washer. A light blue sock was visible through the glass and he watched it move in soapy circles. He kept a count of how many times it reached the top of the barrel and then tried to work out how this related to the number of revolutions per minute. He'd decided it was probably kicking in at around the seven hundred mark when Joanne Walsh returned.

'Right. Well, I found the names for you, but I'm not sure what good they'll do as one of them . . . well, he passed away a few years ago. He was a businessman who used us quite a lot.'

'Oh, no,' Bishop said. 'Well, maybe I can still talk to the one who's still around; the second guy.' Bishop realized his hand was squeezing the phone a lot tighter. 'Do you have his name there?'

'I do. It's Adam Cortiss.'

'Adam Cortiss,' he said. 'That's fantastic, Ms Walsh. Thanks very much, you've been a great help. We'll send your office a copy when it gets printed.'

'Please do,' she said and Bishop hung up, whistling through his teeth. Now he had a name. Adam Cortiss. Things were looking up.

# TWENTY-TWO

Bishop went over to the table and checked the covers of the three current White Pages directories stacked next to the magazines. Brooklyn, Queens and Manhattan. Picking up the Manhattan book, he opened it at the Ts and leafed through the pages.

After a few moments, he smiled as he came upon the sole listing for 'Thorpe, Martin H'. Bishop remembered Thorpe once revealing that the H stood for Heath, and that he suspected his mother of being drunk when she came up with it. The phone number was still the same as before, and Bishop was faintly surprised that Thorpe hadn't gone the unlisted route. Maybe he felt he hadn't reached that level of success quite yet. Still living in the same rent-controlled uptown apartment, too.

Bishop closed the book, picked up the phone again and fed it some more coins. He began dialling the number but when he reached the last digit, instead of pressing the five button to connect to Thorpe, he pressed six.

After a short wait, a deep male voice said, 'Yeah?'

'Hey,' Bishop said. 'It's Frank. Can I talk to Larry?'

'Who?'

'Larry. Larry Foster. Who's this I'm talking to?'

'This is Domingo. Ain't no Larry here, pal.'

'Oh, sorry. Must have misdialled. Thanks.'

Bishop pressed down on the receiver and released it again. After inserting more change, he dialled the correct number and waited as it rang.

Shortly, a familiar voice said, 'Hello?'

Adopting the same lazy Texas drawl as Carmody from this morning, Bishop said, 'Hey, there. Domingo left yet? He was supposed to be here half-hour ago. I can't wait all day.'

There was a short pause. 'You got the wrong number.'

'Aw, hell.' Bishop quoted the previous number and said, 'That's right, ain't it?'

'All except the last part,' Thorpe said. 'This number ends with a five.'

'Shoot. Sorry 'bout that. I'll try again.'

Bishop smiled as he placed the phone back on the hook. While he couldn't be sure the feds were listening in on his ex-colleagues' phone calls, it was better to assume they were. In which case, a quick check on Domingo's number would tell them the last call was nothing more than a genuine misdial.

But Bishop now had the information he needed. Thorpe was at home today. And in Bishop's experience, people were generally creatures of habit in their down time. He checked Cook's watch. 11.39. Getting close to lunchtime for many people this fine Sunday.

And he had a pretty good idea where Thorpe would spend his.

# TWENTY-THREE

Smelling strongly of chlorine, the uniformly grey changing room contained three long aisles with lockers on both sides and four wooden benches running down the centre of each. With the visor of his baseball cap hiding his features, Bishop sat on a bench in the middle aisle and fiddled with the buttons on the diver's watch. It was 13.06, and he was waiting for the skinny teenager ten feet away to finish packing away the last of his gear. Bishop watched him carefully place a pair of grey sneakers with a flashy star design into the locker before finally closing it and moving off towards the pool.

Then the place was quiet except for the muffled sound of running water coming from the next room. That's where Thorpe was. Four minutes ago, Bishop had watched him exit the corridor leading from the pool, wearing a stylish pair of purple and black trunks, and head for the showers.

Thorpe had once mentioned that he'd joined the Asphalt Green Sports Center on East 90th Street partly because it was never crowded, but mostly because it boasted the only Olympic-sized swimming pool in Manhattan. And Thorpe was serious about his fitness. Any time he got a day off, Bishop knew he liked to spend his lunchtime doing laps and he guessed an arm injury wouldn't stop him. In fact it probably helped, so Bishop made a wild gamble and it had paid off.

He had taken the subway into Manhattan, gotten off at the 86th Street station and walked the rest of the way. This far into town no one paid any attention to anyone else; they were all too busy. So as long as he kept moving he reckoned he was safe. At reception, he'd parted with thirty-five dollars and received a day pass and a locker key in return.

Soon, the sounds coming from the shower faucets stopped. Then Bishop heard the unmistakable sound of wet soles against tile. As the footsteps got closer, he got up and turned to the line of lockers on the right. He placed his key in number 317 and waited. The footsteps came to a halt in the adjacent aisle. Then there was the sound of another lock being turned.

Bishop removed his key and walked to the end of the row. He turned left and peered round into the next aisle. A kneeling man with a towel around his waist had his back to Bishop. He was pulling out a folded white T-shirt from a locker and placing it on the long bench behind him. Then came a pair of white Nike sneakers, which he set down next to a pair of damp purple and black trunks.

As the man turned back to pull out the rest of his possessions, Bishop silently walked forward and sat on one end of the bench. Keeping his voice low, he said, 'Hello, Thorpe. Don't bother turning round.'

Thorpe froze, holding a pair of a tracksuit pants in both hands. 'Okay.'

'You recognize my voice?'

'I think so. You been on TV recently?'

'My fifteen minutes, if you believe Andy Warhol.'

Thorpe nodded. 'So, did you get hold of Domingo in the end?'

Bishop smiled. Thorpe still had his sense of humour, at least. 'He never showed. I had to leave without him.'

'He'll get over it. Got to admit, you had me fooled. It sounded nothing like you, but I should have guessed. A wrong number the same day you escape from prison?' Thorpe clicked his tongue and said, 'Any particular reason why I can't turn round?'

Bishop thought about it and decided the cap hid his new haircut well enough. But he kept hold of the Beretta in his jacket pocket. 'Not any more,' he said. 'Go ahead. Take a load off.'

Thorpe turned slowly and got to his feet. He looked at Bishop, dropped the pants onto the white T-shirt and sat down on his side of the bench.

He hadn't changed much in three years. Still in good shape, no doubt due to the swimming. Same prominent jawline. Same comma-shaped scar on his upper lip. The thick light brown hair was as short as ever, but Bishop noticed a few grey strands in there. And maybe there were a few more laugh lines around the eyes.

Thorpe glanced briefly at the jacket pocket concealing Bishop's hand and smiled. 'I know you won't believe me, but it's good to see you.'

'I'm glad to hear that. Makes it easier for me to ask a favour.'

Thorpe frowned and used a palm to pat down a crease in his

tracksuit. 'That kind of depends on how big the favour is. Don't get me wrong, Bishop; it *is* good to see you, but I don't want to end up sharing a cell with you.'

Bishop smiled. 'And here was I thinking you'd be anxious to pay me back after what I did for you in Seattle.'

Eight years before, Bishop's first assignment as a team leader had been to guard a rock promoter on the west coast after he had a major falling out with some local gang-bangers. The three-man team, consisting of Bishop, Thorpe and a man named Romario, had been driving him back from a business meet one evening when their route was blocked by two cars full of armed men who began throwing down fire in their direction. Bishop managed to get out and dislodge a nearby sewer grate and, while he laid down covering fire, ordered Thorpe and Romario to get the principal out of the area via the drainage tunnels.

Amazingly, the cops were on the scene in no time at all and while they went after the shooters, Bishop climbed down into the narrow, dark tunnel and saw that his principal and Romario had gotten away okay. The same couldn't be said for Thorpe. He was still down there, writhing around in a foetal position, calling on Bishop to get him out before the walls squeezed the life out of him.

A fear of enclosed spaces would have ended any other bodyguard's career, but Bishop covered for him in his report. In all other respects, the guy was a natural, so Bishop picked him for his team in all future assignments. He just made sure Thorpe was never put into that kind of situation again.

Thorpe's frown became deeper and he stopped fiddling with his clothing. 'Yeah, you got a point there. I guess I *do* owe you one, at that.' He sighed and said, 'So what do you need?'

'Nothing major. Just some simple information retrieval. I want you to go to the office and dig up everything you can on a man named Adam Cortiss.' Bishop spelled out the surname and said, 'History, current status, everything. The guy's definitely a player and I know you got files on everybody over there. There's bound to be something on him.'

Thorpe said, 'You want to give me a clue who he is or am I working completely in the dark here?'

Just then, a slightly overweight man came in from the shower room and both men paused as he began walking towards them, tightening the towel around his ample waist. Halfway down, he turned and disappeared into the next aisle.

'Cortiss used to work for Brennan,' said Bishop. 'He was also the fourth member of the assault team. The one who escaped without a trace.'

There was a short silence, as though Thorpe was thinking through the full implications of what Bishop was saying. 'That's interesting,' he said.

'Isn't it,' Bishop said. 'And I need it now. Can you do it?'

'Assuming I can, how do you want it delivered?'

Bishop pulled a piece of paper containing his new email address from his pants pocket and handed it over. 'Send it to this address as an attachment. That way we don't need to risk another meeting.'

'Okay.' Thorpe reached into the locker and pulled out a thin wallet. He took out a RoyseCorp business card and offered it to Bishop. 'It's got my business cell number on there in case you need to reach me, but I should have something for you in a few hours.'

'The sooner the better,' Bishop said. He memorized the number without touching the card. Then he stood up, left hand still in his pocket. 'I'll keep checking throughout the day.'

'Right,' Thorpe said. 'But look, if you really didn't . . .'

'Thanks,' Bishop said, cutting him off. Then he turned and left before Thorpe could say anything else.

# TWENTY-FOUR

Returning to the scene was a bad risk in anybody's language. Yet here he was. On Long Island again. At the Brennan place where his life had been turned inside out and seven others had come to a violent end.

But risky or not, Bishop always knew he'd return the first chance he got. He *had* to.

The house had been abandoned since the murders. The widowed Mrs Brennan now lived in one of her husband's town apartments with apparently no intention of ever occupying this place again. Bishop couldn't really blame her. And with her husband's life insurance payout and the money from his will, she now had the kind of bank balance that meant she could afford to leave the estate empty for as long as she wanted.

The bus had brought him to a stop two miles away. After a brief visit to a nearby hardware store where he'd bought a long plastic-handled screwdriver and a small pair of wire cutters, he'd walked the rest. It had been a pleasant enough hike with only a handful of vehicles passing him along the way, none of them law. The same security fencing still surrounded the entire perimeter and Bishop approached it from the north side. A simple touch test with the screwdriver showed there was no electrical current running through it any more. After that, the small wire cutters made short work of the chain link fence and he slipped through the opening, then made his way through the dense, overgrown woods until he reached the gazebo at the back of the house.

As he passed, he inspected the stone floor of the gazebo for old blood stains. Something to indicate Thorpe's presence here three years ago. But of course there was nothing.

Bishop reached the house and just stood there for a moment in the mid-afternoon heat, listening to the singing of birds all around him. In front of him was the rear door and the ridiculously expensive anti-blast picture windows. The door was the same model and same colour as before, but given what had happened it was definitely new.

76

To Bishop's left was the four-car garage that extended out from the house with the roof serving as a balcony for the room overlooking it. And by the side of the garage was a small clutch of oak trees with plenty of low branches. After taking a deep breath and stretching his arms, he climbed onto a low but firm-looking branch and didn't stop climbing until he was able to jump onto the garage roof. The buzz of pain from his stomach pushed him on. It served as an almost constant reminder of what he'd done so far and was now becoming an old friend.

His cellmate, Jorge, had always been eager to pass on his extensive lock-picking knowledge to anybody who would listen and Bishop now used that lesson on the balcony door's lock. Fifty-five seconds later he slid the glass door open and stepped into the room. The floor was still carpeted and there were drapes above the windows, but everything else was gone. No furniture; nothing to give any indication as to the room's previous purpose. But Bishop still remembered. This had been Natalie's den, a room she'd preferred to her second-floor bedroom. The room he'd been running for when the rear door blew up in his face.

As Bishop walked through the house, he wondered if the trip here had been worth the risk after all. The kitchen, corridors, entrance foyer and staircases offered up nothing new. A few stains here and there where blood had seeped past the carpet fibres and lodged in the matting, but nothing more. With a head full of memories related to the day of the attack, he'd hoped that coming back here would trigger something important he'd missed. Something still lodged in his subconscious. But instead the same thoughts and images kept spinning round in a circle. And no new answers to slow the merry-go-round down.

Finally, Bishop climbed the spiral staircase to the second floor and entered the room where it all ended.

# TWENTY-FIVE

The only furniture left in Randall Brennan's office was the desk and the ceiling-high bookshelves. All had been emptied and Bishop saw nothing on the table's polished surface except a few smeared fingerprints. Nothing on the walls either, except pale rectangles where Brennan's celebrity photos once hung alongside framed enlargements of his favourite rare stamps. Bishop knelt down in front of the desk, brushing his fingers over the cream-coloured carpet. This was a replacement. Had to be. No way they could have gotten all the bloodstains out of the old one. No cleaning company on earth was that good. Mrs Brennan probably had it replaced the moment the police wrapped up their investigation.

He walked over to the shelves and swept his fingers over every surface until he found the hidden switch. It sat at the back of the fourth shelf down and looked like a natural swelling in the wood, but was actually made of a hard plastic. Easy to miss, even when you were looking for it. Now that he thought about the layout for this part of the house, it seemed obvious that there was an unaccounted-for space between this room and the huge bathroom on the other side. But then, lots of things only become obvious after the fact.

Bishop pressed the wood-coloured lump and heard a metallic click. After a few pushes the shelves slid apart.

The vault door was a steel panel, about three foot by seven, set into a steel internal frame and a larger face frame. An old-fashioned combination wheel sat in the centre, and next to it was a foot-long steel handle. More a bar, really. Like something on a slot machine, but without the black orb at the end.

He grabbed hold of the bar and tried pushing it down, grunting a little with the effort. But all he got out of it was another jab of pain in his stomach. It didn't budge. Bishop took a step back and looked at it. He wondered how long Mrs Brennan had waited after the crime scene boys had finished up before clearing the office and vault of her husband's things. Probably not long at all. Keeping busy with day-to-day tasks is generally the best remedy for bereavement. In which case, it was likely this safe hadn't been reopened in the last thirty-five months. Mrs Brennan might have even forgotten the combination by now, assuming she ever knew it in the first place.

As he turned back to the room his eye caught a flash of white on the floor in the space between the wall and the right-hand bookcase. Like fragments of paper. He crouched down, reached in until his fingers touched the crumpled pages, and pulled them out.

Bishop scanned the three portions. Two pieces were the remains of an acceptance letter from a Wald College, while the third was part of a communication from some rest home in San Francisco. He tried sliding the shelves further to see if there were more in there but they only moved another inch, as if something was jamming the mechanism. He knelt down on the dusty carpet and probed around under the gap at the bottom until he found the obstruction.

Some more paper was lodged in the railing the wheels travelled on. Gently, he jiggled the bookcase to and fro while he tried to pry the sheets out without tearing them. With each motion, a little more came loose. He was starting to sweat in the airless room when they finally came away in his fingers and he stood up and smoothed out the creased fragments.

They were the bottom sections of the other crumpled-up pages. The college acceptance letter for Philip Brennan was no more than that, although the Dean laid heavy hints that the new library wing was in need of sponsors. The one from Willow Reeves Rest Home was a brief response to a previous enquiry from Randall Brennan regarding an old patient of theirs named Timothy Ebert, explaining that they couldn't discuss the details of former residents.

Possibly just random scraps left behind when everything was moved out, but on the other hand, maybe not. Bishop folded the sheets and stuffed them in his jacket pocket. It couldn't hurt to consider them properly later.

As he looked around the room again, his attention was drawn to four equally spaced marks forming a square in the middle of the carpet. The kind of marks a chair might make. Frowning, he raised his eyes to the sloping ceiling directly above and saw a smoke detector. Just like the ones in all the other rooms. Interesting. So somebody had decided to replace the battery on this one *after* the new carpet had been installed. In a house nobody lived in any more. Yet the indicator light wasn't flashing, and Bishop knew batteries on these things could last ten years or more.

He walked through the doorway to the much smaller adjoining room. Previously Brennan had used it for occasional satellite conferences with his overseas clients. Now it was empty save for two metal folding chairs. The kind that opens up like a slanted capital A. They had cross braces across the tubular steel legs and a single-contoured back and waterfall seat. One also bore the faint, smudged imprint of a shoe with a circular space in the centre of the sole. It looked like a size nine. The same shoe size as Tennison, Thorpe and Chaney. That was a big help. And with over twenty thousand different types of sole in circulation at any one time, he couldn't even begin to guess the particular make.

Bishop picked that chair up and took it back into the other room. He positioned the end of the chair legs precisely on the corresponding marks on the floor. A perfect match.

He climbed up and examined the white, circular device above him. Looked like a good quality alarm. Made of tough plastic with the name *Premier Alert* moulded into it and a grille encircling the perimeter. Reaching up, he tried twisting the casing from its base. It was lodged tight. Ignoring the tearing pain in his lower back, he kept at it and finally got it moving, rotating the device anti-clockwise several times until the bottom half came away in his hand.

Inside, a fragment of metal and plastic was stuck to the base. Both materials were black, and affixed to the side of the plastic was something that looked like a broken lens.

You meet a lot of people in the close protection racket. Some good, some bad. But usually talented in some form or another. And a person with a talent likes to talk about his or her skill. Tennison had been a talented guy who loved to talk. He was great with gadgets and new technologies about to hit the market. Hidden surveillance was his particular thing, and the plastic and metal remnant in Bishop's hand looked just like a part of the cameras Tennison used to show him.

From what Bishop remembered, it could have been the remains of a wireless video capture unit, able to zoom in and transmit footage to a receiver or portable hard drive nearby. Motion-activated, maybe. Or possibly something more advanced, able to transmit real-time footage to its owner.

He tried to pull the piece free, but it wouldn't budge. Probably used superglue. Turning the casing over, Bishop pulled the knife from his ankle holster and made a small nick on the outer part of the alarm, matching the position of the lens inside. He then screwed it back onto its base in the ceiling as far as it would go.

The scratch mark pointed in the direction of the vault. Naturally. Which meant that the person who wanted access to that vault must have obtained the combination before the raid ever took place. Possibly weeks or months before.

So why arrange the raid at all?

# TWENTY-SIX

Sixty seconds after Bishop rang Aleron's buzzer, the door half opened and the girl from the park stared back at him. The baseball cap had been discarded, but her hair was still pulled back from her high forehead. Bishop decided she was one of those rare lucky ones who looked prettier the closer you got.

'Ali's not here,' she said. Her large eyes didn't exactly project warmth, but at least she wasn't closing the door in his face.

'I'll come by again later,' he said, turning away.

'You can wait.' The gap had widened a few more inches. 'If you want.'

Bishop nodded his thanks. She led him into the large living room and he smelt the sweet scent of honeysuckle as he passed her.

In the centre of the room two small leather couches and an easy chair were positioned around a marble-effect coffee table. Underneath, a tortoiseshell tabby was fast asleep and Bishop watched it for a few seconds, envying its contentment. By the large, front-facing window, a forty-inch TV was showing the news and the girl picked up the remote and pressed the red button, allowing them to hear the muffled sounds coming from the street.

'I'm making tea,' she said, running her fingers through the end of her short ponytail. When Bishop didn't reply she added, 'It's just as easy to make for two as for one.'

'Tea's good,' he said and sat down on the edge of the nearest couch.

'Taste it before you decide how good it is. Anything with?'

Bishop shook his head. 'Just as it is.'

She raised an eyebrow at him. 'Just black, huh? A man with discerning taste.' Turning, she walked towards what Bishop guessed was the kitchen, then stopped and turned back with a furrowed brow. 'Did I make a mistake?'

'When?'

'Just now when I let an escaped psycho through the front door.'

Bishop smiled and said, 'Don't hold back, say what you think.'

'Not my words. It's what the TV's calling you.'

'Can't argue with TV, can I? After all, they've never been wrong before.'

'Point taken. But it raises the question of who actually killed those poor people if it wasn't you.'

'I'm kind of curious about that myself,' Bishop said.

'And?'

'I'm still working on it.' He scratched under his chin, feeling a few stray beard hairs, and said, 'I take it Aleron doesn't treat the six o'clock news as gospel, either.'

She paused, then said, 'He told me he's met his fair share of psychos and you don't fit the profile. Said a sociopath tries to charm everyone he meets from the word go, adapting his behaviour to fit in with those around him, but you weren't afraid to be disliked.'

'He notices a lot.'

'So does Owen,' she said. 'He told Ali you might have been the only innocent man in Greenacres.'

'Well, I'm innocent of the crime they put me away for,' he said, studying her eyes. 'But I'm no boy scout. You'd be wrong to think that.'

'Okay. But are you what they say you are?'

'No. That much I'm not.'

'Well, then.' The smile she gave him lit up her face. 'I'm Jenna,' she added before leaving the room.

Bishop sat back on the couch and laid his head against the soft leather. Relishing the feeling he took a deep breath, held it, counted to ten. As he exhaled he stretched his legs out and clenched his muscles. Under the coffee table the cat stirred and stared at him. It seemed everyone was wary of him at the moment. He looked down and stared right back, thinking of that camera remnant he'd found in Brennan's office. And the bonding cement residues he'd found in three other smoke detectors around the house, including the one in Natalie's den. The reasoning behind the one in the office was self-evident, but he was still trying to figure out the significance of the others. After a while, he realized the cat still hadn't looked away. *Don't cats ever blink?*

'You're wasting your time,' Jenna said, interrupting their competition. 'Bud can outstare a statue.' She placed a mug on the table near him and took a few sips from her own. Then she took a seat on the matching couch opposite, stretching out both legs under the table and tickling the cat's head with her toes.

Bishop tried his tea. 'It's good. Thanks.'

'You don't look like a James,' she said.

The comment threw Bishop for a second and he found he enjoyed the feeling. Jenna clearly wasn't afraid to speak her mind and he hadn't met many women like that. Although he did wonder what a James was supposed to look like. Especially as there were so many of them. 'Well, I remember my parents calling me James when I was a kid,' he said. 'But these days most people just call me Bishop.'

'Uh, huh,' she said. 'You and Luke were funny this morning.'

'Lucas?' When she nodded, he said, 'I couldn't help myself. Guys like him just bring it out of me.' About to place the mug on the table, he paused midway. 'You think he'll make trouble for me?'

'Not unless he wants to make trouble for Ali, and he'd never do that. He's hardly in a position to anyway, even if he recognized you. Which he probably didn't.'

'Okay.' Bishop sat back and studied the room. 'I don't see any photos of you and Aleron on display.'

Jenna watched him, then said, 'Well, we've got a long history, you know?'

'Yeah?'

She frowned at the ceiling. 'Let's see now. Next March, it'll be . . . twenty-seven years. Exactly.'

Bishop smiled. 'Okay, I missed that one. You're his sister.'

'Owen's, too. It's not obvious, although I thought the similarity in the eyes might have given you a clue. With Owen out of my reach, I at least try to spend a Sunday morning with my big brother when I get the chance.'

'It's late afternoon now.'

Jenna looked out the window. 'Yes,' she said with a shrug and turned back to him, a faint upturn at the corners of her mouth. 'It is.'

There was a momentary silence and Bishop realized how rusty he was when it came to small talk. There hadn't been much call for it in his previous careers. Even less so inside. But he figured now was as good a time as any to reacquaint himself with the technique. 'You live nearby?' he asked.

'Out in Laurelton. Close enough when you think about it, but you know what siblings are like.'

'Yes. And I get why Luke acted that way now.'

'He's got no claims on me, no matter what he thinks. I make my own decisions about who I want to talk to.' Jenna pulled her feet up to her chest. 'And who I want to spend time with.'

'That I can believe,' he said.

Three heads turned at the sound of a key in the lock and Jenna called out, 'We're in here, Ali.'

A second later Aleron appeared, saw Bishop and said, 'Sorry, man.' He nodded to his sister and said, 'Hasn't the guy been through enough? And don't you have kickboxing class tonight?'

'Don't I every Sunday?' she said. 'Don't worry, I'll get out of your hair now.'

Bishop watched as Jenna stood up. She was about five-four, small-boned with narrow hips and slender legs, but there was plenty of sinewy muscle in there. Probably not an ounce of fat on her. Her body reminded him of a gymnast he'd once known, back when he was stationed at the American embassy in Haiti. Like Jenna, she'd also looked great from every angle.

Jenna noticed the way he was studying her and smiled. 'Don't ever call me petite,' she said. 'I'm stronger than I look.'

'People generally are,' he said. 'You practise around here?'

'The Women's New Hope Center near the airport. Well, not *there*, exactly. More like the gym a block down from it, but lots of women from there come along.' She looked down her nose at him and winked. 'And I don't practise, I teach.'

'Let the man alone, Jenna. We got business,' Aleron said as he walked towards the basement door. 'I'll phone you in the week,' he called out over his shoulder.

Bishop got up and said, 'Thanks for the tea.'

She smiled. 'Hey, that's what Sunday afternoons are for. Look, if I don't see you again . . .' She hesitated for a second and then said, 'Well . . . good luck, James.'

He nodded to her and followed Aleron downstairs. In the basement, Aleron led him to the worktable and pulled out a cheap plastic credit-card wallet from his pocket and handed it over. 'Okay, Mr Allbright, you're all ready to join the human race again. At least, superficially.'

Bishop opened it to the first sleeve containing the replica Social Security card and pulled it out. It had been laminated and looked convincingly worn at the corners, with a further crease running down the red government watermark in the centre. Aleron had done a pretty good job. Better than good, actually. He replaced it and took out the driver's licence and birth certificate.

'Like I told you,' Aleron said, 'these babies'll be good enough for the basics, like checking into a dive or getting past the front door of a government building, but not much more than that. Any place where they cross-reference your name or that Social Security number against a database and you're history. I could supply you with the complete package – that's my speciality – but it would cost a whole lot more. Time as well as money. And I get the feeling you don't want to wait around.'

'These look fine,' Bishop said. He pulled some folded notes from his shirt pocket and handed them over. 'A thousand.'

Aleron counted it quickly before putting it in his pocket and said, 'So you found a place to bed down yet?'

Bishop shrugged. 'Possibly.'

'No need to get suspicious. Maybe I feel I owe you for Owen.'

'Forget about Owen. Nobody owes me anything. I told him I didn't do it for him. If he'd been killed I wouldn't have got what I needed to get out, that's all.'

Aleron grinned. 'A man alone.'

'Life's a lot simpler that way.'

'What kinda life is that? Seems to me you could have stayed inside for all the difference it makes to you.'

'Maybe I just prefer my windows without bars over them.' And maybe he wasn't all that happy about being set up for somebody else's crime, but Aleron didn't need to know that.

'There *is* that, I guess,' Aleron said and handed him a folded piece of paper.

Bishop opened it and read the three addresses on it. 'What are these?'

'Three hotels of the dive variety. I been told they don't scrutinize a person's particulars as carefully as they should. In the current climate, the kind of place that's harder to find than a sixteen-year-old virgin. Especially in New York. Just some information you might find useful. Use it or don't. No skin off my nose.'

'I might do that. Thanks,' Bishop said. He didn't need any more enemies and when a man was offered advice, it made sense to listen.

'No problem.'

Bishop left Aleron in the basement and let himself out of the house. On the street, the sun was approaching its final descent and routine traffic passed back and forth, both vehicular and pedestrian. Everything looked pretty normal. Nothing pinged on his radar. Bishop started walking north.

# TWENTY-SEVEN

Danny Costa had been lucky. The small diner on the opposite side of the street was the perfect spot from which to keep an eye on the house until Bishop finished his business inside. Finding a table near the window was even better.

Costa didn't actually know *why* Hedison wanted this Bishop followed, but that didn't matter. The instruction alone was enough. Hedison tended to keep things close to his chest at the start, but he'd reveal the reason later, as always. As soon as he'd heard of the prison escape this morning, he'd guessed the fugitive would revisit the scene of the crime at some point and had installed Costa near the house on Long Island to keep a lookout. And, of course, Bishop had shown up just a few hours ago. Just as Hedison predicted. Keeping track of him since then had been relatively easy.

And now, some new players on the scene.

Just ten minutes ago, Costa had seen the sexy black piece come out the front door. Very nice, too. Slim and petite; a real stunner. As she'd walked off to the left, hungry eyes had followed her until she left their line of sight. A few minutes later, a Honda cruised by with her at the wheel, slowing down a little in front of the house as though she'd forgotten something before taking off again. Costa had jotted down the licence plate number in a notebook on the table next to a Sunday supplement left behind by a previous customer and continued to wait.

And here was Bishop now, closing the front door and approaching the street. Costa looked down at the supplement and turned a page, aware the target would be scanning the area for anything that looked wrong. By the time it felt safe to look up again, Bishop was already on the sidewalk, walking in the direction the car had gone.

Costa left a five-dollar bill and exited the diner, waiting until Bishop reached the end of the street before following.

# TWENTY-EIGHT

Standing in front of a convenience store, Bishop studied the five-storey building across the street. Straight away he could tell that the classiest thing about the Ambassador Hotel was its name. The building's shabby facade suggested its glory years were far in the past, if they ever existed at all.

It looked perfect.

The hotel was located on a street seventeen blocks north of Aleron's, with several boarded-up storefronts acting as neighbours. Further down on the left was a bleak-looking office complex. On this side, a couple of bars, an all-night diner, a video rental store and the convenience store shared space with apartments and private residences.

Bishop waited for a gap in the traffic, crossed over, and entered the hotel.

The foyer contained eight uncomfortable-looking easy chairs and a couple of tables containing magazines. One man sat watching the TV in the far left corner. Another sat near the windows, listening to his personal music player while reading an old issue of *Entertainment Weekly*. He glanced up briefly at Bishop before returning to it. Straight ahead Bishop saw the elevator bank next to a set of stairs, and a wide corridor that he assumed led to the rear of the building. At his right, a bespectacled man sat behind the long reception counter, watching Bishop as he approached. He looked to be in his mid to late forties and had unnaturally brown hair and the lined face of a lifelong smoker.

'Help you?' he said. The name on the plaque in front of him read *Tyler Marks*.

'I need a room for tonight,' Bishop said.

Marks made a show of looking down at Bishop's missing luggage. 'Last minute decision, huh?'

Bishop smiled. 'The girlfriend came back a day early and didn't like what she found. Had to make do with what I could grab.'

Marks smirked and said, 'Rooms are sixty a night in advance. Checkout's at eleven. All rooms got a TV. I'll need some ID. Rules, you know?'

'Where would we be without them?' Bishop said. He took some notes from his pocket and counted out sixty in twenties and tens. Placed them on the counter along with his new licence.

Marks compared the photo to the face in front of him. Then he took the money and placed it somewhere out of view. 'Just one night, is it?'

'Yeah. Or until Christine gets over it.'

Marks snorted. 'Don't hold your breath, Mr Allbright. You're lucky you still got a pair. Okay, you wanna fill this in and I'll get your key.'

Bishop took a pen from the holder and filled spaces on the registration form. Marks slid a key over with 308 printed on the metal fob. Bishop pushed the form back, took the key and watched Marks compare the details with those on his licence. Then Marks handed the licence back and said, 'Elevators just over there. Enjoy your stay.'

'Sure,' said Bishop. But he saw that Marks had already refocused his attention on the TV and was no longer listening.

# TWENTY-NINE

Bishop decided the room would do. it was located at the rear of the hotel, looked relatively clean and contained a bed, a shower and a TV. There was also a fire escape outside the window with a metal ladder leading to the street below. He'd already checked where the hallway downstairs led and found the rear fire door. Opening it hadn't set off any alarms, either.

He'd visited another internet café on the way here and now he took the nine pages he'd printed out of his pocket and unfolded them. Thorpe had delivered the information as promised. Bishop slipped off his shoes and jacket and lay down on the bed with the pages in his hand.

The top sheet was a photocopied, grainy enlargement of a passport photo. The man looking back at him had a thick neck, short, dark, naturally wavy hair, slightly off-kilter eyes that dropped down at the edges and, of course, the long nose atop a straight mouth and the cleft chin and sunken cheeks Bishop remembered. So here it was, the first step in Bishop's search for who set him up. All in all, an average-looking face you wouldn't look at twice if you passed it in the street. Probably just one of many reasons the CIA recruiters approached him during his last year of college.

The other eight pages gave a brief summary of his agency and post-agency career. Bishop started in at the beginning.

Adam Cortiss joined the agency on August 15, 1984. He spent the next two years at their training facility at Camp Pearly, Virginia with a curriculum that included paramilitary training, countersurveillance techniques, and interrogation methods. He re-entered the world as a newly minted, fully qualified CIA operations officer in June 1986.

His first two years in the field, from 1986 to 1988, were spent based in US embassies in a variety of hot spots like Haiti and Kenya, recruiting suitable assets for his new employers. The résumé was short on specifics, but Bishop assumed 'suitable' in this case meant a combination of guillibility, greed and general hostility towards one's fellow man. The kind of qualities the CIA usually looked for in a source. Code names like 'Operation

Good Girl' or 'Operation Deep Steel' got mentions, but without the actual agency files to hand Bishop could only guess at their meaning.

He assumed Cortiss was successful, as the following two years saw him in Afghanistan helping to arrange the transport of certain Afghans and Arabs to the US for military training as part of 'Operation Cyclone'.

Bishop recognized that code name, all right. The operation that armed, trained and financed what would later become the Taliban had come in for a lot of criticism since the events of 9/11. Most of it deserved, in Bishop's opinion. He'd served for eight years and regretted nothing, but his country's frequent shortsightedness when it came to foreign policy still amazed him. You couldn't keep arming and financing groups like that and not expect it to come back and bite you in the ass in the long run. But the decision makers never seemed to learn. Probably never would, either.

According to the data, Cortiss had arranged entry visas for 'recruiter trainers' and found them apartments on Atlantic Avenue in Brooklyn; in the very same block Bin Laden set up his own recruitment offices for 'freedom fighters'. Bishop once read that he'd utilized the services of the more extreme elements that passed through those doors to lay the seeds for al-Qaeda.

In 1993, Cortiss was part of a multi-agency coalition assigned the task of toppling the Guatemalan president, Jorge Serrano Elias, who'd recently taken it upon himself to suspend the country's constitution. Two months later, Cortiss left Guatemala under the care of its new president, Ramiro de Leon Carpio.

In 1994, he turned up in Afghanistan again on a long-term reconnaissance mission concerning the mujahideen's courier network for smuggling opium out of the country. Bishop had to smile at that one. 'Reconnaissance' could be a euphemism for so many things.

Cortiss also got a mention at a congressional hearing in 1996 as someone who 'might have been present' during the interrogation and torture of six student agitators in the Dominican Republic. And he was ignominiously expelled from Greece in 1999 for behaviour 'incompatible with his diplomatic status'. Which, in Bishop's estimation, could mean almost anything. But probably nothing good.

So it was no real surprise to Bishop to learn of his exit from the agency in June 2001. Budget cuts were the reasons given, but Bishop knew better than that. The adverse publicity resulting from the Greek expulsion just meant it was probably more cost effective for them to cut their losses and pay him off than to keep him on and risk getting more. And then in November the same year, Brennan hired him as an advance point man in his domestic and overseas business negotiations. No mention given to their parting of the ways a few years later, though.

Bishop had to admit, the guy got around. Mixed with some nice company, too.

He kept coming back to one entry in particular. On the fourth page. It was from Berlin in 1990 and concerned the Rosenholz files: a collection of four hundred CDs packed with invaluable info on agents of the HVA, East Germany's foreign intelligence service. They were widely believed to be stored at the Ministry for State Security, headquarters of that country's not-so-secret police, the Stasi. The entry implied that Cortiss had been a member of a small assault team involved in a break-in at the Ministry on January 15. At the scene, the police found seven dead officials and guards with single shots to the head. And no Rosenholz files anywhere on the grounds. It took the guys at Langley a year to admit they had them in their possession, but not how they got them.

A professional, well-organized night raid on a well-protected fortress that resulted in a high body count. The whole operation sounded a little too similar to the Brennan attack for Bishop's liking. He wouldn't have been surprised if Cortiss had arranged other such incursions in the years since. Perhaps not high profile enough to make it into this file. There was a definite modus operandi at work here.

Thing was, if Bishop were to believe the official story, Cortiss was also dead.

A full year before the Brennan raid took place, Cortiss apparently lost control of his BMW while driving back from a restaurant in Washington DC. He crashed into the back of a heavy-duty gravel truck and died instantly. The authorities found plenty of identification on him and a distant cousin living in Massachusetts named Sean Stephenson officially identified the body. Bishop checked to see if there was any reference to where Cortiss had been buried. Unsurprisingly, according to the police report, Stephenson had him immediately cremated. *All very neat and tidy.*

Placing the papers at his side, Bishop yawned and looked at his watch. It was 18.17 now and his eyelids felt like they had weights attached to them. In the last thirty-six hours the only sleep he'd had was the four hours he'd spent unconscious in the prison hospital. His body needed rest. Yawning again, he dropped his head back on the pillow and closed his eyes.

# THIRTY

At 9.13 p.m. two black-and-whites silently coasted down the quiet street before parking diagonally in front of the Ambassador. They were joined within seconds by a third. Then a fourth vehicle, a grey four-door Chevrolet, arrived from the opposite direction and double-parked a few spaces down.

Two women and one man emerged from the Chevrolet all wearing windbreakers with US MARSHAL written in large white letters on the backs. One also wore a black cap. As if on cue, the doors on the other vehicles opened and five uniforms quietly swarmed around the Marshals like a protective detail.

The one wearing the cap gesticulated with her hands as she gave her orders, pointing down the street to the left of the hotel, then in the opposite direction. One policeman followed her first command and ran two hundred yards until he reached the doorway of a boarded-up store. He waited there, hand on his holster. Another did the same in the other direction, this time holing up in the shadows of the entrance to the underground car park that served the tenants of the office building. The other three policemen stayed with the Marshal while she gave further instructions.

Loose groups of pedestrians hung around to stare and a few more waited on the sidewalk opposite the hotel to see what was happening. The two policemen at their guard posts stopped anyone on the hotel side from getting any closer.

A man with a heavily lined face and a bad dye job emerged from the hotel entrance and strode over to the group. The lead Marshal spoke to him briefly and he nodded emphatically. She asked him something else and he shook his head and spoke a few words in response. Then he went back inside.

The Marshal jerked her head up, scanning the immediate area. She pulled a walkie-talkie from her belt and brought it to her mouth. Before she had a chance to speak, a fifth cruiser arrived and just as silently parked in front of the convenience store on the other side of the street. She waited as a patrolman got out the passenger side and ran across the street to her. The driver emerged from his side but didn't follow, just came round the vehicle to the sidewalk and leaned his elbows on the roof of his car.

After a brief conversation his partner returned and gave him their new orders. Then he jogged down the sidewalk to the left and moved the onlookers on his side. The driver turned as two men and a woman exited the convenience store and he told each of them to keep walking to the right. Then he leaned on the car again and watched the hotel.

The Marshal who'd been giving all the orders spoke into her walkie-talkie for a few seconds and then pulled a Glock 19 from her side holster. Her colleagues and the three patrolmen did likewise. Then they all followed her into the hotel.

# THIRTY-ONE

Standing with his back to the convenience store, the patrolman flinched when the barrel of the Beretta pressed against his right kidney, but didn't turn around or move his hands from the car roof.

'That's right,' Bishop said, 'we're all friends here. No sudden moves. You wouldn't believe how nervous I get.'

'I believe you,' the cop said.

'That's a promising start. Hold that thought.'

A sudden spasm in Bishop's stomach had jerked him awake at 20.55. He'd allowed the pain to sit with him for a while, the throbbing concentrating his mind, and then he'd forced himself up. Now, though, he was glad he had. Were it not for the overriding compulsion to buy more painkillers he'd still be in the Ambassador. Instead, deciding the less Marks knew of his comings and goings the better, he had grabbed his jacket and gun and left the hotel via the fire exit out back, circling round to reach the all-night store across the street. He'd just paid for the Advil, along with a Coke and a two-day-old hot dog heated up in the store microwave, when the patrol car came to a stop outside.

Bishop had taken a large bite of the hot dog as he approached the window and assessed the situation outside. He hadn't seen or heard them go in, but the Chevy was the same one he'd seen on the news this morning. Which meant Marshals. With the two cops stationed across the street and the two on this side, he figured two more would take the rear. Maybe one or two on the roof. Another one in the lobby. Delaney and her deputies would no doubt handle room 308 themselves. Bishop looked left and right. He couldn't see any black-and-whites blocking the ends of the street yet, but more cops would come. They always did.

Valuable seconds ticked by as he waited for the driver on the other side of the window to move away from his car and allow him to exit the store and disappear from all their lives without any fuss. But the cop didn't move.

And Bishop couldn't stay here. As soon as they found his room empty they'd lock the perimeter down for witnesses. And more back-up could arrive at any moment. He had to leave. Immediately.

'Okay,' he told the cop, 'I'm gonna reach down for your gun and eject the shells, then place it back in your holster. Just stay still and imagine you're on a tightrope a thousand feet up. The slightest wrong move and you fall. We both will.'

'I understand.'

Glancing around, Bishop saw that nobody was interested in them. Two hundred yards to his left, the cop's partner was in front of one of the bars arguing with three patrons who evidently wanted to stay and watch the show. The other two standing guard across the street were embroiled in their own efforts to keep the growing band of spectators back. Bishop smiled. You just had to love New York.

Keeping pressure on the Beretta in the cop's back, Bishop used his left hand to unclip the safety clasp on the man's holster, pull the .357 out and flip the chamber open in less than two seconds. He shook the gun a couple of times until all six shells fell into the gutter. Then he flipped the chamber home and replaced it in the holster. Bishop still needed this guy and allowing him some semblance of dignity by not taking his weapon would make him less likely to do something stupid.

'That's real good,' he said. 'We're taking each other seriously. What's gonna happen now is we're both gonna get in your cruiser and drive away from here.'

'The world and his old lady's looking for you, Bishop,' the cop said. 'You won't last a minute.'

'Maybe a minute's all I need. What's your name, patrolman?'

'Prior. Cliff Prior.'

'Where are your car keys, Cliff?'

'Left jacket pocket.'

Bishop increased the pressure on the Beretta as he reached round with his left hand and pulled the keys out. He also unlatched the cuffs from the cop's belt and put them in his own pocket. 'Okay, Cliff,' he said, 'bring your arms down slowly from the roof and open the door.'

The cop did as he was told and pulled the door ajar. No interior lights came on, as per regulations.

'On three, get in and move quickly over to the driver's seat with your hands on the wheel at ten and two. I'll be right behind you. Got it?'

'Yeah,' Prior said. 'I got it.'

'Good. Here we go. One. Two. Three.'

Prior ducked into the car and clambered across to the driver's seat, his legs just avoiding the bulky radio equipment and bracketed laptop. Bishop slid into the passenger seat and closed the door behind him. He motioned with his gun for Prior to put his hands on the wheel. As the cop complied, Bishop lowered himself down in the seat.

He turned the radios off and dropped the keys onto the cop's lap as Prior looked back at him. He was in his mid-twenties, clean-shaven, with deep acne scars. No longer a rookie but hardly a veteran. His eyebrows slanted downwards and met above his nose in a permanent V of disapproval. The small eyes burned into Bishop, no doubt committing his face to memory while his mind weighed the options before him. Experience would be telling him he'd probably get through this if he just followed orders.

'Start her up and drive straight ahead,' Bishop said. 'And no screeching of tyres or stalling the engine. You're too smart for that and I'm too fragile.'

Prior inserted the key in the ignition and turned it clockwise. The engine came to life immediately. 'Then what?'

'Focus on the present. Drive.'

The policeman put the car in gear and pressed his foot lightly down on the gas. The vehicle moved off slowly. Bishop felt it gain speed, and when he thought enough distance had been covered he raised himself up on the seat and looked through the windshield. They were approaching a crossroads and a red light.

'Take a left,' said Bishop. 'Screw the red light. You're a cop.'

Prior's walkie-talkie started chattering as he looked left, waiting for a gap in the oncoming traffic.

'Call in,' Bishop said. 'Say you received a possible sighting on Ruscoe Street and you're checking it out. No more than that. Then click off.'

'They won't believe me.'

'They won't disbelieve you, either. Not straight away. Do it.'

Still looking for a gap in the traffic, Prior pulled the radio from his belt and brought it to his mouth. Bishop checked the rear-view as Prior gave his destination. Once he was done, Bishop grabbed the radio and threw it in the glove compartment. The light turned green as they were waiting and Prior drove into 108th Avenue towards Merrick.

Bishop said, 'Turn on your siren and flashers and pull the lead out. You'll take a right at Merrick when we come to it. You guessed where we're headed yet?'

Prior turned on his lights and the accompanying siren got everyone's attention. He swerved left into the oncoming lane and started overtaking. The cars coming towards them got out of the way quickly. 'Jamaica,' he said.

'That's right.' Bishop knew Merrick would take them to Archer. Then another five or six blocks to one of the busiest transit hubs in New York. Ten of the eleven LIRR lines passed through Jamaica before splintering off again. And although it was a Sunday evening, Bishop figured there'd be more than enough commuters for his purpose.

Ahead of them, a long line of cars waited for the lights to let them join Merrick. Prior kept in the oncoming lane and paused at the junction until the flashing red and white lights did their job. He sped off again down the four-lane thoroughfare, veering in and out of traffic like a pro. Bishop suspected a small part of him was actually enjoying this.

'You're doing okay, Cliff,' he said over the noise. 'Just a little while longer and you'll have the vehicle to yourself again.' He looked at the gold band on the fourth finger of the cop's left hand. 'And a bedtime story to tell your wife.'

'Sure. Unless you go psycho on me.'

Bishop looked ahead at the busy six-way junction coming up at speed and sighed. 'Believe it or not, killing cops isn't high on my list of priorities,' he said. 'I got enough problems. Not that I won't if you force me to. Drive straight through this and take a left on Archer. You've done this before. Don't stop; let the siren and the lights do the work.'

The policeman geared down as he approached the intersection. The east- and westbound cross traffic in front slowed at the unwelcome intrusion and Prior used the available space to manoeuvre them through like they were in a game of pinball. When they emerged out the other side, Prior continued down Merrick, gradually picking up speed and raising his eyes to the rear-view every few seconds.

'Something interesting?' Bishop asked. He reached up and swivelled the mirror round. Behind them he made out red and white lights in the distance. Looked like two cars. *Well, that didn't take long.* 'Delaney, right?'

Prior made a face and grunted, as if the very idea of a female in charge marked the beginning of the final days.

'I'd only been there a few hours,' Bishop said, watching his eyes. 'She's better than I thought.'

'Or luckier. The desk clerk at the hotel made you and pressed three buttons on a phone. Yeah, she's talented, all right.'

Bishop smiled to himself. He figured she must be good at her job. Bad cops weren't hated with such vehemence. 'It's a new millennium, Cliff. It's entirely possible she reached her position on merit alone.'

Prior didn't reply. Probably didn't see the irony in their conflicting viewpoints, either.

Bishop looked ahead. Here came Archer. And a green light, no less. It changed to amber as they approached. 'Beat the light,' he said.

Prior accelerated and swept across the line of vehicles waiting to proceed east, tearing round into the westbound lane at forty. '*Shit on a chute*,' he cried and spun the wheel to the right. A large Kawasaki was coming straight at them, encroaching on their lane to get to the head of the eastbound queue. The rider saw their car bearing down on him and swerved to his right at the same time. Bishop grimaced as the bike collided with the rear door of a stationary yellow cab. The police cruiser missed him by a hair as it sped by.

Bishop glanced in the rear-view and saw the rider topple into the street with his machine. A moment later he got up and looked down at his bike, then back at the disappearing police car, while an angry, overweight man climbed out of the taxi alongside him.

'Jesus Horatio Christ,' Prior breathed as he stared straight ahead, too scared to look in his wing mirrors. 'Is he okay? Tell me he's okay.'

'He's fine,' Bishop said, 'as long as the cabbie doesn't kill him.' York College flew by to their left and he looked across at the elevated LIRR lines running parallel to them. 'Maybe he'll stay in his own lane in future.'

The cop glanced in his side mirror and said, 'That's not funny. Jesus. That was *too* close.'

'Forget about it. We're nearly there.' They darted through the 150th Street intersection and Bishop could see the Sutphin Boulevard junction a block ahead. As Prior muttered distractedly under his breath, Bishop started transferring everything from his leather jacket to his pants pockets. In the distance, two more lines of cars waited at the next set of lights.

Bishop said, 'Kill the siren and stop behind that last car.' The cop obeyed the first instruction and began to decelerate. Bishop pulled out his baseball cap and Prior's cuffs. He put the cap on and waited for the car to come to a halt in the centre lane behind a red Toyota. He didn't need to look in the rear-view to make the flashing lights two or three blocks back. Or the din of the sirens. The Jamaica Station terminal lay ahead at the far corner of the intersection. He had about fifteen seconds. 'Give me your handcuff keys,' he said.

Prior hesitated, then pulled them from his pants pocket and tossed them over. Bishop handed him his cuffs and said, 'Through the wheel, Cliff. Hands on either side. It's in both our interests for you to be quick.' He waited while the cop attached one of the bracelets to his left wrist, then pulled the other through the gap in the steering wheel and attached it to his right.

The V was back in place as Prior glared back. 'Maybe I'll see you again, Bishop,' he said.

'Only on TV,' Bishop said and took the keys from the ignition and placed the gun in the waistband of his pants. 'Your jurisdiction ends at the state line.' While Prior chewed on that, Bishop got out and slammed the door shut.

He looked back and saw that the two cars in pursuit had shortened the distance to a block. The grey Chevy was in front, followed by another black-and-white. Bishop turned and ran to the sidewalk, threw both sets of keys into the gutter along with his hotel key, then sprinted towards the five-storey building on the other side of the crossroads.

Bishop figured they wouldn't have seen him exit the vehicle so they'd have to check Prior's cruiser first. Then they'd figure he was making for the terminal and one of the train platforms, maybe even the subway station underneath them. And Prior would confirm it.

When Bishop reached the Sutphin Boulevard intersection he stopped behind the cover of an office building on the corner and glanced back. Both cars had come to a stop behind the cruiser, lights still flashing but sirens off.

Bishop faced front and pulled the cap from his head and slid out of his jacket, making sure his sweatshirt covered the gun. He took the glasses from his shirt pocket and put them on. Then he walked off the kerb between two parked cars, tossed the jacket and cap underneath the one on the left and jogged across the street towards the entrance doors.

Jamaica had recently undergone a major expansion, and the elevated tracks to the left of the station building were now housed under a curved steel and glass canopy that took up a large part of the skyline. Underneath, a long underpass led to the station control centre on the other side of the tracks.

When Bishop reached the doors to the terminal he took another look behind him. His pursuers hadn't reached the corner building yet, so he ignored the entrance and began walking left towards the underpass. A hundreds yards ahead he spotted the mandatory taxi rank and saw a short line of yellow cabs with *On Duty* signs. He turned to look behind him as he walked and saw Delaney sprinting towards the terminal doors with two more Marshals and a couple of uniforms in tow. She yanked the door open and all five disappeared into the building.

Bishop continued until he reached the taxi stand. In the cab at the head of the queue sat a bearded, fifty-something driver reading the sports pages and picking his nose. Bishop opened the rear door and sank into the back seat.

'Just tell me where, pal,' the driver said without checking the rear-view. He flung the paper on the seat next to him and continued picking his nose.

Bishop looked out the side window and considered his answer. It was a good question. If he couldn't trust the staff of a fleapit like the Ambassador, what chance did he have with any of the others? Especially as his new ID was now worthless. So hotels were out. Which didn't leave too many other options.

Except one, maybe.

'Make for Kennedy airport,' he told the driver.

# THIRTY-TWO

'You were somewhere else tonight,' Helen Sook Nam said.

Jenna Falstaff frowned at her friend as she pulled her towel tight across her chest. 'Somewhere else?' she asked.

As usual, they were the only two left in the locker room. Of all her students, the pretty, slight Korean woman had known Jenna the longest, and she always made sure the two of them were the last to shower so they could gossip about the men in their lives. Or, rather, since Jenna was usually lacking in that department, so *she* could gossip about the men in *her* life. There was usually more than one at any given moment.

Helen looped the brassiere over her shoulders and reached through the long mane of impossibly silky black hair behind her to connect it. 'Somewhere nice, I hope,' she said. 'You weren't as focused as you usually are. You seeing someone I don't know about?'

Jenna smiled as she extracted various items of clothing from her locker and began to put them on. As far as Helen was concerned, any change in your behaviour meant the involvement of a man somewhere along the line. And would you believe it? For the first time ever, she was right on the mark. James Bishop *had* been in her thoughts for much of the day.

When she'd suggested to Ali she might hang around the house for a while longer this afternoon he'd just smiled and said, 'There's no future in it. And you the sensible one, too.' She knew that Ali was right on both counts, but she could also tell that Bishop was attracted to her too. She'd considered giving him her cell phone number before she left, but as usual common sense had prevailed at the last moment. If Bishop was picked up with her number on his person, the trail could end with Ali joining Owen in Greenacres and she wasn't about to risk losing another brother.

*Damn*, she thought. Why did she always go for the impossible ones? To her friend, she said, 'The only guys I meet are the ones you try to set me up with. None of whom, I might add, are ever worth a second date.'

Helen giggled. 'You're too fussy is what it is, Jen. At least try them out in the sack. Then if you don't like 'em, throw 'em out with the bacon rinds. Easy.'

'Maybe I've got a few more scruples than you.'

Helen scrunched her nose at the word like it was week-old milk. 'Scruples. What good are they?' She nodded at the Elvis T-shirt Jenna was placing in her bag. '*He* sure didn't have any; that man went for anything that passed in front of him. Although you couldn't really blame him, looking like that.' She gazed at the ceiling and said, 'I wonder if he ever had an Oriental?'

Jenna shook her head as she slipped into her tan suede jacket and reached down for her sneakers. After lacing them up, she said, 'Are we ready?'

'Always.'

They picked up their equipment bags and slung them over their shoulders, then left the changing room and walked through the downstairs gym. It was empty now aside from the owner, who was checking the next day's bookings on the computer at the front desk.

They said goodnight and descended the steps to the sidewalk while the owner locked up behind them. The street below was lined with parked vehicles that were only partly obscured by the large elms that lined the pavement at twenty-yard intervals.

'Can't interest you in a night out at Artisans, I suppose?' Helen said when they reached the sidewalk. Artisans was a new, trendy singles bar cum nightclub that had become her hot place to be seen this month. 'Tonight's manhunt night.'

Jenna smiled. 'Never give up, do you? And tomorrow a work day.'

'Hey, you're only young once. Unless you live in LA, that is. I take it that's a no, then?'

'Ask me again on Wednesday, okay?'

'Hold you to it.' At that moment Helen's cell phone went off and she reached into her bag and brought it to her ear, turning and waving to Jenna as she began her three-block walk to the bus stop. 'Hank, I was gonna call *you* . . . Tonight? Baby, I'm bushed . . . Of *course* I do, but with tomorrow a work day . . .'

*The girl's incorrigible*, Jenna thought, shaking her head as she watched her friend walk away. She turned to go in the other direction, but she'd only taken about ten steps when a man in a hood stepped out from behind the tree a few feet in front of her.

Dropping her right shoulder to let her bag fall to the ground, Jenna immediately gave him her left side and raised both fists. Adrenalin pumped through her body and her heart rate doubled. *Please don't let him have a gun*, she thought.

The man remained still except for the movement of the left arm as it pulled the hood back. Jenna's heartbeat slackened only marginally when she saw his features.

Bishop smiled and said, 'Let's not fight, Jenna.'

# THIRTY-THREE

'Never been out here before.' Bishop waited while Jenna found her keys and inserted one into the top lock of apartment 3C. She looked good under the bright corridor lights. 'It's quiet.'

'Yeah, it's okay,' she said. 'For this town better than okay, I guess. People here mind their own business.'

After a short walk to her ten-year-old Honda Accord, Jenna had driven them to her modern, six-storey apartment block in Laurelton, a leafy suburb of Queens with wide roads and plenty of single-family homes. They'd parked in a small area at the rear with spaces for twenty. Bishop had counted three apartments on each floor, leading off from a single elevator that ran through the centre of the building.

Jenna finished with the second lock and opened the door. She stepped inside and flicked a couple of switches. When the lights came on she said, 'You may enter.'

Bishop followed her down the short hallway, passing a neat bathroom on his left, and came to a stop in the living room.

It wasn't immediately obvious that a single woman lived here. Bishop had expected bright colours and houseplants, but he guessed maybe that was just his sister's taste. Jenna's walls were white and made the place look bigger than it was, while a large picture window took up most of the wall ahead. In the centre of the room a light grey three-seater sofa and two matching chairs sat around a black wooden coffee table whose surface was covered with folders, files, magazines and loose paperwork. On the left-hand wall, next to an archway leading to another hallway, a widescreen TV sat alongside a tall bookcase filled with CDs, DVDs and paperbacks. Another smaller bookcase against the right-hand wall held nothing but computer texts. For decoration, two pen and ink Picasso lithographs dotted the wall behind him, while a third hung to the left of the window.

Jenna drew the drapes and watched Bishop look the room over. She asked, 'Can I get you a drink of something? There should be a pint of Polish vodka at the back of the refrigerator. Just don't ask me how long it's been there.'

Bishop was studying one of the drawings behind him, counting the number of brush strokes the artist had used for the sketch. He decided the pencilled signature underneath had probably taken more effort. He turned to Jenna with a frown. 'Is this a horse or a dog?'

Jenna laughed and said, 'That's a matador.' Tossing her jacket on the sofa, she moved towards him and pointed at the one on the right. '*That's* the horse with its rider. And *that*' – she turned to the one by the window – 'is a sleeping woman.' She turned back to the matador and frowned. 'Although now you mention it . . .'

Bishop leaned closer as she ran a finger over the glass, and then winced as his stomach muscles complained. Jenna looked at him and said, 'What's wrong?'

'I got my ass well and truly kicked yesterday. I'm still feeling the effects is all.' He felt around in his pockets and realized he hadn't transferred everything over from his leather jacket after all. 'I don't suppose you got any Advil lying around?'

'Sure. Follow me,' she said, and led him into the other hallway. It contained two doors, one on each side. Bishop followed her into the joint kitchen and dining room on the right. It was predominantly white, like the rest of the apartment, and split in half. A breakfast bar and two stools separated the kitchen from the dining area, where a large table was jammed against the wall. Bishop guessed Jenna didn't entertain much as a Power Mac currently took up much of the table. Next to the computer were two laptops, a pile of paperwork, a scanner, a printer, a router and additional hardware he couldn't begin to identify.

Bishop leaned against the breakfast bar and removed his sweatshirt while Jenna rummaged through drawers in the kitchen. He also removed the Beretta from his waistband and rolled it up in the sweatshirt before placing the bundle on one of the chairs under the table. He figured it would be easier than answering a bunch of questions.

Jenna turned round and held a packet of tablets in the air like a trophy. 'I knew I had some. You didn't tell me what you wanted to drink with this,' she said, and then made a clicking sound with her tongue. 'You can tell I'm out of practice at this sort of thing. I haven't even asked if you've eaten yet. You feel up to a pizza? There's a really good delivery place nearby that I use occasionally and they're quick.'

'Pizza sounds fine. And I'll take a shot of that vodka too.'

'Sure thing. I think I'll join you.' She pulled out a slim, half-full bottle with *Chopin Potato Vodka* printed vertically on the front from the refrigerator, and grabbed two glass tumblers. She poured two fingers of the clear liquid into each glass, then picked up a cordless phone lying on the counter. Bishop chewed on three of the pills while she pressed a single button on the phone and asked for a large pepperoni and mushroom thin crust. It sounded like Jenna ate a lot of pizza and Bishop smiled to himself when the person on the other end didn't ask for her address. She hung up, picked up her drink and smiled. 'Ten minutes,' she said.

Bishop picked up his glass and they each knocked back a shot. The effect was immediate for him. His system hadn't been near alcohol for three years and his skin tingled as a feeling of numbness rapidly spread throughout his body. 'Whoa,' he said.

'Kicks, doesn't it?'

He looked at the tumbler in his hand. 'I've heard things about this stuff.'

'That old rumour about it doubling for anti-freeze is just an urban myth. It's too expensive for a start.'

Bishop nodded and glanced at the table behind him.

Jenna smiled. 'I'm guessing you've noticed not many people get into my fortress of solitude. I invite some of the girls from work every now and then, but apart from Ali you're the first man to cross the threshold in two years.' She sipped at the vodka and said, 'You should consider yourself honoured.'

'You haven't invited Luke over?'

She sighed. 'Luke would very much like an invitation to visit. More than visit, actually. His problem is he can't accept the past should stay in the past and that mistakes should be learned from, not repeated. Let's not go there, please.'

'All right,' he said. 'So you want to tell me why you're letting me stay here? I mean, you barely know me.'

She paused, then said, 'You helped Owen. It might have been for your own reasons, but my baby brother's still alive, thanks to you.' She shrugged. 'Or maybe I just want to help. People's motives *can* be that simple sometimes.'

Only rarely in Bishop's experience, but he saw no advantage in arguing the point and just said, 'Okay.'

She took another sip and looked at him. 'So, has the real killer got a name?'

Bishop raised his eyebrows. He knew she'd start asking questions soon enough, but it really wouldn't help her knowing any more than she already did. 'I think it's probably best you don't get any more involved. Believe me, the less you know, the better for you.'

Jenna slowly placed her glass on the counter and crossed her arms. He couldn't read her eyes but he saw tension in her muscles as she spoke. 'Oh, really? And you think harbouring a dangerous fugitive from the law isn't placing me in enough danger already?'

'You can explain that away easily enough by saying I held you hostage.'

'Uh, uh. That's not how it works. This is *my* home and if you want to hide out here a couple of days you'd best start talking to me like we're both normal human beings. Otherwise, how do I know you *didn't* kill those people three years ago?'

'Is that what you really believe?'

'What am I supposed to think if you're not gonna talk to me?'

He watched her, both fascinated and a little angry. Mostly with himself. He'd underestimated her determination and it didn't help that she was right. After all, it wasn't her fault she possessed an inquisitive mind. He reached over and poured them each another shot. 'All right,' he said. 'The first guy I need to find is called Adam Cortiss. But that isn't an invitation for you to get involved. I can handle this myself.'

Her face softened. 'See? That revelation didn't hurt, did it? So how—' She stopped at the sound of the doorbell and dashed out of the room without finishing the question.

Bishop heard her exchange pleasantries with the delivery boy, and then she returned holding a flat pizza box. She'd lost her ponytail while out of the room. Her dark hair was now sitting on her shoulders, the curls framing her eyes and high cheekbones. Without speaking, they sat at the breakfast bar and started eating, but after a few mouthfuls Jenna said, 'So how did you find out about this Cortiss?'

Bishop took the papers he'd printed out from his pocket and dropped them on the bar, and she began browsing through them as she ate. He realized he'd already gotten Jenna involved the moment he came to her for help. He found himself feeling like he owed her something, which was a new experience for him. In Aleron's basement, it had occurred to him that he already had enough enemies. And to continue his habit of internalizing everything when help was being offered was tactically foolish. With both Falstaff brothers having already given him major assists, why not allow the sister a chance to make it three for three? At the very least, he'd get a fresh perspective. He considered how much Jenna already knew, and made a choice that he would never have made in his old life.

He said, 'I saw the bottom of this guy's face at the Brennans' house as he ran from the scene. Turns out he used to work for Randall Brennan, so I asked an old contact to dig up whatever he could find. That's it.'

Jenna nodded, continuing to look through the pages. Bishop took another slice. The pizza was really good, and he realized he hadn't eaten properly in over thirty-six hours.

When she got to the end, she looked up. 'A bad, bad boy. So, obviously, if you saw him, what, a year later, it was somebody else in that car when it crashed.'

'Right.'

'But wouldn't the police check fingerprints?'

'Cops don't make extra work for themselves without good reason and there was no suspicion of foul play. Plus they had a relative on hand who could ID the body.'

She turned pages until she found it. 'Sean Stephenson?'

'I'm guessing Cortiss under another alias. He'd be experienced at that kind of thing.'

'Hmm.' Jenna refilled their glasses. 'It's got his last known address here,' she said almost to herself. 'An apartment in downtown Manhattan.'

'Forget about it,' he said, taking another shot of vodka. 'He's long gone.'

'I know. I'm just thinking out loud.'

Bishop studied her profile. 'I haven't asked what it is you do, Jenna.'

She faced him and smiled. 'That's okay, you got other things on your mind. I'm a computer programmer in the city. Not very interesting, but I'm good at it and it keeps me on the straight and narrow. My employers are pretty strict about that kind of thing.'

'Why? Were you a bad girl in your youth?'

She grinned. 'The baddest. I still have my moments.' Turning on her stool, she looked at him. 'Another drink and I might show you what I mean. Your turn to pour.'

Bishop was tempted. He really was. But it would be a mistake. Even if he weren't being hunted by half the civilized world, this was the wrong time. And he was the wrong man. This was just a temporary way station and he couldn't afford to let himself get sidetracked. Not any more. 'Probably not a good idea,' he said. 'Tell you the truth, I'm just about ready to drop and your couch looks good.'

Jenna sat back and looked at him with a half-smile. 'Okay,' she said. 'I can probably find some spare sheets for you.' They both rose from their seats and she left the room, reappearing a minute later to hand him a pile of blankets. 'There's a towel in there for the shower and you'll find a pack of new toothbrushes in the bathroom cabinet.'

He added the sweatshirt containing his gun to the pile and said, 'Thanks,' before turning and making his way towards the living room across the hallway.

'Don't mention it,' he heard her say behind him.

# THIRTY-FOUR

Bishop woke up on Jenna Falstaff's couch with the previous evening's conversation running through his mind. The vodka seemed to have made him a lot more talkative than usual. Or maybe, after spending so much time in his own head, he'd just needed to offload on someone. Either way the damage was done and there was no point going over it. Instead he thought through what he'd learned on his first day as a fugitive.

Adam Cortiss. Brennan's connection to him. The papers stuck behind the bookshelves. The hidden cameras. The shoe imprint on the chair. He got the Cortiss and Brennan connection, and how the vault fitted in; he guessed the motivation had been the money. What he was still left with was who'd gotten him involved. Who out of his team had enough issues to bother setting him up?

Thorpe had come through with the info on Cortiss, but that wasn't sufficient reason to rule him out just yet. He was still a suspect. And there were still Tennison and Chaney to check on. Confronting them would be a lot riskier, especially if Thorpe had decided to cover his ass by reporting yesterday's encounter to the cops. In that case, they wouldn't have to work too hard to guess Bishop's next move and prepare for it. Nevertheless, a little surveillance couldn't hurt. He could check out the situation for himself before making a decision. And there was still the matter of Cortiss, of course. He needed to make inroads on finding him before he did anything else.

Pulling the blanket off, Bishop swung his legs round and sat up. He ran his palm over his scalp and listened to sounds of cutlery and crockery from the kitchen. The thin drapes were still drawn but sunlight made its way into the room. His watch on the coffee table read 10.37. He'd been out for over eleven hours, and despite the pain in his abdomen felt refreshed for the first time in months. Years, maybe.

He pulled on his pants and T-shirt and followed the sounds.

Jenna stood at the breakfast bar, pouring coffee into two mugs on the counter. She was wearing a short white bathrobe tied at the waist, and her damp hair was brushed back from her face. Bishop could practically taste the caffeine from the doorway. She looked up and said, 'Perfect timing.'

'Day off?' he asked.

'What's the point of sick leave if you don't use it up?' she said with a shrug. 'I assume you take your coffee black, as well?'

He nodded, sat on the same stool as last night and took a few sips. It was strong, almost too strong, but the buzz it gave him was worth it. Jenna sat opposite him and added sugar to hers.

'That couch *must* be comfortable. You slept like the dead.'

'Guess I must have needed it.' He turned to look at the Power Mac. 'You mind if I borrow your computer this morning?'

Jenna smiled as she raised her cup and drank. 'If you're planning on searching for Cortiss, I think that's one problem you don't need to worry about any more.'

'Is that right?' He had a bad feeling about where this was going.

'I found him, already,' she said. 'Or at least, the next best—'

'Jenna,' Bishop interrupted. 'Stop.' He put his coffee on the countertop and moved off his seat. She looked up in surprise. 'I said I didn't want you getting involved.'

Without waiting for a response, he walked back to the living room and grabbed his sweatshirt and his gun. He'd underestimated her, and he'd made the wrong choice last night. It had been a mistake to give her a glimpse of Cortiss. He shouldn't have even come here. But sitting in the taxi at Jamaica he'd been fresh out of options. And when you're out of options, you make mistakes. Idiot.

He went over to the window, pulled the drapes apart and was looking out when he heard her enter the room behind him. Without turning round, he said, 'Who else have you told?'

'About you? Nobody, of course.'

'About Cortiss,' he said, facing her. For a second she looked like she might break but her eyes remained defiant. 'You must have had help to locate him so fast.'

'You mean it's impossible that I managed to do it all on my lonesome? You know they disproved that theory about us having smaller brains than men quite a few years ago.'

'That's not what I meant and you know it. I need to be abs—' He stopped and frowned. A comment about Jenna's employers from the night before came back to him. 'Just where is it you work, exactly?'

'You ever hear of the New York State Office for Technology?'

'Not that I can recall.'

'Not many people have. It's a government agency over at Empire State Plaza that provides IT services to other agencies. I'm in their information security department.'

Bishop rubbed his face. 'Did I just hear you right? You're saying you work for the *government*?'

'Kind of.'

'You do or you don't?'

'Don't tell me prison turned you into an objectivist; nothing's black and white, you know. I'm just an independent contractor with the health plan and holiday pay, but without the job security or the pension. Okay?' She shrugged and perched on a corner of the coffee table, sensing his shift in mood. 'Besides, I'm not sure I'd be right for full-on legitimate government work.'

'Why not?'

'And submit myself to a *complete* background check?' She snorted. 'No, thank you.' She leaned forward, resting her elbows on her knees. 'Look, James, I'm sorry I went behind your back, but I'm definitely not working with anybody else on this. I just like solving puzzles, that's all. I can't help it; it's what I do. And let's face it, yours is a real doozy.'

Bishop leaned against the window frame and moved his palm back and forth over his scalp. 'You realize you could have told me all this last night, Jenna, instead of springing it on me now. It all comes down to trust in the end and I'm beginning to think I shouldn't be here. That I made a mistake.'

Jenna pursed her lips and looked at the framed sketch on the wall to his right. The one that was supposed to be of a woman sleeping. 'About four years ago,' she said, finally, 'there was a major news story about how a five-member team of hackers called the Phonebeasts got into the telephone networks and grabbed credit reports, criminal records, and other data from the databases to sell on to third parties.' She turned her gaze to Bishop. 'You remember reading about it?'

Vaguely, he recalled. 'They gave themselves code names, didn't they? I heard the feds caught them all in the end.'

'They caught four of the five and they each earned long stretches in a federal prison. But there was a sixth member they don't even know about who called herself Electra, and I know for a fact the feds would be *very* interested to learn of her existence before the Statute of Limitations comes into effect in a year's time. Especially her real name and what she's doing now.' She raised both eyebrows at him. 'All it would take to get an investigation launched is one phone call.'

Bishop understood what she was giving him. A way of making amends by throwing the ball back into his court. It was a start, at least, and he appreciated the gesture. After all, trust always works best when it's shared.

He moved forward and sat down on the couch a few inches away from her. Her thighs peeked out from the robe and her deep brown skin glistened in the morning sun. Everything was close enough to touch and it took all of Bishop's restraint not to.

Knowing it was too late to go back, he said, 'All right, so tell me what you found.'

# THIRTY-FIVE

She smiled, held up a finger and walked back to the dining room. A few seconds later, she came back holding some notepaper which she passed to him. He read, *Box No. 46533, NY.*

Bishop looked at her and said, 'Are you serious?'

'Now and then. That number's located at the Little Neck post office just north of here and it's a yearly rental, which means he's still active.'

Bishop nodded at the paper in his hand. 'I'd be interested to know how.'

'I told you I had a murky past,' she said. 'After I saw his old address, I started thinking about inherited properties and found my way into the New York Land Registry server. I searched for Adam Cortiss and got three hits. The first two were strike-outs but the third is a four-bedroom house in a nice area of Nassau County. It was owned outright by a Kenneth Cortiss until his death in 1996, whereupon it was passed down to his son, Adam. He immediately sold the property to a company called Siren Associates, whose director goes by the name of Joseph Armitage.'

Bishop frowned and scratched at the stubble on his cheeks. 'Okay.'

'So I phoned the current tenant and told her I was from the Realty Regulation Commission and that I was asking tenants in the area how satisfied they were with their letting agencies. Once she gave me the name, Ashford Properties, I called them up.'

'So I'm guessing Cortiss is still the owner and rents it out,' Bishop said. 'Siren's a ghost company he set up to act as a buffer between him and Ashford.'

Jenna smiled. 'A few thousand every month for doing nothing must be hard to pass up, no matter how wealthy you might be. So anyway, at Ashford I get this self-important little dickweed, and after a lot of wasted energy he finally gives me the name of the property lawyer who handles all matters relating to the house: an Alexander Stillson of Kennington, Hartford & Taylor.'

'A lawyer? He can't have been too talkative.'

'Probably not, but I've learned you don't always get the best results by tackling a problem head on. And the fact I'm a woman doesn't hurt.'

Jenna started to knock her knees together like an excitable kid. Her legs had been distracting enough ~otionless, but this was too much. Bishop forced himself to stand up and move back to the window so he could concentrate on her words.

'I asked for his secretary, a Ms Eileen Turnbull, and said I was a new temp from Accounting. I told her we needed to invoice Mr Armitage for the last quarter, but that I'd labelled his file a dead account by mistake and deleted his billing address from the system. Since he was Mr Stillson's client, would she have it in her address book up there on her PC? And, by the way, could she keep this to herself as I might lose my job if my lapse ever got out? Eileen knows us girls got to stick together and got me that box number in a matter of seconds. She was nice. I liked her.'

Bishop smiled. 'What's not to like?' He nodded at her. 'You're quick on your feet, Jenna.'

'Another echo from my misbegotten youth, although these days they call it "social engineering".'

He thought for a moment. 'So if it's a box number, it means Cortiss has to be contacted somehow when mail arrives, right?'

'Sure. I'd imagine he'd use their text alert or automated call system. I know *I* would. If I knew a cheque was waiting for me, I'd want it now, not later.'

'I agree. So you think a letter will reach him by morning if we make the afternoon post?'

'Should do. Little Neck's only a stone's throw from here. Hold on.' She stood and went back into the kitchen, returning with a pen, a legal pad and some envelopes. Handing them over, she said, 'I'll take it down to the mailbox while you shower. What are you going to write?'

'Nothing,' he said. He tore off four blank sheets, folded them over twice and inserted them in an envelope, sealed and addressed it, and dropped it onto the table. 'I'm kind of glad you're so into puzzles now.'

'Well, I don't *just* like puzzles.' She gave him that half-smile and said, 'I kind of thought you were smarter than that.'

# THIRTY-SIX

Danny Costa sat in the thirteen-year-old grey Volvo in a corner space of the residential parking bay behind the apartment building, and waited patiently for another sighting of Bishop or Jenna Falstaff. The man for professional reasons, the woman for more personal ones.

Last night, when Danny had reported to Hedison after the cops' invasion of the Ambassador, Hedison had looked very interested when Danny brought up the presence of the woman. And her hesitation outside the house before driving off. When Costa had handed over the notebook containing the Honda's licence number Hedison had smiled and said, 'You know, Danny, I'd put even money on Bishop seeking this girl out now he's run out of places to hide. Leave this with me and I'll get her address over to you so you can check her place out.'

Hedison had been true to his word and since then it had been just a matter of keeping watch. Just before midday, the Falstaff woman had come out to her car and driven off. The target had appeared at the living room window shortly thereafter with a towel around his waist. Costa texted Hedison with the news, expecting him to be happy. Instead he was almost indifferent when he called back, as though it was no surprise that events had played out the way he'd predicted. Danny could hardly blame him. In all the years they'd known each other, Hedison had rarely put a foot wrong. He told Danny to attach the tracking equipment he'd supplied to the woman's vehicle when she returned, just in case. They didn't want to lose Bishop a second time.

Costa had done as instructed and all was now well again, for the time being.

One thing was for sure, life always became a lot more exciting when Hedison called. Of course, Costa knew Roy Hedison was merely the alias the man had been using when they'd first met ten years ago. But it still felt natural to think of him under that name, rather than his real one.

When they first met, Hedison was making a name for himself in the Cattrall drug organization for his ability to extract information from just about anybody put in front of him. Instead of the usual brutal interrogation methods, his favoured technique was to kidnap a young female relative of the suspected informer, ply her system with narcotics and then take her in all manner of ways right in front of the subject. The psychological effect of seeing the girl actually seem to be *enjoying* the rigorous physical invasion was usually more than the informer could stand and he'd soon be desperate to tell everything he knew. Once the information was gleaned, Hedison would finish off the subject and either send the girl to join him or arrange for her to be carted off to one of the organization's countless prostitution offshoots for additional training towards her new career. Nothing got wasted.

When Hedison told Costa he needed a right hand he could trust, he hadn't realized how loyal a partner he'd found. That their interests overlapped in so many areas only cemented the relationship and Costa soon became an enthusiastic participant in their subsequent interrogation sessions, offering suggestions and fine tuning their technique in ways that startled even Hedison. But then, Costa had always thought that work should also be fun.

Four years later came the mass arrests of key personnel that signalled the end of Cattrall's dominance in the market. Hedison disappeared just before that happened, then showed up at Costa's door months later, clean-shaven, with his black hair back to its original colour. Whereupon he'd admitted to being an undercover DEA agent all along. He said he'd been forced to make a career change when his bosses had unearthed some of his less orthodox practices while on the job. And that he'd resisted giving them Costa's name since loyalty was a quality he valued above all things. There was always work for loyal people.

He'd kept his promise. In the years since, Costa had always been happy to help out with anything Hedison needed doing. It was a pleasure to work with someone who planned ahead and always had an answer for every problem. And Hedison always paid more than he needed to, especially when things got bloody. The jobs often provided their own little bonuses, as well, like this Jenna Falstaff. A whole range of possibilities loomed there.

Looking up at the apartment windows through the lightly tinted glass of the windshield, the watcher's thoughts turned to what Hedison might have in mind for Bishop. If it were merely a case of removing him a simple 911 call would have done the job, so he was being kept under surveillance for a specific reason. Apparently, there was something Hedison wanted Bishop to do, although Bishop didn't know it yet.

Costa just sat in the vehicle and watched. And wondered what that something could be.

# THIRTY-SEVEN

When Jenna came back from mailing the envelope, Bishop explained what he had in mind for the afternoon and asked if she wouldn't mind helping out. Jenna didn't need much persuading. Less than two hours later, she was driving Bishop down a quiet, residential street in Brooklyn's Ridgewood district. A long row of pre-war, two-storey townhouses lined each side, mostly with well-kept front yards. Sam Chaney's was No. 92. Bishop knew he had a small garden out back, too. He'd come out here once before when Chaney had organized a weekend barbecue for his teammates while they were between assignments. It had been one of the few times they'd all socialized together. To Bishop, it felt like a lifetime ago.

'It's the one on the right with white fencing,' he said. 'But don't slow down.'

'Gotcha,' Jenna said and kept the Honda at a steady fifteen.

Adjusting the visor on his cap, Bishop studied the house as they got closer. He knew Chaney still lived there because Jenna had got into the Land Registry server again and checked. A silver Chevy SUV was parked on the street out front. Same model as his last one. Just newer. Chaney had always been a creature of habit where cars were concerned.

The upstairs drapes were drawn, which further indicated that Chaney was in there right now. The guy was definitely a night owl, which is why Bishop had decided to check his place first. Tennison would wait. Right now he'd be at his office where there were far too many variables. Too many people who might recognize Bishop. Home turf was always better in these situations. Fewer witnesses.

Bishop scanned the other parked vehicles as they passed by. All empty as far as he could make out. But that might not mean anything. He'd have to see.

There was an intersection about a hundred yards up ahead. Bishop saw a small store on the corner with a couple of spaces next to it. 'You want to park up over there for a minute?'

'Sure.'

Bishop liked how Jenna kept unncessary questions to a minimum. Or at least waited for an appropriate time to ask them. Not many people had that ability. Bishop felt she would have made a great soldier. When she pulled in, he turned to her and said, 'Do me a favour, huh? Can you go and grab me a copy of today's *Times*?'

Jenna looked at him and smiled. 'All the way to Brooklyn to buy a paper. You sure know how to treat a girl.' With the engine still running, she climbed out and disappeared into the store.

Bishop used one hand to adjust the rear-view mirror until he could see everything behind him. Specifically, the vehicles they'd just passed on the opposite side of the street. More specifically, the dark grey Crown Vic with tinted windows, parked a few houses down from Chaney's. This time Bishop smiled to himself. *I see you.*

Less then a minute later, Jenna got back in, handed him the paper and said, 'You're still front page news, if you're interested.'

'I'm not.'

'So why did you want the paper?'

'I needed to confirm something and thought it'd look suspicious if we stopped here for no reason. Check the rear-view. See the dark grey sedan back there?'

Jenna moved the mirror to its original position. After a few moments, she said, 'The one with the tinted windows? Is that a guy in there?'

'Uh, huh. He must have ducked down in the seat when we passed by.'

'Police?'

Bishop smiled. 'That's a Crown Victoria. Number one choice for cab drivers and law enforcement, and that doesn't look like a cab to me.'

Jenna puffed out her cheeks. 'So what do you think it means? That Thorpe reported your meet with him yesterday?'

'Possibly. More likely the Marshals are making sure all the angles are covered. That's what I'd do. But it means they'll also have Tennison under surveillance, which means I can't do anything except check back in a day or so and hope they've lost interest.'

Jenna nodded. 'So where to next?'

'Back to yours, I think.'

'Okay,' she said. She pulled out towards the intersection. 'Still, at least you've got the Cortiss lead to follow up. Maybe he'll be able to shorten the list of suspects for you.'

Bishop looked out the window and said, 'Stranger things have happened.'

# THIRTY-EIGHT

'How can they call this rush hour if nobody's *mov*ing?' Jenna said, tapping the brakes. It was Tuesday morning and they were sitting with all the other commuters on the northbound lanes of Cross Island Parkway.

He turned and looked at her as she patted both palms against the wheel. She was wearing a simple tan T-shirt and blue jeans, although her natural curves made the clothes look anything but ordinary. He liked her casual attitude towards her own appearance. It made her even more attractive.

Bishop was wearing one of Owen's suits she kept stored in the back of her bedroom closet, awaiting her brother's release a few years down the line. The arms were a little long, but it was a good fit, overall.

'Relax,' he said. 'It's not even eight thirty.' He knew the post office at Little Neck didn't open until nine.

'I know, but it's at times like these I wish I'd gone for an automatic transmission.'

'A city girl going for a stick shift *is* different. Seems you never take the easy option.'

Jenna looked at him and smiled. 'That's me all over.'

She turned in her seat and reached into her shoulder bag on the back seat, pulling out a small notebook with a picture of a young Elvis on the cover. That was another aspect of her character that intrigued him: this fascination with a white rock 'n' roll icon who'd been dead for over thirty years. She definitely wasn't run-of-the-mill. Far from it, in fact. He watched, amused, as she also retrieved a pair of thin-framed reading glasses and put them on.

'Anybody stares at a monitor as much as I do ends up needing these sooner or later,' she said. 'Usually sooner.'

'They suit you,' he said.

She smiled. 'Flatterer. I don't how interesting you'll find it, but I did a little research while you were asleep. Your Randall Brennan wasn't exactly a saint, was he?'

'Who is?' Bishop said. 'And I wasn't being paid to protect anyone's morals. All I knew about Brennan was that he was a successful arms broker who persuaded developing countries to sign long-term deals for their weapons. And that he was established enough to be able to do most of his work without leaving his upstairs office. And I know that when his family noticed strange people following them whenever they left the estate, he went to RoyseCorp for help.'

'*Fin*ally,' Jenna said as the vehicles ahead started moving, gradually picking up speed. She kept pace and said, 'You ever meet him? Morgan Royse, I mean.'

'Once. Not long after I signed up with the company I got introduced to him briefly. It was pretty uncomfortable. Neither of us had much to say, although I found out later it was down to him that I was offered the job in the first place. Maybe he got a recommendation from some-body and sent the word down. Then a few months later he turned into a recluse. Nobody really knows why. Nowadays he communicates with his top execs, a few VIP clients, the occasional head of state and that's about it. Commutes daily to his forty-storey office building by personal helicopter, never ventures below his penthouse suite and hasn't had his picture taken in years. Unless I missed one while I was inside.'

'Maybe he's shy,' she said. 'You know he and Brennan were in Vietnam together?' She opened the notebook on her lap to a specific page and looked down. 'Both were colonels, too.'

Bishop took a sharp breath as the car in front braked and Jenna followed suit with about an inch to spare. 'You want me to take that?' he asked. She frowned at him, then passed the notebook over. 'Yeah, we heard some rumours they knew each other from the Marines.'

'Okay. How about this, then? I found a twenty-year-old puff-piece in the *New York Times* archives about Alicia Brennan and her involve-ment with a big AIDS fundraiser. Randall gets a brief mention as the proud husband taking time out from his heavy work schedule to support her.' They were travelling at forty now and Jenna removed her glasses. She leaned over to Bishop and tapped the notebook, her finger marking a passage. 'Read the part I wrote down. And the date of publication.'

Aloud, he read, '". . . easier said than done, since the day-to-day administration of the midtown private security firm Randall and his partner started up only three months ago takes up most of his waking hours these days.'" Underneath, Jenna had written *April 17, 1987*. Bishop turned to her. 'RoyseCorp opened its offices in January 1987.'

'January 15, to be exact.' There was a sign for exit 31E and Jenna moved them into the right lane. 'Because the company and Royse aren't mentioned by name, I guess nobody worked out that they had a history when they were investigating the murders. The cops already had you, so they didn't bother digging any deeper. Interesting, no?'

He nodded slowly, digesting the information. 'Yeah, although I don't see how their history is connected to the murders, or me.' He paused, then said, 'I guess Brennan and Royse split up when Brennan went into the arms business. Royse must have bought him out. Although there can't have been too much bad blood between them if Brennan turned to Royse for protection later.'

'He probably figured he qualified for a discount. I doubt we'll ever know for sure; trying to get any kind of concrete info on Royse is almost impossible, and that's a rarity for me.'

'He's probably got an entire staff devoted to covering his tracks. Anything else?'

Jenna took the exit for Northern Boulevard and Douglaston. 'Only an odd obituary in Brennan's home town paper, the *Thornton Gazette*. It turns out Brennan was the sole surviving heir of one Helen Gandy at the time of her death in July 1988.'

Bishop frowned. 'Never heard of her. She famous or something?'

'To conspiracy buffs, Gandy's practically the holy grail. She was J. Edgar Hoover's personal secretary for over fifty years until his death in 1972. She was also the first person called when his body was discovered and was suspected for years afterwards of removing the most inflammatory files from his office before anyone even knew he was dead.'

'Well, it's an interesting footnote. Not much more than that.'

Jenna smiled. 'Not a believer in conspiracies then, I take it.'

'I'm more a believer in Ben Franklin. He was the one who said three can only keep a secret if two of them are dead. Conspiracies work fine in movies. Not so easy in real life.'

She raised an eyebrow at him. 'Still, she might have had *some* files worth stealing when she died and passed them on to Brennan.'

He shook his head. 'I don't buy it. Sure, certain information is worth money, but files from the 1970s? Any government secrets that old would be for curiosity value only. Often the simplest answer's the one to go for, and in this case I think it all comes down to money. Brennan had plenty of it and a secret vault almost nobody knew about. Combine the two and you've found your motive.'

'Yeah, you're probably right,' she said. They stopped at lights on the Marathon Parkway intersection. 'We're almost there.'

Bishop scanned the buildings on the right, past the intersection. There was a large, nineteenth-century-style timber frame building on the corner. Squatting next to it was a small, anonymous-looking, single-storey white building that Bishop guessed would be the post office. Federal funding didn't run to inventive architecture.

The lights turned green and Bishop said, 'Park up in the first available space.'

She did, and after turning off the engine reached back into the shoulder bag again and pulled out a cell phone.

'Forgot to give you this.' She handed it to him along with two spare SIM cards. 'Twenty bucks from a 7-Eleven, but it's not too bad. It's charged and comes with an hour's worth of calls and a few other things, like voice record and camera. I know you probably won't want to use it much, but I programmed my number into it if you need to contact me for any reason.' She shrugged. 'You never know, right?'

'Thanks,' Bishop said and gave it a brief once-over before putting it in Owen's jacket pocket along with the SIM cards.

He pulled out his sunglasses, put them on and reached for the door handle.

'Sure you don't want me to wait? What if he doesn't show up today? You can't just wander around.'

'I'll think of something. This is a situation where I'm better off on my own.'

Finally, she nodded. 'Okay,' she said. 'Be careful.'

'Sure,' he said, and got out. He watched as she pulled into the traffic and drove away. Then he crossed the street to look for a store that sold outdoor gear.

# THIRTY-NINE

At 11.27 on Tuesday morning, the man who used to be Adam Cortiss stood in front of the stamp-vending machine next to the wall of mail-boxes, opened the envelope he'd just taken from Box 46533 and realized immediately he should have sold that house years ago.

Sold it to someone other than himself, that is.

He just couldn't do it, though, could he? Tenants came and went, but his old man's place in Nassau never stayed vacant for more than a couple of weeks. And to be honest, he'd gotten used to that nice little windfall every month. Even after Stillson and the letting agency took their cuts, he still had more than enough to see him through those tight periods that cropped up every now and then. Like now, for instance. Always by cashier's cheque too, as per his original instructions to Stillson. And always a different time each month, since he'd learned from an early age that a set routine could get you killed quicker than a bullet.

And as the house was the only connection left to his previous identity, somebody from his former life had now tracked him through it. No other way it could have happened.

Cortiss gave a deep sigh and lines appeared on his forehead. His face had filled out since Bishop's file photo had been taken, and the wavy brown hair had turned salt and pepper and was cropped close to his skull, receding at the temples and thinning at the back. But the body underneath was still as taut as a man's half his age.

At his right were five cashiers' windows, but only one was currently active. The same two people in the line as when he'd come in less than a minute ago. The patient woman behind the glass window of number two was still serving the stooped old crock dressed in his best suit, and the forty-something mom waiting behind him was attempting to ignore the hyperactive brat at her side. Just two customers and him. So whoever was waiting for him would be outside. And the blank sheets in the envelope meant they didn't care that he knew. As it was, he could name at least three people from his past who'd like nothing more than to see him dead, and any one of them could be out there. He knew the rear exit only led round to the front again, via a side alley, so it was through the front or nothing. Besides, the Lexus he'd parked outside was practically new. Damned if he was going to abandon it without a fight.

Cortiss locked his mailbox and then bent down as if to tie his shoelaces. He pulled up his black jeans a couple of inches and removed his trusty Colt Mustang .380 automatic from the ankle holster before standing up again. Flicking the safety off, he held it in the pocket of his sports jacket and walked towards the front of the post office.

Through the glass double doors he could see a steady stream of traffic flowing past the parked vehicles lining the kerb on this side. His tan Lexus was a few cars down on the right. He scanned the vehicles in front and behind for occupants, but saw nobody.

He pulled one of the doors open and stepped outside, turning his head in each direction. To his left several pedestrians were walking away from him, towards the lights. On the right there was even less foot traffic. Just a guy in a dark suit about a hundred and fifty yards away, moving this way.

With his right hand still gripping the Colt in his pocket, Cortiss made for his vehicle, not taking his eyes off the approaching man. The guy was about six foot, mid-thirties, with glasses and short dark hair. He seemed to look in every direction except Cortiss's and moved at a steady pace like someone with a purpose. Both his hands were in his pockets.

Everything felt wrong and Cortiss's throat felt dry. He increased his pace. Within seconds he'd reached the car and unlocked the driver's door. Then he turned so he was leaning against it at a slight angle to the guy. Twenty yards away, the man casually brought his right hand out and let it swing at his side as he walked. The other hand stayed in his pocket. Cortiss figured he could take this guy out and be on his way before anybody noticed. The Colt was loud, but so was the sound of a car backfiring.

Ten yards away now and Cortiss had the barrel pointed at the man's midsection. He was ready. The guy still looked straight ahead and didn't slow his pace. Cortiss kept watching his left side, waiting for the merest twitch that would serve as his cue to fire.

Five yards and still no movement from the man's left hand. Cortiss kept his eyes on him and then frowned when the man passed by. And continued walking away from him. *What the hell?* Cortiss watched him climb the single step to the post office double doors, push one open and step inside.

The door closed and Cortiss breathed out again.

Okay. So he was mistaken. But whoever wanted him was still around and he was right out in the open. Cortiss reached behind, opened the driver's door and quickly slid in. As he inserted the key in the ignition he thought about what he would do if the positions were reversed. Not enough time to attach a nasty surprise to the starter motor. Best bet would be to place a tracking device under the vehicle and then follow him home and take it from there. Except he wouldn't go home just yet. He knew of an industrial park just two miles from here that would serve him better. He'd drive on over there, see what kind of company he'd attracted and deal with it.

As he started the engine he felt the familiar touch of cold steel against his neck and the man in the back said, 'Good idea, Cortiss. Let's go for a drive.'

# FORTY

Jenna sat down on the nearest stool and tossed her keys onto the dining room table, wondering what it was with men and their damn egos. Why couldn't they just leave their pride at the door and accept help when it was offered? How hard could it be? But no, Bishop could never do anything that obvious. It didn't fit in with the tight-lipped loner thing he had going on.

'Infuriating man,' she said to the four walls.

Still, she'd proved a point by finding Cortiss's mailing address for him. Even Bishop couldn't argue with a result like that. She just hoped Cortiss was the impatient type who *did* subscribe to a notification system, otherwise Bishop was in for a long wait.

Jenna brushed a hand through her hair and got off the stool. She walked into the living room and saw Bishop's clothes on one of the chairs. They were folded and stacked neatly. At least he wasn't a slob. Then she smiled, picked up the sweatshirt and went through the front pockets. So she was the curious type. He'd just have to live with it. It wasn't like he was paying her any rent.

But there was nothing in them. Same with the black pair of chinos. Although she wasn't sure what she'd expected to find. Folding and placing them back on the chair, she came round the coffee table and parked herself on the sofa. And frowned at what sounded like the crinkling of paper. She pulled up the cushion and found some torn, ragged pieces of paper lying there. *Well, now*, she thought. *What are these?*

She looked them over and realized the six pieces made up three complete pages. She sat down cross-legged on the floor, laid them out on the coffee table in proper order and read through each sheet slowly.

The first two pages formed a long-winded letter from an Anthony Cartwright of Wald College in Tribeca, saying how great it was that Randall Brennan had chosen their institution for his son Philip's further education. And how, since the college was always looking for philanthropic supporters who believed in laying the foundations for future scholarship, Brennan Senior might also be interested to learn of the new library wing currently under construction.

Jenna shook her head at the presumptuous tone of the letter. It can't have impressed Brennan much. Especially the part that mentioned how the more generous sponsors often achieved immortality by having whole wings named after them.

The third sheet was a little more intriguing. It was dated March 19, 1989 and came from a Thomas B. Wheatley, director of the Willow Reeves Rest Home in San Francisco. The letter referred to an enquiry Brennan had made about a man called Timothy R. Ebert, whom he believed to be a resident at Willow Reeves between 1968 and 1969. Wheatley regretted that he was unable to divulge any information concerning past clients, not even to confirm whether the person in question ever resided there at all. At the bottom, a line of almost illegible text read. *The Willow Reeves Rest Home is a non-profit organization operating under the aegis of the Kebnekaise Corporation.*

Noticing some bleed-through, Jenna turned both pieces over. On the reverse was a series of letters. Nine consonants and nine vowels, some repeated more than once. They had been jotted down haphazardly in pen as though in preparation for an anagram puzzle. She turned the pieces back again and leaned against the couch. As she tapped the coffee table surface with her fingernails she wondered where Bishop could have picked the papers up, and why he'd hidden them under her sofa cushion.

All she knew was that he'd neglected to take them with him. In which case, she thought, there was no actual harm in checking them out herself, was there?

# FORTY-ONE

From the back seat, Bishop studied the back of Cortiss's head as he drove. His right hand was gripping the Beretta while Cortiss's Colt sat in his pocket. They were heading west on the LIE, on their way to Cortiss's apartment in the Woodside district of Queens. Assuming the address on his driver's licence wasn't as phoney as the name.

After a short search, Bishop had found a camping store and become the owner of a Brunton pocket scope. He'd then entered the modern-looking public library building on the corner of Northern Boulevard and Marathon Parkway, directly opposite the post office, pulled a book at random from the shelves and taken a seat at one of the windows. Every time a man approached the post office across the street, he used the small scope to zoom in on his face.

At 11.25 he'd been wondering how long he could keep watch when the Lexus with the tinted windows pulled up. The face of the driver had aged and the hair was different, but even from a distance Bishop could see it was the same man as the one in the photo. And the jawline hadn't changed since he last saw it three years ago.

Once Cortiss was inside, Bishop left the library, crossed the street and checked under the Lexus's bumpers. A small, magnetized box was hidden at the rear. Bishop smiled to himself. Even professionals were wary of losing their keys.

After letting himself in with the spare and relocking the doors, it had simply been a case of hiding in the back and waiting. He had no idea who the guy in the suit had been, but he was grateful for the temporary confusion he had caused in his target.

Cortiss said, 'And I always thought lawyers were good at keeping secrets. I'm gonna have to have a private word with that Stillson asshole when I get a chance.'

'You only got yourself to blame,' Bishop said. 'Here's a tip: next time you want to disappear, either make a clean break or don't bother.'

'Am I hearing right?' Cortiss said with a snort. 'You're giving *me* advice? Let me write that down.' Then he went quiet again. Just driving. Exit 20 passed them by. Bishop knew the next exit would take them onto Queens Boulevard towards 57th Street and Cortiss's apartment. He thought for a moment, then pulled the cell Jenna had given him from his pocket. He scrolled through until he found the application he wanted and activated it.

'You got any idea how famous you are, brother?' Cortiss asked. He was watching his passenger in the rear-view. 'I swear they got your face plastered all over every channel except QVC, and it'll only be a matter of time before they stick your face on a watch so they can get in on the act. Yes sir, looks like I got me a real life celebrity in my back seat.'

'And you knew me way back when I was still a nobody. You still got that scar I gave you or has it healed over now?'

Cortiss glanced down at his right forearm and said, 'Screw you, Bishop.' Then he lapsed back into silence. As they passed under the sign for exit 19, he looked in his side mirror and began crossing over into the right-hand lane ahead of the turnoff.

'You know, I read your file.' Bishop looked out at the traffic ahead of them. 'Very impressive. The operations you've been a part of. The exotic locales. Above all, the dead bodies. You could write a book.'

Cortiss joined the traffic on the turnoff and said nothing.

Bishop watched Cortiss's eyes in the rear-view. 'Long story short. Three years ago, four heavily armed men storm a protected house. Only one makes it out again, but not before torturing and killing a young girl and her father. Then he disappears, leaving one of the protectors to pay the bills. You're gonna tell me why.'

'Sure of yourself, aren't you?'

'Nothing's for sure in this life. You want to put me straight?'

'What for? You wouldn't believe me, anyway.'

'Try me.'

Cortiss's eyes met Bishop's in the mirror. 'When we get off this I might just ram the next oncoming vehicle. Or take us up to ninety. See what happens.'

'In this traffic? Go ahead. I'm always open to new experiences and it'd tell me more than you've told me so far.'

Cortiss steered them onto Queens Boulevard. 'Try this on, Bishop,' he said as they came to another stop. 'Could be everything you think about me is true. Except for one small point.'

'Yeah?'

'Yeah. Wanna know what I saw when I made it to that top floor office?'

Bishop just looked at him.

'Three dead people,' Cortiss said. 'Same as you.'

# FORTY-TWO

Jenna sat at the dining room table and took a few sips of her Coke as she took in the Willow Reeves Rest Home website. It was very well done. Lots of happy residents smiling at their uniformed keepers on the steps of tastefully designed adobe buildings. And although there weren't any willow trees, there were lots of photos of serene grounds with plenty of green.

Under *About Us*, there was a large amount of text that said little but emphasized their reputation for discretion and quality care for those who needed aid, with lots of testimonials from satisfied family members. The tagline at the bottom read, *Caring for the elderly for over 38 years*. Jenna frowned. That would mean it got its start-up in the early seventies, yet Brennan seemed sure the place had been going for some time before that. In his letter, Wheatley hadn't corrected him on the point, either, which made the tagline even more puzzling. After all, most businesses would have happily traced their origins back to civil war times if they could get away with it. Customers trusted a company with history, so for an establishment to play theirs down was unusual.

Unless their past was something they wanted to keep quiet about.

Curious, Jenna pressed the *Contact* link and was presented with an address in the marina district of the city and three telephone numbers. Further down was a brief list of management personnel, followed by a much longer one of medical consultants connected with the home. Each had a long series of letters after his or her name. She guessed Wheatley must have either retired or died in the last few years as the managing director was now a woman, Irene Ravenscourt. The name alone put Jenna off and she continued down the list for someone who sounded more pliable. *Jeffrey Golden, Records Officer*, she thought. *You'll do.*

She looked at the kitchen clock and saw it was 12.15 p.m., which meant it would be 9.15 a.m. on the west coast. She picked up her cordless, pressed 67 to block the caller ID, then keyed in the first number

135

and got a busy signal. She tried the second, and after two rings a young-sounding female voice said, 'Good morning. Willow Reeves. May I help you?'

'My name is Margaret Huntley,' Jenna said. 'Could I speak with Jeffrey Golden, please?'

'Surely,' the voice said. 'Please hold.'

After a short wait, a slightly reedy male voice came on the line. 'Ms Huntley. This is Jeffrey Golden. What can I do for you?'

'Hello, Mr Golden. I work out of the Illinois office of the IRS and my supervisor gave me your name as a contact for my current case file. I was hoping you could help with—'

'I sent in my return months ago, you know, Ms Huntley. I have video evidence and signed transcripts from witnesses who were there at the time of mailing. Ha ha.'

Jenna rolled her eyes. Sometimes she had to consciously remind herself California and New York were part of the same land mass. 'Um, Mr Golden . . .'

'Jeff, please.'

'Right. Well . . . it's not about you, actually. My call concerns Willow Reeves, or rather its previous incarnation.'

'I don't follow.'

'Well, we're currently putting together a case for evasion of taxes against a man who claims he was a patient at your facility during the years . . .' she noisily crumpled some papers next to her and then said, 'here we are: 1968 and 1969. Yet, clearly, Willow Reeves wasn't established until several years after that.'

'1971,' Golden said.

'Exactly. Can you see our problem? If we charge him with evasion during these years in addition to the others, we'll lose all credibility if he presents the court with papers that prove he was where he claimed to be at that time. We really need to obtain all the facts and trace his movements for those two years before we start making accusations.'

'But if he has papers that prove where he was, doesn't he have to show them to you?'

'Unfortunately, the full disclosure rule doesn't apply to tax-related cases,' Jenna said. She had no idea whether this was true or not. 'But if you could just give me the name of the facility that leased or owned the land before you, and where I might be able to locate any relevant records that would prove or disprove the defendant's explanation for those missing years . . .' She was greeted with silence at the other end. 'Are you there, Mr Golden?'

'Yes.'

One-word answers were never a good sign. Her only comfort was that he was unlikely to tell her to go screw herself. When the taxman asked, you answered. 'Would you have those details to hand, Mr Golden?'

'Will this be a high-profile case, Ms Huntley?'

'Definitely not. The tax office is rarely well served by the media and always plays down the public angle whenever possible.'

After another pause, Golden said, 'The thing is, it wouldn't do our image much good if this got out.'

'I can only assure you that it won't.'

'Okay. Well, the current owners of Willow Reeves bought out the previous owners in 1970, revamped the place, added a few wings and reopened a year later as a non-profit enterprise under its present name.'

'And what was the previous name?'

'Cavendish Private Hospital.'

'Sounds pretty innocuous to me.'

Golden sighed. 'They specialized in treating the mentally disadvantaged.'

'I see,' Jenna said. 'So it was an asylum.'

'That's a word we try to avoid when referring to Cavendish, Ms Huntley. It suggests a Gothic building full of axe murderers. Although before my time, this was a private home with no facilities for housing the more dangerous elements. Many patients actually came of their own volition. Mental illness takes many forms, as I'm sure you know.'

'I didn't mean to offend.'

Golden gave a nervous laugh. 'Of course not. I'm just . . . Anyway, like I said, residents are probably better off not knowing what went on here before. We consider 1971 year zero. Our past isn't exactly a secret, but we see no reason to advertise it.'

'I understand. So are you saying I've hit a dead end as regards accessing old records?'

'Well, obviously we don't have anything here. Maybe . . . Hold on a second.'

Jenna heard the sound of fingers on a keyboard. Golden came back on and said, 'Apparently, all the old hospital files are held in storage in a warehouse back east. Minus the patients' actual medical files, of course; they would have all been forwarded on to the patients' personal physicians. I can give you the address but you'll probably need a court order to gain access to them.'

She'd brightened up on hearing the words *back east*. 'An address would be great,' she said.

He gave her a location in Brooklyn and a warehouse number. She jotted both down on her notepad. 'You've been a big help, Mr Golden.'

'No problem, Ms Huntley. Just remember me come audit time.'

Jenna hung up and looked at her notepad, wondering if she'd just wasted an hour of her life on this. It seemed pretty far-fetched to think a letter written twenty years ago would have anything to do with the bloody events just three years past. But then, you never knew until you checked. She looked at the screen and remembered the other letter. The one from the college. *What the hell*, she thought. *When you're on a roll . . .*

She typed the words *Randall Brennan* and *Wald College* into the same search engine and hit Return. The first link on the results page was for the official Wald College site. She clicked on it and was taken to a section that extolled the virtues of the college's extensive library. Along with its recently constructed annex.

The Brennan Wing.

So he had taken them up on their offer of immortality, after all. That was interesting, if not particularly useful. Still, Jenna experienced the same satisfaction she always felt whenever a particular problem reached its conclusion, and noted down the web address in her notebook. Then she grabbed the cordless again and dialled a number from memory.

The phone was picked up after five rings and the voice said, 'Hello?'

'Hello yourself. You busy?'

# FORTY-THREE

'Sit in the middle, hands in your pockets,' Bishop said from his position at the dirty kitchen counter. He watched as Cortiss did as instructed and lowered himself onto the middle cushion of his own couch. Bishop had already checked under the cushions and found nothing hidden there.

Cortiss's apartment was large and open-spaced, with hardwood flooring and floor-to-ceiling windows overlooking the New Calvary Cemetery. Bishop sat on a stool facing Cortiss, with one elbow on the breakfast bar and his left hand holding the Beretta on his lap. The kitchen counter hadn't been cleaned in days and dirty cutlery fought for space with food-encrusted plates and takeout boxes. Bishop could see a cordless phone buried in a box half-filled with noodles. At least it told him they were unlikely to be interrupted.

'Told you you wouldn't believe me,' Cortiss said.

'You haven't given me enough to form an opinion,' Bishop said. 'So you found out about the vault's existence back when you worked for Brennan?'

Cortiss shrugged and said nothing.

Bishop motioned with the Beretta. 'You gonna make me do this the hard way?'

'Right. You spend all that effort locating me and now you're gonna pop me before you get any answers? That's gonna happen.'

'It might. Somebody owes me three years of my life, Cortiss. And right now, that somebody's you. You won't give me anything, then I might as well finish you off and move on. You know I'll do it. I found you when nobody else could; I'll find your partner too. It'll just take longer, that's all. Talk and I got no reason to kill you.'

Cortiss chewed at his cheek for a moment. Then he turned to the windows and looked out at the sky. Five seconds passed. Ten. Bishop knew he was thinking things through. Working the angles. That's how he'd survived up until now. He'd know Bishop had nothing to lose at this point. He'd also realized a few answers wouldn't cost him anything. That talking might actually gain him something.

Cortiss finally turned back to Bishop and sighed. 'Okay, brother. Let's talk for a while.'

'The vault. How'd you find out about it?'

'The old fool let it slip after a few drinks one day. About how he'd had it built shortly after buying the place. Son of a bitch sent me packing before I got the chance to look for it, though. Bastard.'

'Why?'

Cortiss looked as if he might not answer. Then he blew out his breath and said, 'Natalie Brennan, that's why. How about a smoke?'

Bishop considered for a moment, then nodded. Whatever would keep him talking. 'One-handed. Your left.'

'Figured out I'm not a southpaw like you, huh?' Cortiss smiled and used exaggerated movements to take a packet and a disposable lighter from his shirt pocket with his left hand. He extracted a cigarette, lit it and reached over to place both items on the left arm of the sofa. He blew out a plume of smoke and said, 'You were there, brother. You know what a screw-up she was. Couldn't get her old man to give her the time of day, so she'd latch onto whichever father figure was closest to hand and next thing you know, it's party time. Not that she had to work too hard on me looking the way she did, parading around the house in a tight pair of shorts and a top no wider than a piece of string. Subtle, she wasn't. But you already know that, right?'

Bishop didn't react, but he was pretty sure Cortiss was telling the truth. That was exactly the kind of thing Natalie would do. He made a quick mental calculation and said, 'She couldn't have been more than a child when you were there.'

Cortiss shrugged and took a drag of the cigarette. 'Try fifteen going on thirty. I tell you, they grow up quick these days. Some of the things she wanted to do . . .' He shook his head. 'Hey, I wasn't exactly the first man on the moon, if you know what I mean.'

*Christ*, Bishop thought. *No wonder the girl was so screwed up.* 'So she told her father about the two of you?'

'Nah. She wasn't malicious, just dumb. That silly bitch never bothered cleaning up after us and when Brennan spotted the evidence on her bed sheets one day, that was it for me. For some reason, he didn't want the cops involved so he just let me walk.' He took another drag and said, 'Wouldn't surprise me if *he* was the one broke her cherry and just didn't want family secrets leaking out. The guy was no saint, let me tell you.'

Bishop recalled Jenna using the exact same phrase this morning. He'd always known Randall Brennan was amoral, but accusing the man of incest and child abuse seemed extreme without anything to back it up.

'So he fired you.'

'Right. About a year before you showed up on the scene.'

'But you still had a hard-on for the vault.'

'Oh, yeah. Worse than ever. Enough to want to take myself off any future list of suspects by arranging my car accident.' He smiled. 'It served a few purposes, actually, but that was the main one. The guy in the driver's seat was someone who'd outlived his usefulness, too, so it was win–win all round. You wanna throw me an ashtray?' He pointed his chin at the counter Bishop was leaning on. 'There's one on there somewhere.'

'Use the floor,' he said. 'What then?'

Cortiss tapped some ash at his feet. 'Well, I needed somebody with access to the house and the freedom to search it thoroughly, didn't I? I'd already come up with a vague plan where I'd place Brennan's family under threat, forcing him to hire bodyguards, and buy one off, and then when I recognized one of your team on the news one day I knew I was on the right track.'

'Rebecca Newmarket,' Bishop said.

Cortiss laughed. 'Yeah. You got it.'

The only time Bishop and his team had ever been exposed to TV was during the six months they spent guarding the rabidly right-wing media personality Rebecca Newmarket. Willing to spew forth offensive opinions and racial hatred at the drop of a pay cheque, she'd received so many death threats that nobody but RoyseCorp would take her on any more. She was also the only person to ever cause Bishop to seriously question his choice of career. He'd managed to thwart two potentially fatal attacks just in those six months alone. Frankly, he was amazed she was still breathing.

Cortiss said, 'I saw you all arrive at some awards ceremony and I knew I'd found someone I could work with. Last time we'd encountered each other we were both using different names, but he struck me as somebody who wasn't afraid to get his hands dirty. Turned out I was right. We got reacquainted, I filled him in, told him what I knew and he was like a kid at Christmas. Couldn't wait to get started on all the planning. He picked you out as the fall guy straight from the off, by the way. He doesn't like you much.'

Bishop said, 'His name?'

Cortiss shook his head. 'Uh, uh, brother. That ain't how we're gonna play. Right now, I figure the only thing I got to trade is my ex-partner's identity and current whereabouts. I don't mind answering any other question you got, but I'll be holding back on the big guns until we come to some kind of an arrangement that guarantees I walk.'

'I could force it out of you, Cortiss.' Bishop lifted a trouser leg to reveal his knife.

'You could, but once you started I'd make sure you went all the way. That wouldn't get either of us anywhere, would it? But I *can* be reasonable.'

Bishop saw a determination in the man's eyes. Cortiss would take it to the edge if necessary. He decided to be patient and agree on the reasonable route. It was usually best in the long run, anyway. He said, 'It was you two stalking the family, sending photos of the kids to Brennan and leaving threatening messages.'

'Yeah,' Cortiss said and blew a smoke ring towards the ceiling. 'Needed to make it look like it was coming from somebody wronged by Brennan in the past. And that they were gonna take it out on the whole family sometime soon.'

Bishop shook his head. 'It doesn't add up. How could you predict Brennan would approach RoyseCorp for protection? And if he did, how could you be sure my team would be assigned?'

'Easy. With Brennan's money, who else was he gonna call but the top private security firm in the country? Especially as he helped Royse start the company up in the first place. You know about that?' When Bishop nodded, he said, 'There you go. He and Royse went way back, and that's how we also knew your team would get picked for the job. Don't forget you were the close protection division's golden boy, commanding the only team with a hundred per cent success rate up to that point. Once his old comrade came calling, Royse was bound to assign his most reliable man to the case. Guy like that looks after his own. That's why we timed the threats while you were all on leave and available. And since you always picked the same crew, my partner knew he'd be along for the ride as well.' He stretched both arms out wide and smiled. 'And thus it all came to pass, brother.'

'So when did your partner find the vault?'

'About three months later, in early September. Never told me how he did it, though.'

Bishop didn't respond. He thought back to the slashes on Natalie's body. They'd been deep and frantic cuts from someone who'd had a personal interest in the victim. But when Cortiss had talked about Natalie there'd been no emotion there. Which just left one possibility. Except Bishop hadn't noticed any signs that his men were messing around with the teenager. Even Chaney hadn't stooped that low before.

Bishop said, 'Natalie told your friend where it was.'

Cortiss frowned. 'You think?'

'Sure, pillow talk. He'd been screwing her for a while by then, in that room above the garage. He even risked taking her to my apartment since he knew I rarely stayed there. Setting up the frame.'

Cortiss sucked on the end of his smoke and slowly breathed out. 'Yeah, you could be onto something there. There was definitely some kind of love/hate thing going on. Apparently, she reminded him of an old lover he'd never really gotten over.'

'I'll bet. And he was the one who came up with the idea of an armed assault in the first place, wasn't he?'

'Right. It was the only way we'd get away without suspicion falling on him. And we had to make sure the Brennans ended up part of the collateral damage.'

'And you were happy with that.'

'Hey, brother, whatever gets the job done. Wasn't the first time I'd had to cover my tracks like that.'

Bishop studied Cortiss and suddenly felt the urge to knock his teeth out. He looked so sure of himself, sitting there with his legs stretched out like he was discussing football averages.

Cortiss continued. 'So we knew you guys were due to be relieved on October 15, and decided to use that to get us past the front gate. If the real team were supposed to turn up at seven, we'd turn up at six. Once we had the authentic IDs and codes we were good to go.'

*So the inside man arranged the IDs*, Bishop thought. *Interesting*. And Tennison with his love of technology. How easy would it be to make fake documents to get past Neary at the gate? If you were as good as Tennison, probably pretty easy. And then there were the hidden surveillance cameras, too.

'And the three extra guys in your assault party?' Bishop asked.

Cortiss's face broke into a smile. 'You liked them, huh?' He sniggered. 'They still haven't identified those boys. Never will, either. Romanian ex-army with barely a word of English between them. Poor guys weren't destined to survive that night. If you guys hadn't taken care of them, I would have.'

Bishop kneaded his forehead with his fingers. 'Why'd you waste Neary?'

'That was just one of the boys bringing down the odds once we got in. After that, they each took their assigned man on the perimeter while I made my own entrance and put you to sleep for the allotted time.' Cortiss took a last drag of the cigarette and crushed it under his shoe. 'So there you go. I made it to the top and found Oates shot, and Brennan and Natalie both still dripping from my partner's attentions. I still had your knife so I thought, since you'd be taking the fall, I might as well make it conclusive. Wiped my blood off and smothered it in the Brennans', then dropped it next to the old man. I grabbed the cash and then met you on the stairs soon after.'

Bishop narrowed his eyes, curious about what had stopped his three hollow-points. 'Kevlar?'

Cortiss nodded. 'Covered in blood bags, too. We knew you'd go for the textbook grouping of three in the chest. I'm happy to say you didn't disappoint.'

Bishop had figured as much. But at least now he had the answer as to why the raid took place at all. The whole thing had been nothing more than a diversion to cover up the actual murders that had already taken place *while Bishop was on duty two floors below.*

And he hadn't heard a thing the whole time. Not a single sound. He should have listened harder. He had no excuse. None at all. That was one hell of a bitter pill to swallow.

'So how much did you come away with in the end?' he asked.

'Cash?' Cortiss shrugged. 'Just over five million, I think. Minus the two we planted in that fake account of yours.'

Bishop stared at him. 'Three million? And that was worth seven lives?'

Cortiss tilted his head and smiled. 'Course not, but that ain't exactly what we came for, was it?' Then he laughed hard. 'That's what you thought this was all about? A few million Brennan salted away for a rainy day? Oh brother, that's beautiful. Just beautiful.'

And it came to Bishop that Jenna might have been closer to the truth than he thought. Maybe the vault *had* held something other than money. Perhaps something that was priceless in comparison. Bishop thought of Jenna's comments earlier about J. Edgar Hoover. And of Helen Gandy, a distant relative of Brennan's. 'It was a file, wasn't it? And old FBI file Brennan inherited.'

Cortiss stopped laughing and Bishop knew he'd hit pay dirt.

'How'd you find out about it?' Bishop asked. 'Or did Brennan spill the details the same time he told you about the vault?'

'Sure he told me. Back in the days when he trusted me. Said how some old relative of his who used to work for Hoover had died and willed everything to him. Including this file.' He grinned and said, 'Did a little research of my own once he let me go; you know, some corroboration to make sure I wasn't chasing a rainbow, and I found enough to convince myself he wasn't just blowing smoke.'

'What kind of corroboration?'

'The kind you get by searching dusty old hospital records nobody remembers any more.'

The sound of a barking dog suddenly echoed through the apartment and Bishop instinctively swivelled his head towards the noise, seeing Cortiss reaching for his cigarettes as he turned. Then there was the sound of material being torn. When Bishop turned back Cortiss already had a pistol in his right hand.

Aimed straight at Bishop's head.

# FORTY-FOUR

Your life can change in a second.

That simple fact had been drilled into Bishop so many times in basic training he'd lost count. Let your guard down for just one second and it could be your last, they'd said, so expect everything. If a ten-ton weight falls out of the sky you'll see its shadow first, so move out of the way *before* you look up to see what it is.

Looked like his memory had finally let him down.

Bishop stared at the barrel and didn't move a visible muscle. The Beretta on his lap wasn't even pointing in the right direction any more, and the Colt in his jacket pocket might as well have been in the next door apartment. His right arm was still on the counter, though. Just out of Cortiss's view, thanks to the support pillar in the way. That was something, at least.

Cortiss's own right arm was outstretched with the gun pointing directly at Bishop's head. Unmoving and steady as a waxwork.

Bishop had no doubt he'd shoot at the slightest twitch.

It was a revolver. From this position it looked like a snub-nosed .357 but he wasn't about to lean over for a better view. He could see the chamber was full. Bishop swivelled just his eyes to the left arm of the sofa and silently cursed himself. The tearing sound had been Cortiss punching through his custom-made hole in the arm of the couch where he'd hidden the gun. He must have used a weak sealant to put it back together, as Bishop had seen no sign of a join in the material. Smart. The man had planned for every contingency.

The weird doorbell sounded again. On second hearing it was clear it couldn't be anything but an electronic effect. The barking was too regular. Then came three hard knocks on the door. A voice yelled, 'You in there, Joe? Got a Fedex package here I signed for while you were out.'

Cortiss just looked at Bishop with a smile on his face and pressed a finger to his lips. But he didn't have to. Neither man wanted to advertise his presence. Cortiss would want the guy to go away thinking the apartment was still empty. Bishop didn't want an innocent bystander getting killed if he could help it. And he knew Cortiss would waste them both in a second if it meant his own survival.

More knocking. The neighbour sounded like the determined type and that was good. Bishop needed Cortiss to stay where he was until he was ready. If he got up it was over. He'd see what Bishop's right hand was up to. But Cortiss wouldn't move until Bishop had tossed his gun. And he wouldn't order him to throw it until the neighbour gave up and went away.

'Coulda sworn it was your car I saw pull in,' the neighbour said in a softer voice. Five seconds later Bishop heard someone coughing, but the sound was a lot fainter. The guy had given up. He was going back to his own apartment.

Bishop spoke first to delay the inevitable by a few more seconds and allow his hand to inch closer to his goal. 'How much of what you told me was true?'

Cortiss gave him a look of fake remorse. 'I took care of Neary myself, but everything else was on the level. A surprise, I know, but in my business you don't get to share war stories too often. It can be done but then you've got to waste the other guy after you've finished.'

'Just like the old CIA joke.'

'Yeah. How about you throw your gun? Then we'll talk some more.'

Bishop doubted that. He knew Cortiss couldn't let him leave now. He'd spent years in this new identity and wasn't about to expose himself by turning him in to the cops. Bishop would talk and while the cops wouldn't believe him, they'd check anyway. The Joseph Armitage identity wouldn't hold up under close examination. No. Far easier to kill Bishop. Maybe try to make it look like a suicide. That's how a smart man would play it.

'Thumb and forefinger,' Cortiss said. 'Nice and slow. Toss it in the direction of the windows.'

Bishop slowly lifted his palm away from the Beretta's grip as the fingers of his right hand finally made contact with the handle of the kitchen knife he'd noticed earlier. It was lying on a wooden cutting board, close to where the phone was buried.

With his left hand, he formed a claw with thumb and forefinger and gripped the Beretta by the tip of the barrel. At the same time, his right hand spun the knife around so the blade pointed towards him.

Cortiss's outstretched arm remained rock solid, his eyes glued to the Beretta. Bishop mimicked the same exaggerated movements that Cortiss had used earlier to extract his cigarettes. He very slowly picked the gun up. Meanwhile, his right thumb and forefinger clasped the blade and raised it an inch off the counter, still out of Cortiss's line of vision. It was definitely sharp enough but Bishop couldn't tell how accurate it would be. Kitchen knives weren't designed for throwing and the balance was all wrong. Centre of gravity should be where blade meets handle, but the handle on this one was clearly heavier. And using his right hand, too. This wouldn't be easy.

It didn't matter. The time was *now*.

He swung his left hand as though demonstrating how to draw a tick and, at the end of the tick, released the Beretta. Instinctively, Cortiss's eyes followed the pistol's trajectory and Bishop twisted on the stool in a clockwise motion as he brought his right arm from the counter and pitched the knife towards the centre of Cortiss's head before the Beretta hit the floor. He kept moving after its release and rolled off the stool, dropping to the floor while reaching into his pocket for the Colt, waiting for the shot that would tell him it was over.

But there were no shots. No sounds of any kind. Bishop turned with the Colt now gripped in his left hand and saw why.

Bishop's aim had been accurate, but the knife had turned in midair so that the butt of the handle made contact with Cortiss's forehead instead of the point. Judging by the large, ugly dent in his skull, he'd have a month-long headache when he eventually awoke. But he'd be alive. Which was more than he deserved.

Bishop raised himself up and saw that Cortiss's arm had fallen by his side, gun still clenched in his hand. It was a .357. A shiny Colt Python with a four-inch barrel. He picked up his own Beretta from the floor and then put the other guns in his jacket pockets. He'd drop them in the nearest dumpster once he was finished here.

*The good thing about that one-second rule*, he thought as he rifled through Cortiss's pockets for his car keys, *is that it works the other way, too.*

# FORTY-FIVE

Bishop left the Lexus under some trees on a quiet street four blocks from Jenna's place and walked the rest of the way with his head down and his pace slow. To anyone looking, he was just a relaxed guy taking a stroll.

After a thorough search of Cortiss's apartment he'd found only a single additional item that might prove useful: an M84 concussion grenade. Having experienced its effectiveness firsthand on more than one occasion, he decided to take it with him. Then, after emptying the bathroom of all loose or sharp objects, he had secured the unconscious Cortiss to the radiator with the help of a large roll of duct tape he'd found in the kitchen. He'd want a follow-up discussion soon and figured Cortiss would be more amenable once he'd spent a day or two in his own john, nursing a concussion and a migraine the size of Texas.

When Bishop reached Jenna's building, he took the elevator to the third floor and knocked on her door. Jenna opened it, wearing the same bathrobe as this morning and smelling of flowers. Violets, this time. *Just how many showers did she take a day?*

'Hey,' she said. 'Cortiss showed up, then?'

'He showed up.' Bishop walked through the hallway into the living room and sat on an easy chair. Jenna took the couch. As he took off his suit jacket and draped it over the back of the chair he tried not to let his gaze linger on her bare legs and feet, but it was difficult. He'd known women who'd kill for legs like that. Men, too.

She smiled and said, 'If I ask what happened, will you get mad at me?'

'No, Jenna,' he said. 'I won't get mad at you.' He figured the two major breakthroughs she'd given him so far had earned her the truth, at least. Probably a whole lot more.

Over the next ten minutes he summarized everything Cortiss had given him. When he finished, she said, 'That poor kid. If I'd been her father, I'd have shot the bastard right there and buried him in the woods.' She raked her fingers through her hair. 'Still, at least we know we were on the right track with the Helen Gandy connection, right?'

'You mean you were on the right track. I thought it was simply money they were after.'

'Yeah, well.' Jenna looked out the window and said, 'Sometimes it helps to get another point of view in order to see things clearly.'

'I'm beginning to believe that.' Once again, Bishop found himself looking at her legs and glanced up to see her watching him with a smile on her lips.

She started to play with the ends of her belt. 'Almost two days now since you walked through my door. You given any thought to how long you'll want to stay with me?'

'Yeah, I have,' he said. More than once in the last hour or so, in fact. On the drive back, it had dawned on him that she was probably helping because she liked him, and it had been a long time since he could say that. She'd proved in a very short time that she could be trusted. A rare quality in Bishop's experience. And he realized that the core of his feeling for her was respect. 'Maybe if we see how things develop,' he said, his throat a little dry, 'we can take it from there.'

Her face split into a smile. 'That sounds like a fine idea.' She slowly got up from the couch and walked around the coffee table until she was standing directly in front of him. She took his hand and placed it around one end of the belt and just stood there, waiting to see what he'd do next.

Yesterday Bishop would have made an excuse and let go of it. But that was yesterday. Today, things were different. He kept hold of the belt. Then he slowly pulled until the bow came loose. The robe parted and for a moment he just stared at her smooth brown skin. And the silver, heart-shaped belly button ring an inch from his eyes.

He rose from the chair and pulled her to him. Jenna wrapped her arms around his waist and locked her mouth against his and for a while Bishop was completely unaware of time passing. It was only when he felt her unbuttoning his shirt that he broke contact. Breathing heavily, he helped her pull the shirt from his body.

'*Jeeee-sus,*' Jenna said, staring at his torso with wide eyes. 'You weren't kidding, were you?' She rested her palm on the area where the bruising was darkest and looked up at him. 'I think you need some *special* treatment.'

Bishop watched as she shrugged out of the bathrobe entirely. Then she began walking through the archway and into her bedroom.

# FORTY-SIX

Jenna sank an elbow into the pillow and rested her head on her palm. She looked down at Bishop and traced her fingers over his nose and lips, down his neck and along his shoulders. He closed his eyes. Her fingers on his skin felt nice. They finally came to a stop at the random series of ancient ridges on his left shoulder muscle. Like he knew they would.

'I'm tempted to ask where you got this,' she said, 'but I figure you'll just brush it off like it was a mosquito bite.'

'Not me,' Bishop said. 'I was in agony for weeks. Basic training, one of the assistant drill instructors threw a live grenade during a class on improvised explosive devices. His aim was lousy.'

She clucked her tongue and gently massaged the area. 'Did you like being in the Marines?'

'I guess. For a while, at least. I liked the constant physical challenges, seeing how far I could push myself. Plus I'd always wanted to travel, and I got plenty of that.'

'So what made you leave?'

'Lots of reasons. Mainly, I found myself in too many situations where I'd be thinking *why* and that's not a question for a Marine. Or any kind of soldier.' He shrugged and said, 'It was just time to move on, that's all.'

'And not a single tattoo anywhere on your body. I'm impressed.'

'I'm afraid of needles.'

'Sure you are.'

After a minute's comfortable silence, Bishop could feel her staring at him. He opened his eyes. 'What?'

'I'm scared you'll get mad at me.'

'I thought we were past that. Especially considering our present circumstances.'

'Okay,' she said and took a deep breath. 'I found those letters under the cushion.'

Bishop couldn't help smiling. Expect people to go against their nature and you'll come away disappointed every time. 'And you felt compelled to check things out for yourself, huh?'

She smiled back and he said, 'All right, I'm listening. What did you find out?'

Jenna sat up and crossed her legs. Bishop listened as she described her conversation with Jeffrey Golden about Willow Reeves' previous identity as Cavendish Hospital, and the current location of their records.

'Tax inspector,' Bishop said. 'More of your "social engineering"?'

'Yeah, but those old hospital records Cortiss said he checked? I think it could be this Cavendish Hospital he was talking about.'

'Only because you want it to be.'

'But don't you think it's at least possible? Cortiss could easily have gone to the storage warehouse in Brooklyn and checked for himself.'

He looked at the ceiling and said, 'Yeah, it's possible.' He thought back to what Cortiss had told him, and, more specifically, what he hadn't. 'You know, after everything that went down they couldn't have found what they were after in that vault. Cortiss told me this file was worth a whole lot more than the five million in cash they found, but the guy isn't exactly living in the lap of luxury. Way I figure it, Brennan must have moved the file after he fired Cortiss.' Bishop put his arms above his head. The stretch sent a sharp pain through his stomach muscles and he clenched them in response. The pain became a dull ache. He said, 'Which means if I can find out what's in this file, I can use it to bring the man I'm after out into the open.'

'I was hoping you'd say something like that,' she said and moved off the bed. 'First place to check has to be the warehouse. I'll need something business-like if we're going.'

'You planning on just walking right in?'

'Not exactly,' she said. 'But *we'll* need to make a stop along the way.'

# FORTY-SEVEN

Jenna pressed the doorbell and said, 'You really prefer his late-sixties stuff or were you just leading me on in the park?'

Bishop smiled. He'd borrowed an old baseball cap from Owen's box of stuff and had it pulled low over his face. 'I'm not big on Elvis, but yeah, that '69 album of his was good. "Wearin' That Loved On Look" was a catchy tune.'

She laughed and said, 'And I'll raise you with "Trying To Get To You". You do know that listing old song titles like this is about as original as the apple, don't you?'

He shrugged. 'I've been out of circulation for a while.'

The door opened and Ali's face appeared. He took in Bishop and quickly checked the street behind them before he said to her, 'You lose your key?'

'Didn't want to surprise you.'

'Should have thought of that before you called me earlier,' he said and let them in.

Jenna was dressed in a navy-blue skirt suit and white blouse. Bishop had added a tie to Owen's suit and was wearing his sunglasses. They both looked as though they'd come straight from the office. Except for the baseball cap.

In the hallway, Ali said to Bishop, 'You can wait up here. We won't be long.'

Bishop just shrugged and said, 'All right,' before moving into the living room.

Frowning at her brother, Jenna followed him down the stairs to the basement. She could tell he was annoyed and knew it wouldn't be long before he gave her the reason why.

He pointed to some paperwork lying on the worktable before kneeling down to open the small safe he kept under his desk. She checked through the three-page document, nodding at the official-looking stamps and signatures.

'Not bad,' she said and glanced up. Ali stood watching her. 'Okay, what?'

'This is bad on so many levels,' he said. 'Wanna know exactly how many?'

'Not really,' she said, sighing. 'But I'm sure you'll tell me anyway.'

'Number one,' he said, 'that man upstairs is currently America's Most Wanted. You buy him a cup of coffee and you go down for harbouring. And you got him staying at your *apartment*?'

'This from Mr Good Citizen,' she said, dropping the papers onto the worktop. 'You're the one said he's okay, remember? So what else you got?'

'They're all variations on that one.' He just shook his head slowly from side to side. 'What you trying to do to me? I thought you were way smarter than this.'

'This isn't about *you*, Ali. In case you hadn't noticed, I'm a big girl now and that means I get to choose my own path. James is innocent and right now he needs my help. And if that means letting him stay with me for a while, then fine.'

'*James*?' Ali raised an eyebrow at her. 'Jeez, you're sleeping with him, too.'

Jenna shook her head in irritation. This was getting them nowhere. She glanced at the two wallets in his hand and said, 'Look, why not just give me the IDs and we'll leave you in peace.'

'Hey, take it easy,' he said and handed them over. 'I'm just looking out for you, is all. With Mom gone, all we got is each other, and don't forget, I *am* the older one.'

She softened a little. 'I know, Ali, but I don't need somebody passing judgement on my choices. Even Mom knew better than that. I could use some support, though.'

'Sure, you got it.' He smiled at her. 'So, they what you wanted?'

'They're perfect,' she said, kissing his cheek. 'But I'd expect no less from you.' Behind Ali she saw an open laptop she recognized. 'So that's where my old iBook is. My brother, the thief.'

'Thought I told you. Mind if I hold on to it for another hour or so? I'm transferring some special software.'

'Sure,' she said and began climbing the stairs. 'Maybe I'll come back for it later on the way back.'

'If I'm not here,' he said from behind her, 'you can let yourselves in.'

In the living room Bishop was sitting on the sofa watching CNN. On the screen was a Photoshopped image of himself with his new buzzcut. It closely matched his current appearance.

Jenna and Ali came in from the basement. The reporter was saying, '. . . his escape from Greenacres Prison three days ago, convicted murderer James Bishop is believed to be still in the state of New York. The FBI has released this computer-generated image to all news agencies and believes it to be very close to how he now looks. They also warn that under no circum—'

Bishop clicked the remote and the screen went black.

Jenna said, 'Maybe this trip isn't such a good idea. Ali and I can do it instead.'

Ali said, 'It'd have to be tomorrow; I got a couple of business appointments this afternoon I can't postpone. But Jenna's right. That picture's bad news.'

Bishop shook his head. 'Forget it.'

Jenna watched him, then said, 'Okay, boss.' She tossed him one of the wallets. 'But a makeover wouldn't be a bad idea before we go.'

# FORTY-EIGHT

They drove Brooklyn's streets in silence, Bishop behind the wheel and Jenna next to him with her head down, looking through her notebook. A gauze pad covered his nose. It was held in place by three strips of athletic tape and itched like crazy.

Jenna turned to look at her handiwork and said, 'I'm having second thoughts about this.'

Bishop shrugged. 'Don't. People will be too busy wondering who I pissed off to really look at me. And you'll be doing your part, too.'

As they drove over the Carroll Street Bridge he pressed a finger to the gauze, then reached over and switched on the radio. Brahms's second symphony came on and he raised his eyebrows in silent approval. He'd thought Jenna was only a rock 'n' roller. She didn't comment on the track so he just drove and listened for a while. Or tried to. The reception wasn't too good. Deep in the background there was a high-pitched whistle. The kind that could get annoying pretty quickly.

'Try another one,' Jenna said.

He was about to do just that but, as they were crossing Hoyt, Jenna leaned forward in the passenger seat and said, 'That could be it up ahead.'

Bishop turned the radio off and followed her gaze. The street they were on was mostly made up of industrial buildings, except for a fenced-off section up on the right. As they got closer, Bishop saw a section of the chain link fence had been wheeled across to allow vehicles to pass in and out. A large metal sign with COURT WAREHOUSE CO. written in large type was attached to it. Further in, vehicles had to pass under a security barrier locked in the raised position. There was a small hut next to it and in front of that stood a uniformed guard talking on his cell phone. In plain view behind him were the warehouses – three of them – with a half-full car park in between. To the left of the entrance was a small, single-storey building that Bishop guessed was the front office.

He lowered the window as he pulled in next to the guard. His name tag identified him as Karl Reilly.

'Help you?' Reilly asked, placing the phone in his side pocket and focusing on Jenna. She'd taken off the jacket and undone the top three buttons of her blouse. Bishop could see his bandage hadn't been necessary.

She gifted the young guard a nice view as she leaned across and showed him the new ID Aleron had made for her. 'My name's Margaret Huntley from the Internal Revenue Service, Criminal Investigation Division, with a court order to inspect documents housed in Warehouse C. This is Sergeant George Wright of the NYPD, who's accompanying me as an official witness.'

Bishop opened his new wallet, but Reilly was too busy trying to study Jenna's credentials to notice.

'Is everything in order, Mr Reilly?' she said.

'Er . . . yeah. That's fine.' The guard swallowed and said, 'You want Pearson at the front office just over there. He'll take you.' He sneaked an additional peek at Jenna's legs before straightening up and walking back to his post.

As Bishop raised the window and edged the car forward, Jenna muttered, 'Pervert.'

He stifled a smile as he steered them left and parked in the last angled space in front of the office. 'I'll let you do all the talking,' he said. 'You seem to have a gift for it.'

'Thanks, I think,' Jenna said, grabbing her large shoulder bag and jacket from the back seat. 'You just stay in character then. Your captain's saddled you with this lame babysitting assignment, so you just need to look impatient and generally pissed off.'

'No problem there,' he said and got out.

At the reception entrance, he pulled the door open and let Jenna go through first.

Had Bishop really been a cop, he would have felt right at home inside. A counter separated them from the office area. Three security guards sat at a row of desks. Two were on their computers, the other was speaking into a telephone. A coffee machine, a steel table and three uncomfortable-looking chairs sat on their side of the counter.

Jenna approached the partition and said, 'I'm looking for a Pearson?'

One of the men looked away briefly from his screen and pointed to the grey-haired man on the phone. This guy held a finger up to her as he finished his end of the conversation. Jenna nodded and turned back to Bishop. He was leaning against the wall, looking like he'd rather be anywhere else. He wasn't acting. The grey-haired guy could be a retired cop for all he knew. The kind who liked to chew the fat about mutual acquaintances.

The man approached the counter and Jenna rummaged through her shoulder bag for the paperwork.

He said, 'I'm Pearson.'

She pulled out her ID again and told him their names. Pearson glanced at Bishop before turning back to her.

'So what do you need, Ms Huntley?' he asked.

Bishop watched her unfold the three-page document and lay it on the counter between them. It seemed Aleron kept a portable hard drive containing examples of just about every kind of US official paperwork in existence, including warrants and legal documents for all occasions. Bishop knew the world opened up as long as you looked the part. Pearson would be the litmus test.

'Mr Pearson,' Jenna said, 'this is a court order allowing us to inspect documents relating to Cavendish Private Hospital, pre-1970. I believe they're housed in Warehouse C?'

He watched Pearson skim over the legalese without any real interest. He skipped to the last page with the signatures and yesterday's date. The name of the judge was real, although he'd died five years ago.

'Yeah,' he said, looking up and pushing the paperwork back towards Jenna. 'That's our storage warehouse. A and B are mainly for commercial use.' He walked back to his desk and picked up the cap he found there. 'We'll walk over.'


The warehouse was huge. A series of corridors travelled the length of the building. Each was lined with storage racks filled with large blue crates. The racks stretched halfway up to the ceiling fifty feet above. Wheeled ladders waited at random intervals, and Bishop could hear the hydraulic sounds of forklifts echoing from other parts of the building.

Pearson was leading them down the leftmost aisle. He turned back to Bishop without breaking his stride. 'What precinct you work out of?' he asked.

'77th on Utica,' Bishop said. No need to give him any more.

Pearson faced forward again. 'I thought they would have sent some-body from the 76th on Union Street. They're a lot closer to us, and I know some of the guys from there. Don't know you, though.'

Exactly why Bishop had avoided mentioning it. He knew what was coming next. *Let's just nip this in the bud before it goes any further*, he thought and raised an eyebrow to Jenna walking beside him.

She nodded back and said, '*I* chose Sergeant Wright to accompany me, Mr Pearson, based on who was available at the time. Apparently, the 76th is understaffed to the point where they're unable to provide me with an escort today.'

Pearson snorted and said, 'That sounds about right. *Every*body's understaffed these days.' He came to a stop and pointed down to his right. 'You're in luck, Ms Huntley. We won't need to call one of the forklift guys over for you.'

Bishop and Jenna looked down at the large blue plastic crate at the bottom of the rack. The sticker on the side was stamped *#C7634 – Cavendish Hosp. – Confidential*. Bishop and Pearson both leaned down and carefully slid the heavy crate out of the rack onto the concrete floor. Pearson then ambled over to one of the wheeled ladders fifty feet away and sat on one of the rungs.

'I gotta keep watch,' he said, shrugging. Then he pulled a folded handgun magazine from his back pocket and proceeded to do exactly the opposite.

*Perfect*, thought Bishop. All conversation was finished.

He watched Jenna kneel down and unlatch the top flap and pull it open. Inside was a collection of large cardboard boxes. Each one was stamped with a year. They were all stuffed with paperwork. Jenna raised her eyebrows at Bishop and then picked a box.

# FORTY-NINE

Three-quarters of an hour later, Jenna said, 'Timothy Ebert.'

She was perched on the rung of a ladder with an open ledger on her lap. Bishop was sitting opposite her on a box marked *Jan-Jun 1963*. He was going through a stack of tedious administrative papers and fast losing the will to live.

'What have you got?' he asked, looking up.

She took off her spectacles and said, 'Not sure. I think it's some kind of security log for 1968. The handwriting's pretty bad, but he definitely gets a mention in December. No first name, just Ebert. But how many of them can there be?'

Bishop glanced to his left. Pearson was still on the other ladder, out of earshot and engrossed in his own reading material. 'Why were hospital security interested in him?'

'Seems he disappeared from the home on the evening of the nineteenth. This guy found his room empty while doing his rounds. Says he got some of the nurses to help search the place, but found nothing. No mention of alerting the police, so he can't have been much of a security risk.'

Bishop studied a faded tyre pattern on the floor and said, 'Anything else?'

Jenna replaced her glasses, skimmed over the next couple of pages. 'Yeah, here. Apparently, the missing patient from room eleven turned up again two days later.' She closed the book and stood up and stretched, extending her limbs like a cat. She then came over and dropped the book at Bishop's feet. 'And so ends 1968. Heavy year, that one. Lots of assassinations.'

She bent over and pulled out another book identical in size and colour to the one she'd just finished, this one marked *1969*. She took it back to her makeshift seat, opened it to the first page and began to read.

\* \* \*

Bishop didn't know how much time had passed, but when he looked up Jenna was still in the same position, scribbling something in her notebook as she read a passage from the ledger. There weren't many pages left.

'A real page-turner, huh?' he said.

Without raising her head, she said, 'You could say that.'

He hoped so. After going through all the '68 and '69 boxes he'd found no other mention at all of their mysterious patient. If these were indeed the files Cortiss had gone through, he'd been very thorough. Ebert's existence was almost completely erased. Not even copies of bills paid or records of family visits. Nothing.

Jenna finished writing and came over to sit on a box next to him. She placed the book out of sight of Pearson and frowned. 'It's weird, right? If Cortiss was so good at covering his tracks, how did these two security logs get past him?'

Bishop had already looked through a few pages of the '68 journal. 'I think the main reason is these aren't official logs. There are no daytime entries for a start, and he keeps going off on tangents. And the guy's handwriting isn't just bad, it's abysmal.'

She nodded. 'Yeah. And some of the prose is almost flowery. Hardly what you'd expect of an official record. In fact, there might not have *been* a security log. This place wasn't exactly a hotbed of activity. Yeah, now you mention it, these read like the personal diaries of a bored night watchman. If he'd bothered to put his name on them they would probably have been returned to him. I'm not surprised they slipped past Cortiss's radar; I had to wade through a lot of stream of consciousness crap to get to the interesting stuff.'

She looked around, found her shoulder bag and pulled it towards her. 'On top of that, Ebert's only actually mentioned by name once.' Watching to make sure Pearson wasn't looking her way, she opened her bag and dropped the 1968 ledger into it.

Smiling, Bishop said, 'But he *is* mentioned again?'

'Yeah, but only as "Eleven".' Jenna picked up her notebook and turned back a page. 'Mr Eleven discharged himself from the home at least five more times in '69 without telling anybody beforehand. On each occasion he'd return a few days later, like before. February 17, May 5, July 3, September 26 and October 11.'

'Okay,' Bishop said, rubbing his palm over his scalp. 'That's it?'

'Not quite.' She opened the '69 diary to a page marked with a Post-it note and said, 'Listen to this entry from November 13: "Some excitement at last, or at least what passes for it in my nocturnal existence. Agent Mandrake's returned with written authorization to inspect certain patients' files. He doesn't say much, just requests that I unlock the door to the records room. I leave him in there at 11 p.m. and he doesn't emerge again until 2 a.m."'

'*Agent* Mandrake?' Bishop said. 'A fed?'

'Doesn't say. He's not mentioned before this. Maybe his previous visits were during the day.' She continued reading aloud. '"He asks for my thoughts on the patient in room eleven and I tell him I haven't had much contact with him. Just that he's as moody as everyone else here, and that he has a habit of flying the coop every once in a while on the sly. I can see he finds this particularly interesting but he doesn't say why.

'"He also asks about the hospital routine and if we ever arrange outside excursions for the patients. Sure, I say, there's usually something planned every month for those who want a change of scenery. Museums, ball games, that sort of thing. I tell him Eleven usually puts his name down for these before he asks me and he cracks a smile and asks when the next one's due. This Friday, I say. He thanks me for my help and then departs eastwards."'

Jenna took off her glasses and said, 'And that's about it. If this Mandrake came back to search Ebert's room, it wasn't during this guy's shift or it would have made it into the book. Everything else seemed to.'

After another glance at Pearson, Jenna slipped the 1969 diary into her bag, zipped it closed and grinned at him. 'Don't know about you, but after all that, I'm famished.'

'Help me put this all back,' Bishop said, getting to his feet, 'and I'll treat you.'

# FIFTY

Bishop pulled into the drive-thru off Court Street and ordered them a box of chicken wings, a large cheeseburger, two large seasoned fries and two iced teas. They parked in a space on the next street along to eat, under the shadow of an elm tree. The guy who'd handed them their order hadn't even looked at Bishop's face, but as suburban streets had nosy neighbours he decided to keep the bandage on.

As they ate, Bishop thought about Mandrake. If he was a fed, then it indicated they were getting somewhere. Which meant that Jenna's hunch was right and Timothy Ebert was the key, somehow. But how he linked to the man who set Bishop up wasn't clear yet. Tennison had never been one for old FBI cases. None of them had.

Grabbing some fries, Bishop said, 'You know, there can't be that many Mandrakes around.'

Jenna nodded. 'There was the magician, but other than that . . .' She wiped her hands on a napkin and pulled out her Motorola. After pressing a couple of buttons, she brought it to her ear.

'Hey, Crys, it's Jenna . . . Yeah, I'm okay. You know, headachy, feeling a bit sluggish. I should be back in by the end of . . . Ha. That'll be the day. Listen, can you do me a favour, no questions asked? . . . Well, you're still working on that new package for the Feebies, aren't you? . . . Who's your contact over there? Rafferty? . . . And how heavy you been flirting with him? . . . Don't give me that, Crys. You're the same any time you talk to a guy with a badge. Look, if asked where a retired agent of theirs named Mandrake might be, you think he'd tell you?'

She turned to Bishop and rolled her eyes. 'Didn't I say no questions asked? . . . Okay, *okay*. Well, just tell him I'm seeing a guy who says he had an uncle who worked for the FBI in the sixties and wants to get in touch with him again . . . No, not really . . . No, Mandrake's all I got . . . Well, it's not exactly a common name . . . Right . . . Right . . . Cool. I owe you one, Crys.'

'She sounds a handful,' Bishop said when she hung up.

'Yeah, but she's a good programmer and the best at getting information out of people. Especially men. Hopefully, she'll get back to me within the hour.'

Bishop nodded. She paused, took a bite of chicken, wiped her hands again. 'So, you any closer to figuring out why you were set up?'

In his mind, he saw the faces of Chaney, Thorpe and Tennison lined up like fruit in a slot machine. He shrugged and said, 'Not really, but I figure it's got to be personal.'

'So, what, you pissed one of them off and ended up on the guy's hate list?'

'I had to reprimand Tennison, Thorpe and Chaney for various reasons over the years. So, yeah, any one of them could have decided to take it personally.'

'But then why would Thorpe have helped you with Cortiss?'

Bishop shrugged. 'He owed me. Doesn't cross him off the list, though.' He sipped some iced tea and looked at her. 'You were real good back there, Jenna. In another life, you could have been an actress.'

She smiled. 'I'm not nearly neurotic enough, but thanks. I aim to impress.' She fiddled with her straw and after a few moments said, 'You don't think we're wasting our time on this, do you?'

He shook his head. 'I think whatever lead this Agent Mandrake was following up at Cavendish is too good to ignore. Especially as Cortiss says this was about more than the money. I've never believed in coincidence and Brennan kept that Willow Reeves letter in his vault for a reason.' He shrugged. 'It could all lead to nothing, but it's all I got right now.'

'Yeah, I guess so.' She collected together their wrappers and went to put everything in a nearby trashcan. When she got back to the car, Bishop had the engine going.

She said, 'Can we stop off at Ali's first? I left something there I'd like to pick up.'

# FIFTY-ONE

Bishop was in Aleron's living room taking off his tie and jacket when Jenna's cell went off in the hallway. He heard her say, 'Hey, Crys,' and then she came in and sat down on the sofa. The cat hovered around her legs as she placed the phone on the coffee table and pressed the loudspeaker button.

A young, female voice said, '. . . of applause, please, as Crystal Rogers hits pay dirt once again. Not only does she succeed in her mission, but she also gets a date out of it.'

Jenna rolled her eyes again and said, 'I'm currently on my knees, bowing before your magnificence. So gimme.'

'Okay, there was a William *Mendrick* who worked out of the Washington office and retired in 1967. He finished up—'

'That's not him,' Jenna said.

'Didn't think so. And he died fifteen years ago. Our next and final contestant is Arthur Mandrake, who retired from government work in 1986 to go into the tourist business.'

Bishop raised his eyebrows. Jenna said, 'Tourist business?'

'Right. Metroblade Helicopter Charter and Tour Services, it's called. Out in Hoboken, not far from the river. Brad says he's the kind of ex-agent they all want to be when they retire.'

Bishop heard pages being turned at the other end.

'*Brad?*' Jenna asked.

'Yes,' Crys said. 'Brad. Shut up. Let's see, hard to read my own writing sometimes. Okay. Apparently, he got together with a guy who flew with him in Korea and they resurrected an abandoned private heliport to use as a base to fly executives to and from the city as well as show tourists the sights. They got a loan and bought a couple of helicopters, while Mandrake used his federal contacts to grease the wheels and breeze through the city zoning laws and get the necessary planning permissions. Good enough?'

'Better than good.'

'And get this. Brad's got tickets for that new play on Broadway, *The White Door*, starring Eloise Anderson for the first four weeks of its run. Opening night. Guess who he's taking.'

'Truly, your light shines brightly,' Jenna said.

'Well, duh. Just get well so you can tell me what this is all about, okay?'

'Okay,' she said and ended the call.

Bishop said, 'Jersey isn't too far.'

Jenna nodded. 'That's what I was thinking.'

'You mind going solo on this one, Jenna? I don't want to push my luck with a fed, retired or not.'

'Sure,' she said. 'I was gonna suggest it myself, anyway.'

When Jenna got up and disappeared into Ali's basement, Bishop sat back and stared at the ceiling. He tried to count all the reasons an FBI agent might have for travelling the width of a continent to research some patient in a private hospital. He'd reached four when Jenna reappeared holding a white laptop and another baseball cap. It was so new the metallic, circular logo on the front still had a shiny gleam. It looked expensive, too. She placed the laptop on the coffee table and threw the cap at him. He caught it and pulled it on. He knew nothing about fashion, but he guessed Aleron might have something to say about someone wearing his new headgear.

He watched her type for a minute and a half. Then she looked up and said, 'I guess he runs his business on word of mouth. There's no actual website, but there are plenty of directories listing the address and phone number.' She reached into the shoulder bag and pulled out the familiar notebook and a pen. Having scribbled down the information she picked up the cell again, keyed in the number and activated the loudspeaker. She sat back and tucked her legs under her. An otherwise innocent move that still had him thinking impure thoughts.

They listened to the ringing tone a couple of times before a ragged female voice said, 'Metroblade Charter and Tours.' She sounded fiftyish. Maybe older.

'Hi,' Jenna said. 'Could I speak with Mr Mandrake, please?'

'Which one you want, honey?'

'Um, Arthur?'

'Art? Does he know you?'

'No. My name's Jen—'

There was no 'hold, please'. The phone just went silent. Jenna shrugged. 'I *guess* I'm being put through.'

She was. 'Can I help you, ma'am?' The voice sounded young, even though Bishop guessed Mandrake must have been in his sixties or seventies by now. But the use of the pronoun was pure old school.

'Hello, Mr Mandrake. You don't know me; my name's Jenna Falstaff and I was hoping I could come speak with you, if that's possible.'

'All things are possible, Jenna. I'd be grateful for a little more information, however. Are you a journalist?'

'No, sir. The only stuff I write is computer code.'

'My name's Art, not sir. And if you're calling with an offer to design a website for us, I'm afraid you're wasting your time.'

'No, I'm not selling anything. This is about something else.'

'I see. Something to do with me, personally?'

'That's right.'

'Hmm, curiouser and curiouser. Well, fortunately for you, my daily duties here, or lack thereof, afford me ample time to indulge in extraneous pursuits such as enigmatic interviews with pretty women. You *are* pretty, I take it?'

Bishop nodded. She smiled and said, 'As a picture. I like the way you speak, Art.'

'High praise indeed, coming from a woman with the family name of Falstaff. And if you're under fifty you're already pretty, in my opinion. When would you like to see me?'

Bishop looked at his watch. 16.34. He mouthed *now* and she said, 'How about today?'

'No time to waste, eh? If you're in the area, I don't see why not. One of us usually closes up around seven, so any time between now and then is fine with me, although six or just before would be best. Ask Alex at the front desk and she'll point you in my direction. In the meantime, I'll try to imagine what you look like.'

'I'll see you then,' she said. 'I hope I shape up.'

'I've no doubt you will, Jenna. Goodbye.'

She pressed the disconnect button and said, 'Well, that part was easy. It's already rush hour, so I better make a move. What are you going to do?'

Bishop reached across for her notebook and turned back a few pages.

'If you want to lend me your apartment keys, I'll get a cab back to your place. Do a little research of my own.'

'A cab? What if the driver recognizes you?'

He pulled the nose bandage from his pocket and tapped the visor of his cap. 'He won't.'

Jenna smiled and said, 'I gave Ali a spare set of all my important keys for emergencies. I'll go get them for you.' She looked down at her suit. 'I might change out of this while I'm at it; I should still have a few clothes lying around upstairs.'

'Can't do any harm,' Bishop said, smiling. 'Mandrake doesn't sound like the kind of guy who stands on ceremony where women are concerned.'

# FIFTY-TWO

Peering out the driver's side window, Danny Costa sat waiting for Jenna Falstaff to emerge from her brother's house and silently gave thanks for the wonders of modern surveillance technology.

Being freed from having to keep your quarry constantly in sight made shadowing so much less stressful. Especially when all you had to do was attach a miniature GPS tracking device to the target's vehicle and let the ultra-powerful signal it sent out do the job for you. Right now, that little box was busy transmitting its location in the form of regular SMS transmission bursts, which were then converted into a form that could be superimposed over a detailed map stored on a particular website. As long as you knew the specific address, any web-enabled phone could access it.

So Costa didn't have to physically scan the area to know that Jenna's Honda was parked on the kerb about thirty feet away. Not when a simple glance at the screen of the cell phone affixed to the dash gave the same information.

Earlier, after following the Lexus from the post office to an apartment building in the Woodside district, Costa, deciding further instructions were called for, had sent Hedison a text message giving the address and explaining the situation. Hedison had called back quickly and said, 'Sounds like our boy might have found Mr Cortiss. Stick with him for a while and keep me updated.'

Of course, that was easier said than done in New York. When the same Lexus eventually emerged from the underground car park with Bishop at the wheel, the journey back to Jenna's place had been more than a little nerve-racking, with Costa in danger of losing him at every traffic light. So when Bishop finally parked it on the street and walked to the girl's apartment a few blocks away, Hedison had recommended the placement of another tracking device to the undercarriage in case Bishop decided to use it again. Problem solved.

Now, here they were, back at the brother's again. Where to next? Costa wondered. And at what point was Hedison planning to gatecrash the party and liven things up? Costa could think of far more enjoyable pursuits than spending the day sitting in a car – many of them involving the Falstaff woman – and could only hope it was sooner rather than later.

And speak of the devil; here she came. Dressed in a leather jacket, blue T-shirt and black jeans. She was clutching a shoulder bag as she locked the front door and ran down the short path to her car parked four spaces ahead. Once she got in, it took less than a minute for her to ease the vehicle into the street and move off.

Costa glanced at the moving red dot on the little screen, smiled at it as one would an old friend, and followed.

# FIFTY-THREE

Bishop paid the cab driver and entered Jenna's building. The bandage and cap had done their job. Often the simplest things worked best.

Inside the apartment, he dropped the cap onto the kitchen counter and ripped off the bandage. He then changed out of Owen's suit and put on his own clothes. Sitting in Jenna's chair at the dining table, he turned on the computer and router and wondered if he'd made a mistake letting Jenna go. But really, what choice did he have? Mandrake was old-school FBI. He'd have seen through Bishop's disguise in a second. Besides, Jenna would be fine. She had a talent for getting people to talk and an interview with an elderly tourist operator was unlikely to cause her problems.

Right now, though, he wanted to find out the significance of the dates Jenna had jotted down at the warehouse. Everybody seemed to be interested in this Ebert, and Bishop had a strong feeling the dates he went missing from hospital could prove to be key in finding out why. There had to be something there.

Opening up Google, he typed in *December 1968 February May July September October 1969*. He thought of the hospital's location and added *San Francisco*, then hit Return.

The first page of results contained links for sites listing old concert dates for Janis Joplin, Cream, Jimi Hendrix and Deep Purple, as well as some Vietnam memorial sites, an Andy Warhol chronology, and, of all things, a Charles Manson fan site. The next few pages had more of the same but with even wider frames of reference. Not exactly what he'd been hoping for, but then he hadn't really expected to hit a home run in his first inning.

He kept at it, typing in various combinations of search words. Sometimes he inserted some of the full dates Jenna had written down. Sometimes he left off a month entirely. But the links became even more wide-ranging, many of them containing only the barest connection to

San Francisco. He shook his head, leaned back, and stared at the ceiling.

The logical answer was to refine the search parameters, and to do that he'd need to add more information. He worked through everything they'd gotten so far and a smile began to form at the realization that there *was* a word missing. And a pretty obvious one when you took into account Mandrake's presence at the old hospital.

Bishop sat forward, added the word to his original grouping and pressed Return.

He stopped smiling when he saw the hit halfway down the first page. It was so unexpected that it stood out amongst everything else.

'Ho-ly shit,' he whispered as he read the two-line description of the site. *This can't be for real.*

He clicked on the link and was taken to the home page of a site devoted entirely to its subject. The design was basic, no frills. The occasional photo here and there to break it up. There was a list of options running down the left-hand side. One in particular caught Bishop's eye and he clicked on it. The screen then filled with paragraphs of tightly spaced copy and no images. Just white text on a black background. What Bishop read made him forget everything else. His set-up. His escape. Jenna. He was totally absorbed in the words onscreen.

By the time he reached the author's list of sources at the bottom, he finally understood the FBI's interest in the patient.

Of the six times Ebert had been missing from the hospital, four of them matched up with the recorded dates listed on the site. It was more than a coincidence. Although what it meant was so messed up it was hard to believe. He checked Cook's diving watch and figured Jenna would have reached Metroblade already. And she needed to know about this, especially if Mandrake needed a little prod to open up about his past.

He pulled the cell phone from his pocket and sent her a text with the web address. He added a line telling her to check it ASAP and sent it off.

As he sat back in the chair he realized all he could do now was wait until Jenna contacted him. Not a very satisfactory situation. Perhaps now was the time to move on to Tennison. He'd be finishing work soon and making his way across the river to his home in Guttenberg. Might be a good idea to see if he also had his own police escort, like Chaney. Couldn't hurt to check. Bishop glanced over at Aleron's cap, wondering if it would be disguise enough, and found himself studying the large, circular emblem on the front properly for the first time. And then it all clicked into place.

The Lexus was still where he'd left it under the trees. He kept his head down as he approached the driver's door and relaxed a little once he was inside. Jenna might have been right about residents here minding their own business, but he couldn't afford to take unnecessary chances. He started the engine, and as he sat back his palm accidentally pressed against one of the buttons on the steering wheel. The radio came on in the middle of an old Beach Boys song. A nostalgic back-to-roots thing about doing it again. But he was more interested in the high-pitched whine just noticeable in the background. Exactly the same as when they'd been in Jenna's car. He tried another station and there it was again. Bishop drummed his fingers on the steering wheel, then opened the driver's door and got out.

He checked under the Lexus's wheel arches. The first three gave him nothing. But at the rear passenger side he found a black, magnetized transmitter. It was about the size of a matchbox and he knew exactly what it could do. Somebody was using it to keep track of Bishop. Jenna, too. And obviously not someone who wanted him caught, as a phone call to the cops would have been simpler and cheaper.

Bishop walked over to a storm drain and dropped the device through the grate.

He had mixed feelings about the transmitter. On the one hand, it told him he was on the right track. Obviously an early warning system in case he was getting too close. Which he clearly was. But with Jenna's car also under surveillance, it meant he was putting her in danger as well and that was the last thing he wanted. She'd already helped enough and he wanted her out of the way and safe while he handled things alone from now on. But first, he needed to get rid of the other transmitter.

# FIFTY-FOUR

Jenna gave a huge sigh as she switched off the engine, unconsciously matching her breathing to the ticking of the muffler as it cooled down. She knew how it felt. As usual, the Holland Tunnel had been the worst. Rush hour, too. It wouldn't have been so bad if she'd had the radio to listen to, but that annoying high-pitched tone in the background merely stressed her out even more.

At least Mandrake's address had been easy to find. Metroblade was a two-storey building with a small car park out front at the end of a gently curving cul-de-sac off Newark Avenue, near the turnpike bridge. The left-hand side of the road was taken up with a vast auto salvage business. The other side was taken up by a noisy recycling site.

Jenna got out, locked the vehicle, and walked over to the portico entrance. Inside, the reception area was filled with comfortable chairs arranged in circles of four. Framed enlargements of aerial views of the city covered the walls. The place felt subdued and relaxed. Two couples sat in one of the circles, deep in conversation with each other. They looked like tourists waiting for their ride. None looked up at her entrance. Directly ahead, a bespectacled woman with dyed-blond hair sat behind a large desk working on her computer. There was no name plaque, but Jenna guessed this was Alex.

The woman saw her approach and said, 'Help you?'

'Hi, we spoke on the phone. Jenna Falstaff. Here to see Art.'

'Oh, yeah,' Alex said, looking her over. She rose from her chair, leaned over the desk and pointed a finger towards the wide hallway to Jenna's right. 'Down there, honey, and up the stairs. First right at the top is Art's office, okay?'

Jenna thanked her and walked down the hallway, then up the stairs. At the top, she rapped her knuckles against the door with Arthur Mandrake's name on it, and a voice said, 'Come in.'

The room she entered was longer than it was wide, with a row of shuttered windows along one side that overlooked the car park. A long, rectangular conference table took up much of the central floor space. At the far end, a smiling Art Mandrake rose from behind his computer and came around his kidney-shaped desk with hand outstretched. 'Jenna,' he said.

She walked over and took his hand. 'Hello, Mr Ma— Sorry. Art.'

Art stood at around five-nine and wore a well-tailored black suit. He looked about seventy and his face contained deep lines and creases that Jenna figured resulted from a life spent closer to the sun than most. The skull was almost entirely free of hair, apart from a few white wisps above the ears but the clear, brown eyes held a sparkle that was ageless. Jenna couldn't help smiling back.

'Anything you'd like, Jenna?' He went over to a small refrigerator next to his desk and said, 'I've got water and soft drinks, or I can get Alex to bring you up a coffee if you'd prefer.'

'Water's fine,' she said and waited as he filled two glasses with Evian and ice. He motioned for her to sit down in one of the chairs surrounding the conference table. 'Thanks. This is a little out of the way for a tour company, isn't it?'

He sat down next to her and crossed his legs. 'It's worth it for the cheaper rent. Besides, a large part of our business comes from high-level executives who believe avoiding New York traffic is worth almost any price. We've got three helicopters that rarely stay on the ground for very long. Two of them are due back soon, in fact. You're even prettier than I imagined, Jenna. If there's a man in your life, I hope he appreciates you.'

She felt herself blushing at the compliment. 'I'm not sure what he thinks. The strong silent type, you know?'

'Hmm. If he's not careful, he'll develop an ulcer.' He brushed some imaginary lint from his sleeve and said, 'So how can I be of service?'

She took a sip of water and said, 'Well, it has to do with a visit you made to the Cavendish Hospital in San Francisco in late 1969.'

Art looked at her for a few moments. 'What makes you think I was ever there?'

'Your name was mentioned in a private diary belonging to their night man at the time. Here.' Reaching down into her bag, she pulled out the 1969 book, opened it to a page marked with a Post-it note and placed it before him.

He pulled his spectacles from his shirt pocket, perched them on his nose and read the entry without touching the book. When he reached the end, he took them off and sat back. 'I think if we are to proceed,' he said, 'I need to know what your interest is in this. Do you think that's fair?'

Jenna had known the question was coming but still hadn't come up with a decent answer. And Art would see through the usual snow job in a second. She cleared her throat and took another sip of water. The truth, then. As far as possible. 'That man in my life you mentioned?'

'Yes?'

She kept her attention on the glass of water in front of her. 'He's . . . well, he's in a lot of trouble. Please don't press me for specifics, but we're both trying to find the person responsible for putting him there. One way to do that is by finding out what this person was actually after and why. Our digging so far has led us to a patient who stayed at Cavendish Hospital forty years ago. And from there to you.' She turned to Art and smiled. 'Could I be any vaguer?'

Art took a sip of his own drink and said, 'This man of yours sounds intriguing. I'd be interested in meeting him.'

'I don't know. He's got a lot on his plate at the moment.'

'Of course.' Art placed his glass next to hers and said, 'Do you know, Jenna, I was an agent for the Bureau during the last ten years of Hoover's life and in all that time I met him only the once, and even that was one time too many. He was not an impressive figure, either as a human being or as a boss. Nevertheless he *was* my boss, and when he called me in to his office in late '69 and assigned me to fly down to San Francisco to visit this hospital, I did as I was told. Once there, I was to inspect the billing records of each patient and write a detailed report of my findings. For Hoover's eyes only.'

'And that's all he told you?'

He smiled and rubbed a hand over his bald pate. 'If you've read anything about Hoover you'll know he was a man with issues, not the least of them being his pathological distrust even of the people under his command. I certainly didn't need to know *why* I was to do it. The verbal order from the great man himself was deemed reason enough.'

Jenna heard the sound of rotary blades and turned in her chair. Out of the window, she saw a helicopter heading towards the city. 'Final trip of the day?' she asked.

'A brief journey to see the sights during magic hour.' He squinted at a speck in the distance. 'And here comes Mr Rafe Stevenson, if I'm not mistaken. Returning from another profitable day at the exchange.'

He had good eyes. Jenna saw the speck gradually turn into another copter and asked, 'So did you find anything?'

'I found out who paid the bills for each patient and took photocopies, or what passed for them in those days. Then I typed up my findings and sent it all off to Hoover's office. If you're asking whether I found anything suspicious, then no, I didn't.'

'But Hoover must have. He sent you back there.'

'My, you *have* done your homework. Well, whatever Hoover found he didn't let me in on the secret. He just sent me one of his infamous memos and ordered me to go back and find out everything I could about one patient in particular, including a thorough search of his room when the opportunity arose.'

'Timothy Ebert in room eleven.'

He arched his eyebrows at her. 'Not bad. Yes, Timothy Ebert. Well, I inspected the man's medical records – something I'm not too proud of when I think about it now – and discovered he'd been admitted two years before, in 1967. He'd been diagnosed with an extreme form of manic-depressive illness. My youngest daughter works in a hospital and I've learned this is now referred to as bipolar disorder. Back then, though, they really had no idea how to treat it.'

'Isn't that like schizophrenia?'

Art shook his head. 'A common misconception. Bipolar disorder's a disease caused by a chemical imbalance and characterized by intense mood swings. Some patients suffering from the disease in its most extreme form can experience full-blown psychosis where they feel they're on a special mission, but it's actually treatable with the right medication. True schizophrenia, on the other hand, is quite rare and is based around continual hallucinations and delusions. Much harder to treat because the patient simply stops taking his medication if one of his hallucinations tells him to.'

'Okay. So who was footing the bills? His folks?'

'No, not his parents. Do you know, I can't quite remember the person's name. Although I do recall it was quite a mouthful. Maybe that's why it didn't stick.'

'Shame,' she said. 'The night man wrote that you were interested when he told you about Ebert going AWOL.'

'Of course I was. Any behaviour that was out of the ordinary got my attention.'

Jenna pulled her notebook from the bag at her feet just as her phone sounded a message alert. 'And he gave you the dates Ebert went missing?'

'Certainly,' Art said. 'But if you expect me to remember . . .'

'No need,' she said. 'He wrote them down himself. There were six in all. Here.' Jenna turned to her notebook's most recent page and handed it to him as she pulled out her phone. Art studied the dates before looking up at her with a blank look on his face. 'They don't mean anything to you?' she asked.

'Should they?'

'I don't know,' she said, experiencing uncertainty for the first time. 'I was hoping . . .' She paused. What *was* she hoping for, exactly? That he'd remember every detail from an obscure assignment four decades ago and wrap everything up for her in a nice little package? *Yeah, right, Jenna. Good plan.*

She glanced down at her phone and saw she'd received two messages, not one. Both were from Bishop. After asking Art to excuse her for a moment, she opened them up. In the first, he'd given her a web address to check. In the second, he told her to remain at Metroblade and that he'd meet her there. She frowned, wondering what had caused him to risk exposure by coming here. Although it couldn't be too serious or he would have said so. Oh well, she'd find out soon enough when he arrived. But she could check the link right now. Maybe he had gotten somewhere.

'Well, it looks like you might get to meet the man in question, after all,' she said.

'He's coming here?'

She nodded and looked at Art's PC. 'That thing's connected to the web, right?'

He followed her gaze. 'Naturally. Why?'

'You mind giving me a few minutes to check on something?'

'Go right ahead.' He slid the 1969 diary over and opened it to a random page. 'I can amuse myself with this gentleman's private thoughts in the meantime.'

Grabbing her cell and notebook, Jenna walked over and sat in front of the monitor. Just beyond the keyboard, under a shapeless chunk of polished glass, lay a folded copy of today's *New York Times*. With the three-year-old mugshot of Bishop in plain view. After a quick check to see if Art was watching, she picked up the paperweight and turned the newspaper over. Right now, Bishop needed all the help he could get. Then she grabbed the mouse and opened a web browser, keyed in the web address from her phone and pressed Return.

And as sudden as a car crash, there it was. A big, fat piece of the puzzle laid bare right in front of her. The whole timeline from 1968 through 1969. Bishop had found it. She fell silent as she speed-read through the text, her heart beating faster with each sentence. Occasionally she glanced at her notes to compare the dates and marked each one with a tick or a cross where appropriate. When she reached the end, she leaned back in the chair and stared at the ceiling as she digested the information. Or tried to.

After a while she looked over at Art. From between the pages of the 1969 journal, he'd extracted one of the letters Bishop had found at the Brennan house and was reading through it slowly.

'You better come take a look at this, Art,' Jenna said, standing up. She waited as he rose from his seat, still holding the letter in his hand, and came round the desk to join her.

He sat down, looked at the screen and said, 'Is that . . . ?'

'Why don't you compare the dates in my notebook before you ask questions? I copied them down earlier from the two journals.'

He dropped the letter next to the newspaper and began reading through the onscreen text, referring to Jenna's notations as he navigated down the page. She watched his face in the light of the monitor, and when he reached the last line she couldn't tell if he'd gone pale, but thought it likely. She gave him a few moments to take it all in.

He eventually looked up at her and said, 'Well.'

'In a word,' she said. 'Now you can understand why Hoover wanted you out there.'

'Yes.' He licked his lips and tapped the notebook. 'Four of the dates Ebert went missing . . .'

'. . . match up with the dates of the murders,' she said. 'You should feel good, Art. Now you know what Hoover knew all along. After all this time, you've finally discovered the identity of the Zodiac killer.'

# FIFTY-FIVE

As he made his way down Canal Street towards the Holland Tunnel, Bishop wondered how he was going to get around Mandrake. It didn't matter how old the guy was, it was a good bet he'd make Bishop the moment he saw him. And since Jenna couldn't very well claim ignorance of Bishop's fugitive status, she could face prosecution for associating with a known felon if Mandrake decided to go down that route.

He decided the simplest solution was to wait for her outside reception and avoid Mandrake altogether.

Once again, his thoughts returned to what he'd found on the website. He felt sure there was still a piece missing. There had to be. With the exception of Jack the Ripper, the Zodiac was modern history's most notorious serial killer. Even now, forty years later, Bishop had no doubt one of the major media corporations would pay big money for actual proof of his identity. But enough to warrant a massacre? When there were already millions for the taking in Brennan's vault? Bishop thought it unlikely.

Which meant it came back to Timothy R. Ebert himself. Clearly, the guy was still walking around as nobody would be too interested in a dead man, unless there was a family connection of some kind. Bishop considered the distinct possibility that he was somebody known to both Cortiss and his partner. Somebody well off, financially. And prepared to pay a hell of a lot more than five million to ensure his secret remained hidden. But who was he?

Still too many questions and not enough answers.

As he joined the small queue of vehicles waiting at the tunnel's westbound entrance, Bishop looked up into the darkening sky to see a helicopter in the distance heading in the same direction as himself. Metroblade couldn't be far now.

# FIFTY-SIX

Standing at the window, Jenna watched the approaching helicopter steadily grow in size and thought about Timothy Ebert. And why his identification as the Zodiac had proved so costly to so many people. At least she wasn't short of questions to ask Art now. When the chopper finally passed by overhead, she turned to see him still engrossed in the website, and nodded her head at the ceiling. 'That your other exec?'

'Yes,' Art said, frowning at the screen. 'Interesting.'

Jenna came over and perched on his desk. 'You find something else?'

'Do you know anything about the Zodiac's ciphers, Jenna?' he asked, turning to her.

'Some. He'd send coded messages to the papers, demanding the front page, right?'

'In a nutshell. In late July 1969, he sent the first one to San Francisco's three main newspapers, claiming it would identify him once decoded. It didn't, of course; just more gibberish about being reborn in paradise with the victims as his eternal slaves. But the code ended with a series of eighteen seemingly random letters that have puzzled cryptologists to this day. Take a look.'

She came to his side and read through the translated cipher. There, right at the end, were the letters EBEORIETEMETHHPITI.

'It's a stretch, I know,' he said, 'but if you kind of read it backwards . . .'

Jenna stared at it for a few seconds and then turned to him with her mouth open. 'Pity Timothy Ebert.'

He nodded. 'Not exactly conclusive. But if you know where to start and don't mind bending the rules a little, it *does* contain a signature, of sorts.'

'Or a call for help,' Jenna said and looked down at the letter Art had been reading. It was the one from Willow Reeves. She reached over and picked it up. Turned it over. And of course the nine vowels and nine consonants written on the back were the same as those on the screen.

She saw Art looking at the letter with narrowed eyes, then at her. 'Randall Brennan,' he said softly. Then he glanced at the newspaper and turned it over so the top half with its photo of Bishop was showing again. He leaned back in his chair and looked at her. 'Your man's taking a bit of a risk coming here, isn't he?'

And right there, Jenna could tell he knew. That he'd put it all together and come up with the only possible answer. Didn't anything get past this guy? She sighed and said, 'That kind of depends on you.'

'I guess it does.' He clasped his hands together and chewed part of his lip. 'Although I admit I'd be interested to hear his side of the story.'

Jenna thought he might say more but he just faced the screen again and said, 'I didn't think websites like this existed any more. I expected pages of wild theories, but the author just lists the facts, often taken directly from police records. Very impressive.' He turned to her and said, 'Would you mind turning on the lights, Jenna? It's getting dark.'

'Sure.' She went over to the doorway and pressed the wall switches, and three oval ceiling lights came on. 'So does the stuff in there jibe with what you found in Ebert's room?'

Looking at the screen once more, Art said, 'I didn't search his room.'

'But I thought . . .'

'Oh, I was *supposed* to. But as soon as I reported back to Hoover with my findings regarding Ebert's medical history and the disappearances, he ordered me back east immediately.'

'He didn't want to follow it up?'

Art smiled. 'I didn't say that, did I? In fact, I can guarantee he *did* follow it up; he just used an agent other than myself to do it. I told you he didn't trust anybody. He especially didn't like the right hand to know what the left was doing. If I'd found something in Ebert's room I might have made the connection between him and the Zodiac, and Hoover couldn't afford that possibility. I never saw the room and I never saw Timothy Ebert.'

'But somebody must have.'

'No doubt. And I'm sure Hoover built up one of his famous files . . .'

'Later, Art,' somebody bellowed from downstairs.

To her surprise, Art shouted back, 'Go easy, Jake.'

Jenna leaned against the conference table with her arms crossed, smiling at him.

Art smiled back. 'Sorry. Our daily routine, come quitting time. Only Cory and the tourists to go, and then we'll shut up shop for the night.' He tapped a finger against the letter. 'So this Willow Reeves is the name Cavendish is operating under now?'

Jenna nodded. 'But under different ownership. Some non-profit organization bought them out in 1970.' She scrunched her eyebrows together. 'Kaiser something or other. Foreign-sounding. It's at the bottom of that letter.'

Without looking, he said, 'Kebnekaise.'

'Hey, that's it. How'd you know?'

'I told you it was a mouthful.'

She stood up. Uncrossed her arms. 'Hold up. Are you saying . . . ?'

'Yes,' he said. 'It's the name I saw next to Ebert's on the billing records. I thought it was the name of a person, but it looks like I was wrong.' He shook his head. 'Isn't that always the way? Answer one riddle and another takes its place.'

'You're not kidding,' Jenna said, almost to herself. 'Just who the hell is Kebnekaise? And who's Timothy Ebert?'

She walked over to the window and looked through the shutters again. There was barely any light left in the sky now. Magic hour was definitely over. She lowered her gaze to the car park down below and saw a Porsche pull out of the gate and gently accelerate away down the solitary road with its headlights on. Probably the pilot, Jake, on his way home. The only cars left now besides hers were a Discovery, a Chrysler, a Chevy and a Mercedes. She continued watching the Porsche's progress until it passed another set of headlights, headed this way.

Jenna turned to Art. 'He's here,' she said.

# FIFTY-SEVEN

Bishop parked the Lexus a few hundred yards down the road. After wiping down everything he'd touched, he locked the doors and walked towards the Metroblade building. Both floors still had lights on and five vehicles were still parked in the spaces outside. When he got closer, he made out Jenna's Honda. He passed through the open gate and headed for the covered entrance on the left. Keeping out of the light, he peered through the glass doors and saw a well-lit reception area but no movement of any kind.

He moved in closer and saw the reason why.

Reaching back under his shirt for the Beretta, he pushed the door open and stepped inside. As he walked towards the front desk he smelt it. And then he reached the woman he'd seen from outside. She lay sprawled on the floor next to an overturned chair. She had two large-calibre holes in her forehead. He bent down and touched her arm. Still warm.

With his gun leading the way, Bishop crept down the passageway on the right. Through the glass doors at the end, he saw three empty helipads. The middle one was illuminated by ground lamps, while four elevated floodlights further out bathed the whole area in amber.

Bishop backed up against the left-hand wall and peered round the first open doorway. He saw a long, thin room with charts and maps all over the walls. A large desk held what looked to be ground-to-air communications equipment. Sitting in a swivel chair was a male figure. Bishop didn't need to check his pulse. Both legs were stretched out and his head was tilted back, eyes gazing sightlessly at the ceiling. There was a wide slit where his throat used to be.

He moved to the second doorway and glanced in. This room held a sofa, four desks arranged in a square and a kitchen at the far end. A body lay face down on the floor, next to the sofa. Bishop could see it was another male. A pool of black liquid surrounded him.

Bishop turned, entered the stairway alcove opposite and slowly climbed the steps, banishing from his mind all thoughts that history was repeating itself. He wasn't responsible for these people or their safety. He couldn't have done anything to stop this.

But Jenna was another matter entirely.

At the top, a door bearing Mandrake's name was ajar. He pushed it open with a knuckle and stepped inside, gun first. At the far end, near the desk, he saw an old man in a suit lying on the floor. He guessed he was looking at Mandrake.

Bishop squatted at his side and saw a deep gash in the skull. Up close he could see that Mandrake's chest was still moving. He checked his pupils, then reached into the man's jacket and pulled out his wallet. He found an expired pilot's licence and grabbed the desk phone. As he leaned over to dial 911, he saw a small notepad open on the floor.

'What are you reporting, sir?' a female dispatcher asked.

'Medical emergency.' Bishop gave the address and said, 'Patient is male, sixty-nine years of age and unconscious. Name is Arthur Randolph Mandrake. Violent head trauma due to assault with a blunt instrument. Likely occurred within the last fifteen or twenty minutes. Breathing is shallow and dilated pupils suggests possible coma. He's in the front office on the second floor. There are bodies downstairs, too.' He hung up, remembering to wipe the phone with his sleeve. Then he reached down and picked up the notebook. A stylized, two-colour headshot of Elvis looked back at him.

Which only confirmed what he already knew. Jenna had been snatched. Bishop had missed her by a matter of minutes. He should have gotten here faster, or spent less time going through that damn website. Or he should have accompanied her out here in the first place, regardless of the risks. He was at fault. He knew that. And it didn't take much guesswork to figure out who'd taken her. Or what might happen to her if he didn't get her back. As he placed the notebook carefully in his pocket, he made himself a promise that he'd return it to Jenna by hand. Whatever it took.

Then white light filled the office and Bishop squinted at the approaching helicopter lights. Looked like somebody was coming in for a landing. He dropped his gaze to the road below. He could make out red and white flashing lights in the distance, coming this way. And they didn't look like the ones you found on ambulances.

Bishop had a feeling they were for him.

# FIFTY-EIGHT

Behind the door, Bishop saw a coat hanger bearing two Metroblade windbreakers. He slipped one on and then ran down the stairs as the *whup, whup, whup* of the helicopter vibrated through the building. A small voice in his head warned that Jenna could still be there. But his gut knew otherwise. She would have been with Mandrake, and she wouldn't have left her notebook by choice.

In the comms room downstairs, he found a set of ear protectors and added them to his outfit.

He slammed the rear doors open and ran the two hundred yards to the helipad, stopping just outside the perimeter of ground lights. Looking up, he saw the copter coming in at a steep angle less than a hundred feet above him. Slipping his gun into the windbreaker's pocket, Bishop lowered his head as the landing lights passed over him towards the large H in the centre of the landing area.

Turning, he saw the red flashing lights were more intense. They were possibly already in the parking area. He figured another minute at most and it was game over.

He faced forward, counting seconds and calculating distances in his head. The small, single-engine helicopter was descending on the H with about fifty feet to go. He glimpsed a man and two women in the back and a bearded man in front next to the pilot. They were all staring past Bishop at the light show out front. The fixed skids were already thirty feet above the landing zone. Then twenty. At fifteen feet, Bishop ran forward with his head lowered and met the copter at the exact moment it touched concrete. He pulled the passenger door open, then slid the rear door back so the whole left side of the copter was exposed. The passengers ignored him for the action behind him. The bearded man in front said something, but Bishop couldn't make it out over the noise of the rotors.

He pulled the gun from his pocket and kept it at his side while his right hand unlatched beard man's safety belt. 'Okay, people,' he yelled.

'Seatbelts off and an orderly exit, please. Let's make it quick.'

The three in the back began to undo their belts in unison and the pilot looked at Bishop with his mouth open. Before he could say anything, Bishop laid the Beretta on the floor by beard man's feet. The pilot looked down and saw it. When he looked up, Bishop made a whirring motion with his right index finger. 'Keep the engine running, pal. Police emergency.'

He moved back a foot to let beard man out and said, 'Heads down as you walk back to reception, people.' To the pilot he said, 'Are we go?' Receiving a single nod in reply, he turned to the rear passengers and said, 'Snap it up, folks, we got a situation here.'

The woman nearest the door jumped out, closely followed by the other two. As soon as they were clear Bishop slid the rear door shut and dived into the front seat, latching the door closed behind him. Then he pulled the ear protectors off and replaced them with the headset at his feet. The sound of the engine and rotors immediately became background noise. Bishop plugged the cable into the comms unit and heard the sound of breathing. 'Where's Gregg?' the pilot said in his ears.

'In the comms room,' Bishop said and looked out the window. He saw beard man waiting at the perimeter for his wife and friends to join him. Further back, the building's rear doors opened and silhouettes emerged with guns drawn. Bishop counted four. Two wore windbreakers similar to his. They weren't running yet, but they would once they realized the copter wasn't powering down. Bishop clicked the safety belt home and turned to the pilot. 'Let's get going,' he said.

The pilot was in his early thirties. Short thinning blond hair and a gaunt face with downcast mouth. He said, 'You want to show me some ID first?'

'Sure,' Bishop said and pressed the barrel of the Beretta against the man's knee. 'How's this? Now take us up before I forget you're a civilian.'

The pilot started flicking switches on the panel above his head. 'I'm on it. I'm on it.'

'Back the way you came,' Bishop said, pushing his frame further down into the leather seat. The outlines were now running towards them and had already halved the distance. He turned back to the pilot. 'And you should know, if push comes to shove, I can fly one of these things myself. So you're not indispensable.' Bishop pointed a finger skywards. 'Take us up. Now.'

Bishop hoped his captive wouldn't call his bluff. He'd ridden in plenty over the course of his life, but never as the pilot. Maybe he'd take lessons if he ever got out of this. It was always good to have a goal.

He kept the gun in place and shifted his position as the pilot flicked switches and pulled back on the stick. The four cops – no, two cops and two Marshals – were shouting at them now. Bishop could hear their muffled cries above the escalating whine of the engine. They were almost close enough to touch and Bishop saw the pilot hesitate slightly.

And then Bishop felt the back end rise, tilting the chopper forward slightly before the pilot levelled it off. He lifted the machine slowly into the air, at the same time turning it clockwise so they were pointing east. Bishop took the gun away from the man's knee and looked down. They were already fifteen feet in the air and rising. He saw both cops and one of the Marshals brandishing their weapons. The other Marshal, a female, had a hand above her eyes, blocking out the landing lights as she yelled into a walkie-talkie. Delaney. Had to be. Calling for air support, no doubt. *How the hell did they track me here so fast?*

They were fifty feet above the helipad now and still rising. As the pilot steered them over the Metroblade building, he said, 'Where are we going and what the hell's going on?'

'Just keep us in this direction,' Bishop said, turning to him. 'Towards downtown. What's your name?'

'You're no cop.'

'That's right. What's your name?'

'Cory . . . Cornell Mandrake. Where's Gregg?'

*Mandrake*, Bishop thought. So this had to be the old man's son. Carrying on the family business. 'If that's the guy in the comms room,' he said, 'he was already dead when I arrived a few minutes ago.'

'*Dead?*' Mandrake swung his head round to Bishop and the chopper tilted to the left before he righted it again. 'What do you mean? I don't—'

'The woman at the front desk, too. Your old man was just knocked unconscious. I found him upstairs.' Bishop thought it wisest not to mention the dilated pupils. Or the third body he'd found. 'I called for an ambulance. He should be okay.'

Mandrake faced front. 'Art?'

Bishop kept his eyes on the hand holding the stick. Waiting to see how Mandrake would react. 'Paramedics know how to move him,' he said. 'You don't. Let's keep this thing in a straight line, okay?'

'You killed them,' the pilot said in a monotone.

'I got no reason to, but I'm after the guy who did.'

Mandrake grunted. He didn't sound convinced, but he didn't change direction, either. 'And what's he to you?'

'A woman came to meet your father earlier. Mid-twenties. Pretty. You see her?'

Mandrake frowned. 'No.'

'She was the one the killer came for. Your people just happened to be in the wrong place at the wrong time.'

Bishop watched Mandrake for a few moments, then removed the headset and pulled his cell phone from his pants pocket. He keyed in a specific number he'd memorized earlier.

The voice that answered said, 'That you, Jimmy?'

'Who else?' Bishop said.

'Thought so. Gotta admit, you always did have a fine eye for women.'

'And what would you know about that, Thorpe?'

# FIFTY-NINE

'And here I was, just about to call you,' Thorpe said, amused. 'How'd you guess?'

Bishop said, 'Let me speak to Jenna.'

'You'll speak to her when I say so. She wouldn't make much sense at the moment, anyway; not in her current state. So back to my question. Cortiss couldn't have given out my name or you would have come for me before now, so how'd you know?'

Mandrake took off his headset to listen in. Bishop said, 'You should have taken better care at covering your tracks. I found a chair in Brennan's office that had your stamp on it. You always did like designer sneakers. Especially those worn by Eddie Sorokin, that Cardinals player you always liked. He must be wearing Nike these days, right? Like the ones I saw you take out your gym locker?'

The Converse All Stars logo on Aleron's baseball cap had been the spark that helped him make the connection. A circle with a star inside. Simple and memorable, like a good logo should be. At the gym on Sunday, he'd seen that kid's sneakers with all those stars over them, but no circles. But Bishop guessed they were still Converse sneakers. He figured the designers of famous brands could afford to be a little more creative when it came to logo placement. As long as the complete, intact logo was present somewhere. Like on the soles, maybe. And an indented version of that particular logo would leave a circular space when seen as an imprint. Like the one he'd seen on the chair. He recalled a throwaway comment from Thrope during the Brennan job about how he hated the Converse sneakers Sorokin was wearing at the time, but felt compelled to wear them anyway. A real fan.

'Good memory,' Thorpe said. 'You're too smart for me, Jimmy, I'm gonna have to watch out for you. Still, at least you found Cortiss for me. I'd been trying to locate my old partner for a while now and you led me straight to him. All trussed up like a turkey for Thanksgiving.'

'You kill him, too?' Bishop asked, already knowing the answer. Not that Cortiss's death would be any great loss to the world.

'What do you think? Oh, man, you've no idea how glad I am you made it out. Life was starting to get monotonous and you've already tied up one loose end for me without even being asked.'

Bishop noticed Mandrake pulling on his headgear. Probably the cops trying to contact them on the two-way from the comms room. He reached over and turned the radio off. Mandrake shrugged and removed his headgear again.

'Hey, what's that noise in the background?' Thorpe asked. 'You making use of Metroblade's aerial services?'

'Yeah.' The Hudson was visible in the distance, and beyond that the twinkling lights of the Manhattan skyline. About three or four minutes before they hit town. 'The cops conveniently showed up just after I arrived. I got you to thank for that?'

'Uh, uh. Not me, partner. I want you free as that whirlybird for the time being.'

Bishop nodded to himself. So Art Mandrake had seen through Jenna's story and notified them somehow, or maybe he'd refused to talk unless she came clean. But then, he couldn't realistically expect a fed to do anything else. Retired or otherwise. 'So why kill those people back there?'

'Forget about them. We got business, you and me.'

Bishop snorted. 'Not in this life.'

'Don't tell me you've forgotten about Jenna already.' When Bishop didn't respond, Thorpe said, 'I didn't get what I was after three years ago, Jimmy. This time it's gonna be different. You're gonna make sure of it.'

'Is that a fact?'

'Yeah, it is. Now I'm guessing you know what it is I'm searching for by now, right?'

'Some kind of FBI file on the Zodiac killer,' Bishop said, shaking his head at the thought of all the lives it had cost so far.

'Clever lad.' Thorpe laughed. 'Brennan had it. I want it. You're gonna get it for me. The little lady's banking on it.'

'You seem pretty sure I'll risk everything for a woman I've only just met,' he said.

'Well, we did work together for almost five years straight, and you learn a lot about a person after that amount of time. These days, I can pretty much predict how you'll react to almost any given situation. And the way I figure it, this sweet thing came under your protection the second you started exchanging bodily fluids. It's one of your weaknesses, Jimmy. People like you can't change your nature, so don't even try pretending otherwise. You've seen what I'm capable of, so don't force me to describe the things I'll do to her if you don't come through.'

Bishop saw they were over the Hudson and about to reach the verboten financial district. He covered the mouthpiece with his hand and said to Mandrake, 'No encroaching on Manhattan airspace, we got enough trouble. Take us around the shore and head for Brooklyn.' Without waiting for a reply, he took his hand away and said, 'So how do I find this file?'

'That's better. I was starting to think I'd have to do something regrettable before you took me seriously. And you don't need to search for it; I already know where it is. You're gonna love it.'

'I doubt that. So where is it?'

'In the private offices of your old boss, Morgan Royse.'

# SIXTY

'You still there?' Thorpe asked when Bishop didn't immediately reply.

But Bishop was already thinking of RoyseCorp Tower at East 66th and First. The headquarters of his ex-employers. He'd only been there three times, but he'd seen enough to be impressed.

'You're talking about one of the most secure private buildings on the island,' Bishop said.

'It gets better,' Thorpe said. 'You'll find it somewhere on the uppermost level where mere mortals can never set foot. Not even yours truly. In a special vault old Morgan had built up there a while back. What do you think?'

'You don't want to know. Why me? In case you haven't noticed, I'm no safe-cracker and I've got half the country out for my blood.'

'But you *are* resourceful. Given the right motivation, a man like that can accomplish anything. And I figure the safe return of your woman is just the kind of inducement that works best on you. But just in case I'm wrong, I'll offer you additional incentive: footage of you three years ago in Brennan's kitchen. Before, during and after your fight with Cortiss. How's that sound? Definite proof that you couldn't have killed the Brennans. Your passport to freedom.'

'Sounds almost too good to be true. Especially coming from you.'

'But you know it *is* true, don't you, Jimmy? If you saw the shoeprint, you must have found that broken lens in the smoke detector.'

'I found it.'

'And if you found that one, you know there were others,' Thorpe said. 'Now I've managed to collect schematics and plans of the RoyseCorp building, including the top floor. And I've made plenty of notes of security arrangements throughout the building and other odds and ends. I've sent everything to that email address you were kind enough to supply. Now, what else?'

'What's my time scale? It'll take me three or four days just to scout the place.'

'You got till midnight tomorrow,' Thorpe said.

Bishop almost laughed out loud. He looked at his watch. 19.27. Midnight tomorrow was less than twenty-nine hours away. 'That's funny,' he said. 'And impossible.'

'Nothing's impossible. You, of all people, should know that. To be honest, my colleague here has taken a shine to Jenna and I'm not sure I can put off the inevitable any longer than that. Danny's proclivities are a little . . . off the wall, shall we say? Midnight tomorrow, that file will be in your hands or she won't be the same person you remember when you get her back. Either physically or mentally. I might even join in if you don't come through, although I usually prefer them a *lot* younger. Am I making myself absolutely clear?'

Bishop watched Mandrake ease them round Battery Park towards Brooklyn. 'Yes,' he said.

'That's the word I like best. Now listen to me. I even *smell* a cop in my vicinity within the next thirty hours and the deal's off. I can't see you tipping them off, but I figure you're gonna need help with this, so you'll need to be real careful about who you talk to from now on. Loose lips and your lady friend gets an identity change she didn't plan on.'

'Put her on,' Bishop said, 'or forget it.'

'Why, of course, Jimmy. Just don't expect riveting conversation.'

While he was waiting, Bishop covered the mouthpiece again and said, 'You see an apartment block in Brooklyn with a roof large enough to land on and we'll part ways.'

Mandrake nodded once as they passed over Prospect Park, and began to lose altitude.

'James?'

The voice was slurred, but Bishop knew it was her. 'Hey, you hang in there, okay?'

'Heybaby,' she said in a singsong voice. 'Dopey dope. Doped right up. Poor Art. Sorry. Kyzatoo.'

*Kyzatoo? What was she talking about?* 'You got nothing to be sorry about,' Bishop said. 'I'm gonna get you out.'

'See what I mean?' Thorpe broke in.

'What did you give her?'

'Just one of my special concoctions to keep her out of mischief for a while. Don't worry about her, partner, focus on the problem at hand. We'll talk again real soon, though.'

The line went dead.

Bishop pocketed the phone and slowly picked up his headset from the floor. He took the time to place the earpieces so they fit precisely over his ears. He made sure there were no gaps. Then he made minute adjustments to the mike so it was positioned an inch away from his mouth. Exactly one inch. As he made the adjustments, he stared ahead at the night lights of New York and thought through the various methods he could use to ease Thorpe's departure from this world. Because that time was coming. Soon.

'You found us a place to land yet?'

'You're Bishop,' Mandrake said. 'The one on the news.' When Bishop didn't reply, he said, 'That was the man you're after, right? Who is he?'

Bishop breathed a sigh. 'If I tell you, you'll have to tell the police and that puts my friend at risk.' He turned to face him. 'Look, I need your help here, Cornell. As far as you're concerned, I didn't call anybody on my cell just now and it'd be best if you don't even mention my friend's presence when you get back. Cops might check the vehicles parked out front and get her name from that, but that's out of my control.'

Mandrake paused, then said, 'If I don't tell them, they'll figure you killed Gregg and Alex, won't they?'

Bishop shrugged and said, 'I'm used to it.' But Mandrake's comment raised an important question. Once things slowed down, the cops might realize Bishop didn't have much in the way of motive to shoot a bunch of strangers. They might start delving deeper into Art Mandrake's appointments for today and find the mention of another Falstaff more than just coincidence. Again, beyond his control. He could only hope Jenna's visit hadn't been logged.

He pointed down at his left towards a five- or six-storey apartment block with a long flat roof and external fire stairs at the rear. 'Over there looks good.'

Mandrake nodded and circled the building as he dropped altitude. As he got nearer, he switched on the landing lights.

Bishop kept his eyes on the rooftop, which was sprinkled with satellite dishes, but his thoughts were on how close he'd come to getting his hands on the man he'd set out to find. And how little it mattered now that Thorpe had Jenna. His own problems had immediately taken a back seat to the new situation placed before him. Getting Jenna back in one piece was all that counted now. And his increasing feelings for her were only part of the reason why. Mostly, it was because she'd ignored all the evidence against him and believed in him when nobody else would. That was something he'd never forget. So now, since he'd placed her in harm's way, it was up to him to get her back. It was that simple.

Thirty seconds later, the skids touched concrete. Bishop took off the headset and unbuckled his belt. He was reaching for the door latch when Mandrake said, 'What vehicle does she drive?'

Bishop frowned. 'Honda Accord. Why?'

'If they ask, I can tell them it's my girlfriend's I'm borrowing while mine's in the shop.'

A corner of Bishop's mouth lifted and he said, 'Thanks. That would help. And I hope your old man's okay.' He pushed the door open and stepped out with head lowered. Then he slammed the door shut, nodded once at Mandrake and ran for the stairs.

# SIXTY-ONE

Martin Thorpe slotted a new SIM card into the phone and flicked the old one out into the busy street. Now that Bishop had contaminated his old business number he no longer had any use for it. He pressed the button that raised the tinted window, concealing them from any curious onlookers as they made their way towards East 3rd Street.

Not that there would be any. It was a common enough Ford work van he'd purchased almost a year ago. The streets were filled with them. He turned to smile at Danny in the driver's seat, then swivelled round with his left arm over the back of the seat to watch their guest.

Jenna was currently sitting cross-legged against the side of the van with her hands bound together in front of her. Rocking her head back and forth. Thorpe had to admit she was very cute. Not really in his age bracket, but he could see why both Bishop and Danny were drawn to her. Not only that, but she had brains, too. Not that you'd know it by looking at her now.

If somebody had asked him why he'd picked now to grab her he wouldn't have been able to explain it. It just *felt* like the right time after Danny's regular reports had shown just how close Bishop and Jenna were getting to the truth. Far too close, in fact. Sensing they might not get a better opportunity, Thorpe had decided to take the van and meet up with Danny at Metroblade and take Jenna while Bishop was out of the picture. He hadn't figured on there still being staff around, but he and Danny had been able to dispose of them with a minimum of fuss.

'How we doing back there, Jenna?' he said. 'Nice and comfy, are we?'

Jenna stopped rocking her head and looked up at him with an unfocused expression.

'Won't do it,' she said.

'Who? Bishop?'

She shook her head. 'Mnothintoim.'

Thorpe made a clicking sound with his tongue. 'Now that's negative,' he said. 'You better hope you do mean something to him, Jenna, or it's never going to get better than this.'

He gave her a big smile and said, 'Do you know, there's an old Buddhist principle that speaks of a limit to the amount of pleasure the physical body can experience. For example, you can gorge yourself on good food for as long as you like, but eventually you'll feel sick. Or you can screw yourself till you're blue in the face, but at some point your weenie'll start aching. It's a fact of life. Conversely, it states the amount of *pain* a body can withstand before packing up is practically limitless. Imagine that, Jenna. *Limitless.*'

He faced forward, still smiling, and said, 'Now that's something to think about, isn't it?'

# SIXTY-TWO

'Does *every*thing you touch turn to shit, Bishop,' said Luke Shelton, 'or did you just decide to save up all that bad karma for the first good woman to cross your path?'

Bishop let out a long sigh. They really didn't have time for this.

They were facing each other in the small living room of Luke's four-room apartment in Brooklyn's Loft Street. A widescreen TV showed a movie with the sound turned off. Aleron sat slumped on a faded blue couch. Bishop turned to him, eyebrows raised.

The muscles in Luke's jaw tensed. 'Like you even care, asshole,' he said. 'I make one call . . .'

'You won't call anybody, Luke,' Aleron said. 'And I didn't bring him here for a dick-swinging contest. Jenna's in trouble. You gonna help or bitch?'

Bishop saw Luke visibly sag at his friend's words and almost felt sorry for the guy. Almost.

Aleron hadn't been too happy to see Bishop when he showed up at his house and explained the situation, but Bishop knew he couldn't save Jenna and do what was required alone. He needed them both. He also had a strong feeling that Luke was the fifth member of the hacking network Jenna had been talking about before. The one who'd escaped the FBI's clutches, along with Jenna. Which meant his computer skills were probably on a par with hers. Bishop hated to admit it, but he felt those skills might soon be needed. They didn't have to like each other. Jenna was all that mattered.

Bishop sat on the couch next to Aleron and Luke pulled his La-Z-Boy round to face them. He still didn't look happy, but Bishop guessed that this was just his natural state anyway.

Aleron said to Bishop, 'So what we got to do? You make this RoyseCorp building sound like Fort Knox. Why? What are they protecting?'

'Information, mostly,' Bishop said. 'You got to realize they're the largest private security organization in the country, which basically translates as the largest in the world. My old racket, close protection, is only a small part of what they do. Their main bread and butter comes from general combat and law enforcement training at their massive compound in Virginia. And if you get through the course, it's pretty much guaranteed they'll find you high-paying work somewhere in the world along with the twenty thousand other contractors on their books. They're at the top of a very short list when friendly foreign governments need highly trained personnel to keep the peace during times of civil unrest.

'On top of that, Royse has negotiated over twenty billion dollars in federal law enforcement contracts that I know of. And that doesn't include those black contracts that slip through the cracks.'

Luke shrugged. 'So?'

'So they've got lots of fingers in lots of pies, with lots of sensitive information picked up along the way. The CIA, for one, would just love to get a crack at the stuff stored on their servers, so you can imagine how other countries might feel. All of which means they take their internal security very seriously.'

Aleron nodded. 'And we've got to find a way through it to get Thorpe's file.'

'And we will,' Bishop said. He just hoped it was true. He turned to Luke. 'But first, I need to check my emails. Where's your computer?'

# SIXTY-THREE

'That could be it,' Bishop said, pointing at the screen. He and Luke were in a converted bedroom, with most of the wall space around them taken up by seventies-era movie posters. He watched as Luke zoomed in on the only unmarked area they'd seen so far on the penthouse level. All the other rooms on the floor plan were named for their purpose and had the symbol of a partly open door inserted into one of the four walls. This one's central location meant it had no windows and there didn't seem to be an entrance or exit, either.

'Huh,' Luke said, inching his face closer to the screen. 'Unless it's his secret bowling alley. He's already got everything else up there. Library, bathroom, gym, steam room, projection room, shooting range. Christ.' He shook his head and continued scrolling down, stopping at another unmarked box. 'Hey, what's this?'

'Elevator bank running through the centre of the building,' Bishop said. 'Probably blocked off at the penthouse level years ago.'

'So how does he get to his office? Teleportation?'

'Pilots his own chopper,' Bishop said. 'Enters through the roof so he doesn't have to meet any other human beings along the way. A Howard Hughes for the digital age.'

'Huh, so they're allowing night-time flights in Manhattan again?'

Bishop shrugged. 'Probably safe to assume he bought somebody off and got special dispensation from the city.'

Luke grunted and closed that file and opened another marked 7. He scrolled all the way down until he reached a dark blue bar that ran across the bottom. 'Fill me in, Bishop. Every floor plan except the first floor and the penthouse has got a coloured bar like this on it. Floors two to four are purple, five through eight are blue . . .'

'Colour-coded departments,' Bishop said. 'The lower floors are Accounting, I think. They've got access to the other accounts levels, but nothing beyond that. Close Protection was green and took up three floors somewhere in the early twenties. Same deal, with no access to other floors. There were nine in total, I remember.'

'Unless they added more while you were away,' Luke said. 'Who knows how old these plans are?'

'Let's assume they're current,' Aleron said, walking in with the rest of the printouts in his hands. He sat down in the room's only other chair. 'Bastard's done his research, I got to give him that. I've already lost count of how many problems we're up against here.'

Bishop turned and leaned against the wall. 'If it were easy,' he said, 'Thorpe would have done it already. What kind of window we looking at?'

Aleron looked up. 'Seems all that money hasn't changed Royse's work ethic any; unless he's got overseas business he keeps fairly regular hours. Gets in at eight, leaves at nine in the evening, seven days a week. So unless you're planning to go in right now, we got a three-hour window tomorrow between nine and midnight.'

Bishop tapped his head lightly against the wall, eyes raised to the ceiling. 'Cutting it fine.'

'Razor thin,' Aleron said. 'And it gets worse. Building's got forty floors and, penthouse aside, each one's got at least six armed watchdogs on constant patrol. Count on at least twice that many on the first floor. We got fingerprint scanners and CCTV everywhere, including in the elevators, and they only go as far as the thirty-ninth floor. Then we got more cameras in the stairwells, which do actually go up to the fortieth, but then you're faced with an inch-thick steel fire door that doesn't open from that side. And, yeah, I know that's illegal, but it seems Royse makes his own rules and screw anybody who doesn't like them. And if you're thinking of crawling around the air vents like they do in the movies, forget about it. At their widest, you got twelve square inches to play with and nobody's that skinny.'

'All that's for keeping intruders out of the main building,' Bishop said, and saw Luke turn from his screen to listen. 'We don't want anything below the fortieth, so we use the roof access, same as Royse.'

'Right,' Aleron said. 'Which then presents its own set of challenges. Luke, what can you show me?'

Luke swivelled round to search through the folder he'd downloaded. Bishop and Aleron came over to stand behind him. 'All I got,' he said, 'is a single aerial shot of the building.' He clicked on an icon and the screen was filled with a high resolution image of a skyscraper's flat roof.

'Thorpe must have been thinking the same thing and hired a chopper to make a flyover,' Bishop said. He rested a palm on the worktop and leaned in, taking note of every detail. From the position of the shadows, Bishop guessed the photo had been taken some time in the late morning. The top five floors were in view and showed reflective glass running around the building, except for the south side of each odd-numbered floor, where windows were replaced by concrete. Most of the roof itself was taken up with the various air conditioning systems and two plain utility buildings. He could also see intricate scaffold pulleys on the north and south sides.

But the most notable feature was the large green circle that had been painted on the east side of the roof, with a white H inside it. Just above that was a sloping concrete structure, jutting out of the roof at a fifteen degree angle like a giant wedge. Bishop figured it was the entrance to the penthouse. The vertical end of the wedge was partly shrouded in shadow due to the overhang that extended out a couple of feet at the top and sides, but Bishop could see it contained a door shape. Next to it was a wall device that could have been a keypad or intercom.

Aleron nodded as he took in every part of the photo. 'Yeah, it matches up with his notes,' he said, and pointed at the shadowed part of the entrance. 'See here? Numeric keypad by the side to get in. And although you can't see it in this shot, there's another closed circuit camera just under the overhang, covering the helipad and a large part of the roof area beyond it.' He moved his hand over the area in front of the entrance. 'They've also got motion sensors built into every inch of the roof except for the actual helipad itself. Once Royse leaves that circle he's got sixty seconds to reach the door and key in his code before he trips the alarms.'

Bishop leaned back against the wall and rubbed his scalp. 'Those scaffold pulleys there. How often do they get their windows cleaned?'

Aleron smiled. 'Thorpe checked that, too. Apparently, they got two guys on retainer. They've been through a thorough security check and get paid a good salary to be available at a moment's notice. The Local 2 Union doesn't even get a look in. Everybody knows them by sight and they don't use replacements.'

'All right.' Bishop turned to Luke. 'Aleron told me you used to be a real hotshot hacker back in the day.'

Luke kept his eyes on the screen. 'If that's what he said.'

'As good as Jenna?'

He was silent for a moment, then shook his head. 'Nobody is.'

'Okay. So how are you with numeric keypads?'

'Huh. They're duck soup if you've got time to play with them. I got a program that'll interface with the keypad's programming port, then run a number sequence until it hits the right combination. No way it can be done in sixty seconds, though. Ten minutes, minimum.'

'Fair enough,' Bishop said. 'The main problem is once we get in, how to break into a vault we know nothing about. I already told Thorpe I'm no safecracker, for all the good it did me.' He turned to Aleron. 'Tell me he's not throwing us in blindfolded. He must have found out something we can use.'

Aleron shrugged. 'Only that RoyseCorp has an open-ended contract with Ulysses for all its safes. He's also seen a large vault in the basement for paperwork too sensitive to store in cyberspace. Also made by Ulysses.'

Luke said, 'So, what, we're just gonna gamble on Royse's vault being the same make?'

'I don't think we've got much choice at this point,' Bishop said.

'Hey, look, I been thinking,' Aleron said, biting his bottom lip. 'A year ago I helped out a guy in your situation who wanted the full makeover. But when it came time to pay up he was a couple thou short. I let him go with a promise I knew he wouldn't keep, but a few days later his brother paid me a visit to thank me personally. A useful guy to know in the safe business. Said if I needed a favour in the future he might be able to help out. You know, lend a hand. He gave me a cutout number I could reach him with. His name's Wilson.'

Bishop raised an eyebrow. 'I might have heard of him, if it's the same Wilson.'

'*I* haven't,' Luke said, frowning. 'Who the hell you talking about?'

Aleron turned to him. 'You remember that nationwide manhunt a few years back after thieves made off with fifteen mill from the Pacific Continental in Seattle? It was the main story for about a week.'

Luke nodded. 'This Wilson was one of them?'

'The one who got them into the bank vault, if you believe the rumours. The cops couldn't pin anything on him. He had people who swore he was in another state when it happened, just like on every other job he's pulled in the last twenty years. It sure is good to have friends, ain't it?'

'So people tell me,' Bishop said. 'Okay. Set up a meet for me tomorrow if you can.'

'Got it.' Aleron paused. 'How did Jenna sound when you spoke to her?'

'Unharmed, I think, but totally out of it. Hard to tell on what, exactly. Some kind of opiate, maybe, to keep her passive.' Bishop frowned. 'You think you could you get your hands on some naloxone?'

'Maybe. If I knew what it was.'

'It's a drug that reverses the effects of narcotic poisoning, assuming that's what he's given her. Sometimes it's called Narcan. Try to get a hypo of the stuff; it'll look like the ones they use for insulin. In fact, get two. We'll need to get Jenna moving quickly when the time comes. It might make all the difference.'

'Consider it done,' Aleron said. 'But there's still a couple more issues. Like that camera above the entrance.'

'Leave that with me,' Luke said. 'But I'll need your help, Ali.'

'You got it. Which just leaves the small problem of getting up onto the roof in the first place. Bishop?'

Bishop was staring at one of Luke's movie posters, his thoughts on what Jenna had said at the end. 'Kyzatoo', it had sounded like. Then he thought of that line on the Willow Reeves letterhead. The part about it operating under the aegis of the Kebnekaise Corporation. *Kebnekaise, too*. Was that what she'd been trying to say? Turning to Luke, he said, 'See if you can find out about something called the Kebnekaise Corporation when you get a spare moment, okay?' He spelled the name. 'Probably nothing, but I want to make sure.'

'All right,' Luke said.

'I was saying we still need to get to that roof, somehow,' Aleron said.

Bishop pushed off against the wall. 'That's my department,' he said.

# SIXTY-FOUR

Thorpe removed the last padlock and raised the shutters to the under-ground parking lot at the dilapidated five-storey office building on East 3rd Street. He waited as Danny steered the van into the darkness. With a last look at the quiet street outside, he closed them again and used the same padlocks to seal them from the inside.

They were excellent locks. Military grade. Made by Sargent and Greenleaf. Supposedly resistant to every form of attack, including liquid nitrogen. Retailed at over a thousand bucks apiece. Thorpe had bought them at a considerably lower price and exchanged them for the old ones four years ago. There weren't many hidey-holes left in Manhattan these days, but this was a good one to keep handy for emergencies and he didn't need undesirables finding their way in.

He got back in the passenger seat and they continued down into the subterranean garage. At a push, he figured there was enough space for forty, forty-five vehicles. At the going rate for parking in this town, it was probably worth as much as the real estate above them. He was just glad the owners were still locked in a divorce court with all their assets frozen. He'd be sad if they ever settled.

The van came to a halt in the far corner of the lowest level, outside a one-room structure that had housed the car park attendant in better days. Danny cut the engine, but left the headlights on. Leaving Jenna in Danny's capable hands, Thorpe walked into the office and found the portable industrial lamps. He turned them both on, placed them on the ground in opposite corners of the room and examined his surroundings.

An ancient radiator sat against one wall. In front of the glassless window was an old desk and chair. The butane stove and portable heater were both new. Thorpe had brought them when he brought the lights. The room would do for the next twenty hours or so before he moved Jenna to another location he had in mind. Storing a kidnap victim in the same place for too long was just asking for trouble.

He looked up as Danny came in with one arm around the girl's waist and sat her down next to the radiator. Thorpe pulled a pair of cuffs from his pocket and attached her right wrist to the steel pipe that disappeared into the wall, making sure there was little leeway around her wrist. While Danny walked back to the vehicle to retrieve some supplies, Thorpe joined Jenna on the floor with his legs outstretched, back against the wall. Taking her left hand in both of his, he watched as she slowly raised her head and looked at him.

'Sorry for the drab surroundings, Jenna,' he said, 'but it's for the best. I need to know you're safe and sound for the next few hours and nobody'll bother you here.'

''Cept you.' She attempted to wrest her hand from his before finally giving up.

'Not me, I've got work to do. Danny here will be taking care of your immediate needs, so be a good girl and you'll be treated accordingly. I should add that the reverse also holds true.'

'Why?' Jenna asked, her eyes barely open.

Thorpe looked at her and knew the question referred to more than her current situation. But if she expected him to pour out his motives to her, in her condition, she was mistaken. It would just be dead air and it would take far too long, anyway. Besides, pointless navel-gazing had never been his thing, although he wasn't averse to the occasional dip back into the past to relive a specific triumph or success. He supposed the Brennan operation qualified as a success of sorts. Despite not actually finding the file he'd been searching for, he certainly came out of the mess no worse off.

If you ignored the arm injury that forced him out of the field, that is. He definitely hadn't planned on *that*. But then, he hadn't been planning on remaining a bodyguard for much longer, anyway. Not when he had a new mission in life that outweighed all other considerations.

Which reminded him. Thorpe took the cell phone from his pocket. He keyed in a number he'd memorized and waited for the ringing tone. He didn't have to wait long for an answer.

'Yes?'

'It's Martin,' Thorpe said.

'Martin. I did not recognize the number.' Although the words were clear, the accent behind them was thick.

'I change numbers a lot. It's safer that way.'

'So. I didn't expect to hear from you again, my friend. I had long given up.'

Thorpe smiled. 'I told you I'd find a way and I have. I expect to have it within twenty-four hours. It'll be available to you shortly after that. Assuming you still want it.'

'Of course we do, my friend. But I am thinking why you are calling me now instead of twenty-four hours from now. When you will know for sure.'

'Well, I've decided the price is now double what we originally agreed. I imagine you'll need time to get the funds ready.'

'I see. Double, you say?' The foreign man sounded amused. 'Considering the sum we agreed on, I would think that is unlikely.'

'You should think of it as a priceless wine that only gets better with age. Don't tell me you didn't expect some kind of renegotiation with the passing of time?'

'Little surprises me, to be sure, but that is not the same thing, is it? And I do not drink wine.' The line went silent for a few moments before he added, 'I will have to consult the others.'

Thorpe stroked Jenna's head and said, 'I'd expect no less, my friend. But don't consult too long. There are plenty more fish in the sea, especially in your part of the world.'

'You will get a definite answer very soon,' the man said. 'This I promise.'

'Until then,' Thorpe said and ended the call.

He leaned his head back until it touched the wall and closed his eyes. Not long now. He knew they'd go for it. They had to. And with Cortiss dead, he wouldn't even have to share the spoils.

# SIXTY-FIVE

When Cortiss first approached him with his proposal and the bare bones of a plan, Thorpe and the rest of the team were in LA, helping to keep that suicidal Newmarket bitch from getting her head blown off.

It had been a while, but Thorpe remembered the ex-spook from his DEA undercover days working for the Cattrall drug cartel. Their paths had crossed only once, but the man had impressed Thorpe as someone with absolutely no morals who'd do just about anything for money. This time, when he told Thorpe about the existence of the forty-year-old file, what it contained, and what they'd need to do to get their hands on it, Thorpe came on board immediately. He knew a great opportunity when he saw one.

Of course, it also helped that Randall Brennan's daughter shared certain similarities with Fiona Stretton. The first girl he'd ever felt anything for. And the last. The resemblance was clear in every photo Cortiss showed him. The long black hair. The spray of freckles across the cheeks. The large, blue, condescending eyes. The contemptuous turn of the mouth. It was really remarkable. And it wasn't too long before his desire for Natalie Brennan matched his desire for the file itself. He saw absolutely no reason why he couldn't have both.

He and Cortiss worked together on the plan over the ensuing months, going over every step in detail, refining it to the point where absolutely nothing was left to chance. Then, when their next assignment after Newmarket came to an end and the team were sent home for some well-earned rest, Thorpe and Cortiss began their hate campaign against the Brennan family in earnest. And as Cortiss had predicted, Brennan bypassed the cops entirely and went straight to his old partner, Morgan Royse. Demanding round-the-clock protection for himself and his family. The best men available. Which just happened to be Bishop and his team. Who just happened to be in between assignments right then.

It wasn't until they all showed up at the Long Island house to meet their new principals that Thorpe finally got to see Natalie close up. Physically, she was everything he'd hoped for and he found it hard to take his eyes off her. They were all in the living room and he was watching her coolly inspect each of them when her gaze fell upon Bishop. And then her eyes lit up. The almost feral desire in her expression left little doubt as to what was going through her mind, and at that moment Thorpe's resentment of Bishop moved up another couple of notches.

Right from the start, he and Cortiss had agreed they'd need a patsy for everything to work. Cortiss didn't care who, as long as it was somebody from the team. After Seattle, Thorpe already had a good reason to nominate Bishop for the role. Natalie's attitude towards him merely confirmed the decision.

All in all, it took Thorpe almost two months of subtle manoeuvring to get her into bed. Most of the time they used the room above the garage, and for a while there it was like he was actually with Fiona again, but without the verbal abuse and the humiliations she'd subjected him to throughout their brief, and ultimately tragic, relationship.

But Thorpe never forgot that his main reason for being there was to find the vault. He knew it was somewhere on the property, but after three months had failed to find any sign. Until Natalie just came out with it one day, as they were lying next to each other after a particularly energetic session. About how her father had the vault built shortly after his purchase of the property. Right in the space between his third-floor office and the bathroom. Thorpe was amazed he hadn't noticed before and had to tip his hat to whoever did the interior design.

The next day, Thorpe placed a motion-activated camera in the ceiling of Brennan's office to catch the combination the next time he accessed it. He also placed another one in Natalie's den for his own enjoyment, and two more in the kitchen and living room as a precaution.

Thorpe stepped things up after that. The visit to the Queens apartment Natalie believed was his and the accompanying photo session was easy. Thorpe knew Bishop only ever stayed at his apartment in between jobs, so the chances of his noticing their presence were non-existent. He took the opportunity to plant the evidence on Bishop's hard drive at the same time. The fake IDs for Cortiss and his Romanian team took a little more work, but he got them in the end. Then, with less than a month to go before their planned assault, Danny sent word they'd gotten footage of Brennan entering the vault. And the combination was clear enough to make out.

A few days later Thorpe was able to check for himself. Inside the vault he found over five million in cash, plus hundreds of sensitive files that were probably worth even more. But the one he wanted wasn't among them. The Zodiac file simply wasn't there. He couldn't believe it. All their work and planning for *this*?

It took an extreme effort of will to rein in his anger and think clearly again. If it wasn't here, it had to be elsewhere. Somewhere not on the property. Once this mess was behind him he could concentrate on the elsewhere, but right now they had to stick to the plan they'd already set in motion. And they'd still end up with a million and a half apiece after depositing the two million in Bishop's fake account, so it wouldn't be for nothing.

When Friday, October 15 finally came around, Thorpe spent the early hours dismantling the safe room's control system and emptying the vault of all Brennan's files for later study. The money he left. The files went over the electrified fence for Danny to pick up later. Then he inserted a remotely activated jamming device in the kitchen capable of disrupting Bishop's communications.

After that, it was just a matter of waiting. At 5.35 p.m., Thorpe left his post, climbed the tree next to the garage and accessed Natalie's room. She was on the bed listening to her iPod with her eyes closed. He still remembered her surprised expression when he suddenly inserted a syringe into her neck and depressed the plunger. And then the mild sedative kicked in and she was quiet.

The rest happened exactly as he'd imagined it. First, their cautious, stumbling journey to her father's office, followed by Thorpe's demand that Brennan face the bookshelves or his daughter died. Then the red fountain as Thorpe slit his throat from behind, tying Natalie to the chair and taping her mouth while the old man's life poured out of him. Then his opening of the vault door in preparation for Cortiss's arrival. Sending that message to Oates's pager, ordering him to get Brennan to the safe room immediately without alerting the others. The look of shock when Oates showed up thirty seconds later and saw the blood. The look of total disbelief when Thorpe showed him the silenced gun and fired three rounds into his chest. It all went just beautifully.

After erasing the message from both pagers he checked his watch and saw he still had plenty of time. From his pocket he unfolded a thin polyethylene disposable coverall and put it on. The next part would be messy, but necessary. He stood in front of Natalie and tore the shirt from her body. Then he made the first slash across her chest and heard her muffled scream under the tape. He watched her eyes pop and her body arch and jerk as she fought against the bonds holding her down. He slashed again. And then again.

By the time Thorpe was finished a couple of minutes later, he was breathing heavily and his knife was sticking out of the girl's belly. Her chin lay on her chest and she was rocking her head from side to side, uttering meaningless noises in her throat. Everything below the neck was crimson and there were far more cuts on her body than could be accounted for by a controlled attack. But that was okay. It would just look like Bishop had let his emotions get the better of him while cutting his girlfriend up.

Thorpe plucked the blade out and ripped the duct tape from her mouth. Then he moved behind her and pulled her limp head back by her hair . . .

He flinched at the sound of a vehicle door shutting and returned to the present. He saw Danny come through the doorway and drop the other mattress on the floor. Thorpe turned to Jenna. She was dozing. Her head slumped forward, just like Natalie's after he'd slit her throat.

Luck had been with him for the most part that day. Outside, he'd activated the jammer, set the charge on the rear door and made for the gazebo. It would have been perfect cover had he actually reached it before one of Cortiss's goons got two lucky shots off.

A lesser man would have gone down when he took the shots in the arm and shoulder. But Thorpe remained conscious and kept the kitchen window in sight at all times. Waiting for the exact moment when Bishop began running towards the rear stairs before blowing the charge on the door, knowing Cortiss would take care of the rest.

Thorpe stood up, brushed the dust off his pants and made a hand motion to Danny to signal he was leaving. He looked down at Jenna and said, 'But it's those moments that separate the winners from the losers, isn't it?'

# SIXTY-SIX

Cornell Mandrake leaned forward on his chair in the Palisades Medical Center waiting room and watched the figures of Deputy Marshal Delaney and Agent Wagner until they turned right for the elevators and disappeared from view.

Wherever Bishop was, Mandrake didn't envy him.

Delaney seemed to know everything about the guy from his birth on up, and it had only taken a couple of minutes in her presence for Mandrake to realize failure wasn't part of her vocabulary. Her younger male colleague, Wagner, clearly idolized her and not just because of her looks. Mandrake had found himself answering every question with an attention to detail he hoped would cause her to think well of him. And that wasn't like him at all.

Except he hadn't quite told her everything.

A movement of white in his peripheral vision brought his head around. The slim, bearded Dr Akhtar was approaching the waiting area with his hands in his coat pockets. Mandrake stood up and walked over, meeting him halfway.

'Is your sister still here, Mr Mandrake?' the doctor asked, looking around as he adjusted his glasses.

'Lisa's had to take the kids to her ex-husband's for the night. She'll be back soon.'

'All right. Well, there's been no change as yet, I'm afraid. Your father's out of ER and stable, but it's still too early to tell how seriously the blow's affected him, although the coma is not a deep one, so it's possible he could wake tomorrow, or it could be weeks from now. We'll conduct more tests through the night and probably know more in the morning.' He looked up at the clock on the wall. The shorter hand was just edging past the twelve. 'Later *this* morning, I mean.' He gave a weak smile.

'But he *will* wake up?'

'Guarantees are worthless currency in a hospital, I'm afraid, but he's strong and otherwise healthy for a man of his age and it was called in quickly. I feel positive; more than that, I cannot say. Now, if you'll excuse me . . .'

Mandrake nodded. 'Thanks, doctor. I'll be here all night, so if you can keep me updated . . .'

'Of course. And if I don't, one of my colleagues will.'

The doctor turned and walked back the way he'd come. Mandrake went back to his row of empty chairs, sat down in the same warm seat and thought about tomorrow. Or today. The police had assured him they'd clear the crime scene before daylight, but had asked him to shut the place down for the next couple of days until they were sure they had everything they needed. That was fine by him. He didn't feel much like flying at the moment. He'd just lost three people he'd known for years, and his father was currently in a place where nobody could reach him. Christ. All this within a few hours. It was almost too much to take in. He closed his eyes, rubbed his hands over his face and considered getting a cup of coffee from the machine down the hall.

'How's he doing?'

He jerked upright. Bishop was looking back at him from the next chair. *Damn*, Mandrake thought, *how did he do that?* The guy was as silent as a ghost. He was wearing chinos, a jacket and a baseball cap. He looked like a regular Joe rather than America's Most Wanted.

'He's still unconscious,' Mandrake said. Glancing around, he added, 'Look, no offence, but why do you care?'

'I care about finding the man who put him there,' Bishop said. 'Good enough?'

Mandrake shrugged and leaned forward again, an elbow on each knee. 'I guess so. What's it matter what I think, anyway? Look, I was going to get a cup—'

'Her name's Jenna Falstaff.'

Mandrake turned to look at him. He knew exactly to whom Bishop was referring. He said, 'I'm sorry about your friend, but I've seen three of my own—'

'They're dead,' Bishop said. 'You can't do anything for them now and your old man's under the care of professionals.'

'Yeah, thanks for the update. Look, as far as I'm aware they don't know anything about this Jenna and they believed me when I told them the Honda was my girlfriend's, but I've got enough . . . How'd you find me, anyway?'

'Wasn't difficult. I called every hospital until I found one that held a Mandrake. I figured you'd be here, too, and just waited until Delaney and her sidekick left.' Bishop leaned forward so they were level. 'I came here for your help, Cornell.'

'Nobody calls me Cornell except Art when he's in a patronizing mood. And wasn't getting you across the river help enough?'

'Only you can answer that. Were they rough on you?'

'The Marshals? Why would they be? I was an innocent victim held at gunpoint by an escaped murderer.' The brief grin he gave Bishop stopped before it reached his eyes. 'She's got a major hard-on for you, you know. Doesn't seem to care that you were the one called 911 for Art, either.'

Bishop shrugged.

Mandrake took a deep breath and let it out slowly as he sat back in his seat and looked at the ceiling, listening to the sounds of the hospital around him. It was mostly quiet now except for the occasional message over the speaker system, requesting a doctor's presence in another part of the building. A nurse walked briskly past the open area with her arms full of pillows and sheets. Mandrake watched her until she was out of sight.

Then he motioned his head towards the couple sitting three rows in front. 'See those two? I've been here for hours and they were probably here long before me. Haven't said one word to each other the whole time.'

Bishop followed his gaze and said, 'Somebody they both care about is sick. Maybe dying. Could be that's the only thing they got left in common.'

Mandrake nodded and looked down at the floor again. After another minute, he sat upright and said, 'So which law you want me to break this time?'

# SIXTY-SEVEN

'Look, let's get one thing clear,' Wilson said, stopping on the path and turning to Bishop. 'I don't know what you think's gonna happen here, but if you're expecting me to take part you got the wrong guy. I'm paying off my debt to Falstaff just by talking to you. And don't expect me to have second thoughts at the last minute and decide to go for that one last job to prove I still got it. Ain't gonna happen. A good friend of mine once told me my luck was gonna run out sometime and he was right. That last job was four years ago. I don't miss it and my wife loves me for it.'

'I wasn't expecting you to come along.' Bishop said. 'I know your rep.'

Wilson just looked at him for a few beats. Then began walking again. 'Okay, just so you know.'

On Bishop's return from the hospital early this morning, Aleron had informed him he'd set up a ten o'clock meet with Wilson in Central Park, near the Alice in Wonderland sculpture. Bishop got to the statue fifteen minutes early to scout the area and saw only dog-walkers and joggers. At 10.03, a heavy-set man in his late forties wearing a thin raincoat approached from the east. Without slowing, he nodded once at Bishop and kept walking along the path.

Bishop joined him and they strolled in silence for a while. The sun was already out, but there was a morning chill in the air. Good weather for walking. Seeing Wilson close up, Bishop added five years to his first guess. The man looked in his early fifties. His forehead was ridged with lines and the close-cropped hair a lot greyer than Bishop had noticed at first glance. But the grey eyes were clear and missed nothing.

'I can't even hook you up with someone in the game,' Wilson said. 'People in my line don't work with amateurs. Especially when there's no chance of a payoff at the end of it. No time for prep, either. Oh, yeah, and you don't even know the make of the vault for sure.' He shook his head. 'Christ, it sounds even worse when you hear it out loud.'

Bishop agreed, but didn't bother saying anything.

'Okay,' Wilson said. 'So your guy has his own private vault built somewhere on the top floor of his building, that right?'

'Right. Probably a Ulysses, since they built the one in the basement. No way to know for sure.'

'Course not. I mean, why make it any easier for yourselves? So you wanna get inside, you got one of two ways to go. Wanna guess what they are?'

'Drilling through or breaking the combination.'

'Man knows his movies. That's the one thing they got right. Manipulation of the lock also falls under the second category, but you can forget about that. You ain't got the touch, but don't slit your wrists over it; not many people do.' Wilson nodded towards an empty bench coming up on their left. 'Here, step into my office.'

Bishop sat down at one end, Wilson a few feet away. With enough space between them to look as though they weren't together. Wilson took a clear plastic baggie out of his raincoat pocket and started to unwrap it. On cue, a pigeon landed directly in front of them. Then another.

'Friends of yours?' Bishop asked.

Wilson looked at him askance. 'Let them get their own food. This stuffs too good to waste on dumb birds. Here, try one.'

Bishop took a cookie from the bag and took a bite. Chocolate chip. It tasted wonderful.

'Great, ain't they? Just another reason why I love my wife.' Wilson took a bite of one and said, 'And you can forget about drilling through. That was my game and it took me years before I got it right. Plus, the kind of plasma cutters you'd need you couldn't find in a week, let alone the next twelve hours.'

Bishop leaned back. 'So it's finding the right combination or nothing.'

Wilson grinned. 'Simplifies things, don't it? For high-paying customers, manufacturers will personalize your vault to your specifications, but what you'll probably be faced with is an electronic lock where you gotta key in a code on a keypad. Usually just numbers. You'll get three attempts and then it'll kick you out for a few minutes before you can try again. They're standard on most private vaults these days. I know Ulysses uses them on nearly all their models.'

Bishop took another bite of his cookie as two young men passed by in front of them.

Once they were alone again, Wilson said, 'Now we got three ways to get that combination. One: every manufactured safe or vault comes with a factory-set code, usually six to eight digits, to allow the customer to get in so he can then set his own personal code. Thing is, a lot of customers use that pre-set one a few times until it becomes habit. "You know," thinks Ted J. Poindexter, "this one's got enough numbers in it to mean nobody's gonna guess it, so why set a new code when I've already memorized this one?" Believe me, it happens more times than it don't.'

'I don't have access to the factory codes.'

'But I do,' Wilson said. 'Or I can get them. I'll give you my cell number and when you're in, you look until you see the model number or serial number and call it in. It'll be somewhere in plain sight. Give me five minutes and I'll tell you what the factory code is. That much I can do for you. Does your guy sound the type who'd be that dumb?'

Bishop watched as the pigeons decided they had better things to do and took to the air. 'To be honest, no.'

'Well, you never know, it's worth a shot. Okay, let's move on to method number two. How good a guesser are you?'

Wilson offered the bag again. Bishop grabbed a second cookie and said, 'Are you serious?'

'Not so much since I retired, but I am about this. Look, if it ain't the pre-set code, nine times out of ten it'll be a number that's important to the client. People often forget human nature where memory's concerned. Don't automatically assume the owner's gonna come up with a series of random numbers just to fool you. Life ain't Hollywood. He's got enough on his plate with his Social Security number, bank account number, PIN numbers, passwords to his Big Booty porn sites and everything else in between. One more random six- or eight-digit number to remember he can do without, believe me.

'You want to study up in the next few hours. The more you know about your guy, the better equipped you'll be. We're talking loved one's birthdays, important anniversary dates – both personal and business related – and like that.'

'So what's the third?'

Wilson gave his half-grin again. 'The third is what you use if the first two don't work: a good hacker. You're now gonna tell me you haven't got access to one of those, right?'

'I got one. I just don't know how good he is yet. He talks the talk, and if actions were words . . .' Bishop shrugged.

'I gotcha. He give you any indication he can tell the difference between his rear end and a decent sequencer program?'

Bishop threw the last piece of cookie into his mouth. 'Yeah. We're relying on it to get past Go.'

'That's something. And it might get you past more than that. Depends how good the program is. And the programmer, of course. None of them are infallible, but your man'll know more about that than I do.' Wilson returned the bag to his pocket and stood. 'So there's your three options. Was anything I just said worth the half-hour it took out of your life?'

'I don't know,' Bishop said. 'But I've always believed any edge is better than no edge at all.' He stood as well, and they both began to walk back towards Alice. 'So what happened to your friend with the career advice?'

Wilson made a harsh sound through his nose. 'Serving eighteen to twenty at Sing Sing for his third strike; a goddamn two-bit robbery at a gas station. Can you believe that? Full of wonderful counsel for his pals, but ain't got the sense of a gnat when it comes to his own circumstances.'

'Sounds like he just made the wrong choice for that particular moment.'

'Yeah,' Wilson said. 'All it takes is one.'

# SIXTY-EIGHT

Aleron hadn't figured on RoyseCorp's lobby being so open. Once he pushed through the revolving doors there was little between him and the bank of elevators half a football field away. And if the ceiling two or three storeys above him wasn't imposing enough, they'd constructed the interior floor out of marble to accentuate every footstep. Behind him, a wall of heavily tinted glass faced out onto First Avenue and transformed a sunny morning into a shadow of itself.

He stepped out of the way as more worker bees pushed past him and glanced to his left. There was a chest-high, crescent-shaped counter about two hundred feet away, with a wall of monitors behind it. One lobby guard stood and watched everybody entering and exiting. Two more sat at their stations behind the counter, where he guessed the more sensitive screens were located. Either that or they were playing computer games under there.

Aleron walked towards the station while the upright guard watched his every step. This clearly wasn't a business that encouraged the casual visitor. As he came nearer he saw, lying atop the counter at one end, three evenly spaced piles of glossy brochures. He angled his approach towards them.

The guard was dressed in a navy-blue uniform and looked to be in his late twenties. As Aleron got closer, he could see the RoyseCorp logo on the man's right chest pocket. Aleron's improvised courier uniform felt tawdry in comparison. He wore a black windbreaker over a white shirt and grey chinos, while an ID wallet hung from a chain off his belt.

He said, 'How you doin'?'

'Help you with something?' the guard said.

Aleron smiled and placed a large manila envelope on the counter beside the brochures. 'Delivery here for a Martin Thorpe that needs your autograph.' He placed a clipboard next to the envelope and turned it round. He was momentarily distracted by something he'd apparently spotted in the space between two of the piles of brochures in front of him, but quickly put the disarming smile back on his face when the guard came over and picked up the envelope.

As the guard turned to pass it to one of his seated colleagues, Aleron brought his right hand up, laid his palm over the space he'd been looking at and slid it back, putting his hand and whatever it now contained in his pants pocket.

The guard spotted the movement and said, 'What you got there, guy?'

Both seated guards looked up at the man's tone. The nearest one looked to be the senior guard here.

Aleron's expression was as guileless as a child's. 'Come again?'

The older guard said to the first, 'Something up, Deke?'

The one called Deke smiled and said, 'Let's see.' He turned back to Aleron. 'The item you just took from the desk here and put in your pocket. What was it?'

'Just my pen.' Aleron frowned. 'What's the matter with you?'

Deke's smile became a grin as he came round the side of the counter. He stood directly in front of Aleron, reached down to the wallet hanging off his belt and snapped it open. 'Well, Samuel Arthur Willis of Eastside Logistics,' he said, 'either you show me what's in your pockets or we're gonna have to make a scene here.'

Aleron didn't have to look to know the senior guard was slowly making his way round the other side of the counter. The loud footsteps finally stopped about two feet behind him and Deke said, 'What's it gonna be, guy?'

After a short pause, Aleron slowly reached into his pocket and pulled out an inch-long flash memory stick with *2GB* written along the side. He handed it over.

Deke frowned at it and then offered it to his other colleague, who was watching the proceedings from behind the counter. The seated guard did something out of view and nobody said anything for a minute. Then he looked up and gave a barely noticeable shake of his head. Deke turned back to Aleron. 'You got a record, Mr Samuel Arthur Willis?'

'Hey man, I'm just a working Joe, like you guys. No harm done, right? Let me go before I get towed, huh?'

Deke looked over Aleron's shoulder. 'Wanna get him checked out, Ham? You still got friends over at the 31st.'

The man behind Aleron said, 'I don't know. I'm thinking maybe Samuel Arthur Willis here now understands how idle hands do the devil's work. And to keep them to himself from now on.'

Deke tilted his head. 'That right, Samuel Arthur Willis? You a quick learner?'

'The quickest,' Aleron said.

The guard picked up the clipboard from the counter. He scribbled a signature halfway down the sheet and slammed it against Aleron's chest. 'That's the stuff. Now get your ass out of here while I'm still in a good mood.'

'Thanks, man.' Aleron took the clipboard and walked towards the revolving doors without looking back. Once outside, he kept pace with his fellow pedestrians until he was out of sight of the building. Then he pulled out his cell phone and pressed some buttons before bringing it to his ear. It took two rings before it was picked up.

'You're in,' he said and hung up.

# SIXTY-NINE

Sitting in Ali's basement, Luke smiled as he placed his cell back on the work desk, and returned to the algorithms on his laptop while he waited for the program to do its work.

Ali's call meant one of the gurads had just taken the bait and plugged the memory stick into their system. From their end, all they'd see was an empty flash drive. But the malware Luke had put on it last night would already be in their security surveillance server. Right now, it was creating an undetectable hole in their firewall and sending all their previously secure CCTV footage to an internet site accessible only to Luke.

For the next twenty-four hours, anyway. After that, the program would patch up the firewall, close off the connection to the URL and erase itself from their system before they even knew it existed. It was an ingenious little program that impressed with its simplicity. Luke only wished he could lay claim to it, but then Jenna had always been the gifted one.

The thought of Jenna gave him a sick feeling in his stomach. Bad enough that he was still in love with her. Worse still was the fact that he couldn't confide his feelings to anybody. Least of all Ali. Especially not with Bishop around. Thank God he'd taken down the photos of her from his living room a few weeks before. Nothing sadder than a man obsessed with his ex.

*Ping.*

At the sound of the alert, Luke moved his finger along the touch pad and went to the special URL address he'd bookmarked. After he'd typed in the username and password he'd set last night, it took a couple of seconds for the page to start loading.

In front of him were two columns of silent video screens showing real-time black and white footage of the RoyseCorp building's lobby. Each miniature screen had basic navigation controls surrounding it to enable the user to pan the camera left and right, up and down, or zoom in and out. He began scrolling down the page while it continued loading.

He turned at the sound of the basement door opening and watched Bishop descend the stairs for a moment before turning back to the screen.

Bishop came over and saw the feeds. 'Aleron got us in, then.'

'Looks that way, don't it?' Luke continued scrolling through the screens in silence until curiosity got the better of him. 'How'd it go with Wilson?'

'He gave me enough to make it worth the trip. How useful it'll be it's too early to tell.' He looked at Luke. 'He also said you'd play an important role in getting us in. You and your sequencer program.'

Luke smiled. 'That piss you off much?' The front view of a helicopter on top of a roof came onscreen. 'Ker-ching. There's our baby.' He noted the camera number on a pad and then continued on down the page until he reached the bottom. 'No other rooftop cameras,' he said, scrolling back up to the chopper, 'so just this one to worry about.'

'Can you do anything now?'

Luke shook his head. 'Once I get within range, I can upload to their server. But until then it's all look, but no touch. All we can do is wait for your ex-boss to finish another long day at the office.'

'Not quite all,' Bishop said. 'How good are you at digging up information on people?'

# SEVENTY

Jenna had no idea of the time. The room had no natural light and although her mute captor was probably wearing a watch, she decided she wasn't *that* curious. Thorpe was bad enough, but Danny scared the hell out of her. Jenna remembered the facial bruise she'd seen earlier and smiled. At least she'd gotten in a good kick before she went down.

She'd woken up half an hour ago and decided it was in her best interest not to make a sound. Hazy though much of it was, she recollected some of the events of last night after she was doped up. She also remembered the extra hypodermic Thorpe had left behind. Aware that keeping a clear head was the only chance she had of getting out of this, she hoped that staying quiet might influence whether she got a second dose or not. But who was she kidding? The hypodermic had been left behind for a reason. It would be used.

Her free hand felt along the wall until it reached the plastic bottle of water that had been left within reach. She unscrewed the cap and swallowed a few mouthfuls before putting it back. No food around, but she wasn't hungry anyway.

She leaned her head back against the cold concrete wall, unable to believe how quickly her life had turned inside out. Or how long she might have left if Bishop couldn't get what Thorpe wanted by midnight.

Jenna stared straight ahead and frowned. And wondered why she was assuming Bishop was doing *anything* to help her. Everything had been one-way so far. *She'd* been the one doing all the helping, not the other way around. *And* he'd just got out of prison and you don't inherit many virtues from those kinds of places. So why did she think he'd help? Just because she was good in bed?

She shook her head and forced herself to stop. This wasn't like her at all. Which meant it must be the drugs talking. Whatever it was they'd given her. She'd only ever smoked the occasional joint in her teens, but each time the grass had made her feel paranoid. Just like

225

now. She closed her eyes and breathed deeply for a few minutes, like she did before every class. Clearing her mind and focusing on nothing but the sensation of air entering and escaping her nostrils. In. Out. In. Out.

Bishop had told her he was coming for her, so she had to believe in him. No doubt he'd bring Ali in to help, too. Maybe Luke as well, if he could raise himself from his pool of self-pity.

The sudden pressure of a hand gripping her right arm forced her eyes open. Danny was kneeling before her, syringe in the other hand. Before Jenna could react with coherent thought, Danny inserted the needle into the same vein as before and depressed the plunger. There was a brief stinging sensation and Jenna brought her free hand up to pull the needle out, but she didn't reach it in time. Her reflexes were far too slow. Within seconds, the drug was coursing through her system and she dropped her hand back onto her lap like a dead weight.

She leaned back and looked at her tormentor's face as it swam in and out of focus. And before surrendering herself to the narcotic entirely, she offered up a silent plea that if her time was really coming, she would at least be allowed the opportunity to take Danny with her.

# SEVENTY-ONE

On the thirty-fifth floor of RoyseCorp Tower, Martin Thorpe sat at his rosewood desk in his spacious office and finished his last duty of the day. He saved his most recent report on the situation in Kabul – where three RoyseCorp contractors currently languished in jail after killing a local taxi driver and his two passengers – as a PDF file and then emailed it to the man upstairs.

Not *the* man, of course – nobody at his level reported directly to Royse – just his immediate superior, Woodfield, who'd use it to brief *his* boss, Geller, head of Foreign Operations. Royse might get to hear about it, but only if Geller deemed it worthy of his attention. Knowing Geller, probably not.

Thorpe found it hard to care one way or the other. Especially when he was now so close to achieving his aims. When you were a kiss away from being richer than Solomon it made all other day-to-day problems fade into insignificance. He had absolutely no doubts Bishop would succeed in penetrating the vault five floors above him. The man was nothing if not inventive. That's what made him so dangerous and the whole situation so exhilarating.

He walked over to the window and looked down at East 66th Street. Watching the New York minions scurrying about on their little errands. Thinking of ways to deal with Bishop once he had the file. And Jenna, of course.

The vibration of his cell phone lying on his desk interrupted his thoughts. He walked over to pick it up and smiled when he saw the caller's number. 'I expected you to call back sooner,' he said, sitting down again.

'I am here now,' the familiar voice said simply.

'With positive feedback, I hope.'

'You guess correctly, although I was not sure they would agree to such an amount. One hundred million is a vast sum, even for us.'

Thorpe forced himself to stay cool, but it was difficult. He'd just doubled his money in the space of a few hours. *Doubled* it. Straining to keep the delight out of his voice, he said, 'That's excellent news. I knew you wouldn't let me down. And the money . . .'

'Be assured the money is, at this moment, waiting to be wired over to an account of your choosing at the appropriate time. Now it is your turn, my friend. It will cause much consternation if you do not follow through with your promise. Hopes have been raised in certain people whose emotions it is unwise to meddle with.'

'I'm sure they have. And with good reason. Once I have it in my hands, sometime in the early hours of the morning, I'll contact you with the meeting point. Satisfactory?'

'Satisfactory,' the man said.

Thorpe put the phone down and leaned back in his chair. Happy with the world and his place in it.

He looked up at the ceiling and wondered if kids felt like this on Christmas Eve.

# SEVENTY-TWO

Bishop and the others arrived at the darkened Metroblade building at 20.14, where Mandrake was waiting for them outside the front entrance. All three were wearing black. Shirts and sweaters under nondescript windbreakers, dark combats, and rubber-soled boots. As Bishop emerged from Aleron's Jaguar, he glanced over at the Honda in the parking lot without comment. He knew without looking that the others were doing the same. He hefted his knapsack and went inside.

Luke went straight for Art's office upstairs, while Bishop stayed downstairs and forced Mandrake and Aleron to go over their part of the plan with him again. And again. And again. Strictly speaking, Aleron didn't need to be here at all, but Bishop wasn't entirely convinced of Mandrake's commitment. He felt the presence of Jenna's brother would dissuade Mandrake from getting the jitters at a critical moment.

Once Bishop finished rechecking his and Luke's equipment for the sixth time, they all made their way upstairs. On Art's monitor they watched the static image of a helicopter. Now and then the radio scanner transmitted brief exchanges between the air traffic control tower at La Guardia and nearby aircraft.

At 20.52, Bishop saw a man come into view on the screen. He was carrying a slim briefcase as he walked towards the copter under the glare of the floodlights surrounding the helipad. He moved with a military bearing and his profile showed an aquiline nose and a full head of close-cropped hair.

Aleron leaned in closer. 'That's definitely him, right?'

Bishop nodded. 'It's him.'

He watched Royse get in and place his briefcase on the passenger seat before fastening his seatbelt and slipping on his headset. Then Royse leaned forward and adjusted various controls before sitting back again.

'Air Traffic Control, this is Helicopter November Romeo Charlie One. Do you read? Over.'

Bishop closed his eyes as he listened to the voice coming from the speaker. It sounded the same as he remembered. The tone was clipped and precise. There were traces of New Jersey in there, too. The pitch was a little deeper than Bishop's and contained a grating quality you'd find in a heavy smoker. Or maybe one who'd just given up.

The tower came back quickly. 'November Romeo Charlie One, this is Tower. We read. Over.'

'Tower, this is November Romeo Charlie One holding at rooftop helipad. Ready for departure. Over.' The sound of rotor blades starting up could be heard in the background and Bishop opened his eyes to let sound and vision merge together.

'November Romeo Charlie One, that's a roger. You are clear for takeoff. Have a safe flight, Mr R. Over.'

'Tower, this is November Romeo Charlie One. Roger that. Departing. Same, same, tomorrow, Gary. Out.'

'Maybe sooner even than that, Gary,' Bishop said in a fairly decent imitation, although it lacked the grating quality. Aleron glanced at him and raised an eyebrow.

He watched as the chopper rose, hovering a couple of feet off the ground before making a precise, hundred and eighty degree axial turn in readiness for departure.

Mandrake reached over and switched off the radio. 'Single-engine,' he said. 'Looks like a Colibri. Nice machine.'

Luke swivelled round in his seat. 'And yours is what?'

'A Colibri.' Mandrake gave him a thin smile. 'The professional's choice.'

'Same, same,' Bishop said, watching as the chopper shrank to nothing onscreen. Then he turned to Mandrake and said, 'Hey, you wouldn't have any smokes lying around, would you?'

At 21.13, Mandrake held them stationary at just under a thousand feet above the East River. The lights of New York City were laid out before them like a picture postcard. Bishop took a final drag of his fourth cigarette, opened the door a crack and flicked the butt out. He kept it open for a few moments until the last dregs of smoke were gone, and then latched it shut again.

He coughed deeply a couple of times and tested his voice. He certainly sounded like a smoker now. He nodded once to Mandrake, who switched on the radio with his free hand. Bishop said into the mike on his headset, 'Air Traffic Control, this is Helicopter November Romeo Charlie One. Do you read? Over.'

The response was almost immediate. 'This is Tower. We read, November Romeo Charlie One. Over.' It was still Gary, although Bishop could hear a question mark in his tone.

He turned and saw Aleron shift in his seat and glance at Luke. Bishop continued, 'Tower, this is November Romeo Charlie One. Am holding at the northern end of the East River. Request permission to return to RoyseCorp helipad. Over.'

'November Romeo Charlie One. Something wrong, Mr R? Over.'

'Tower, this is November Romeo Charlie One. More than you could know, Gary. Over.' Bishop arched his eyebrows at Mandrake and waited.

'November Romeo Charlie One, continue holding, please. Over.'

Bishop checked the time. 21.17. He breathed out slowly and looked at the Manhattan skyline. If this didn't work, they'd need to consider the fallback option. Mandrake wouldn't be happy about it, but Bishop wasn't about to go back empty-handed now. Not with Jenna's life in the balance.

Mandrake clasped his free hand over the mike and said, 'The police turning up at Metroblade so fast.'

'What about it?' Bishop said.

'That Marshal. She told me Art sent an email alert to the police, saying you were on your way to see him. Forgot to mention it before.'

Bishop smiled. He'd guessed as much. 'And no reference to Jenna?'

Mandrake shook his head. 'They showed me the email. No mention of her.'

'Good.' He went back to studying the skyline for a while before checking his watch again. 21.19.

'November Romeo Charlie one, this is Tower.'

Bishop said, 'Go ahead, Tower. Over.'

'November Romeo Charlie One, you are clear to proceed. Over.'

Mandrake grinned as Bishop said, 'Tower, this is November Romeo Charlie One. Roger that. I owe you, Gary. Over.'

'No problem, Mr R. Be safe. Out.'

Bishop took off the headset and leaned back in the seat. He felt a large hand pat him on the shoulder. 'Go,' he said.

Mandrake went.

# SEVENTY-THREE

When they reached RoyseCorp Tower, Mandrake held them steady at fifteen feet above the angled, ramp-like structure. The floodlights were still on too, which was a bonus Bishop hadn't counted on. Probably on a timer.

Bishop turned to Aleron in the rear and made a horizontal twirl with his forefinger. They switched places, then Bishop swapped again with Luke and slid the rear passenger door open. A strong current of September night wind swept through the chopper and Bishop took a deep breath of the city air. He took a quick look over the side, then reached under the front passenger seat and pulled out a thirty-foot length of knotted climbing rope.

Next to him, Luke splayed his hands into leather gloves and yelled, 'I'm not liking any part of this, Bishop. The height part, mainly.'

Bishop finished tying one end of the rope securely to the steel snap ring attached to the ceiling of the cabin. 'It's only a ten foot drop,' he said, testing his weight against it. 'You're almost that tall standing up.' He threw the rope out the door and watched it coil on the roof of the entrance structure. 'Just follow me,' he said, and waited until Luke reluctantly nodded back.

Bishop put his own gloves on and made sure his knapsack was tight on his back. Then he grasped the rope with both hands and turned so he was facing Luke. Stepping onto the fixed skid, he gave a thumbs-up and lowered himself out into the sky.

With his legs entwined round the swaying rope, Bishop descended using just his arms and in less than ten seconds his feet touched concrete, just a few feet from the overhang. He knelt down, held the rope in place with one hand and gestured for Luke to follow. The taller man stepped out onto the skid. A few moments of hesitation and then he was making his way down the rope at a pretty good speed.

When he landed next to him, Bishop said, 'Not so bad.'

'Yeah, right,' Luke said, out of breath. He looked terrified. 'Nobody can make me do that again.'

Bishop smiled and waved up at Aleron, who began pulling the rope back in. Once it was up, Mandrake rose a few more feet, but kept the copter directly above them.

Luke puffed his cheeks out and took off his knapsack, laid it on the ground and pulled his laptop out. He also pulled out a slim metallic box the size of a cigarette pack and connected it to the computer with a long USB wire. He handed the box to Bishop and said, 'Wireless transmitter. Doesn't need to be touching the camera, as long as it's within a couple of feet of it.'

Bishop nodded, then crawled to the far left of the overhang and peered over. He was about ten feet above the roof. Further along, he could see the featureless black steel entrance door in the centre of the wall and the entry keypad on its right. Directly above the door, a few inches under the overhang, was the oval camera in its fixed position, looking straight ahead. Bishop moved across until he was directly over it and placed the wireless transmitter an inch from the edge.

Luke was busy working on his laptop when Bishop returned. Bishop looked at the screen and saw the roof footage he'd been downloading ever since Royse had left. 'We've only got about fifteen minutes' worth,' Luke said. 'I'm giving it a loop command now, so if my little box of goodness is doing its thing . . .' The picture vanished, to be replaced by lines of code. Luke's fingers tapped out their concerto across the keyboard and Bishop saw a smile slowly play itself out on his lips. 'We're in,' he said, finally.

Bishop still saw only code. 'How can you tell?'

'Check it out, non-believer,' Luke said. He opened his internet browser and accessed his bookmarked web page. It showed the same empty rooftop as before. 'That's what's being transmitted to the building's security right now,' he said, and stood up and walked over to the overhang. Kneeling down beside his magic box, he swung his hand back and forth in front of the camera. 'Well?' he shouted back.

Bishop watched the screen and saw the same bare rooftop. No hands. Bishop nodded at Luke and looked up at the chopper. Aleron was looking down at them from the open door. Bishop pointed to the helipad and made landing motions with his arms. Luke came over and they both watched as Mandrake momentarily hovered over the circle before landing directly on the H.

While Mandrake began powering down, Luke brought out a second metallic object from his knapsack, similar in size to the transmitter. It was finished in matt grey with a series of ports at one end and one side covered in adhesive pads. He used another long cable to connect it to his laptop.

Bishop took his own knapsack off and pulled out a length of thin knotted rope with a different-sized loop tied at each end, a black steel rock hammer, and some two-inch long universal mountaineering pitons. He moved to the edge, in line with the keypad, and lowered the end of the rope with the larger loop until it hovered a foot off the ground. Then he put the knapsack on part of it to keep it in place while he brought the other end as far back as it would go. About ten feet from the overhang. Where the rope ended, he took out a marker pen and drew a dot on the concrete.

Luke had finished setting up, and watched as Bishop came back for the tools then returned to his mark and hammered one of the pitons halfway into the concrete. Next he picked up the rope and placed the miniature loop over the exposed pin. After pulling at the rope with all his strength he turned back to Luke, who held out the box to him.

'Wireless data transceiver,' he said. 'Same rules. As long as you position it a few inches away from the keypad, we're good to go. Give me fifteen, twenty minutes and I'll get us in.'

Bishop placed the box in his top shirt pocket and looked at his watch. 21.34. 'You told us ten before,' he said.

'Maybe I exaggerated. So sue me.'

Shaking his head, Bishop picked up his knapsack and pulled out two small items which he put in another pocket. Looked like it was down to him to narrow the timescale.

With the rope in both hands, he carefully lowered himself over the side until his feet were within a few inches of the rooftop surface. Then he inserted his left foot into the stirrup and gradually relaxed his arm muscles. His body hovered just clear of the ground.

The door to his left was a black steel monolith set into the stone. No handle, no lock to pick and no hinges. Which meant it must open inwards once the right code was inputted. The keypad was at chest level and Bishop had to bend his left leg a little to bring his face in line with it. The keys were laid out in the standard three columns of one through nine with the fourth row made up of a star, a zero and a hash. No letters, thank God, but also no other signs to indicate whether it was armed or disarmed. Bishop looked up and saw Luke with his head over the side, watching him.

He pulled the transceiver from his shirt pocket, ripped the seals off the adhesive pads and stuck it to the wall beside the keypad. Then he reached into his pants pocket and pulled out the tube of aluminium fingerprint powder and the fibreglass brush he'd asked Aleron to get for him earlier. He opened the tube, tapped a large quantity of powder into his gloved palm and blew it directly onto the keypad until the fine particles covered the surface. Then he used the brush to gently dust away the excess. He was left with just five keys with silver powder markings on them. 1, 5, 7, 8 and #.

'There we go,' he said.

Then the stirrup came loose and he hit the ground with both feet.

# SEVENTY-FOUR

'What the hell?' Luke said.

Bishop raised his hand to forestall further talk and checked his watch. 21.37.12. No flashing lights or sirens yet, but he knew there would be sixty seconds from now without the right code.

*All right*, he thought. *Either you make it through this first hurdle or it's over before it's begun. No pressure.*

He stared at the keypad. He knew the keys Royse had pressed, but not the order. Or which of them needed keying more than once. Wilson had said you usually get three shots before being kicked out. And less than sixty seconds in which to do it. *So you better make them count.*

1, 5, 7, 8. So if Royse subscribed to Wilson's theory, they would likely make a date. Luke had dug out a few more biographical details that afternoon, but not nearly enough to satisfy Bishop. And none of the dates he'd seen contained the four numbers in front of him.

And then he remembered one date *did* match. When he read that piece about the AIDS benefit Brennan attended in April of 1987, Jenna said the company had been formed three months earlier on January 15. That made 1/15/87. With a hash after the final number, maybe. Or before the first number. Or to separate the month, day and year.

Bishop licked his lips, then pressed 1, #, 1, 5, #, 8, 7.

No result.

He tried adding a hash at the start, followed by the same number sequence and another hash at the end.

Still nothing. He checked his watch again. 21.37.47. One more try and twenty-five seconds left.

Bishop closed his eyes and willed himself to come up with something. Anything. There was always an answer. Always. You just needed to think. Two seconds later, he opened his eyes and leaned in closer to the keypad. And frowned when he noticed a small amount of residue on two of the other keys: the zero and the nine. He should have taken more notice the first time. Stupid. He pulled the tube out again and emptied the contents into his palm, then blew the remaining powder against the lower half of the keypad.

He didn't need the brush this time. The nine key had even less residue now, but the zero was almost entirely covered in silver particles.

21.37.58. Less than fifteen seconds.

Time enough for one last try. The placement of the zero was obvious, but where to put the hash marks? Bishop thought of Royse's precise, clipped manner when he'd conversed with the tower. And the zero that had to go before the month of January. Like most military men, he liked things neat and in their place, so Bishop had to assume his first instinct had been the correct one: that in the absence of a slash symbol a hash mark had to suffice.

This time, Bishop pressed 0 first. Then 1, #, 1, 5, #, 8, 7. Then he waited for the click of a lock opening.

Still nothing.

Bishop checked his watch again: 21.38.11. Time was up. He watched it change to 21.38.12.

Then he heard a metallic click to his left. He let out a breath he hadn't realized he'd been holding.

The door had opened.

# SEVENTY-FIVE

'Wanna tell me what that was all about?' Luke said from behind Bishop.

They were halfway down a sparsely lit concrete stairwell that came to a stop two levels below in front of another door. Bishop said, 'The rope was slippery. It just came loose is all.'

'Don't tell me that. Not after I just rappelled out of a helicopter.'

'Forget it. We're here now.' But even as Bishop said it, he reminded himself not to get too cocksure just yet. That he'd gotten them this far by a hair's breadth. The vault wouldn't be anywhere near as easy. Plus they had to find the damn thing first.

He reached the bottom of the stairs and studied the solid steel door in front of him. This one had a handle, but no keypad or visible lock.

He grabbed the handle, pulled the door open, but didn't step inside.

He couldn't make out much in the darkness and the lightspill coming from behind wasn't much help. He reached into his pocket and pulled out his Maglite, playing the beam around the interior. He saw plenty of glass and a few pieces of furniture here and there. No obvious traps or alarms. Switching the light off, he lay down on his stomach and tried to see any sign of a laser grid close to the floor. Nothing. He got to his feet and turned to Luke, who was standing close behind him.

Chewing his lip, Luke looked at Bishop and said, 'We gotta go in, right?'

Bishop nodded. The guy could be a jerk but Bishop couldn't fault his logic. After all, what other choice was there?

He stepped into the room.

And immediately realized there were motion sensors in here. But not for reasons of security. The room was slowly getting lighter and Bishop guessed it was some kind of automated light enhancer. It began at subdued and over the next sixty seconds grew in intensity to become a near perfect approximation of natural daylight. Bishop looked around and saw the lights were hidden in recesses in the walls and ceiling. Very tasteful. Probably cost a fortune like everything else in here.

'Huh. If this is what you call a Howard Hughes complex,' Luke said at his side, 'I wanna be just like him when I grow up.'

'You got a few years to go yet,' Bishop said.

'Bite me.'

Royse's penthouse looked like a first-class lounge. There was thick, dark grey carpet everywhere and most of the décor was a gleaming white. Shutters covered the windows on the east and west sides and foundation pillars fell at regular intervals, while tinted glass partitions separated the space directly in front of them into three distinct sections. There was a reception area, with six black leather easy chairs surrounding two glass coffee tables. Next was a conference area with a long oval marble-effect table, overlooked by a huge projection screen. Then a spacious kitchen area with facilities for the preparation of snacks or refreshments. Bishop wondered if anyone other than Royse had actually sat in any of these chairs recently. Knowing Royse's aversion to human contact, probably not.

Further back, a tinted glass wall with sliding doors travelled the width of the building. Through it, Bishop could see a wide passageway.

'Let's see where we are, exactly,' he said and reached into Luke's backpack.

'What, we haven't died and gone to executive heaven?' Luke said over his shoulder. 'How the hell does he keep this place clean?'

'Probably flies in his own cleaners once a week,' Bishop said, pulling out the floor plan and unfolding it. He found their current location on the sheet and looked up. 'Okay, most of his playrooms are in that section past the glass, along with the one we think could be the vault.'

He turned to the wall behind them. It ran from one side of the building to the other and alongside the door they'd just come through was another to its left. With a keypad. He pointed and said, 'That'll lead to Royse's office area.'

'Same code as outside, you think?'

Bishop thought about human nature and said, 'Don't see why not.'

He walked over and tried the same numbers. A second later, the door opened inwards. He turned to Luke and said, 'You check those rooms back there. I'll see what we've got in here.'

'Way ahead of you,' Luke said.

Bishop walked down the hallway into a huge office. It looked like something out of *Dr Strangelove*. Taking up the rear wall a hundred feet away was a huge digital map of the world set on a black background. Bishop saw electronic notations against most of the countries. In front of it was Royse's enormous, black marble work desk. On it were three widescreen monitors.

He turned to the wall behind him and understood why Royse had left the central part of the office so bare.

When Bishop had been stationed at the London Embassy during the early nineties, he and an English girl he'd been dating flew to Spain for a long weekend. On her recommendation, they'd ended up visiting the Queen Sophia Museum in Madrid to check out the recently acquired Picasso masterpiece, *Guernica*. He remembered standing before the monochrome mural for almost an hour, oblivious of everything but the abstract depictions of suffering in front of him.

And here it was again, even bigger than before. Maybe twice up. Starting a couple of feet to the right of the hallway, the photographic enlargement went from floor to ceiling and stretched fifty feet across.

Bishop stepped closer to the photograph until his nose was an inch away. He tapped the wall with a knuckle. Felt solid enough. He stepped back and looked at the wall to the left of the hallway. He knew that behind there was the stairwell from the roof. But what lay behind this? He unfolded the schematic again and looked it over carefully. And then he groaned. He'd been right when he said Royse had long ago blocked off any elevator access to this level. This was where it used to be. Right behind the photograph.

He turned away and walked towards the map wall. As he got closer, he noticed door-shaped recesses at each end, but no handles. He made for the one on the left, glancing briefly at the desk and a black, futuristic-looking ergonomic chair as he passed by. When he was within five feet of the door, it slid silently to the right and he stepped through without breaking stride. More motion sensors, he guessed.

He was in the library. More white. No decorations, just a single, oval-shaped black desk in the centre of the room accompanied by three leather easy chairs. Ten-foot-high bookcases lined two walls, along with two steel sliding ladders. The bookcases were full.

Moving to the windows at his left, he opened his backpack and pulled out an electronic tape measure. He switched it on, pointed it towards the opposite wall, and looked at the figure displayed on the LCD screen. One hundred and eight feet. Hundred and ten once you accounted for the bookshelves.

Bishop left the room and walked to the other side of the map wall. That door slid open too and Bishop stepped down into the bathroom, spa and gym area.

No carpet here, only tiles. The bathroom took up half the space and in the centre was a marble-topped unit with shelves for towels and lotions. Behind it was an enormous Jacuzzi. More shelves covered the map wall and Bishop checked over the toilet, bidet, washbasins, step-in shower and larger, closed-off shower. In the far corner by the window was a white marble chamber. He figured that had to be a steam room.

In the other half of the room was the gym. Through the wide opening Bishop saw various expensive items of fitness equipment.

He pointed the tape measure through the gap and read the result. Eighty-six feet. Meaning both spaces came up to a hundred and ninety-six feet in total. Bishop added on another three or four feet to cover the exterior walls and reached the building's total width of two hundred feet. No hidden vault in here. Unless that steam room was more than it pretended to be. He went over and opened the two-inch-thick door. The room was ten by twenty. Two marble benches faced each other and there was a small drain in the centre of the floor. Aside from a control panel set into the wall by the door, that was it.

Bishop turned as Luke walked through the doorway. He looked even less happy than usual.

'You're kidding,' Bishop said.

Luke shook his head. 'I wish.' He held up an electronic tape measure similar to Bishop's. 'Every inch covered and they all check out.'

'And the unmarked room?'

'The big man's home from home. Jumbo bed, bathroom, fully stocked kitchen and a living room bigger than my whole apartment. Might not have had doors before, but it's got 'em now. Everything a billionaire could possibly need for a night away from the wife.' Luke sighed and leaned both hands on the towel unit. 'But no vault.'

# SEVENTY-SIX

'I don't buy that,' Bishop said, moving towards the gym area.

Luke snorted and waved an arm at the doorway behind him. 'Hey, be my guest, man. The numbers don't lie.'

'I believe you,' Bishop said. He was scanning the gym and saw nothing that even remotely resembled a vault. And no hidden areas. 'I just don't accept the conclusion. You still got all the floor plans on your laptop?'

'What you take me for?' Luke said. He took off the backpack, pulled out his laptop and placed it on the unit. He opened a folder and said, 'You gonna check every floor?'

'Just one.' Bishop came over and looked at the file names. He scrolled to the bottom and double-clicked on *F-39*. The schematic for the floor beneath them opened up and Bishop zoomed in on each room before moving on to the next. 'There,' he said, when he found another room with no name and no door symbols. It was located on the south side, directly underneath their feet.

Luke raised his eyebrows. 'Huh. For all you know, it could be another love nest in there.'

'He's already got one of those,' Bishop said. 'Don't forget we're in a centrally located Manhattan office building. Up here is Royse's private little Xanadu, but every office below is prime real estate with a specific reason for being.' He tapped the screen with a knuckle of his index finger. 'And this one's too big for an office, especially for one with no windows.'

'What are you talking about? It's got to have windows.'

'Remember that aerial shot of the roof?' Bishop said. 'The odd-numbered floors we saw, there were no windows on the south side. Just white concrete.'

Luke nodded slowly. 'Okay. Maybe a conference room then.'

Bishop scrolled left and stopped at a large space on the north side with the designation *Conf. Hall.* 'Two on the same floor? I don't think so.'

'So how do we get down there and check it out?'

'The same way Royse does.'

'Fire stairs?'

Bishop took in their surroundings. 'I can't see it. Too much chance of encountering another human being. No, he'd want to be able to access it directly from up here, somehow.'

'And he's got the kind of money to make it happen,' Luke said as he also scanned the room.

Bishop's gaze finished up on the steam room. The only anomaly left.

Luke was looking at it, too. 'Could be nothing more than what it says on the label,' he said.

'Or could be a whole lot more,' Bishop said.

They walked over and Bishop pulled the door open. 'This feels magnetic,' he said. 'Wouldn't be surprised to find steel underneath.' He let go and the door slowly began to close. When it clicked shut, he opened it again and stepped inside. Discreetly placed ceiling lights instantly came on. Luke stood in the doorway while Bishop inspected the control panel affixed to the wall.

It looked like a blown-up version of one of the early iPod models. Bishop had had one briefly before he gave it away. A small token of thanks from a grateful client. The top half consisted of an LCD display, while the lower section contained a protruding steel click wheel with the legend *Temp -/+* next to it. In between was a row of four buttons. Underneath them were the words *On/Off, Timer, Display* and *Clean.* Bishop pressed the on button and the display lit up dark blue. He pressed the other buttons, but nothing else happened. The screen remained blank. Turning the wheel achieved nothing either.

Frowning, Bishop studied the room in more detail and immediately saw what was missing. 'No way can this be a steam room. There are no air vents.' He turned to Luke and said, 'When you buy an expensive piece of equipment, you keep hold of the manual, right?'

Luke shrugged. 'Sure. Everybody does.' He paused, then said, 'So why should the rich be any different?'

'You called it. Might be something in the library next door to tell us how to work this. Or the desk outside. It's worth a look.'

'On it,' Luke said. The door gently closed behind him.

Bishop sighed and turned the wheel anti-clockwise again. Nothing happened.

He turned it clockwise instead. And heard a deep electronic humming coming from under his feet. And then the whole room started to descend.

# SEVENTY-SEVEN

Bishop crouched as the floor descended slowly. This wasn't exactly what he'd expected, but then Royse had always had the power to surprise. He stayed low as the tiled walls became steel and used the nearest bench for balance. When he'd covered twenty feet, the bizarre elevator came to a stop.

He was in a stainless steel room. The wall ahead curved gently inwards like a bubble. A seam ran down the centre from ceiling to floor. Bishop figured this had to be the vault entrance. Attached to the wall on his left, at chest level, was a forty-inch LCD display, currently inactive. Illumination was provided by eight fluorescent oval lights mounted in the ceiling. On the right-hand wall, he saw another control panel with a small display and a single red button underneath.

Bishop looked up as a steel layer silently extended out from the wall and sealed the room. That couldn't be good. Reaching into his pants pocket, he pulled out his cell phone and looked at the display. No bars. Naturally. So now he no longer had Wilson as a back-up, although he had a feeling this would have been a new one on the veteran safe-cracker. Bishop checked the time. 22.08. He just hoped he could still get Luke down here for the next part. He turned and walked towards the panel on the wall, and the moment his foot came into contact with the steel floor both displays lit up simultaneously.

On the small display screen, Bishop saw white text appear against the blue background. *Time limit for vault entry currently activated. Time remaining before lockdown: 04.56 . . . 04.55 . . . 04.54 . . .*

Bishop pushed the button, but nothing changed except the numbers.

He ran over to the large LCD screen. This display was set on a white background. At the top, big black digits counted down the remaining time. Most of the screen was taken up by a colour spectrum wheel, like the one he'd seen at Aleron's. Underneath that was a thin bar that graduated from black to white, with every shade of grey in between.

To the right of the wheel were five long blank bars. Ten more smaller blank boxes were lined up across the bottom.

Bishop stared at the thing as though he were looking at ancient hieroglyphics.

*04.41 . . . 04.40 . . . 04.39 . . .*

# SEVENTY-EIGHT

04.38 . . . 04.37 . . . 04.36 . . .

Bishop knew he couldn't rush this. There'd be a logical system. He just had to relax his mind and take the time to figure it out.

First, the spectrum wheel. It started with yellow at twelve o'clock before graduating through orange, then red, then magenta and various shades of mauve to purple at the six o'clock spot. By seven thirty, that colour had transformed itself into blue, then cyan, then green and lime before turning into yellow again at the top. The colours were also at their most vibrant along the outer edge of the circle and steadily grew fainter the nearer they got to the centre, which was white.

Bishop took off his leather gloves and dropped them on the floor. Then he touched his left index finger against the yellow section close to the outer edge. Four of the boxes on the right immediately filled with percentages, while the fifth one duplicated the actual colour he'd touched. No letters to guide him, but these had to be the CMYK values Aleron had told him about. The first and fourth bars, presumably cyan and black, were at zero per cent, while the second and third – magenta and yellow – read seven per cent and ninety-six per cent. That made sense. The colour in the fifth bar showed a bright yellow with a hint of orange coming in. Bishop touched that bar and the first of the ten boxes underneath flashed red briefly before turning white again.

So the whole thing was clearly a colour combination lock. Find the right percentages, press the sampled colour and hope it gets accepted. Once you hit ten, you're in. Bishop figured there was nothing simpler if you had an afternoon to play with.

04.01 . . . 04.00 . . . 03.59 . . .

Beneath the spectrum was the graduated grey bar with a small virtual arrow located in the white section. Bishop placed his finger on the arrow and slid it slowly to the left. As he did so, the entire colour wheel became progressively darker as black was added to the mix. The centre

247

changed from white to grey, while other colours such as red morphed into brown, blue became navy blue and so on. Bishop nodded to himself. That was the contrast setting for the darker hues. He slid it all the way back to white again.

*03.49 . . . 03.48 . . . 03.47 . . .*

So, ten colours to find. With the time now remaining, that worked out at just over twenty-two seconds per colour. *How the hell is that even possible?* Bishop knew he had to bring down the odds somehow. He also knew Royse would have the same time limit when he came down here, or near enough. Which meant they wouldn't be colours with complex values. Simple flat colours seemed the obvious bet. The kind Royse could put his finger on instantly.

*03.42 . . . 03.41 . . . 03.40 . . .*

Bishop touched the yellow part of the spectrum and moved his index finger closer to the edge until the third bar read a hundred per cent, making sure the first, second and fourth bars remained at zero per cent. He took his finger away and used it to touch the yellow sample in the fifth bar.

The same box on the bottom left of the screen flashed red again, momentarily. Then, instead of reverting to its original white, it turned green. And stayed green.

Bishop smiled. He liked green in these kinds of situations. Green could only signify good things.

He tried the same method with cyan. A hundred per cent cyan, zero per cent everything else. The second box also changed from white to red to green. He'd just found two colours in twelve seconds. Not bad. Only eight more to go. Maybe it *was* possible to do this, after all.

*Why not try for three in a row?* He did the same for magenta and pressed the sample bar containing the pink hue.

The third box flashed red before reverting to white. Not accepted.

*03.19 . . . 03.18 . . . 03.17 . . .*

Refusing to lose heart, Bishop simply changed tack. If he could figure out what the colours represented, he could figure out the colours. Something meaningful to Royse, probably. Martial arts belts came to mind, but Bishop had read up as much on Royse as was available and didn't remember any mention of an interest in karate. Or any other martial arts.

Then it hit him. Colour coded departments.

What else besides the colour coded floors beneath his feet? Had to be. Luke had asked him about them only last night. He remembered seeing the yellow and light blue levels in the building years before, although he had no idea what departments they housed. He knew for a fact there were no pink floors, which explained magenta's absence from the combination. Which left what?

What about green? His old level.

*03.01 . . . 03.00 . . . 02.59 . . .*

Bishop moved his finger around the green section until he found a spot where both cyan and yellow bars were at a hundred per cent, while the other two remained at zero per cent. He touched the fifth bar and was awarded another green box. *Excellent. Now we're getting somewhere.*

He thought back to what Aleron had told him on Sunday. *Say you mix a hundred per cent of yellow with fifty per cent magenta. That gives you bright orange. Whack the magenta up to a hundred and you got warm red.* Bishop had seen both colours on Luke's plans, so he tried them next. Nice, obvious colours. Each one took him ten seconds to locate on the display and he finished up with two more green boxes. Making five in all. Halfway there. He was making good progress.

*02.25 . . . 02.24 . . . 02.23 . . .*

Last night, Luke had mentioned a couple more before asking Bishop what they meant. What had he said? *Floors two to four are purple, five through eight are blue.* Bishop now tried the blue first. He touched the area that offered up a nice, deep blue before it turned into navy and read the values. A hundred per cent cyan, forty-five per cent magenta and four per cent yellow. Not obvious enough. He got rid of the yellow and brought the magenta up to fifty per cent. There. He touched the sample bar and got a sixth green box in return.

*02.06 . . . 02.05 . . . 02.04 . . .*

He moved on to purple. Six o'clock. Outer edge. A hundred per cent cyan. A hundred per cent magenta. Zero everything else. Looks good. Press the colour.

The white box remained white. Wrong purple. Too deep.

He kept the magenta where it was and reduced the cyan down to fifty per cent. The colour in the sample bar became a rich mauve. This time, when he touched it the seventh box turned green.

*01.43 . . . 01.42 . . . 01.41 . . .*

Three left. Foreign Operations next. Thorpe's department. He hadn't done those guys yet. Along with Law Enforcement Training (red), they were close to the top of the heap at RoyseCorp. Both figuratively and physically. Bishop was probably on one of their floors right now. So what colour were they? He hadn't scrolled down enough on the F-39 schematic to notice a coloured bar, although he'd been told each office up there had its own uniquely crafted pine or rosewood desk. One of the perks. Brown, maybe?

*So how come there's no brown on this wheel?*

*01.26 . . . 01.25 . . . 01.24 . . .*

Then he remembered. The contrast bar. First he found that warm red again. A hundred per cent magenta and a hundred per cent yellow. Then he slid the arrow on the contrast bar across and watched the black come into play, changing the red into brown. He checked the values for black. Forty-seven per cent. He brought the slider up to fifty per cent. An easy-to-remember number. There.

He pressed the sample bar.

The seven green boxes became eight.

*01.01 . . . 01.00 . . . 00.59 . . .*

Bishop took a deep breath. Just two more to go. And a whole minute in which to do it. Easy. Except he had no idea what came next. He looked down at the colour wheel and tried to recall which departments were left. He'd told Luke there were nine when he'd been here before. *Unless they added more while you were away,* he'd replied.

*Forget about that,* Bishop thought. *What colour was next? Think.*

He stared at the steel vault entrance in front of him and went through them in his mind. Accounting. They were purple. Close Protection were green. Legal were orange. Training were red. Recruitment were . . . what?

Bishop frowned. *That* was the missing department. So what colour was that section? And then he smiled. The answer was right in front of him. What was stainless steel without the shine?

Grey.

Keeping the slider arrow at fifty per cent black, Bishop reduced everything else to zero per cent and pressed the sample bar. The ninth box flashed red. Then turned green.

*00.21 . . . 00.20 . . . 00.19 . . .*

Bishop was sure the numbers were speeding up. No way did that take forty seconds. *What was left?* There were no more departments and he couldn't see the lobby being part of the equation. Which meant the tenth colour would be personal to Royse. Which left the penthouse.

*00.14 . . . 00.13 . . . 00.12 . . .*

His mind turned to *Guernica* upstairs and he wondered how you could get any work done with that thing in your line of vision. Maybe all the white around it balanced things out. He thought of balance. Yin and yang. Black and white.

*00.09 . . . 00.08 . . . 00.07 . . .*

It had to be black or white. One or the other. That whole *Guernica* wall upstairs was black. So was the map wall. Most of the furniture, too. But the overriding décor was white. So Bishop slid the slider arrow on the gradient bar all the way to the right. To its original position.

*00.03.*

The centre of the wheel was white again. Just as it was when he started. Bishop touched it with his forefinger.

*00.02.*

His glance shifted to the colour value bars on the right. Everything was at zero per cent. The fifth bar was white. Bishop touched it with the same finger.

*00.01.*

The tenth and final box flashed red.

# SEVENTY-NINE

At 00.00 it changed to green.

And nothing happened.

Bishop looked around the room. It was still the same. Other than his breathing, the only sound in the room was the faint whistle of air making its way through the vents. Had he made it in time or not? For all he knew, the whole place could be locked down and the first he'd know about it would be when they found him in this steel tomb.

Bishop kept staring at the display as he put his gloves back on, waiting for a clue or prompt, a *game over*, at least, but there was nothing.

He walked back to the panel on the wall, but the screen was blank. No *entry code successful*. Nothing. Then he felt a current of air against the back of his head. He looked up and saw the steam room far above him.

So something *had* changed. He had an exit route again. Which meant he should also have a signal. He brought out his cell and saw three bars in the top corner. Luke answered on the second ring. 'Yeah, I know,' he said. 'Still looking.'

'I'm already in,' Bishop said. 'But look before you walk through the door.' Pocketing the cell, he sat down on the bench while he waited. He wasn't about to congratulate himself just yet. He'd beaten two combinations already, but he still wasn't in the vault. He breathed deeply for a few moments and calmed his mind. Conserving his energy for whatever came next. The clock was still ticking in his head.

It took fifteen seconds for Luke's face to appear in the doorway above. He looked down at Bishop and said, 'So do I jump or what?'

Bishop stood and said, 'I'll send this thing up. To come back down, close the steam room door and turn the click wheel on the panel clockwise.'

'Right.'

Bishop pressed the button on the panel and the mechanism began to hum again before rising off the floor for its return journey.

Luke joined him sixty seconds later and looked around the steel room with wide eyes. 'Whoa,' he said. 'Intimidating. So what's the deal?'

'Colour code,' Bishop said and led him over to the LCD display. 'Five minutes to find ten specific colour values. Each time you get one right you get a little green box.'

Luke nodded. Then he turned to Bishop with a frown. 'But they're already green.'

But Bishop's attention was already on the vault door. He ran his hand over his hair and said, 'I know.'

'You're *in*? But I thought . . . You mean you cracked the combination?'

Bishop shrugged. 'It's hard to tell.'

Luke turned to the vault. 'Huh. I see what you mean,' he said, and started walking towards it. 'Maybe you didn't—' He stopped. The seam running down the centre was turning into a gap. And it kept getting wider.

# EIGHTY

Bishop watched the steel doors slowly slide apart and finally allowed himself a mental pat on the back. He'd done it. One more obstacle out of the way. That was how you got through everything in life. One step at a time. But there were still plenty more steps to go yet.

When the gap was five foot wide, the doors stopped.

'More motion sensors,' Bishop said. 'We just needed to get closer for it to activate.'

'I guess so,' Luke said.

Bishop checked his watch. 22.21. Less than a hundred minutes to go. 'Come on, we need to move,' he said and entered the vault. Luke followed.

The interior was circular and fifteen feet in diameter. It was lit by a single, large oval light mounted in the ceiling ten feet above. Melded to the centre of the floor was a three-foot-square steel cabinet with ten file drawers, each one six inches deep. Built into the north, east and south points of the inner wall were three airtight steel frames, each containing a piece of art. Bishop ignored them. Only the cabinet interested him. Behind it, a steel plate grew out of the wall at waist height to form a work desk, with a mesh office chair underneath.

Luke was inspecting the framed pieces, one by one. 'Hey, this guy actually owns that Leonardo da Vinci sketch they auctioned a few years back. I remember seeing it on the news. Almost twenty million, it went for. Will you look at this?'

'I've seen enough art today,' Bishop said and pulled out the top drawer. It contained eight neat piles of bearer bonds. The top ones were all for a hundred thousand dollars. Each pile looked to be about fifty sheets deep.

Luke had come round and whistled softly behind him. 'And that's gotta be thirty mill, at least.'

*More like forty.* Bishop closed the drawer. 'Start at the bottom and we'll meet in the middle.'

As Luke knelt on the floor and slid the bottom drawer out, Bishop moved to the side and opened the next one down. Inside was a locked glass case containing an ancient hardback book with nothing written on the cover. Next to it, a Sotheby's catalogue was folded back to a page describing the 1623 first edition of the collected works of Shakespeare. Bishop hadn't realized any of those even existed any more. He couldn't see any cotton gloves lying around, though, which told its own story.

The third drawer contained numerous stacks of high denomination bills in different currencies, but the fourth held the kind of paper he was looking for: stacks of unlabelled cardboard folders.

Bishop picked them all up and carried them over to the desk while Luke rummaged through the lower levels. He opened each one and quickly flicked through the paperwork inside. He saw federal contracts containing signatures from the President's office. Reams of overseas contracts, bearing signatures from foreign royalty or senior government officials. Three large folders contained the personnel files of highly placed military staff. Two more folders held nothing but photos of unidentified elderly men and much younger women in various states of coitus. Some elderly women, too. Bishop shook his head. Nobody ever said billionaires got where they were by playing by the rules.

It took him less than five minutes to scan through everything. There was no end of sensitive material in there, but nothing about the Zodiac killer. Nothing at all. Bishop sighed and turned to see that Luke had already reached the fifth drawer from the top. He saw him pull out a small hardback book and slowly flick through the pages.

'Anything?' Bishop asked.

'Everything,' he said. 'Except the file.' He came over to the desk and placed the book on top of some of the folders. 'More cash. More shares. A couple more old books in glass cases. One of them's called *Cosmography* by some foreign guy.'

'Ptolemy,' Bishop said. Another perennial on most World's Rarest Books lists.

'Whatever. So how about you?'

Bishop just looked down at the mess on the desk and shook his head. He nodded towards the leather spiral-bound book Luke had brought over. 'What's that?'

Luke shrugged. 'Guess the guy's a stamp collector.'

Bishop frowned and picked it up. The book was nine inches by six with no lettering on the cover or spine. He opened it up. Inside were forty or fifty thick card pages, each one covered in plastic to protect the wealth of stamps on every sheet.

'So what do we do now?' Luke said as Bishop began to go through it. 'Something tells me Thorpe ain't the kind who'll believe us when we tell him his file ain't here. I'm thinking we should take as much cash as we can carry and renegotiate with the bastard. Money always talks with people like that. Bishop. Hey, Bishop, you listening, man? I'm saying Jenna's only got ninety minutes before—'

'I heard you,' Bishop said, still paging through the book. 'And we're not thieves.' He looked up at Luke and asked, 'Does Royse strike you as the collector type?'

'Are you kidding? Look around you.'

'Did you see any cotton gloves in the book drawers? Or in any of the others?'

'Gloves?' Luke frowned. 'What's that got to do with anything?'

'It means Royse doesn't care what's inside those books. You want to look through a priceless manuscript hundreds of years old without the grease in your fingers destroying the pages, you wear cotton gloves. And if he were really interested in the pictures, he'd have them on the walls of his office or apartment. Not locked in here where he can't see them. It's not like they're stolen or anything. Everything in here, it's all just various forms of currency.'

Luke pointed at the paperwork on the desk. 'What about those files?'

'They count as currency too. Maybe even more so.'

Luke thought about that for a second. 'So?'

'So, it takes a certain mentality to become a serious collector in anything and Royse doesn't seem the type.'

'And?' Luke nodded at the book in Bishop's hand. 'Chances are, they're rare, and rare equals money. Why can't that be an investment too?'

'Because it doesn't hold a candle to the rest of the stuff in this room. I don't see a British Guiana One Cent Magenta in here. Or a Cottonreel. Or a US Franklin Z-Grill. None of the really exceptional stamps that would make this book worth keeping in a vault.' He turned to a page near the back. 'It's got a pristine Penny Black, though.'

Luke gaped at him. 'Which is worth what?'

Bishop shrugged. 'Five grand, maybe.'

'How do you know all this?'

'Brennan gave me a crash course in it one evening when he was in his cups and I was the only other person in the house. Rare stamps were a hobby of his, although he wasn't obsessive about it. He had money, but nothing compared to Royse, which makes me think this collection belonged to him.'

'So why would he want Royse to look after it when he had his own vault at home? Especially when it ain't worth that much.'

'Maybe it was to him. There must have been a good reason for Thorpe to zero in on this vault. This could be it.'

Bishop upturned the book so the pages flopped down, but nothing fell out. That would have been too obvious anyway. He sat down on the chair and went through it again, methodically moving his fingers over each page until he reached the end. Nothing. He did the same with the thin leather on both inside covers. There was nothing at the front, but when he felt the inside back cover, he said, 'There's something in there.'

He pulled the knife from his ankle holster and made a slit in the leather. Then he gently pulled it away to expose the thick cardboard underneath. Right in the centre, a small section of the card had been cut away and an intricate Yale-type key had been inserted in the space.

'Well, how about that,' Luke said.

Bishop pulled the key out. A small sticker had been pasted on the face with E2110 written in blue pen. He turned it over and saw a second sticker. 3975642 was scrawled on it in the same colour pen.

'So what's it supposed to open?' Luke asked.

Bishop looked up at him and said, 'I have no idea.'

# EIGHTY-ONE

Nobody spoke on the return trip. Bishop spent the journey looking at the city passing beneath them, consumed with his own thoughts. He guessed Aleron and Luke were doing pretty much the same.

They reached the Metroblade helipad by 22.43. Mandrake stayed with the chopper while Bishop led the others into the reception area and took a seat in one of the chairs.

'So that's it?' Aleron said. 'I just kiss my little sister goodbye?'

Luke wouldn't look him in the eye. Bishop looked at his watch and said, 'Not for another hour and a quarter.'

Luke took a step forward. 'Goddamn you—'

'Get a grip,' Bishop said. 'I'm saying she's still alive right now.'

He took the key from his pocket and rotated it between his fingers. 'I been thinking, there aren't many places left with long-term lockers. Gyms. Schools. Anywhere else?'

Aleron sat down opposite and said, 'Some libraries and colleges, I guess. You got somewhere in mind?'

'Not yet,' Bishop said. 'But Jenna might.' He reached into his rucksack and pulled out her notebook.

Last time he'd looked, he'd only focused on the notes she'd made from their warehouse visit, but now he scanned the entries before that. And saw the names, numbers and addresses Jenna had jotted down during her search for Cortiss. An address in Nassau County. *Joseph Armitage/ Siren Associates. Ashford Properties. Alexander Stillson – Kennington, Hartford & Taylor. Box. No. 46533, NY.* After all that came the newspaper quote concerning Brennan and the obituary tidbit mentioning Helen Gandy. Then the warehouse address in Brooklyn, followed by a web address from Wald College's site. Then the dates Ebert went missing from the hospital. And, finally, Metroblade's number and address.

He looked up to see Aleron and Luke staring at him. 'Well?' Luke asked.

'Haven't seen this before,' he said and handed the notebook over, his index finger underlining the web address.

Luke took it and pulled his laptop out of his bag. He sat down and got to work. In less than a minute, he said, 'Okay, it's a page all about some library annex at Wald College in Tribeca. The Brennan Wing.'

Aleron looked at Bishop. 'Go on,' Bishop said.

Luke inched his face closer to the screen and said, 'It's off campus a few blocks away from the college and got opened in 2000. Says Randall Brennan was the main sponsor and put in twenty mill towards its construction. Lots of crap about extra shelf space, a couple more lecture halls, extra reading rooms, computer terminals, things like that.' He read silently for a few moments and then smiled and turned the laptop round to face them. 'Check the photo at the bottom.'

Bishop leaned forward while Aleron came over and crouched next to him. The screen showed a close-up colour shot of the ribbon-cutting ceremony in front of the new library. In the foreground, slightly to the right, a smiling Brennan stood with an oversized pair of scissors in his hand, the blades already halfway through the mauve ribbon stretching across the open entrance doors. Bishop thought the smile couldn't have looked any more unnatural if he'd tried. On the left, a bearded man, possibly the Dean, was in the process of clapping whilst laughing at something. Probably his own joke. Through the open doors, Bishop could make out a wide hallway leading to a slightly blurred reception desk in the background. Lining each side of the hallway were stacks of steel lockers.

Bishop looked up. Mandrake had come back in and was standing behind Aleron, looking at each of them in turn. Luke said, 'Colleges and libraries, Ali. Looks like the Brennan Wing ticks *both* boxes.'

Aleron nodded. 'Yeah, yeah. It's something, all right.' Both men turned to Bishop.

'I can't see it,' he said.

Luke snorted and rolled his eyes. 'Why don't that surprise me? How about you enlighten us then?'

'Look,' Bishop said, 'if that wing was opened in 2000, then that photo was taken before 9/11. Lots of changes after that date. Like no more lockers in public buildings. You won't find any in Grand Central any more. Same goes for JFK and most other places you can think of.' He nodded at the laptop screen. 'I figure those ones there lasted another year, eighteen months tops, before they got taken away too.'

Luke said, 'And you know that for sure, right?'

'I didn't say I did. But let's assume the lockers *are* still there. We know Brennan arranged it so the key was hidden in a steel tomb nobody knows even exists. So where does he decide to hide the priceless file itself? In a public building, of course. Where thousands of people walk past it every day, and its only protection is a lock my twelve-year-old niece could open with one of her hairpins. That sound logical to you?'

Luke snorted again. 'What, you never heard of hiding something in plain sight?'

Bishop sighed and turned to Aleron.

'You been on the up so far, Bishop,' Aleron said. 'I'll give you that. And if you got a better lead than this, I'm listening. Otherwise . . .' He shrugged.

'I'm still thinking,' Bishop said.

Luke's laugh sounded like a dog's bark. 'You'll be sure to let us know what you've come up with an hour or two from now, though, right? Keep us updated?'

'Step off, Luke,' Aleron said. He grabbed a Metroblade business card off the table and reached into his pocket for a pen. 'What were the numbers on that key again?'

Bishop said, 'E2110 and 3975642.' Aleron wrote both numbers down on the back of the card.

'Okay,' Luke said. 'To me, that means locker 2110 on the east side of the building. And I think you're right about one thing: those locks will be next to useless. So the second number is for the extra combination lock he put on there. You got any more great advice before Ali and me get going?'

Bishop looked at them. 'You thought about how you're gonna get in? There'll be cameras. Guards, too.'

'Don't worry about it, Bishop,' Luke said. 'You just sit back and keep that brain of yours whirring while the seconds tick away to nothing.'

Aleron rubbed a thumb over his brow and looked at the key in Bishop's fingers. 'You better keep hold of that in case you think of something. I've learned a few tricks with locks myself, so we should be okay.'

'I hope you're right,' Bishop said. 'If you are and you get the file, text me so I've got something concrete when Thorpe calls at midnight to set up the exchange. Text me either way, but don't call; I want to keep the line clear for him.'

'Okay,' Aleron said.

Luke looped his bag over a shoulder and was already halfway to the entrance doors when he stopped and came back. He pulled a folded piece of paper from his pocket and dropped it on the table in front of Bishop. 'What you asked for,' he said and walked back to the doors. He unlatched one and stood there, waiting.

Aleron got up and put out his hand. As Mandrake shook it, he said, 'Thanks for your help. And I hope your old man's okay.'

Mandrake gave a thin smile. 'Thanks. And let me know when you get Jenna back. I feel like I know her already.'

'You'd like her,' Aleron said, and gave a nod to Bishop. 'Everybody does.'

Then he joined Luke at the door and they both walked out into the night.

# EIGHTY-TWO

Bishop barely registered their exit. He just sat there, the key in his hand. Thinking. 22.53. Sixty-seven minutes to come up with something.

He hadn't lied to Aleron. He really did hope they'd prove him wrong, but he thought it highly improbable. The file had to be someplace else. Had to be. He just needed to figure out where.

And to do that, Bishop needed to discover the meaning behind these two numbers. E2110. 3975642. One on each side of the key. Which indicated they referred to two entirely different things, connected only by their common purpose: the location of the file. They clearly weren't map coordinates, but maybe they were pointing towards its location in a less obvious manner. And they felt faintly familiar to him. No, familiar was the wrong word. But there was definitely something there that struck a chord in his consciousness, and it sure wasn't anything to do with a combination lock.

A hand entered Bishop's field of vision and placed an opened bottle of Dr Pepper on the table. 'Art swears by the stuff,' Mandrake said. He sipped from his own bottle and sat down opposite. 'Calls it lubrication for the mind. Course, he gets off on the sugar rush, too.'

Bishop nodded his thanks and picked up the bottle. He took a few sips, hoping Mandrake would lapse back into silence. Instead, the pilot said, 'It'll come. You can think too hard on a problem and then it's right in front of you.'

'Sure,' Bishop said with a sigh.

He glanced down at the key in his left hand and studied the sticker. And he frowned. In the conversation with Aleron and Luke he might well have overlooked the simplest thing. He pulled at the sticker and saw engraved letters on the face of the key. *Price.*

Keys usually had a manufacturer's name on them. Like Yale or Chubb. Or nothing at all. He'd never heard of Price. So maybe locksmiths had the option to personalize their keys themselves when they ordered them from the manufacturer. To Mandrake, he said, 'You got a Yellow Pages here?'

'Sure, Alex keeps—' Mandrake stopped. And tried again. 'There should be some in the desk behind me. Which borough?'

'Let's try Manhattan first.'

Mandrake walked over to his receptionist's desk. It was still cordoned off by bright yellow crime scene tape and he ducked under and rooted around in the drawers. He came back and handed over a directory that looked thinner than Bishop remembered. He guessed the internet had all of life's answers these days.

Opening it to the Locksmiths section, he flicked through it until he came to the Ps and started turning the pages more slowly. And then he stopped. There, at the bottom of the left-hand page, was a quarter-page ad. *All Your Lock Problems SOLVED!* it screamed in large red text across the top. Under that, in slightly smaller letters, was the name: *Price Locksmiths*. Bishop skipped over the text and focused on the photo of the premises that took up the left third of the ad. He saw a small, well-stocked store with a glass front and a single glass door. Apartments above it. And then he looked at the address.

110 East 2nd Street.

If you needed to fit that on a small sticker you might shorten it to 110E2. Or E2110. Possibly. He just hoped the shop's owner had one of those apartments above.

Bishop checked his watch again. 22.59. He'd have to get moving. Ripping the page from the directory, he grabbed his knapsack, placed Luke's note in his pocket and rose from the chair. 'Looks like you were right,' he said to the pilot. 'This could be something. What you did for us, I won't forget.'

'Me neither,' Mandrake said. 'Next time, I charge you.'

Bishop smiled and strode over to the doors and pushed into the car park. Jenna's Honda and Mandrake's Mercedes were the only vehicles left. No sign of Cortiss's Lexus on the road, either. The cops must have taken it away. When he reached Jenna's vehicle, he pulled out the emergency set of keys she'd given him and used the one with the Honda logo to unlock the door. He threw the knapsack on the passenger seat and was about to get in when he stopped, pulled the Maglite from his pocket and walked to the rear of the vehicle.

He lay on his back and pulled his upper torso under the car. He felt a twinge in his stomach muscles and paused, willing it to go away. The Three Bears already seemed like months ago. Back at a time in his life when getting out and finding who'd set him up was all he cared about. Strange how things changed. He could never have imagined the situation in which he now found himself.

He switched on the flashlight and shone it at the undercarriage. It was only a few moments before he found the magnetized transmitter box next to the exhaust resonator. He detached it from the vehicle and slid his body back out. He stood up, tossed the box towards the fence and then got in the car.

# EIGHTY-THREE

Situated on the edge of Chinatown between Canal and Franklin, Cortlandt Alley is one of New York's few remaining alleyways. The narrow, grimy side street spans two blocks and is almost always dark. During the day it serves as a commercial access to the five- or six-storey warehouses and factories on either side. At night it serves as a haven for crack addicts and the homeless. In recent years, the alley has also become the location of choice for music video directors tasked with lending their baby-faced employers some semblance of street credibility.

None were present at 22.57 on Wednesday, though, as Martin Thorpe steered the van slowly northwards down the cobblestoned street. He passed fire escapes, sweatshops, padlocked doorways and raised, shut-tered entrances until he came to a stop outside two of the latter, both emblazoned with graffiti.

'Okay, you two,' he said, putting the vehicle into neutral as he scanned the street ahead. 'Out you go.'

He turned in his seat and watched Danny exit the rear doors before reaching back in to pull Jenna out. Thorpe had already cuffed both hands behind her back at the car park, but he needn't have bothered; she was still too doped up to be a problem. But she'd start coming out of it soon, and then she'd quickly wish she were under again.

Neither he nor Danny had used this place much recently, not since his undercover days, when they'd interrogate suspected informers here without fear of the screams reaching the outside world. The Cattrall organization still owned the lease, but these premises had been unused for years now since their operations had been moved out west. He was surprised they hadn't sublet it, but he figured waste not, want not. There was a wealth of hidden spots in even the busiest of cities, but only if you knew where to look. And Thorpe made it his business to know.

As Danny removed the second padlock securing the brown metal door next to the shutters, Thorpe said, 'Remember what we agreed.

There needs to be enough light so there's no mistake, and I don't want you going to work on her until I give the word, okay?'

Danny gave him a nod and a smile, then pulled the door open and shoved Jenna into the darkness before turning to watch him drive away. Thorpe knew it wouldn't be dark in there for long. He'd checked earlier to make sure the lights on the first floor were still working and stashed Danny's favourite tools and instruments in plain view, ready for use later.

He smiled to himself as he pulled out his cell and accessed the web page they'd been using to track Jenna's vehicle. Maybe that was why the two of them worked so well together, their little sexual peccadilloes making them outsiders to the rest of the world. Although he couldn't help thinking his appetite for the young stuff was probably a little healthier than Danny's more sadistic tendencies. At least Thorpe's bed partners woke up in the morning. For the most part, anyway.

Still, each to their own. And it wasn't as if Jenna ever had a chance of coming out of this alive. Not after she'd seen their faces. Besides, everybody died. The only difference was that the process was going to be a little more painful for her than for most. Okay, a *lot* more painful. But it would only last a few hours and then it would be over.

He kept an eye on the cell phone screen as he carried on up towards Canal Street. The red dot was still in the same place. Still over the other side of the river at Metroblade, where Bishop had returned earlier to avail himself of one of their choppers.

Oh, well. His hope that Bishop might use her car to get back to the city had been a long shot at best, but he'd leave it on, anyway. There was still an hour to go.

Things might change between now and then.

# EIGHTY-FOUR

Bishop turned into East 2nd Street at 23.43 and found the locksmiths' a minute later. There was little traffic at this time of night, and even fewer pedestrians. He slowed to a crawl as he passed the storefront while searching for a nearby space. The only one was at the end of the block under a No Parking sign. Ignoring the sign, Bishop parked up then jogged the two hundred yards back to the shop.

The brownstone looked thinner in real life. Shutters covered the windows and door he'd seen in the photo. On the left was a second door up some steps. Bishop saw a single, new-looking buzzer and intercom built into the brickwork next to it, which indicated a sole tenant rather than a bunch of separate apartments.

He kept his finger on the button for about ten seconds. When he got no response, he kept at it for half a minute more before a deep male voice erupted from the speaker. 'I got ears,' it said. 'Give me a reason.'

Bishop said, 'A friend of Randall Brennan's.'

A short pause. And then, 'Wait there.'

Bishop counted forty-nine seconds before he heard the sound of bolts being pulled back from the other side. The door finally opened inwards to reveal a thick-shouldered, dark-skinned man. Bishop guessed early fifties. He was about two inches taller than Bishop and wore flip-flops and a black Oriental-style kimono that couldn't completely hide his paunch. There was a small amount of grey showing in the close-cropped beard and at the temples, but his face still looked young. His right arm remained behind his back, out of view.

'What was that again?' he asked.

'Randall Brennan,' Bishop said.

'I got that part. I didn't get your connection to him.'

The man tried to look and sound casual, but Bishop instantly knew the guy was ex-military. The erect bearing, the obvious gun behind his back, the way his eyes checked the surrounding area and the occasional vehicle passing by. Probably Corps if he'd known Brennan. And then the significance of the second number hit Bishop like a bullet. '3975642,' he said.

'That supposed to mean something to me?'

'A soldier never forgets the serial number of his first rifle,' Bishop said, and pulled the key from his pocket and held it up. 'Mine was 6758296. Yours is written on this along with your name and address. You're Price?'

The man scrunched his eyebrows together. 'I know you?'

'I doubt it,' Bishop said. 'You planning on shooting me or inviting me in?'

The man studied Bishop for a few moments. Then he smiled and pressed himself against the wall with his right hand in plain sight. It was holding a .45 semi-automatic, pointed at the floor. 'Just follow the light,' he said.

Bishop walked past him and heard the door close behind him. The passage was lit by a single bulb. More light came from a small reception room at the end. When he got there, he saw a single window overlooking a small yard. He turned and watched Price approach with his hand and gun now in his dressing gown pocket. Directly at Bishop's left was a closed door that he guessed provided access to the shop. There was a stairway to the right of the hallway, which Bishop assumed led to the living quarters above. Neat stacks of magazines, newspapers and junk mail filled the reception room floor and five large potted plants were lined up against the right-hand wall, like a parade at attention. Attached to the same wall was a red and black payphone that looked older than Bishop, with its receiver hanging off a hook at the side.

'I know where I've seen you now,' Price said, head tilted slightly as he studied Bishop. 'You don't *look* like a psycho.'

'You're not the first person to notice,' Bishop said. He knew soldiers and cops were trained to observe more, but he was still impressed by how quickly Price had placed him. 'Although that might change before daybreak.'

Price nodded. 'Payback's something I understand. If it's warranted. What was your unit and rank?'

'Initially, 1st Battalion 3rd Marines, Bravo Company out of Hawaii. Later, C Platoon at 2nd FAST Company, based out of Yorktown. Sergeant.'

'Yeah, I heard of them from buddies still in. Fleet Antiterrorism Security Team. *Deter, detect, defend*, right?'

'That was one slogan we used, sure.' Bishop frowned and said, 'You knew

Brennan well enough to care what happened to him, and now you know who I am. How come you're not pointing that .45 in my direction?'

Price shrugged. 'Someone with your history couldn't have killed the colonel. Or his daughter. You and I know that, even if the judge didn't.'

'Thanks. I could have used you on the jury.'

'You're welcome. So I'm assuming you're closing in on the real killer?'

'I was, until he snatched a friend of mine as insurance.' Bishop looked down at the key in his hand. 'But I'm hoping this can provide me with something to help get her back. Thing is, I don't have much time left.'

'Then I guess you better follow me,' Price said. From the same pocket that contained the gun he took a large set of keys and used one to unlock the door at Bishop's left. He opened it, reached in to switch on the lights and stepped through.

Bishop did the same and found himself halfway down the first of two long aisles that stretched to the rear of the shop. The place was as well stocked as the photo had indicated. Turning left, he followed Price and passed by examples of every kind of safe, door viewer, buzzer, intercom, door holder, chain guard, mail box, pivot, alarm, cylinder, padlock, deadbolt, key type or door closer he could imagine.

'I own this whole building outright, you know,' Price said, his flip-flops making a clapping sound as he walked in front. 'Thanks to him.'

'Brennan, you mean?' Bishop checked his watch. 23.48. Wouldn't be long now before he got a call from Thorpe. Probably a text message from Aleron, as well.

'Right. About five years ago I was struggling for reasons I won't bore you with. The usual country song shit. Couldn't keep up repayments and got served with repossession papers. Then all of a sudden, my whole mortgage gets paid off in one swoop.' Price stopped outside another door at the rear of the premises and searched through his key chain. 'That ended the drinking for me, at least. Turns out the colonel had been keeping tabs on his old sergeant since the war and stepped in to save the day.'

'Vietnam?' Bishop asked. 'You don't look old enough.'

'Good genes and regular exercise, I guess.' Price found the correct key and unlocked the door. He opened it to reveal a thin stairway, with light coming from the basement. He entered first and said, 'Anyway, the colonel showed up at my door a few days later, and once he picked me up off my knees, told me he only wanted one favour in return.'

Bishop joined him at the bottom of the stairway and looked around.

They were in a low-ceilinged, narrow room that ran the length of the property. Three fluorescent tubes in the ceiling provided light. There was a large wooden workbench at this end, most of its surface taken up with the inner workings of various locks. The brick wall to Bishop's left was covered with shelves full of various tools. Five metal filing cabinets were lined against the wall ahead, next to a long black desk with mandatory computer and accessories. Built into the same wall was a waist-high safe with a keypad lock. To Bishop's right, a sliding wall sectioned the room off from a smaller area at the street end. He could make out weights and gym equipment back there. Which explained Price's comment about regular exercise.

'What was the favour?' Bishop asked.

Price walked over to the safe, knelt down and keyed in a twelve-number code. 'Told me I was to be his personal safety deposit box and that if ever somebody came along and quoted me the serial number of my first rifle, I was to give him this and leave him to it.' He opened the safe door and pulled out an old, metal, military-style footlocker about two feet in length and a foot wide. The lid's locking hasp was secured to the steel loop on the front by a simple key padlock.

'Weird thing is, me and the colonel never really got on when he was my CO. Never anything concrete, but I always had the suspicion he was one of those who thought a brother should know his station and be satisfied with Private First Class.' He shook his head. 'Shit, I dunno. Maybe he changed over time.'

'People do,' Bishop said. 'And you don't have to like somebody to trust them.' He nodded at the lockbox. 'You look inside after he died?'

'Be easy, wouldn't it?' The locksmith stood up and shrugged. 'Part of the deal was that I not give in to temptation, even if that happened. He guaranteed there was nothing illegal in there, just some kind of inheritance, so I gave him my word and that's how it's been ever since. Whatever's in there doesn't belong to me. I get curious every now and then, but not enough to break my promise. I'm stupid like that.'

'Nothing stupid about keeping your word,' Bishop said and crouched down in front of the locker. He placed the padlock in his palm and inserted the key into the lock. It fit perfectly. He turned it clockwise and the padlock clicked free.

Bishop worked the padlock through the loop, placed it on the floor and took the metal hasp in his hand. Then he opened the lid.

# EIGHTY-FIVE

The footlocker contained a simple black box file, like the ones found in almost any stationers. It was made of stout board with wooden ends, and had a flush-fitting lid with a press button lock on the side. This particular one was worn with age, with no labels to identify its contents.

Bishop reached in and pulled it out. It was heavier than he'd expected.

'Here, use this,' Price said and slid his ongoing projects and tools to one side of the workbench. Bishop brought the file over and placed it on the heavily scarred surface, along with his cell phone. Then he pressed the lid lock and opened the file.

The interior was packed tight with paperwork, all held in place by a metal spring-loaded clamp. Everything was in plastic sealed evidence bags or clear wallets. He released the clamp, gathered everything in both hands and spread it all out on the worktop.

Standing on the opposite side, Price said, 'Want me to leave you to it?'

'Up to you,' Bishop said with a shrug. If Price felt the need to stick around Bishop wouldn't stop him. Besides, he figured the man had a right to see what he'd been guarding all this time.

Bishop picked up an evidence bag containing a single sheet of paper. Inside was an abandoned draft of a letter. The almost childish handwriting tilted heavily to the right, but every word was clearly legible.

It read: *This is the Zodiac speaking. I am the killer of the taxi driver by Washington Square* . . . The words 'killer' and 'Square' had been crossed out and replaced with 'murderer' and 'Street'. It continued: . . . *and Maple Street last night and* . . .

The letter finished there.

Ebert must have changed his mind, or started another draft. Either way, Bishop knew he'd found Hoover's Zodiac file. At some point, these things had all been in contact with the serial killer. Even though the letter was sealed in an airtight evidence bag, Bishop felt dirty just holding it.

Bishop saw Price still standing there and handed him the letter before pulling out another evidence bag. It contained a piece of folded black material with no markings. Frowning, he put it to one side and picked up two more bags, each containing a hardback book. The larger one was a manual on ciphers and codes. The smaller one gave a history of the Roman alphabet.

*Busy boy*, Bishop thought. He could almost picture the patient in his hospital room, sitting on his bed, patiently teaching himself the perfect system with which to screw with the press while he randomly picked off members of the public.

'Hey, is this for real?' Price said, studying the unfinished letter with wide eyes.

'I sure hope so,' Bishop said and glanced down as his cell phone made a beeping sound. A message had arrived. He opened it up and read, *No luck. U?* It had to be from Aleron. He quickly keyed in a reply: *Yes. Talk later.* and sent it off.

He grabbed another wallet and pulled out a three-page typed memo addressed to Director Hoover. It was dated November 17, 1969. Bishop saw Arthur Mandrake's name and signature on the last page. According to the report, Ebert had admitted himself voluntarily in December 1967, complaining of frequent blackouts and gaps in his memory after smoking a few joints with friends one night.

Bishop had known plenty of people who smoked. Which meant he was aware that weed was no more dangerous than alcohol, and far less addictive. And it certainly didn't have the power to turn a person psychotic. But he guessed maybe it could act as a catalyst for someone with an underlying psychological condition. It seems the docs thought so too and a diagnosis of 'manic depressive illness' was made shortly after his admittance.

Attached to the memo was a hospital report listing the dates Ebert went missing, as well as his final discharge papers from the hospital. He released himself and re-joined society on December 17, 1969. Bishop knew the killings had stopped by then, so they must have finally found a drug that worked. Or at least one that kept him on an even keel. Bishop hoped so. He didn't like to think what might have happened if

Ebert stopped taking his medication. Or how many other unsolved murders there'd been during the last forty years.

'You should find this interesting,' he said to Price, slipping the sheets back in the wallet and passing them over.

Then he picked up a file labelled *FBI Forensics Report*. Inside were blood results from a black, cotton executioner's-type hood found in Ebert's room with a crosshair logo stitched on the chest. Which explained the mysterious evidence bag he'd just handled. Bryan Hartnell, the surviving witness of the murder of Cecelia Shepard at Lake Berryessa, reported that the killer had worn a garment just like it. The test results showed traces of Shepard's and Hartnell's blood on the cloak, as well as hair samples that matched Ebert's. They also found Ebert's prints all over the two books and stationery.

From Bishop's viewpoint, it was all pretty damning. Even though his own case had taught him the danger of jumping to conclusions, this kind of evidence was hard to ignore.

Bishop checked his watch. 23.58. Thorpe was due to call in two minutes and he had a strong feeling the bastard would be punctual. Unless he wanted to play games. Either way, he knew Thorpe badly wanted these files, but he still hadn't discovered why. What was it about Ebert that made this information so valuable?

'This is some unbelievable shit, ain't it?' Price said as he went through Mandrake's paperwork. 'News networks would pay big money for this.'

'I guess,' Bishop said and dropped the forensics folder in front of him. He reached for one of the polypropylene wallets and pulled out six flimsy carbon copy sheets held together by a paper clip. They were copies of Ebert's billing records from November '68 to December '69. They stated that all his bills were paid for by the Kebnekaise organization.

*Kebnekaise.* There was that name again. Bishop suddenly remembered the note Luke had given him and reached into his pocket for it. He'd not had a chance to check before now.

Unfolding it, he saw a page of double-spaced text giving a brief profile of the company. Bishop assumed Luke had hijacked it straight from some government server. It confirmed its current status as a non-profit organization and listed the Willow Reeves Rest Home in San Francisco, California as its sole holding. It also recorded the company's date of registration, August 7, 1967 and the fact that it was awarded tax-exempt status the next year on May 19. Then came a year-by-year listing of the organization's gross turnover. The figures weren't impressive. To Bishop, it looked as though the place was just getting by. Then came the names of its current board of directors. None of the four names did he recognize.

But there was one more line of text underneath, giving the name of the person who originally registered the company. That was a name he *did* recognize. And if it meant what he thought it meant, Bishop could understand why Thorpe was so obsessed with the file. And why he'd gone to such lengths to obtain it.

Bishop pursed his lips as he sorted through the two remaining items on the worktop. There was a report by an Agent Gilbert Deveraux, listing everything found in Ebert's room on November 20, 1969, most of it on the table in front of him. Underneath that, Bishop found Ebert's original hospital admission sheet. It was inside a beige card folder with Ebert's name and date of birth typed on the front. Inside, glued to the top right corner, was a forty-year-old black and white headshot of 'Timothy Ebert'.

Bishop felt the hairs on the back of his neck stand up. This was it. Once you had the final piece, everything fell into place. Everything. But even though it only confirmed Luke's findings, it was still a jolt seeing the faintly familiar face staring back at him. The family resemblance was remarkable. Last time he'd seen it had been almost five years before. On the evening news. A brief piece covering the guy's death from natural causes, with some predictable speculation on how his son was taking it. But the fact that he was dead made absolutely no difference to the file's significance now. Bishop knew that. It was what that particular face represented that mattered most. This file would be worth a fortune to the right people. Which meant the *wrong* people would almost certainly pay even more for it.

Just then, a brief gasping sound made Bishop look up. Price threw the papers he was holding on the floor and placed both hands on the edge of the table with his arms straight out. His lips moved, but no sounds came out. He stared at a point above Bishop's head for a few moments, then he slumped to the floor.

At the bottom of the stairs stood Thorpe. A silenced Glock in his hand.

# EIGHTY-SIX

Bishop's instincts took over and his left hand pulled the Beretta from his waistband in less than a second. He aimed it dead centre on Thorpe's forehead. The sight on top of the barrel remained perfectly still, as though connected to its target by an invisible rod.

'Drop it,' Bishop said.

'Sure thing, Jimmy.' Thorpe smiled, made a star of his hand, and the piece fell to the floor with a loud clunk. Then he came forward, stooped down to pick up the papers Price had dropped, and approached the desk.

With the barrel of the Beretta never wavering from the man's head, Bishop circled him and backed towards the stairs.

Thorpe laughed and moved into Bishop's previous position, rummaging through the wallets as though the gun didn't exist. 'So you found the tracking device, huh?' he said. 'Bet you quit looking after you found that first one, right? Come on, Jimmy, you should know by now I never do anything half-assed.'

Bishop picked up Thorpe's gun and knelt down next to Price, still keeping an eye on Thorpe. Price's left leg was bent at an angle under the right and a small pool of blood crept out from under the silk of the kimono. He placed his fingertips at the man's jugular and it was a few seconds before he felt a pulse. Bishop couldn't see where the bullet had entered, but unless Price received help straight away he didn't see much hope.

'Don't waste your time,' Thorpe said. 'A locksmith who doesn't secure his own front door properly deserves everything he gets.'

'You're real good at shooting people in the back, aren't you?' Bishop said, rising. 'But then, you've had plenty of practice.'

Thorpe smiled. 'Now, now, Jimmy. You wouldn't be trying to bait me, would you?'

'Maybe you should just tell me where Jenna is. Before we see how many parts of your anatomy you can do without.'

Thorpe glanced up from the papers in his hands, still smiling. 'You know, they say a man with a gun can get almost anything he wants, unless the man without one has an edge. How about it, Jimmy? You think I just blundered in on impulse, or could it be I've got something up my sleeve?' With exaggerated slowness, Thorpe put his hand in his pants pocket and brought out a cell phone. Bishop watched him place it on the workbench and felt his advantage slipping away like water down a drain.

Thorpe said, 'You can send it now, Danny,' and pushed Bishop's phone across. He went back to reading and fifteen seconds later Bishop's own cell beeped twice. 'Pick it up, partner. Danny's sent you a midnight movie.' Thorpe looked at his watch and said, 'Actually, ten past.'

Bishop grabbed the cell with his free hand and accessed his messages folder. It contained an MPEG file and he opened it.

The footage was shaky and showed a medium shot of Jenna. She was fully dressed and bound to a sturdy wooden chair in the centre of a well-lit, high-ceilinged, windowless room. From the refuse strewn across the floor and general air of neglect, Bishop guessed it was a disused warehouse somewhere. The only other furniture was a long wooden table next to Jenna's chair. On the table was a black box and a selection of sharp-looking cutting implements laid out in a neat row. There were two more equally neglected rooms in the background, each one divided by a wall containing an entranceway wide enough to accommodate a large truck. In the last room, Bishop could make out a human figure lying in a foetal position on the floor. Maybe a homeless person had found a way in and never had the chance to regret it. Beyond him, or her, was an open doorway with a couple of steps just visible, leading up.

The camera moved in closer on Jenna. She was slumped in the chair with her face towards the floor, hair falling over her cheeks. Bishop couldn't tell if she was conscious or not. Then Danny panned down to her feet and Bishop saw the electrical wires wrapped around her big toes, held in place with medicinal bandages. The camera moved along the wires until it reached their source on the table: the black box with four dials on the front. Bishop could swear he actually heard it humming. Danny pulled the camera away and a blurred hand came into view and touched one of the dials before the picture returned to Jenna in the chair.

Bishop closed his eyes. Then opened them. He knew what was coming.

Jenna's head suddenly snapped back hard. The high-pitched scream that came from the phone's speaker made Thorpe jump, and then laugh. Bishop's grip on the phone tightened so much he thought it might break. He watched her body fight against the bonds as the voltage surged through her. He counted twelve seconds before the screams ended and the electricity was turned off.

He watched Jenna dry-heave and spit repeatedly on the floor, before she finally fell back against the chair, exhausted. He knew she'd been trying to rid herself of the acid-metallic taste in her mouth. It was a peculiar taste, Bishop knew. One that stayed in your mouth for days as a nice little reminder.

Then Jenna's eyes opened and she turned her head towards her tormentor. She stared directly into the camera for a moment and then screamed, *'You goddamn freak dog! This is what gets you off, is it? Are you so—'*

The movie clip ended, cutting her off in mid-cry.

Bishop looked up. Thorpe hadn't moved. But nor had his own hand. The gun was still pointing at Thorpe's head. His finger was still on the trigger. *An ounce of pressure*, he thought. *Maybe two.* Just that much and Thorpe's trail of bodies would stop. But it wouldn't yet, of course. Not quite yet. With Danny listening at the other end of the line, Bishop understood who was in control for the time being.

As Bishop slowly lowered the gun, Thorpe said, 'The left hemisphere in charge now? Okay, that was just something to soften her up a little. You saw the knives on that table? Well, Danny's gonna take great pleasure in using them on Jenna unless we come to terms here.'

'What terms?' Bishop said. 'Your file's right there. Just tell me where she is.'

Thorpe shook his head. 'Guns first.'

Bishop stepped forward and placed both pieces on the workbench, then took a step back. Thorpe slid them over to his side, picked up his Glock and pulled a disposable hypodermic from his jacket pocket. He placed it on the table near Bishop.

'Hang fire for a while, Danny,' he said and closed the connection on the phone. Then he picked up a file on Ebert and started reading like he had all the time in the world, only looking up every now and then to check Bishop hadn't moved. Bishop watched him and thought of the knife in his ankle holster. He thought of how he could reach it before Thorpe put a bullet in him. And once he reached it, he could practically guarantee Thorpe would talk. Bishop knew how to make him sing like a lark.

'It's this last batch of papers that really seals the deal, don't you think?' Thorpe said. He was staring at the admission sheet like a man in love. 'I gotta tell you I'm impressed. Didn't I say how resourceful you could be when you set your mind to it?'

'And it's all thanks to you,' Bishop said. 'Was it worth it?'

'You tell me,' Thorpe said, meeting Bishop's gaze. 'What's the going price for conclusive evidence that this country's most infamous serial killer was Timothy Hemming, the current US Attorney General's father?'

# EIGHTY-SEVEN

'You call that conclusive?' Bishop said.

'I call it close enough for government work,' Thorpe said, smiling. He flipped through some pages again, speaking almost to himself. 'Man, Cortiss told me what this file contained, but it's still something to see it all first-hand. The Hemming family are really something, aren't they? Three US Attorney Generals out of the last four generations. That's some history right there, huh?'

Bishop said nothing. He was aware of the Hemming family's reputation. And the influence they exerted amongst the power players on Capitol Hill. He also knew their family-owned law firm was the most respected and most expensive in Washington. Had been for most of the twentieth century. Ever since Aaron Hemming became Attorney General in 1933 under Roosevelt, holding the post for a remarkable six years. Then Eisenhower appointed his son, Matthew, to the job from 1953 to 1957. That was some history, all right. So it hadn't surprised anyone when, six years ago, the current president appointed Matthew's grandson, Robert, to the lofty position. It was almost a family tradition. Almost. Only Timothy missed out on the prize. Bishop guessed he had his own reasons for wanting to stick with the family firm and stay out of the limelight. Although his face did get on TV when he died. And the President still showed up at his funeral.

Thorpe went on, his enthusiasm undiminished. 'You know old Aaron Hemming and Hoover were pals way back in the thirties? I read up on it. Hoover was so impressed with Hemming's spin-doctoring skills, he used the same methods to promote the FBI when he was starting it up. He probably knew Timmy from when he was a baby. Think of that.'

He looked up from the papers and smiled at Bishop. 'But it's the sixties where it gets interesting, huh? Our Timmy must have been acting *real* weird if his old man, Matthew Hemming, felt it necessary to send him to an asylum on the other side of the country under an assumed name. And then set up this Kebnekaise company just to pay his bills. And then, once he decided to enter the family business, to buy up the home and erase almost all references to his stay there. Makes you wonder if he ever suspected how screwed up his son really was. What do you think?'

Bishop shrugged. He didn't really care about Timothy Hemming. Or the Zodiac. Only Jenna mattered.

'I'm playing nice, Jimmy, so don't piss me off. I asked you a question, which means I want your opinion.'

Bishop sighed and said, 'I doubt even he knew. He came back to the hospital each time unable to remember a thing.'

Thorpe frowned. 'But he sent letters to newspapers afterwards, as well as pieces of bloody clothing. He must have had some awareness.'

'Maybe. I'm no expert.'

'No shit.' Thorpe laughed and shuffled the papers in his hands. 'So once he's well again, he gets married and has kids. Then he grooms Robert for the job he missed out on. I bet Hoover must have been praying he'd decide to go for the position himself eventually. He must have stayed awake nights imagining the hold he'd have over the Prez with that kind of information at his fingertips. I got to hand it to the old bulldog, his decision to hold all this back as the ultimate bargaining chip was a piece of genius. That man always thought five steps ahead.'

'Sounds like he was one of your childhood heroes.'

'He knew what he wanted and didn't let anything stop him from getting it.'

'No matter what the cost,' Bishop said.

Thorpe smiled. 'Exactly.'

'And now it's your bargaining chip. Or are you planning to sell it on? I can see al-Qaeda going for it big time. You're in Foreign Operations now so it can't be hard to find the right contacts.'

Thorpe laughed. 'You hit the nail there, Jimmy. That's where the money is these days and, believe me, they want this so bad it's giving them a rash. Even those morons realize you can't go on blowing up tower blocks for ever. They've finally wised up to the idea that the best weapons are those that hit right into the heart of the enemy with the minimum of effort. Soon as they get their hands on this, they'll hold a press conference that instantly changes the world's attitude towards the last remaining superpower. Maybe for ever.'

'And you'll provide them with the bullet.'

'Hey, a good businessman merely finds a gap in the market and fills it.'

'Businessman. That what you're calling yourself now?'

'Why not? I imagine that's how old man Brennan pictured himself when he shaved in the mornings, and he helped arm these idiots in the first place, don't forget. He was no innocent.'

'And Natalie. How about her?'

Thorpe looked at a point beyond the walls. 'Ah, sweet Natalie with that cute little ass of hers. Wasn't she something? Unfortunately, whenever I'd be pounding away at her I knew she'd be thinking of you. It took some of the pleasure out of it, let me tell you. And I got so sick of being under your shadow, Jimmy. Parading around like we were all friends. Making out I owed you for that sewer incident. You were right about that, but not in the way you thought.'

'So that's why you hate me. Because I saw you at your most vulnerable.'

'No,' Thorpe said and his smile changed to a sneer. 'Because you used that knowledge against me. I know how your mind works; you enjoyed having that power over me. You loved it. That's why you always picked me for your team, so I'd always be reminded of how inferior I was to you. Knowing I couldn't ever turn down the assignments if I wanted to stay employed. Always taking sole credit every time we completed a successful job. Making sure I could never get my own team.'

Bishop shook his head. 'You're deluded,' he said.

'Sure, Jimmy. It's all in my mind. Anyway, the reasons don't matter. It all came down to us needing a fall guy from the team and I picked you. But as much as I enjoy going over old times like this, I think we need to focus on the present. See that hypo in front of you? I want you to pick it up and choose a vein.'

Bishop didn't move.

Thorpe said, 'It's a clean needle, if that's what you're worried about.'

'I see your word's as reliable as ever,' Bishop said. 'Why not just shoot me?'

'Shoot you?' Thorpe raised both eyebrows. 'No, no, Jimmy. If I wanted you dead, I could have nailed you when I got the locksmith. No, I want the cops to stay focused on their pursuit of a living, breathing fugitive, and not get distracted by stuff that's taking place on the sidelines. I'm keeping my end of the deal. Well, part of it, at least. Can't give you that footage of you and Cortiss like I promised. Sorry.'

'I never believed that part, anyway. You know your name will be the first word out of my mouth if I ever get caught.'

'And what do you think their response will be? *Oh, really, sir? So he actually arranged all this so he could get his hands on files that prove the Attorney General's old man was really the Zodiac from forty years ago? Nurse? Straitjacket, please.* And since Jenna hasn't seen mine or Danny's faces, don't count on her backing you up, either.' Thorpe motioned with his head at the syringe on the workbench. 'All I've done is prepare a little something to keep you docile for an hour or so while I get on with my business. So the sooner you do what I say, the sooner I can tell you where she is and we can all move on with our lives.' He pointed his gun at Bishop's head. 'Or we can finish it all now. It would complicate things for me, but it's your choice.'

Bishop rolled up his right sleeve, reached over and took the syringe from the table. Removing the plastic cap, he flicked the barrel several times and depressed the plunger until the first drops of the clear solution squirted forth. He inserted the needle into the crook of his arm and said, 'I should have left you down there in the sewer where you belonged.'

'Too late for regrets,' Thorpe said, keeping his eye on the needle. 'All of it. I've measured the amount precisely for somebody of your size. And put it back on the table when you're finished. We both know what you're like with sharp objects and I don't want you getting any ideas.'

Bishop depressed the plunger all the way. When the syringe was empty, he tossed it on the table.

'Probably take a minute for the effects to kick in,' Thorpe said, 'so my advice is to find a spot on the floor before you fall on your ass and embarrass yourself.'

Bishop thought for a moment and looked around. Then he walked past Price's body towards the wall with the tool shelves. He sat on the floor with his back against the bricks, legs angled so their right side was hidden from Thorpe's view. He began to reach slowly into his right pants pocket.

Aleron had only been able to get one syringe of Narcan that afternoon and it was still there in his pocket. Thing was, without knowing what he'd just introduced into his bloodstream, there was no telling how effective it might be. If it was the same dope Thorpe had used on Jenna, he had a chance. At this point, all Bishop could do was inject it and hope for the best.

His fingers touched the syringe and he felt his way along the barrel until he was able to pop the plastic cap over the needle. He was in the process of taking it out when Thorpe put the papers down and moved around the table towards him, still holding the Glock.

Bishop stopped. He'd have to wait until Thorpe left before using it. He watched Thorpe pause briefly to check Price's pulse, or lack of one, and positioned the syringe so the plunger protruded from the pocket slightly. He placed his hand over it just as Thorpe, apparently satisfied, came over and crouched down in front of him.

'Tell me where Jenna is,' Bishop said. He could already feel his heart beating faster, and yet his body felt sluggish all over. It felt like he had a cotton ball lodged in his throat.

'One track mind, you know that?' Thorpe said. 'Okay, okay, she's in a warehouse on Cortlandt. Happy now?'

'Which one?' Bishop said. There was a distinct slur in his voice now that made him uneasy. Every muscle in his body felt numb and he was finding it difficult to move his lips. And his heart was definitely beating a *lot* faster.

'Hmmm.' Thorpe frowned and scratched his forehead. 'You know, now that I think about it, I don't believe I ever saw a number on the door. Lots of graffiti, but that's no help; they've all got graffiti over them. Hold still, it might come to me.' He pretended to search his memory for a few seconds then said, 'No, it's gone. Sorry, Jimmy. Tell the truth, I sort of promised her to Danny and I wouldn't want to break up that particular party. Oh yeah, and she *has* seen our faces. I lied about that part too. Probably best if you forget about her altogether and worry about your own situation.' He was watching Bishop closely. 'Starting to kick in yet?'

Bishop had things to say, but could no longer speak. Or swallow. Or move any part of his body. The whole world was numb. He couldn't even feel his heartbeat any more, although he was still breathing so it had to be working in there still.

'Stuck for words?' Thorpe asked. 'Good dope, isn't it? I first tried it out on a sweet little thing a while back and within a minute or two she couldn't move a single muscle except her eyelids. Lasted nearly an hour, too. Enough time for me to try out all sorts of things she wasn't too happy about. Amazing. I'd patent it if it wasn't so full of banned substances. See, the main problem with paralysing agents like vecuronium or succinylcholine is they shut down *all* the muscles, including the diaphragm here.'

Thorpe pressed his fingertips into Bishop's stomach to stress the point, but Bishop felt nothing. All he could do was stare at Thorpe.

'Fine if you're in a hospital where they can intubate you. Not so good anywhere else. That's where my special blend comes in. The vecuronium turns off the muscles, but accelerates your heartbeat to dangerous levels. The morphine slows it down enough to keep it from jumping out your ribcage and bouncing up those stairs. While the third element keeps the automatic motor functions ticking along without affecting the secondary muscles. Impressive or what?'

Bishop blinked at him. He didn't plan it. His lids just chose that moment to open and close. Providing moisture to the eyes he could no longer use in any direction other than straight ahead. Everything but Thorpe was just a part of his peripheral vision.

'Well,' Thorpe said, rising, 'enough gabbing. Last thing I wanna do is bore you.'

He watched Thorpe return to the workbench and gather up all the material and place it back in the box file. Bishop could hear him humming an unidentifiable tune to himself. Then he picked up both cell phones and put one in his pocket while he keyed in a message on the other. Bishop heard the electronic burp a few seconds later that signified the message had reached its destination. He prayed it wasn't a green light for Danny to go to town on Jenna.

Thorpe turned to him and said, 'Your cell comes with me, Jimmy, but I'll leave your Beretta. I figure you'll need it more than me.'

*Yes, I will*, Bishop thought. *And maybe I'll grant you a similar courtesy when the time comes, Thorpe. Maybe not. But whatever else happens, the debts you've racked up will be paid in full. One debt, in particular. I found you once, and once I get Jenna back I'll find you again.*

Thorpe gave the basement a final glance and nodded. 'Okay, pard. Onward and upward. My new life awaits. Stay out of trouble now, y'hear?'

Then he climbed the stairs, humming to himself all the way to the top.

# EIGHTY-EIGHT

Jenna wanted nothing else in life other than to somehow break free from her own skin. Please God, anything to escape her burning insides. She tried to vomit, but she'd had no solids in the last twenty-four hours. And the dry-heaving only caused her stomach to become just another source of pain in her tired and weakened body.

How much more of this could she be expected to endure? The first jolt had been bad enough, but the small residue of the drug in her system had protected her from the full effects. The second surge had been indescribable. The objective part of her mind knew it had only lasted ten or eleven seconds, but at the time it felt infinite. But she wouldn't cry in front of the freak. She'd find enough strength for *that*, at least.

Jenna no longer thought of her tormentor as Danny. That was a name for humans, not for the thing now sitting cross-legged and silent on the floor in front of her. Watching her as a biology student studies a frog that's being dissected.

Her one flicker of hope had been the sight of the cell phone. Knowing it would be used as leverage on Bishop, she'd immediately begun hurling abuse as a way of getting her one pathetic clue across to him. Her main concern was that the filming might have ceased before she could say what needed to be said. And even if Bishop *did* hear her, would he even realize what she was giving him? He needed a starting point and she didn't know enough about her location to provide him with that. All she had was a detail.

That was the last time she'd spoken in this place. She wouldn't beg.

Jenna shifted her gaze to the prostrate human figure on the floor in the other room. Her memory of the journey through the building was fragmented at best, but she thought she'd seen two figures in there when she'd been dragged in. One of them had even looked female. Maybe that one, there. It was so hard to focus.

285

Who were they? A homeless couple? Were they even alive? Knowing her keepers, she thought it was unlikely. Her screams should have woken the dead, yet the figure hadn't moved from its position once. Could be a store mannequin for all she knew. But what did it matter? She cursed her wandering mind and tried to focus.

Movement in front pulled her attention back and an ice-cold palm pressed her forehead back and pulled her eyelids up. This was the third time they'd gone through this procedure. Jenna didn't want to know what was so interesting about her eyes.

And then it came to her. This was a waiting game. Waiting for all traces of the drug to leave her system so she'd be aware of everything that was happening to her when the real fun started. In a feeble effort to deny their existence, she'd purposely not looked at the knives and needles over there, but that no longer worked. Jenna almost hoped for another turn of that dial. Maybe one more surge of electricity would be more than her heart could take and then all her problems would be solved.

She'd come to realize death was no longer the worst thing that could happen to her. Just the last.

After a while, Jenna heard the familiar beep of a message and watched her captor walk over to the table again and pick up the cell. Knowing it was useless, she tried once more to move her limbs. But the electric cords binding her to the chair gave her no leeway and she soon gave up. Instead, she turned and saw the freak nod at whatever was onscreen before putting the phone down. And the warm smile that lit up that previously blank face scared Jenna more than anything else that had happened to her in the last thirty hours.

# EIGHTY-NINE

Thorpe got in the van he'd parked a block away. He placed his prize on the passenger seat and just looked at it. Savouring it.

So there it was. Finally. Everything he ever wanted in one convenient package. Unbelievable. Maybe he'd lease an island in the South Pacific, stock it up with nubile flesh and live off the interest while he screwed himself silly. He'd have to give it some serious thought. With his money now doubled, the options open to him were almost limitless.

It was weird, though. Thorpe expected to feel a sense of relief, elation or *some*thing at the successful culmination of three years' work, but at the moment all he felt was casual indifference.

But perhaps it was a little too early for victory runs. After all, he didn't actually have the money yet, did he? He still had to arrange the handover with Sayyid, his al-Qaeda contact, and that was a meeting he wasn't going to take lightly. Like him, whoever showed up would want to part with as little money as possible and Thorpe had to prepare for a multitude of potential double-cross scenarios. He shouldn't ever forget the kind of animals he was dealing with.

At least the location for the exchange would be up to him. That was something. Maybe the most important thing. And, of course, Danny would be there to cover his back once the woman was taken care of.

Thorpe took out his phone and keyed in the number. When the call was picked up on the third ring he said, 'It's me.'

'Martin, my friend,' the familiar voice said. 'And using another number, as is your wont. I have been waiting. Are we to do business?'

'That we are. I've got it with me now and it's everything I promised. One of the sealed items actually places our friend at the scene of one of the murders.'

A moment's silence at the other end. 'I see. I have to admit I had my doubts, but you have done as you said, Martin. I am most impressed. So can I assume you have decided upon a location for the handover?'

Thorpe put a smile in his voice and said, 'That I have, my friend.' He relayed the details and asked, 'That good for you?'

'Since I have never set foot there,' Sayyid said, 'that remains to be seen. But it is acceptable. What time shall we meet?'

'Five a.m. And one more thing.'

'Yes, my friend?'

'I don't expect a one-on-one, but if I see more than four people at the site, I'm outta there and you can add another twenty per cent to the price.'

'It shall be as you say, Martin. Don't worry. I will be in touch if there is a delay for any reason.'

'I never worry,' Thorpe said and ended the call.

Then he keyed in a brief message, located Danny's number and sent it across. *Almost there*, he thought. By daybreak he'd be a man with money to burn and a future without limits.

With a satisfied grin on his face, Thorpe started the engine and began driving towards it.

# NINETY

*Move*, Bishop thought. *I want the index finger to move. I want it to start tapping against the cloth of my pants. I order you to override the effects of the drug and move.*

It didn't. He would have seen it at the lower reaches of his vision if it had, but he saw only stillness.

Bishop knew almost nothing about paralyzing agents, but he figured when mobility returned it would reach the extremities first. So he continued to concentrate all his energies on the index finger of his right hand in an effort to speed up the process. Just like he'd been doing for the past eight minutes since Thorpe left.

He kept trying. Again and again. Refusing to give in to the drug. Each time he pictured the action in his fuddled mind and each time he willed the muscles to obey him. It was his body and the mind controlled every aspect of it, just as it would do now. *You belong to me*, he thought. *You're a part of me. Start tapping against the material. Do it now. Show me . . .*

This time, the forefinger twitched.

He willed it to do it again and it did. He also felt a sensation in the fingertip as it touched the cotton. He kept tapping out a rhythm that he imagined matched his heartbeat.

Next came the thumb. *Follow the finger's lead*, he thought. *It's easy. I want to feel the plastic of the syringe against the skin. Tap, tap, tap. It's the easiest thing in the world.*

There was no movement. He concentrated harder, visualizing it. He kept the image at the forefront of his mind. Nothing else existed. Only the thumb as it tapped. Seconds passed. Then minutes. And for every second he pictured his thumb tapping. And soon Bishop realized he wasn't just picturing it. It was actually moving in unison with the index finger. Tap, tap, tap. He could feel it. He still felt dead everywhere else, but that didn't matter. Things were starting to move in the areas that counted.

Patiently, he went through the same painstaking process for each of the other three fingers. Each one responded quicker than the one before it, until eventually he had the use of all five. That would have to be enough. He'd already used up fifteen valuable minutes.

Bishop used his thumb to slowly pull the thin hypodermic the rest of the way from his pocket. There. Next, he clamped the syringe between his index and middle fingers, using the thumb to hold it in place. He then used the last two fingers to drag his hand and forearm over his leg until the needle was pointed towards the left inner thigh. Then he carefully pressed the syringe against the material of his combats until he sensed the needle penetrate the cotton.

Now came the tricky part. Since his legs were totally numb, he'd have to stab inwards with as much force as four fingers and a thumb allowed and trust he'd pierced the skin.

Visualizing the action in his mind, Bishop tightened his grip, took two deep breaths, and on the third *pushed* and drove the hypo towards his leg with all the strength he could muster.

Of course, he felt nothing.

But as he relaxed his hold on the hypo it was clear it had penetrated *some*thing. The syringe was jutting out at an angle. He had to assume he'd done it. If he'd misjudged, he'd be here for another forty-five minutes and Jenna would be beyond help.

Bishop pressed his thumb down on the plunger until it was empty.

And he waited. And tried to recall how long it took to produce results. Inside, when he'd been admitted to the infirmary with food poisoning, he'd seen three guards come in carrying a big white lifer who looked dead already. The prison physician had injected the drug into his arm and it seemed as though the con had regained consciousness immediately, but Bishop knew that couldn't be right. So he played the whole scene through in his head at double speed to make sure and nodded to himself when it finished. It had been about two minutes. Maybe less.

It took Bishop a moment to realize what he'd just done. He nodded again. And smiled.

He pressed one hand against the concrete floor and slowly got to his feet, rolling his shoulders and stretching his arms as he rose. Relishing the sensation. Everything seemed to be working just fine. His head was a lot clearer, too.

He went over to pick up his Beretta from the worktable and checked the magazine. Still full. He placed it in his pocket and checked on Price. The older man's face was ashen, but when Bishop checked his pulse he found a beat. Faint, but it was there. The guy was a bull. He left Price and jogged up the stairs and through the shop floor until he reached the vintage payphone. Upon hearing the dial tone, he dialled 911, gave the details of Price's injury and the address and hung up.

Then he ran down the hallway to the front door. And once he was outside he kept running.

# NINETY-ONE

Danny Costa inserted the acupuncture needle into the fleshy part of Jenna's left thumb and watched as the visibly throbbing veins in the girl's temples gradually ebbed away to nothing. The woman audibly exhaled at the relief from the pain.

Hedison, or Thorpe, had been correct when he'd said pain was limitless, but it was also true that pain without respite was pointless. Too much and the body started to accept it as the norm, gradually acclimatizing itself to the new status quo and so diluting the desired effect. No, much better to offer up some relief at unexpected moments to remind the body of what it was missing. That way the subsequent physical distress could be appreciated all the more.

So let her enjoy this quiet moment before things took a turn for the worse. And they would get much worse very soon. Jenna had been sneaking glances at the knives laid out on the table more and more in the last few minutes. Especially the one purposely placed apart from the others: a Japanese hunting knife with a razor-sharp, three-inch-long, curved, stainless steel blade. Perfect for skinning animals. And not *just* animals.

This Jenna really was very beautiful, and the mental image of the knife cutting into that perfect brown skin and peeling it away from the muscle membranes caused Costa to shiver. She'd speak soon enough. She'd beg and she'd scream. They always did.

Choices, choices. What to do? The second message sent ten minutes ago had ensured there was no rush, but Costa had learned from Thorpe the necessity of preparing for all eventualities. And Bishop had proved annoyingly capable. With Thorpe admitting earlier that he had no specific plans to kill Bishop, that meant there was always a chance, however slight, that he might show up here.

Well, there were ways to prepare for that. But the tempting sight of Jenna helpless in the chair was fast overriding all sense of caution. After all, there were numerous warehouses running the length of this alley. What were the chances of Bishop actually picking out this one?

Thinking about it, not much chance at all.

So, after extracting the needle from Jenna's hand and throwing it on the floor, Costa walked over to the table and picked up the hunting knife.

And smiled.

# NINETY-TWO

Bishop had covered the two miles between East 2nd Street and Cortlandt in less than ten minutes, but it was only as he drove slowly down the sparsely lit alley that he realized the enormity of his problem. It was lined with nothing *but* warehouses. Most were four or five storeys and they all looked pretty much the same.

He figured that since Danny was inside with Jenna, he was looking for a door with no padlocks on the exterior. So far, he'd spotted two possibles, but that wasn't good enough. He needed to narrow it down to one. And fast.

He stopped the vehicle and looked out at the darkness ahead. He thought back to that movie clip. All he'd seen were three filthy ground floor rooms in a derelict warehouse. That wasn't much help. At this hour all the warehouses looked abandoned.

Bishop leaned forward with his arms over the wheel, tapping his fingers against the plastic. He allowed himself to think about Jenna, but tried to ignore her pain and rage. Instead he concentrated on her words. She hadn't spoken until the end of the clip, when she screamed *You goddamn freak dog*. Which was kind of a weird thing to say. Why not just 'freak'? It was simple and got the point across.

And then he remembered that brief moment of hesitation just before the abuse, when she saw Danny recording her. Like she'd just spotted an opportunity she could use.

He sat back and thought of the two doors he'd passed without padlocks. They'd been pretty standard doors with graffiti all over them.

*Freak dog.*

He put the vehicle in gear and moved slowly forward, examining the doors on each side. He reached the White Street intersection and waited for the late night traffic to thin before driving straight across to the second section of the alley. He continued crawling, checking each side.

As he passed a brown metal door on his left, he noticed it had no padlocks and tapped the brakes.

The steel shutters that covered the delivery entrance were covered in more street art. Most of it amateur stuff, but a cartoon near the bottom stood out. It was a headshot of a well-known beagle wearing a pair of headphones. Next to it was a yellow speech balloon. Inside, the lettering read *MC Freakdog.*

*Good girl, Jenna.* Bishop backed the car up and pulled in close to the neighbouring warehouse. He pulled out his Beretta and opened the car door. The warehouse he wanted was a five-storey building, with a door at each level to allow access to the exterior fire stairs. The doors above had padlocks on, meaning they wouldn't be of much use in an emergency.

But if the place was abandoned, that wouldn't matter.

On the second floor level a fire ladder was fixed to the exterior. It looked pretty old and rusty but definitely usable. He got back in the Honda and moved it forward. Placing the Beretta in one of the windbreaker's pockets, he went to the trunk, pulled out a tyre iron and tucked it in his waistband. Then he climbed onto the Honda's roof.

He took a deep breath in preparation for the discomfort to come and then jumped. He grabbed hold of the lowest rung and pulled himself up. The pain in his abdomen was worse than he'd anticipated and air hissed through his teeth as he clenched his stomach muscles. Using only his arms he pulled himself up to the next rung, and then the next, concentrating only on what was before him until his foot finally touched the bottom rung. Then he kept climbing.

When he made it to the top, he rolled onto the latticework landing and took a few breaths before he got to his feet. Set into the wall in front of him was a metal door with a sliding bolt. It was secured with a rusting padlock. Bishop took out the tyre iron, inserted it into the semicircular bar of the padlock and yanked down. There was the sound of metal scraping against metal and then the lock snapped open. Bishop left the tyre iron on the landing and pulled his Beretta and flashlight out. Then he slid the bolt across.

Inside it was dark and silent. There was an old decaying smell, but nothing fresh and Bishop took a slight comfort from that. Holding the door open, he flicked the Maglite on and saw a long, cavernous room that stretched back a hundred and fifty yards. At his immediate left, directly in line with the shuttered doors down below, was a disused freight elevator shaft. In the far wall, he could see a set of windowless double doors.

He had the flashlight in his right hand. The Beretta in his left. He criss-crossed them into the Harries position, aimed them at the double doors and entered the building.

# NINETY-THREE

Bishop kept to the right as he advanced across the cluttered floor space. The building was unusually quiet. Older structures usually made a few noises, but he guessed these warehouses had been built to last. Apart from him, there was just stillness and silence. When he reached the pair of wooden sliding doors, he switched off the flashlight and waited, listening. Still no sound. But under the doors he noticed a faint residue of light creeping in. He was on the right track.

He gripped the handle on the left door and gently slid it open until he had enough space to fit through. On the other side was a stairway landing, partly illuminated by light from the floor below. To his left, more steps led upwards into darkness. Bishop went over and aimed the flashlight into the wide stairwell. The smell of damp wood and old faeces hit him, but he saw nothing but concrete until the next turn. No sounds, either. Not even from rodents trying to escape the light. He switched the flashlight off and pocketed it, then crossed to the other steps. The ones leading down. Holding his gun in both hands, he descended.

At the bottom, he looked through the opening into the rooms beyond.

He was seeing the room from the reverse angle of the movie clip, but he was definitely looking at the same three rooms. The same walls with the large entranceways separated them, allowing him to see right to the end a hundred yards away. Three grime-covered fluorescent fixtures along the central beam provided light.

Jenna sat just to the right of a pair of huge double doors at the end. Next to her was a table containing knives of different shapes and lengths. She was still bound to a chair and her head was slumped forward. Her shirt had been ripped from her body and her left arm was covered in blood. There were dark stains on the floor all around her. From this distance, Bishop couldn't tell if she was breathing or not.

Every part of him wanted to run over and check, but she'd been left alone for a reason. Which meant Danny was still here somewhere, waiting for him. He needed to secure the area before he did anything else.

Directly in front of him was the figure he'd seen in the video. Still in the same foetal position. He couldn't see the face, but it was clearly female. She was wearing shapeless jogging pants and a filthy, baggy, hooded sweatshirt. But it was the second figure lying nestled against the right wall twenty feet away that got his attention. That one was male.

Bishop checked the girl first. With his gun covering the man, he crouched at her side and placed his fingers beneath her ear. She was all skin and bone, so there was no problem locating her pulse, which was slow, but regular. He looked down at her profile. Late twenties, possibly, with prominent cheekbones, filthy long brown hair and body odour bad enough to make him breathe through his mouth. Yet she seemed quite pretty, or could have been if she'd given up the drugs. He noticed two recently used condoms near her feet, as well as a disposable syringe that looked new. He shook her shoulder, but got no response. She felt like a dead weight.

He got to his feet and approached the man. He was wearing a thick overcoat and lying on his side, right hand tucked into his pocket. Bishop used a foot to push him onto his back. He looked the same age as the girl. He had blond shoulder-length hair and good, symmetrical features. The hair looked as though it had been washed recently. And apart from a nasty bruise above the right cheek, his face showed none of the wear and tear of someone who lived on the streets. That overcoat didn't look like a cheap make, either.

Keeping a foot on the man's right elbow, Bishop crouched and placed the gun barrel against his forehead. He raised the man's eyelids. The rapid eye movement indicated unconsciousness, but Bishop knew that that could be faked easily enough.

He slammed the side of the gun into the guy's right temple. The man groaned and his head slumped to the left, bleeding a little from the wound. Bishop checked the eyes again and got the same results, although his breathing was now a lot louder. Bishop looked down, pulled the man's hand from his coat pocket and reached inside to see what he'd been holding.

And pulled out a hunting knife. An expensive one by the looks of it. Japanese or Korean and used for skinning game. The curved blade had blood on it. A lot of blood.

Taking the knife with him, Bishop approached the entranceway to the second room and peered round the wall. Seeing it was empty, he crossed to the next opening, looked round and saw only Jenna. Still in the same position.

But this time, he could see her chest rising and falling. She was alive.

He jogged towards her, listening out for movement from behind and keeping an eye on the doors ahead. As he got closer, he saw that Danny had only started. A two-inch-long section of her upper right arm had been stripped away, exposing the defined bicep muscle. The length of skin was still attached and hung down, swaying with each exhalation. He gently touched her cheek. She had a large, red bruise just below her left eye. He guessed Danny must have knocked her out when he heard Bishop break in.

There wasn't as much blood as he'd first thought, but enough had run down her arm to create a pool on the floor. Glancing at Jenna's bare feet he saw the burnt skin around her toes and the medicinal plasters, but the electrical wires had been removed. He also noticed that each chair leg had a metal hinge that had been bolted to the floor, and wondered how many others had suffered slow, painful deaths in its arms.

He gently lifted the hanging piece of skin until it covered as much of the wound as possible, and held it there for a few seconds until he felt sure the blood would help it stay in position. Then he used the hunting knife to cut at the thick cords binding her right arm to the chair. Jenna began to stir and her eyes opened to slits when he was halfway through. They focused on Bishop and she whispered, 'You came.'

'I said I would.'

Then he watched Jenna's eyes become circles and she screamed '*No!*' and that awful body odour filled the air again.

The girl. *It was the goddamn girl all along.*

Bishop tried to turn, but a bony knee jammed into his back and the gun fell from his grasp as he dropped to the floor. Still gripping the knife, he began to rise but another agonizing stomach muscle spasm hit him and he dropped to his knees. He gasped for breath and something knocked against his wrist and he saw the knife fall onto Jenna's lap.

Then he saw Danny's clenched fists on either side of his face. There was a length of electrical wire between them, stretched taut.

And then the wire was at his throat.

# NINETY-FOUR

Bishop instinctively brought his right hand up and managed to get his two end fingers between the wire and his larynx before it tightened. Immediately, Danny began twisting while dragging him back along the floor. Blood spurted from both digits and ran down his forearm as the pressure increased. He tried slamming his right elbow into the weight at his back. Each time, Danny avoided the blow without loosening her grip.

After about twenty feet, Bishop fell on his side and Danny wrapped a leg around his waist and came down with him. He could already feel the wire start to cut into his neck near the Adam's apple. Where was her strength coming from? The scrawny bitch was half his size. Less than half.

In the struggle, he thought he heard shouting, but couldn't make out the words. Had to be Jenna. He knew it wasn't coming from Danny. He figured she was a mute. The only noise she made was something that resembled hissing as she squeezed the life from him. As if she was excited, like this was a turn-on for her.

Bishop reached down to his ankle holster with his left hand. But Danny kept punching his elbow away with her knee until he was forced to give up. He scanned the floor for something else he could use. Anything. But there was nothing except some ancient batteries and old cardboard and newspapers. But his Beretta should be nearby. He'd gotten part of his foot on it when he was being dragged, and it had come at least part of the way. He was sure of it. So where the hell was it? Unable to move his head, he used his legs and free arm to manoeuvre his body so it faced the table. And there it was. On the floor just a few feet away. He dragged himself towards it with the world on his back, but the moment it came within reach a boot came into view and kicked it away.

The wire was cutting into his neck now and he felt blood running into his shirt under the jacket. It was getting harder to take in air and his breath came out in rasps. He reached his free arm around but she skittered over him like a spider. He couldn't get near. Any time he veered off and went for his ankle, she knocked his arm away with her knee before he could make contact.

*Forget the direct approach then.*

Bishop dragged himself back towards the table and she wriggled around on top of him, her right knee pressing into his side. The pressure didn't let up at all. The more exertion he put into surviving, the more she got off on it. His trapped left arm was completely wet now as it dragged underneath him and he knew he was leaving a trail of blood across the floor.

Another foot. Then one more. He was past halfway. Momentarily, he thought of Jenna. He hadn't heard her in a while and he couldn't see her chair. It was just out of his vision. He moved another foot. And another. And there, in front of his face, half covered by some scrap paper, was a metallic object. An acupuncture needle. Three inches long with a thin steel handle. His fingers closed around it and he stopped crawling.

Danny began rubbing her body against him in a grotesque parody of ecstasy. Bishop felt her knee dig deeper into his side as she tightened her grip on the wire. He'd stopped trying to take in oxygen. No point now. His vision had deteriorated to the point where he could barely see the floor an inch from his face. Everything was turning grey. His only lifeline was the small amount of air still remaining in his lungs. Gripping the needle in his fist, he brought his arm back to rest against Danny's leg, his closed fist on her knee. She didn't bother trying to move it out of the way. Bishop guessed she relished the extra contact with her victims during their final throes.

Relying on feel alone, his forefinger located the lower part of the vastus lateralis muscle, just above her knee. All muscles were sensitive, but he knew that particular one was in a league of its own. Just ask any sportsman. Utilizing his last vestige of strength, Bishop raised his fist as high as it would go. Then he plunged the needle into the muscle all the way up to the handle.

The pressure against his neck was gone and the weight on his back fell away. Bishop rolled over and coughed as he filled his empty lungs with oxygen. He used his unharmed hand to pull the garrotte out of the groove in his neck and raised his injured fingers to stem the blood.

He'd lost the top of his little finger, but his ring finger was still there, but only just. He turned to Danny. She sat on the floor next to the table, her right leg stretched out before her. She was slowly pulling the needle out of her knee with both hands, her face a picture of agony.

'That's what real pain feels like,' he said. 'How do you like it?'

Behind her, Bishop could see Jenna cutting at the cords binding her feet with Danny's Japanese knife. Still coughing, he reached down and pulled his own knife free from its ankle holster. It was time to end this right now. As he rose to his knees, he watched Danny throw the needle away before glancing down at her side. She picked up something off the floor.

His gun.

With her left hand clamped around her knee, she pointed the Beretta at Bishop's groin. And the smile she gave him was one of the most beautiful he'd ever seen.

Jenna suddenly launched herself from the chair. She leapt on Danny and plunged the hunting knife deep into the girl's back, between the shoulder blades. Danny's smile turned into a grimace and she dropped the gun and fell forward.

'*Die, you sick bitch*,' Jenna screamed as she got to her feet. She reached for another knife on the table.

Bishop moved closer and picked up his gun. 'No, Jenna,' he said as he pulled the knife out of the woman's back and threw it under the table. Danny's sweatshirt was already drenched in her blood. 'Turn away.'

Jenna looked at him. Her arm continued to bleed and her body was bruised and battered, but she didn't look scared or in pain. She looked almost wild. He couldn't blame her.

'This isn't my first time,' he said. 'And I don't want it to be yours, either. Turn away.'

Jenna opened her mouth and then paused. Slowly she turned, dropping the knife. She leaned against the table and Bishop saw her shoulders shaking.

Bishop rolled Danny onto her back. The floor turned red beneath her and she looked up into his eyes. Her mouth was parted and her teeth were covered in blood. Her eyes met his and she smiled at him again.

'Goodbye,' he said, and snapped her neck.

# NINETY-FIVE

Leaning against the table, Bishop watched Jenna reach into the jacket he'd given her and tear a long strip from the inner lining. She began wrapping the material around what remained of his two end fingers before extending it around the width of his hand.

He hadn't been feeling too hot since Saturday, and he felt even worse now. But it was worth it. Jenna was worth it. He watched her working on him and smiled. The relief he felt at finding her in one piece far outweighed the physical pain, and would be enough to keep him going for a while yet. With Jenna safe, that was all he cared about now. Just staying on his feet a little longer. He still had things to do.

As she secured the ends of the strip tightly with a knot, Bishop noticed she never once looked at Danny's body lying a few feet away. Although she did occasionally glance towards the double doors. Bishop had already checked the room beyond and found the girl he'd seen in the video. Danny had cut the poor girl's throat and propped her next to the grate covering the elevator shaft. Then she must have planted the knife on the boyfriend and taken the girl's place.

'This time you *do* need a doctor,' Jenna said, inspecting the bandage. 'But what do I know, right?' She studied the black strip of cloth around his neck and he felt her fingers gently touch the wound underneath. They came away clean. She frowned, then leaned forward and kissed him on the lips. 'Thanks.'

'You're welcome,' he said and touched her face. He kissed her again. Longer this time. The feel of her lips on his worked better than any balm and he didn't want it to stop. But he broke away finally and then crouched next to the corpse, checking the pockets. 'Can you remember if Thorpe said anything about where he was meeting his buyers?'

'No.' She paused. 'But I was out of it most of the time.'

He found Danny's cell phone and stood up. Handed it to Jenna. 'Here, use this. Your brother and Luke had their own lead to follow, so their nerves are probably shot to hell by now. You're in Cortlandt Alley, by the way.'

Jenna took the phone, keyed in a number and put it to her ear. A second later, she said, 'Ali, it's Jenna. I'm okay. I'm safe.' She smiled and Bishop heard a yell at the other end. 'I know, I know, I'll explain it all when you get here,' she said, and gave the location. 'I need to call the police now . . . Right . . . Don't be long.' She handed the phone back to Bishop and said, 'Ali promised to name his firstborn after you. I am calling the police, aren't I?'

'The moment I leave here,' he said, and scrolled through the phone's menu until he got to the message inbox. 'Tell them everything that happened and remember, *I* stabbed her with the knife. You never touched her.'

'But it was self-defence.'

'We both know that, but the wound in her back will open up questions you don't need. Just lay it at my door, Jenna. Believe me, with what they already got on me, it won't make any difference.'

Bishop smiled at the phone. Danny hadn't gotten around to deleting her messages. He saw the most recent communication had been sent less than an hour ago and opened it up. *Exchange at 0500. BH. Meet me 0400.*

BH. He should have known. Brennan's house. You set up an exchange, you want the territory to be a place you know like the back of your hand. And the house certainly qualified as that. For both of them. He checked his watch. 00.51. That gave him plenty of time. *Okay, Thorpe*, he thought. *I'll meet you there, but you won't like it.* He deleted the message and gave the phone back to Jenna.

She brought her hand to his cheek. 'Once I tell them what's happened, they'll have to know it wasn't you.'

He shrugged. 'It doesn't matter. It's not about me any more.'

'What do you mean?'

He dismissed the question with a shake of his head. 'You'll be okay on your own until Ali gets here?'

She waved a hand at the table. 'I'm pretty handy with these now.'

Bishop smiled and nodded towards the back room. 'There's a guy back there who'll probably need stitches because of me.'

'I think the freak can take the blame for that one, don't you?' She shook her head and said, 'How the hell does anyone get like that?'

He looked down at the body and shook his head. 'Some people are just wired wrong from birth.'

'Yeah, I guess.'

He had begun walking towards the double doors that led back to the alley when she said, 'James . . .'

Bishop turned back. The expression on Jenna's face could have been interpreted in any number of ways. He chose one and said, 'I know.'

Then he opened the door and left.

# NINETY-SIX

Thorpe looked out from the third floor window and adjusted the magnification on the night vision field glasses. As the four-wheel-drive passed through the open gates, he could clearly see the figure drop off the back and disappear into the overgrown foliage surrounding the property.

He shook his head and came away from the window. Assholes. They just couldn't do it, could they? Tell them four, maximum, and they bring five. All right, fine, let them think they had the upper hand. He'd planned ahead for just this contingency.

At the moment, he was more concerned with Danny's absence. He'd sent another message without any response and was loath to use his cell any more. Or either of the others. He could guess what had happened. She'd gotten carried away with the Falstaff woman and lost track of time as she tried to make the fun and games last as long as possible. He'd seen it happen more than once. Even joined in a few times, back in the days before her constantly evolving tastes got too much for him. Problem was, that girl was just *too* damned addictive and he knew all too well where that sort of thing led. He still felt pangs of desire whenever she aimed that movie-star smile at him, and for that reason distanced himself from her whenever he didn't actually need her for a job.

But she could have handled the one outside for him. They'd obviously left him there to take care of Thorpe once he emerged from the house. Probably to 'persuade' him to reveal his account details once they had the files in their hands. That's what Thorpe would have done. They didn't realize he could stay here for days without being discovered.

Thorpe stepped through the doorway to the vault and switched on the small battery-powered lamp on the floor. He noticed the light was dimmer than before. Probably another hour before he'd need to replace the batteries. Pity he hadn't been able to find a replacement bulb for the one in the ceiling, but the lamp would do for the short amount of time he'd be in here. Because without some kind of illumination, this would be unbearable.

He went back and slid the bookcase over but kept the vault door open a crack, telling himself it was because of the cell phone reception and for no other reason. He forced himself to ignore the all-consuming terror that threatened to take over, the fear of being buried alive that had been with him since childhood. He told himself he was still in control of his surroundings and could slide the bookshelves over any time he got the jitters too bad. He glanced at the tins of food and the bottles of water he'd brought along and assured himself this wasn't so hard. He wouldn't starve, and he had light and enough extra batteries in his pocket to last for days, if it came to that.

Sitting cross-legged on the floor, he opened his laptop. Footage from four of the six cameras he'd hidden around the house filled the screen: the foyer, the kitchen, the living room and one of the upstairs rooms. He'd found the fuse box in the basement earlier and now the house was awash with light. Good old Alicia Brennan, still paying the electricity bills for an empty house. It was a wonder the rich stayed rich.

He watched the foyer camera showing the front door. After a short wait, he saw it open and a muscular, clean-shaven Arabic man entered, wearing a dark suit that strained at the seams. Thorpe enlarged the image so it filled the screen and watched the man look around for a few seconds with his hand under his jacket. He said something to the ones outside. Then came a man sporting a precisely cut goatee and wire-rim glasses. This one wore a far better-tailored suit. The third was similarly dressed. He had a full beard and carried a large briefcase with him. Finally, another one entered, even bigger than the first and wearing a polo-neck and dark slacks. He stood just inside the doorway, looking in every direction.

Then the first three marched through the double doors at their left and went out of shot while the fourth stayed by the door. Thorpe reached for his walkie-talkie, shrank the screen and enlarged the one for the living room. He watched as the three men approached the centre of the empty room, where Thorpe had left another walkie-talkie for them. The bespectacled man reached down and picked it up off the floor. That would be Sayyid, then. Thorpe checked his watch and pressed the transmit button. 'Almost perfect timing, my friend,' he said. 'Two minutes early, in fact.'

Sayyid looked in all directions before bringing the radio to his mouth. 'This is . . . unexpected, Martin. We do not meet face to face?'

'I'm shy, Sayyid. And there's only one of me while there are four of you.' Thorpe smiled at that part. 'Don't worry, I can do this remotely. Now I've placed parts of the file in four separate locations somewhere on these grounds. How we do this is I'll tell you where I've hidden the first piece so your man mountain can bring it back for your bearded friend. As soon as he's verified its authenticity, you can wire a quarter of my fee to the account number I gave you. Once I get confirmation from my bank, I'll give you the next location and . . . well, you can guess the rest.'

'Yes. Although it does raise the question of how we arrange the last payment. I will have the final part in my hand before it is paid, yes?'

'Kind of,' Thorpe said. 'But let's cross that bridge when we come to it. I've had time to think this all through so we both end up with what we want.'

'As you say. Please begin.'

'Okay. If your friend goes back to the entrance hall and climbs the stairs, he'll take the left-hand corridor. There are three doorways on the left. He'll take the second one. There's a walk-in wardrobe against the room's far wall. If he pulls up the carpet in there, he'll find a floorboard that comes away with a little effort. Tell him to bring you what he finds.'

'Very well.' On the screen, Thorpe watched Sayyid saying a few words to the bigger man, who then marched off.

Thorpe leaned back against the wall and waited. For the most part he was in good spirits now that everything was working out as he'd planned. But the anger he felt at Danny's failure to show up soon threatened to override his satisfaction. The stupid, smelly bitch just couldn't keep her mind on the end game, could she? She was trustworthy in so many other areas, why did she have to give in to her addictions so easily? Once this was over, she'd need to be taught a lesson or two. Thorpe closed his eyes, and after a few moments his good humour returned as he considered ways in which he might punish her. Painful ways.

He opened his eyes and the big man was already on the living room monitor again and in deep conversation with his boss. He'd missed him entirely. *Careful, Martin. Keep your thoughts on the job at hand.* He watched Sayyid bring the radio to his mouth and say, 'There is nothing there.'

Thorpe frowned. So the big one *was* as stupid as he looked. He got the sigh out before he pressed the transmit button. 'I put it there less than two hours ago, Sayyid. *Left*-hand corridor. *Second* room on the left. *Loose* floorboard in the wardrobe. Explain it to him. It's not rocket science.'

'That is unnecessary. Naji speaks your language far better than I and he followed your instructions to the letter. He found the loose floorboard already open, but nothing inside.'

Thorpe's mouth opened as he finally understood why Danny hadn't showed up. Bishop. And if he'd taken her cell, that meant . . . 'There's somebody else in the house, Sayyid,' he said. 'Name of Bishop. He must have heard the directions and got there first.'

'Who is this man?'

'I used him to get the file,' he said, shrinking the cameras down so he could fit all six on screen. 'He's dangerous.'

'So what do you suggest?'

Thorpe thought for a moment. 'I suggest, since you're all probably armed, that you find him and take him out.'

Sayyid looked at his colleagues and said, 'This is your problem, Martin. We are not your personal assassins.'

'Not even for ten million bucks?'

Sayyid lowered the radio and spoke to the others. A minute later, he raised it to his lips again. 'My associate, Hanif, has offered up a far more acceptable solution. The original arrangement was fifty million dollars for the file, yes? If you are willing to stick to that agreement, we would be more than happy to help you in this situation. In effect, Martin, you lose nothing, depending on how you choose to look at it.'

'Be serious,' Thorpe said, trying to ignore the sick feeling he was getting in his stomach.

'I generally am about such matters. Come now, my friend, as a businessman you must realize the scales have shifted in our favour. And unless you are willing to take on this man by yourself . . .' He let the sentence hang, knowing he held the winning hand.

Thorpe closed his eyes and banged his head against the steel wall. *Shit. Shit. Shit.* He tried to think of another way around it, but knew it would ultimately mean giving away his position. And he couldn't do that. Not for any price. Without Danny at his side, Sayyid's offer was the only option left open to him. Which meant Bishop had just cost him fifty million dollars. Fifty *million*. He couldn't believe it.

He raised the walkie-talkie and said, 'You're a goddamn thief, Sayyid.' A pause, and then he said, 'Do it.'

'Consider it done,' Sayyid said. 'But please refrain from blas—'

At that moment, all six cameras went dark.

# NINETY-SEVEN

Bishop took his hand from the ruined fuse box and ran up the basement steps. He passed through the utility room and turned left for the rear stairs. At the turn halfway up, he climbed two more steps and crouched down. He kept his gun and flashlight aimed at the bottom of the stairs.

Wherever Thorpe was, and Bishop had his suspicions, he'd be giving this Sayyid his location right now before assuming radio silence. One or more of them would undoubtedly be along in a matter of seconds to check it out.

Bishop was counting on it.

He'd entered the house the same way as before and hadn't had long to wait before the terrorists showed up. After logging each face as they'd entered, he'd listened in on the conversation and beaten the one called Naji to the first location. Right now, the abandoned Zodiac letter, the envelope, the medical report on Ebert and the book on codes and ciphers were safely hidden in the wardrobe in Natalie's den.

Six seconds had passed since he'd plunged the house into darkness. He figured they'd just send one to check the basement and cover him from a distance. About thirty yards directly ahead, the rear windows let in just enough light for him to make out basic shapes in the darkness. And then he saw a movement.

The silhouette of a machine pistol was gradually coming into view from the left. For a second Bishop thought it might be another Heckler & Koch, but the extended magazine wasn't curved. Maybe a Steyr of some kind. Then came the hand holding it and part of a big forearm. Bishop heard no sound at all and he knew these weren't amateurs.

Part of the big man's body came into view and Bishop heard a faint breath as the silhouette changed, the profile morphing into a shapeless mass as the man turned towards the stairwell.

Bishop aimed his flashlight at the head area and clicked it on. The man squeezed his eyes shut against the light and Bishop pulled his trigger twice. He saw two roses instantly bloom in the centre of the man's forehead before he switched the light off. Then Bishop ducked into the steps at his left, pulling his feet out of the line of fire as a stream of bullets ploughed into the wall and ceiling behind him. Small particles of plaster erupted at each hit, striking the back of his neck like hailstones as the dying man reflexively emptied his gun.

Bishop ran up the rest of the steps and took the right fork at the top. As he ran through the dark hallway towards the front of the house he heard short, controlled bursts of gunfire in the stairway behind. He pocketed the flashlight and pulled out a five-inch-long steel hexagonal tube instead. The M84 stun grenade he'd found in Cortiss's apartment and stashed in his knapsack. Perfect for taking out the man stationed at the front door.

But as Bishop passed the last door on the right, something big slammed into him. He landed face down on the floor without his gun, but still holding the flash-bang. He rolled onto his back and a pair of hands grabbed his collar and pulled him to a standing position. Then the man's arms wrapped themselves around him and squeezed, trapping his arms hard against his side and lifting him off the floor. *The fourth guy*, he thought. The man must have raced upstairs the moment he heard the shots and waited for Bishop to run right into him.

The man's strength was remarkable and Bishop felt a rib snap under the pressure as his breath exited his lungs in a single burst. In response, he slammed his head forward and felt it connect with something soft. It felt like a nose giving way. The man gave a sharp grunt and took a step back and his grip loosened enough for Bishop to pull his left hand free.

Bishop took the stun grenade and smashed it into the man's mouth, jamming it in as far as it would go. The man choked and let go of Bishop as his hands went to his busted face. Bishop pushed the man's hands away and grabbed hold of the grenade's primary and secondary pull rings. He yanked them free, then pulled the man's polo-neck up over his face to keep it all in. He took two steps back, dropped his shoulder and aimed a side-kick at the man's stomach. The man doubled over, and as he fell backwards on to the landing Bishop turned and dived to the floor, clamping his eyes shut and pressing both hands against his ears.

The grenade detonated inside the man's skull and a brief, thunderous explosion of sound and light reverberated throughout the open space.

Taking the Maglite from his pocket, Bishop got up and swept the beam around the floor. Ignoring the man's body as it rolled down the stairs, he found his Beretta a few feet away and picked it up. He turned off the light and ran back down the corridor. He turned right at the end, past the rear stairs, then right again until he was in the next hallway along.

Bishop remembered the house layout well enough. There were three rooms on the left side. On the right, opposite the middle doorway, was the door to a windowless storeroom. That would be okay, except the door had always been locked before, and he needed to move quickly. And the first and third rooms on the left both contained floor-to-ceiling windows. No good, either. Too much chance of throwing light on his position when he opened either door. But the one in the centre had just a normal-sized window facing some trees. Not much light at all. Bishop jogged down the hallway and brushed his fingers against the right wall. When they felt the storeroom door, he gripped the handle and pushed. As he'd suspected, still locked. Instead he entered the door opposite and closed it behind him.

Bishop leaned against the door and touched his left rib, wincing at the sudden flare-up of pain. Felt like it was cracked. He was falling apart at the seams. But he was alive, while the terrorists were down two men. Just the ones called Sayyid and Hanif left. And they wouldn't be as careless now they knew what they were up against. They'd search the rest of the house together, each covering the other's back.

He raised his eyes to the ceiling and the familiar shape there made him wonder if Thorpe was watching him now. Bishop knew top-end surveillance cameras could make the most of low-light situations, but even if Thorpe *could* see him, so what? He couldn't transmit anything by radio without making targets of the other two.

But nothing was stopping them from conveying messages via cell phones. And sooner or later Bishop would have to pass through the kitchen or some other monitored area where Thorpe could see him. He couldn't stay here and wait to be cornered like a rat. Not when they had automatic weapons and ammo to spare.

Bishop closed his eyes. And thought of ways of turning a liability into an advantage.

# NINETY-EIGHT

Thorpe watched the miniature screens and asked himself why he hadn't put a camera in every room. The answer was obvious: because he'd banked on Danny being here with him to take up the slack. So much for covering all bases.

At least he had decent equipment, although the one he'd placed in the hallway directly underneath had become next to useless. He'd shut all the doors down there and with no natural light coming in from the windows the screen just showed black.

But the living room monitor showed movement as the two surviving terrorists made their way to the entrance hall. Sayyid was in the lead while Hanif covered the rear. Then Thorpe's attention was drawn to the monitor showing the hallway underneath him. For a moment there, he thought he'd seen a flash of something from one of the doorways. He kept his eyes glued to it. Then a vague movement around Naji's body on the kitchen monitor diverted his attention. He peered closer to see if it happened again. The man's legs were sprawled on the kitchen floor while the top half lay in deep shadow on the bottom four steps. The left arm was still in an unnatural position behind his back. Sayyid had moved it there to retrieve some extra magazines from one of the pockets. Thorpe watched, fascinated, as the arm slowly slid off and came to rest on the stairs. There was no more movement after that.

Possibly gas escaping from the body. Or something else?

He frowned and, without taking his eyes from the screen, reached over and picked up Bishop's cell phone off the floor.

# NINETY-NINE

As soon as he heard the floorboard creak, Bishop knew his text message to Sayyid had worked. He'd used the cell he'd taken from Naji's suit pocket after replacing the SIM card with one of the spares Jenna had given him. So the message pointing them to Bishop's supposed location wouldn't be seen as originating from a dead man's phone.

The moment he heard the muffled sound of a door being kicked in, Bishop pulled his own door open and saw the two figures framed in the doorway of the room opposite. They had their weapons raised as they scanned the room.

Bishop raised his Beretta and squeezed the trigger three times at the figure on the left. Two centre mass, one in the head. All three hit home and he saw blood spurt from the head wound as the man went down.

He shifted his aim to the second one and saw the glint of spectacles on his face as he turned. The man was quick. Bishop fired off two shots at his chest section and saw him fall. He landed on the floor with his weapon pointing in Bishop's direction. Bishop aimed for the head area and fired twice, but the man was still moving and both shots went wide.

Then Bishop felt the pitter patter of rounds hitting the wall above his head, he leapt back and crawled to the wall at the left of the doorway. The terrorist's machine gun spat a chain of bullets at the spot he'd just vacated, punching holes in the doorjamb and wall and littering the carpet with plaster and wood. Bishop heard the ejected shells clattering against a wall in the hallway, and then there was just a clicking sound. The man's gun was empty.

Bishop got to his feet and heard a magazine being pulled from its housing. He slipped around the doorframe, Beretta pointed at the spot where he'd seen the man fall.

It was Sayyid.

The terrorist lay on his back amidst a pool of blood. In the darkness it looked like black oil. His free hand struggled with a spare magazine that had gotten snagged in his well-tailored jacket pocket. He looked up at Bishop as he finally got the magazine free and snarled, '*Yela'an mayteen ahlak.*'

'How would *you* know?' Bishop said, and shot him in the left eye.

His Arabic was poor at best, but he'd gotten the general gist of what Sayyid was saying. Something about God placing a curse on his family's graves. Not that it affected Bishop one way or the other; insults were better left in the schoolyard. Bishop just hoped he'd meet his own end with a little more dignity.

He turned to the other one. The one called Hanif was lying on his stomach with his arms outstretched, head on one side and dead eyes turned towards his associate. Placing the Beretta in the back of his waistband, Bishop leaned down and plucked the weapon out of his hand.

It was a Steyr TMP. A lightweight, compact, Austrian machine pistol he'd used once in another life. Deadly accurate with almost no recoil. No wonder terrorists loved it. Removing the magazine, Bishop saw there were still six rounds left. He replaced the magazine, then leaned down and pulled his knife from its ankle holster.

Then, with a weapon in each hand, he walked to the staircase that led to the next floor.

Towards Thorpe.

# ONE HUNDRED

By the time Bishop reached the third floor landing, he was still holding the Steyr but not the knife. He checked the bathroom and the old fitness room, then pushed open the double doors to Brennan's office and stepped inside.

There was enough light coming through the window to see the large desk straight ahead. He glanced briefly at the entranceway to the adjoining room at his right before he stepped over to the bookshelves. Inserting his hand into the fourth shelf down, he pressed the soft area on the side and slid the whole bookcase across.

'No sudden movements, James,' Thorpe said from behind him.

Bishop stood motionless.

'Know how much you've cost me?' Then, without waiting for a reply, Thorpe said, 'Drop the hardware, keep your arms high and turn around real slow.'

Bishop opened his left hand and dropped the Steyr. He raised his arms and turned to face Thorpe, who was standing six feet away with his Glock aimed at Bishop's face.

'A fortune, I hope,' he said.

Thorpe shook his head. 'No. Much more than that. But don't worry, there are plenty of other groups who want what I've got and you won't be around to screw it up next time. I figure you've got your Beretta under the shirt, right? Get rid of it in slow motion.'

Bishop sighed, reached back with his left hand and pulled it out. He threw it towards the desk and heard it land on the floor by one of the legs.

'Now the knife. The one you always keep on your ankle.'

Left arm stretched out for balance, Bishop leaned down and pulled the left trouser leg up with his bandaged hand to show him the empty holster. 'Not any more,' he said, rising again. 'I found it a nice new home.'

'Where is it?'

'Lodged in the space where Danny's vocal cords should have been.' Bishop smiled, hoping Thorpe could see it. He raised his right hand with its blood-soaked bandage before lowering both arms to his sides, keeping the left one slightly angled at the elbow. 'Skinny bitch took one of my fingers, but it was worth it. I slashed at her face a few times before I finished her. Pay her back in kind for what she did to Jenna.'

Thorpe's gun hand wavered a little, and in the low moonlight Bishop watched him blink. 'Couldn't bear touching it again,' he said. 'Not with her stink on it. You know, I think she probably smells better now than when she was alive.'

'I don't believe you,' Thorpe said, and his gun moved slightly off its target.

'Oh, she's dead all right.'

'Not that,' Thorpe said, and the gun moved back again. 'The face slashing. That isn't your style at all.'

'Don't count on it. You tend to bring out the worst in people.'

'I don't buy it. You don't have the strength of will for that kind of work.'

'Strength of will? Is that all you need to torture a helpless victim, or does there need to be a personal element, too?'

'We talking about Natalie Brennan now?'

'Who else?' Bishop said. Cupping the fingers of his left hand, he began to straighten his arm down and said, 'She must have really got her hooks into you, for you to slice her up like you did.'

'Maybe just a little,' Thorpe said, moving his gun around again to underline the last word. 'Who knows? Just a shame I didn't have more time to play with her, but I was working to a deadline that day.' He shook his head. 'Man, don't you just hate deadlines?'

Bishop said nothing. With his left arm now straight, he allowed the knife to slide down his elbow until the polymer handle landed on his middle two fingers.

Thorpe said, 'To be honest, she reminded me a lot of a girl from my past, and I always get carried away when that little whore rears her pretty head.'

'Yeah? You kill her, too?' The blade had snagged against the shirt cuff and Bishop stretched his arm to try to free it. No good. He couldn't extend it far enough.

'I had to, before she dragged me down with her. You must have known girls like that, right?'

*Not really*, Bishop thought, but he shrugged and the shoulder movement allowed enough space for the blade to come free of his cuff. Then he began using his fingers to carefully rotate the knife like the second hand on a clock, so it was pointing towards the floor. *Just keep talking, Thorpe*, he thought. *Let it all out. I'm a real good listener.*

'Sure you have,' Thorpe said. 'Every man meets his female nemesis at some point in his life. Fiona was mine.'

'Doesn't sound like she was,' Bishop said, flinching as the blade cut into his pinkie finger. 'Yours, I mean.'

'Ha. Ain't *that* the truth. Any guy who crossed her path was fair game for her, and she couldn't wait to tell me about each and every one of them.' Thorpe shrugged. 'It was just Natalie's bad luck she looked so similar.'

'You sure taught her a lesson, though, right?' Bishop said. He manoeuvred the blade carefully along until he had it lodged tight between his index finger and thumb. The other three fingers lined up next to the index finger for support. He was ready.

'Yeah, well, I admit I went a little crazy with the knife at the end there.' Thorpe chuckled to himself. 'Heat of the moment, you know?'

Bishop was only partly listening. Most of his attention was on the barrel of the Glock. Waiting for something in Thorpe's speech pattern that would cause the gun to point away from Bishop's head. Just for a second.

'So if you think you can bait me by telling me how you killed Danny,' Thorpe said, tapping his gun in the air like a drumstick on every third or fourth word, 'well, I can't deny I'm a little pissed off, but life goes on. Or at least, *my*—'

And when the gun barrel moved this time, so did Bishop.

# ONE HUNDRED AND ONE

He had to throw it underhanded, which wasn't his favoured style. But he'd already picked out his target, and the moment the gun barrel wavered an inch to the left of his head, he bent his knees, brought his left arm back and, keeping his wrist straight, swung it towards Thorpe. At the last possible moment, he let go of the knife.

He didn't actually see it leave his outstretched hand. One moment it was between his fingers, the next it was in Thorpe's right shoulder, just beneath the collarbone. Thorpe grunted in surprise and looked down at the weapon protruding from his body as his gun hand jerked upwards in reflex and fired a shot into the ceiling.

Bishop rushed towards Thorpe and rammed his shoulders into his chest, his left hand grabbing hold of Thorpe's right wrist as they both fell back through the doorway to the connecting room. Bishop got a foot under one of Thorpe's to trip him and both men landed on the floor in a jumbled heap. He lost his grip on Thorpe's gun hand and Thorpe quickly rolled to the side and plucked the knife from his shoulder with his free hand.

Bishop saw the last folding chair a few feet away. He got to his feet and picked it up. He slammed it shut and saw Thorpe bringing the Glock round in his direction. Grabbing the flattened chair by its legs, Bishop raised it above his shoulders and swung it like a tennis racquet at the side of Thorpe's head, hearing a satisfying crack as it made contact. Thorpe slammed back against the floor while the gun skittered across the carpet into one of the corners.

Bishop dropped the chair and placed his heel on Thorpe's left wrist, grinding it hard into the skin until the hand opened and the knife fell out. Thorpe groaned in pain and clutched his ruined wrist. Bishop knelt down, retrieved his knife and pressed it against Thorpe's throat, the blade digging into the flesh just above the Adam's apple.

'Don't,' Thorpe said.

'Shut up,' Bishop said, and ran his hands over Thorpe's clothes. He found two more syringes inside the jacket. Each was unmarked and held a clear solution, just like the one he'd been given in Price's basement. Bishop put them in his pocket. He also found a pack of batteries, a set of keys and two cell phones. He tossed the batteries and keys and checked the phones. Jenna's Motorola and one that had to be Thorpe's. He pocketed the Motorola and tossed the other.

'Stay right there,' Bishop said and got to his feet.

Thorpe remained on his back with his left hand clutching his shoulder wound and the other hand gripping the left wrist. Watching Bishop.

Bishop went over and picked up the Glock. Then he went over to the window and looked down. A three-storey drop. No ledge. Same as before. Not exactly a viable means of escape. Especially not in Thorpe's current condition. Satisfied, he walked into the next room. With one eye on the entranceway, he picked up his Beretta and the Steyr. He stuck the Beretta in his waistband, emptied the Glock of ammunition and placed the shells on Brennan's desk. Wiping his prints from the gun, he pulled the vault door open and tossed it inside. Same procedure with the Steyr, although this he threw into the hallway outside.

Bishop walked back into the adjoining room and saw Thorpe was trying to sit up.

'Don't bother getting up,' Bishop said. He grabbed hold of Thorpe's collar and dragged him along the floor into the other room. When he reached the bookshelves, he let go and just waited while Thorpe propped himself against them.

Thorpe touched his left cheek and winced. 'Look, I wasn't lying about that footage of you and Cortiss,' he said. 'I got it in storage. I can take you right to it.'

'Later,' Bishop said. 'First, tell me where you hid the other three parts of the file. We'll be going through the house together and if you're lying about any of the locations, I'll remove your thumbs. To start with.'

'Hey, no problem. First one's in the kitchen, behind the back plate of the oven. Just need to click it free and you'll see it. Next one's in the room those two idiots broke into. The space under the windowsill.'

'And the third?'

'That gazebo out back. Under one of the paving stones. Want me to take you now?' Thorpe placed a hand on the floor and began to rise.

Bishop motioned with the gun. 'I told you not to get up.'

'What? But I thought . . .' Thorpe's eyes widened and he raised his palm towards Bishop. 'Hey, hey, don't forget the footage. I swear I wasn't lying about that. You think I'd get rid of something I could use against you? On that key chain you took from my pocket, there's a key that opens a unit at a place called Armistad Storage. It's on Southern Boulevard in the Bronx, and they got thousands of units there. You'll never find it without me.'

Bishop shrugged and said, 'You're probably right.' He reached into his own pocket, pulled out the two syringes and dropped them on Thorpe's lap. 'But right now, I want you to take your pick of these and choose a vein.'

Thorpe looked down at them, his mouth open. Then back at Bishop.

'I'm giving you the same choice you gave me, Thorpe. Assuming they contain the same junk, you'll have an hour before you can move again. I figure it won't take the cops long to figure out where I've gone, especially if somebody saw this house lit up earlier. You might beat them, which is unlikely, or you might end up with a lot of explaining to do. But you'll be alive.'

Thorpe just stared at him and said, 'Hey, come on now . . .'

'Or I can shoot you right now.' Bishop aimed the gun at his head. 'I'd recommend the second choice. It's quicker and cleaner, but it's your decision. No more talk. You got thirty seconds.'

Thorpe just stared at the syringes in his lap, shaking his head as he picked one up. He rolled up his left sleeve and Bishop watched him pop the protective cap off and insert the needle into his arm. Then he depressed the plunger until there was nothing left.

'Good. Now break the needles off against the floor and put the hypos in your pocket.'

Thorpe did as he was told and said, 'You'll never find that storage locker on your own.'

'It doesn't matter any more,' Bishop said. 'What does matter is that Natalie died right here in this room. And she died hard.'

He crouched down and Thorpe flinched.

'See, that's the part that bothers me most,' he continued. 'Natalie was just a kid with a life full of choice ahead of her. Until you came along and cut it short like it was nothing. And you made her last minutes on earth a living hell, while I was maybe a hundred feet away.

That's some debt I owe her. Today, we're gonna balance the books a little.' He waved a hand in front of Thorpe's face, but the eyes just stared straight ahead. He picked up Thorpe's hand by the index finger and watched it drop back onto his lap like a lump of clay. 'Looks like your special cocktail's really kicking in now. Anything to say while you're still able?'

Thorpe blinked and visibly swallowed a couple of times. Then, without moving his lips, he said, 'You'll . . . kill . . . ee . . . ow?'

'Sorry, Thorpe. Unlike you, I keep my promises. You'll stay alive a while longer, but I guarantee you won't like it. Here, I'll show you.'

Bishop stood up, took hold of Thorpe's collar again and dragged him through the doorway into the vault. He propped Thorpe against the wall, then pulled out his flashlight and shone it around the interior until he found the lamp on the floor. He walked over and switched it on. The light was dim, but it allowed him to see the vault interior clearly enough. The room was about ten foot by twenty. No visible air vents and a ceiling close enough to touch. Nice and cosy. He looked at the bottles of water and dried foods Thorpe had brought in. And the open laptop in the middle of the floor and another cell phone that looked familiar. Walking over, he picked up his Nokia and said, 'You won't need this any more.' He put it in his pocket and then stamped on the laptop. 'Or that.'

The food and water he left.

Bishop examined the three-inch thick door from this side. Its only feature was the inner handle. There were no emergency release or alarm buttons in sight. Banks had them, but Brennan had clearly decided they weren't needed in a private vault. No combination settings units either, so any changes presumably had to be done via the outer dial while the door was open.

'You know, if I was a betting man,' he said, 'I'd wager you reset the combination on this a while back, so only you could access it.' Bishop looked around the chamber again. 'That'd be the smart thing to do, and you always were smart. I wonder how long the air will last once the door shuts. I'm guessing thirty-six hours. Forty-eight at a push, although it'll probably seem a lot longer. Still, it'll give you time to think.' He nodded at the lamp on the floor. 'And you've got that. I wouldn't want to leave you completely in the dark.' He crouched down before Thorpe. 'Walls beginning to close in yet?'

Thorpe's lids blinked automatically. The rhythmic rise and fall of his chest was just visible, but nothing else moved.

Bishop said, 'When I was in that basement you left me my gun, so I thought I'd grant you the same courtesy.' He pointed a finger at the empty Glock lying near the broken laptop. 'You'll find it just over there.'

Then he stood and checked the vault one final time. He turned, and was about to step through the doorway when he remembered the Beretta in his waistband. He pulled it out. The bullets in three of the bodies could be matched to this gun, but without serial numbers it couldn't be traced to him. Not if it wasn't on his person. He ejected the six remaining rounds and pocketed them. Then he wiped the gun and magazine of prints before dropping it on the floor. As he stepped through the entrance he turned and said, 'When you pull the trigger, I want you to think of Natalie.'

He pulled the steel door shut, pushing the handle down until he heard the locking bar click into place with a heavy, metallic thud. He spun the dial anti-clockwise a few times, then tried pulling the handle into the open position. It wouldn't budge. Bishop placed his palm on the vault door and smiled before pulling the bookcase across to cover it up again.

*Sweet dreams, Thorpe.*

Turning to the desk, he took the six rounds from his pocket and added them to the rest. Might as well leave them here. No point taking them with him if he no longer had a gun. Although the casings would still have his prints on them. Bishop needed to split before the cops showed up, but he could spare a few seconds to wipe them off first. Having the law place him at the scene of another bloodbath was the last thing he needed. He grabbed hold of his shirt tail and was using it to pick up the first shell when he heard the soft scuffle of feet and turned round.

An Arabic man in a black tracksuit stood in the doorway. His arm was outstretched towards Bishop and at the end of it was a gun.

Bishop saw a flash and then something punched him in the solar plexus. He fell against the desk and collapsed to the floor, both legs stretched out before him, head propped against a table leg. He saw another flash and his body jerked as something slammed into his left thigh. He coughed and felt the metallic taste of blood in his throat, and he wondered why he hadn't heard either of the shots.

He looked up and saw the man enter the room and point the gun at his head. And he understood. Silencer. At the same time, weird pulsating colours started to appear at the edges of his vision and he wondered what they meant. He closed his eyes and the colours disappeared. That was better. They were beginning to annoy him.

Bishop decided to keep his eyes closed for a while. He already had a good idea of what was coming next.

# ONE HUNDRED AND TWO

When Bishop opened his eyes agian, the room was bathed in light and the gun had been replaced by three others. They were all pointing at his head and looked to be Heckler & Koch MP5s. Longer versions of the machine pistols used by Cortiss and his band of mercenaries three years before. The owners of these ones wore ski masks and dark jump-suits. *Looks like we've come full circle*, Bishop thought, and smiled.

The man in the centre moved aside. In the gap, Bishop saw a woman in similar battle gear walking towards him. Instead of a ski mask, she wore a black cap that didn't entirely hide her blond hair. Deputy Marshal Delaney crouched down in front of him and he saw she was another one of those women who looked prettier close up. She didn't look as stern in real life and the intense, dark brown eyes reminded him a lot of his sister Amy.

Bishop slowly stretched his arms out towards her with his wrists held together.

A corner of Delaney's mouth turned up and she pushed his arms down again. 'You don't have much respect for our intelligence, do you, Bishop?'

He said nothing. Just watched her look at the bandaged hand before her gaze turned to the gunshot wounds in his side and thigh. The blood had clotted while he was out and it looked as though the bullets hadn't hit any vital arteries. Everything still hurt, though.

'Try not to move. Ambulance is on its way and should get here in another ten minutes. I think you'll live in the meantime, tough guy like you.'

Bishop cleared his throat and asked, 'How'd you find me?'

'We checked all the messages on Daniella Costa's cell and found a reference to something known as BH. It took a while but I thought this house seemed worth a look.'

'There was a fifth man . . .'

'Yeah,' she said. 'He thought he could blast his way out. He was wrong.' She turned to the men surrounding her and said, 'Okay, guys. I think I can handle him from here.' The men lowered their weapons and silently walked out of the room, one by one. She watched them go and turned back to Bishop. 'Everything here shouts a deal gone wrong. I'm guessing the dead men were Thorpe's buyers for the file you found?'

Bishop creased his brow together. That hurt, too. 'You know about Thorpe?'

'I told you we're not stupid. Even before Miss Falstaff told us her story, I knew there was something wrong with the guy. The past ten hours have been illuminating, to say the least.'

'Go on,' he said.

'I'm the one with the badge,' she said, 'which means you go first. Try to be concise.'

Bishop took a breath and then gave a condensed account of the last four days, leaving out Aleron, Luke, Wilson, and the break-in at RoyseCorp. As for his presence here, he'd come to confront Thorpe and found himself caught in a crossfire between the two parties. He'd been searching the house for Thorpe when the fifth man shot him.

When he finished, Delaney said, 'I noticed a few gaps in there. For instance, you don't have a gun on you. Just how were you planning on confronting Thorpe exactly?'

Bishop nodded towards the holster at his ankle. 'Got a knife.'

'Uh, huh. So you're saying Thorpe shot them all?' Without waiting for an answer, she asked, 'Any idea who they are?'

He shook his head. 'In Price's basement, Thorpe intimated al-Qaeda. Don't know for sure.'

'Okay. So what was in the file?'

'Various FBI files relating to the Zodiac killer from forty years ago. I'm guessing his identity's in there and it's somebody important, but Thorpe broke up the party and put a bullet in Price before I could find out. How is he, by the way?'

'Price? He's still unconscious, but I hear they got the bullet out okay. They told me a fraction of an inch to the left and he'd be in a wheel-chair for the rest of his life. So it was Thorpe who killed Cortiss?'

'Right.' He pulled his Nokia from his pocket and handed it to her. 'But I recorded my conversation with him on this. He managed to fill in quite a few blanks before Thorpe got to him.' He paused, then said, 'Okay, I showed you mine.'

Delaney sighed and got to her feet. Putting the cell in her pocket, she walked over and leaned her back against the bookshelves. 'After it became obvious you weren't following the usual pattern of a fugitive, I looked deeper into the events of three years ago to see if I could find something there. And that's when things began to look flaky.'

'Flaky?'

'Definitely flaky. Things didn't add up for a lot of reasons I won't go into now, although your previous spotless record was a big stand-out. So I delved further into the lives of the other three survivors and Martin Thorpe came up with a big red flag. You know he used to be a DEA agent?'

Bishop shook his head. Thorpe had told him he used to work for the Justice Department but had never gone into specifics. But the DEA made sense. It also explained Thorpe's fascination with drugs and what they could do.

'Well, he was with them for almost five years until he left to join RoyseCorp. His record was sealed, too, which raised my antennae further.'

'You mean it isn't any longer?'

'Not since I got a Supreme Court judge to unlock it last night. I'm not telling tales out of school when I say Martin Thorpe is a *very* bad man. He worked undercover within the Cattrall drug organization in the nineties under the alias Roy Hedison, and from all accounts he adapted to his new identity a little too easily. Seems he had a particular talent for extracting information from suspected informers. His favoured method was to kidnap the victim's teenage niece or daughter, dope her up and then rape her in front of him. Once the poor bastard talked, Thorpe would kill him and pass the kid on to one of their prostitution outlets.'

Bishop nodded. This was all news to him, but it fit with what he now knew of Thorpe's character. He also figured the cocktail's effects had to have worn off by now. He pictured a terrified Thorpe less than ten feet away, smashing his fists against the walls and screaming to be released from his soundproofed tomb. It had to be a living hell in there for him. Bishop almost smiled at the image. 'After what he did to Natalie Brennan,' he said, 'that doesn't surprise me.'

'Well, it surprised his superiors when a couple of low-level runners who got arrested named him as the one who tortured and killed a Manuel Rose and raped his fourteen-year-old daughter. And probably a whole lot more besides.'

'Let me guess,' Bishop said. 'They decided a trial would taint the whole agency for years to come and that a simple resignation would be best for everybody.'

'Close enough. They also forbade him from applying for any kind of job in law enforcement and then sealed his file for good measure. So the last few hours have seen us using warrants to search his two apartments. One of them, we found two naked, underage hookers desperate for their next fix. More important as far as you're concerned, we also found a receipt for a storage locker registered to one Roy Hedison.'

Bishop raised his eyebrows. So Thorpe had been on the level. About that, anyway.

'Want to know what we found in there?'

'Since I'm not lying here in cuffs, I'm guessing something that puts me in the clear. Maybe footage from the cameras he'd placed around the house?'

'And then some,' Delaney said. She turned as a man in a black windbreaker came in. Bishop recognized him as the one who accompanied Delaney to the hospital. His voice was too low for Bishop to hear anything and after a few seconds Delaney sighed and said, 'But I'd like one more go round to make sure, okay, Mitch?'

''Kay, chief,' he said, and after a brief glance at Bishop he left the room.

Delaney narrowed her eyes at Bishop and said, 'No sign of Thorpe so far.'

'Probably miles away by now,' he said, and heard the sound of squeaky wheels on the carpet outside. The paramedics were here. 'I'd be surprised if we ever heard from him again.'

'Uh, huh.' Delaney turned to the bookcase at her back and tapped her knuckles against the wood. 'Didn't Brennan Senior keep his vault behind here?'

'Yeah.'

'Hmm.' She turned back to Bishop with the same frown, and a second later two paramedics appeared in the doorway with a gurney in tow.

The taller one said, 'Gunshot victim.'

Delaney waved a hand at Bishop. 'Among other things.'

The men entered and lowered the gurney next to Bishop, then knelt down on either side and carefully transferred him onto it. All the while, Bishop kept his eyes on Delaney. He watched her turn back to the bookcase with a pensive expression. She rested one hand on a shelf and he heard her tapping her fingernails against the wood. The gurney was raised to its normal height and Bishop felt compresses against his thigh and side. Then the shorter paramedic pointed the wheeled stretcher towards the double doors.

The taller one grabbed hold of the front and said, 'Okay, Marshal?'

Delaney was silent for a few more seconds. Then she gently slapped her palm against the shelf and said, 'Okay, let's go.'

They began wheeling Bishop towards the doorway and Delaney came over and walked alongside. Looking down at him, she asked, 'You suppose there's anybody left who knows the combination to that thing?'

'Can't think who,' Bishop said and turned his face to the ceiling. 'Far as I know, the only man who did took it to his grave.'

# EPILOGUE

When the whistle blew, both sides trudged off the playing field. They made their way back to their respective changing rooms, ready to face the music for the goalless first half. Spectators all around the stadium rose to get drinks or empty their bladders. Or both. Bishop did neither. He just stayed in his lower level seat and unfolded his afternoon edition of the *New York Times* to the front page again.

The bold headline hadn't changed. It still read, US ATTORNEY GENERAL ROBERT HEMMING RESIGNS. Underneath, the sub-headline read, *Long-term supporter of President steps down after five years for undisclosed personal reasons*. The photo at the top was taken from the press conference this morning. Robert Hemming looked as though he'd aged ten years overnight.

Bishop read a little more of the story, but when it started regurgitating the same few facts in an effort to fill up space he gave up. Dropping the paper onto his lap, he leaned back, whistling through his teeth as he extended his aching right leg out in front. A few people were already returning to their seats on either side of him, but he ignored them and looked through the translucent roof to the cloudless sky above. He kind of missed the old Giants Stadium, but at least the new arena here in Harrison *felt* like a soccer stadium. There were no football lines on the turf, for a start. And it was real grass, too. The only thing missing was a beer, but the doctors had warned him when he left hospital last week that unless he wanted a new stomach he'd need to abstain for at least another month. He was willing to concede they knew their business.

After removing the two 9mm rounds from his left kidney and right thigh, most of the surgeons' efforts had been spent working on his abdominal wounds. One said he was amazed Bishop had stayed upright for so long with so much intestinal bleeding. They'd done a good job on him, though. Good enough to mean he was no longer coughing blood with every breath. His throat and ring finger were also healing, although he'd probably continue to sound like a poor man's Clint Eastwood for a while yet. Other than that, all he'd really lost was the top half of his pinky, which he'd never used much anyway.

Halfway through his two-week hospital stay, a detective named Kinneman had come to visit. He'd handed Bishop official notification of his overturned conviction, saying it was mostly thanks to the material found in Thorpe's storage locker. It seems he'd transferred his 'greatest' moments onto DVD for his personal viewing pleasure. In addition to the attack on Bishop by Cortiss, they found countless movies of Thorpe having sex with Natalie, as well as footage of Thorpe cutting Randall Brennan's throat in front of the vault.

A nationwide manhunt was still under way. Bishop wished them luck.

Kinneman also said no charges would be filed against him for Daniella Costa's death. That one came straight from the mayor's office. With the city edgy about a possible wrongful arrest suit, 'self-defence' worked for everyone. Especially once Jenna told the police her side of the story. Bishop was also currently involved in negotiations regarding compensation for the three years he'd spent inside. That is to say, his lawyer, Miles Pascombe, was involved. Pascombe seemed optimistic that they'd end up with a respectable figure at the end of it. Which would satisfy Bishop. Financially, at least.

And as for Jenna, well, they were both taking things at a slower pace now they had time to get to know each other, although he had a dinner invite tonight he meant to keep. She'd called earlier to say she couldn't go to the game with him as she wanted to visit Art Mandrake now he'd regained consciousness, but that she'd cook Bishop his meal of choice later. As long as he chose chili. God only knew what that was going to do to his stomach.

Most of his time, however, had been spent musing on what to do now the world was open to him again. He was currently resting at his folks' place on Staten Island, but he'd need to find work sooner or later. He just had no idea what. Close protection held no attraction for him any more. And besides, Bishop was no longer the same person. For one thing, he wasn't planning on taking orders from anybody ever again. He'd done that already and look where it got him. But he couldn't deny the decision limited his options somewhat.

'Penny for your thoughts, Sergeant,' said the man in the seat to his left.

'They're not for sale, Colonel,' Bishop said with a faint smile.

He turned to study his ex-employer's profile. Morgan Royse studied the stadium, his colourless lips set in a straight line. The Red Bulls cap he wore hid most of the salt-and-pepper hair, but the hooked nose was unmistakable. Up close, the bags under his eyes made him look older than his supposed sixty-five years.

'I didn't know you were a Bulls fan,' Bishop said. 'Excluding the guy sitting at my right, how many people you got around us?'

'I'm not,' Royse said. 'And four, but don't take it personally; they're my second skin when I'm away from the office.'

'The people who were sitting here might want their seats back.'

'They can afford to find others now. How are your wounds?'

'I'll walk with a limp for a while and I try not to laugh too much.' Bishop picked up the paper and tapped it against the empty seat in front. 'I figure Hemming's resignation is your doing. How'd you know about the files?'

Glancing at the newspaper, Royse settled back into his seat and said, 'Sergeant Price was happy to share his side of the story once I told him RoyseCorp was paying all his medical expenses; I was able to fill in the gaps myself. And a mostly empty house doesn't offer up a wealth of hiding places once you know what you're looking for. You know, I had a very uncomfortable meeting with Robert yesterday. He certainly didn't need much convincing when I urged him to step down. I don't think I've ever seen anybody look so devastated. The kind of knowledge he's been carrying around must weigh heavily on a man's soul.'

'Politicians don't have souls,' Bishop said. 'That's why they're politicians. So he knew, all this time?'

Royse nodded. 'Without going into specifics, he said he found out twenty years ago and hadn't spoken to his father since. He told me it was the main reason he'd wanted to gain public office. He figured serving his country would somehow make amends for his father's sins.'

Bishop arched his eyebrows. 'Somehow, I don't think entering politics was the answer. You find Thorpe's body, too?'

'And disposed of it. I didn't want Alicia to stumble upon it by mistake, assuming she ever goes back there. Nasty way to go. From the looks of it, Thorpe spent most of his final hours trying to pull the door open with his bare hands like a man possessed. His fingers were just raw stubs of meat. It must have seemed a lifetime in there.'

'He earned every second.'

'I couldn't agree more.' After a short silence, he said, 'I had an interesting chat with Gary at Air Traffic Control as well.'

'I can imagine.'

'Yes, you probably can. I've since changed the combination to my vault, although I'm sure Randall would want you to keep the stamp album as a memento. I must admit it puzzled me when he originally asked me to safeguard what seemed to be an essentially worthless stamp collection. I immediately forgot all about it until the moment I realized it was the only item missing. So would I be correct in assuming it somehow led you to the file itself?'

'Yeah, you would.' Keeping his gaze on the pitch ahead, Bishop said, 'You ever leave a man behind, Colonel?'

'Not once.'

'So I'm the first.'

Royse sighed. 'I'm not infallible, Bishop, although many people seem to think otherwise. After you'd been sentenced I admit doubts crept in. I researched your life and the circumstantial evidence didn't fit with what I read. I kept a close eye on you at Greenacres after that and as soon as I heard of the lawsuit you instigated I lent my weight to the proceedings. Didn't you ever wonder why the case ended so quickly in your favour?'

'It crossed my mind once or twice.'

'I knew you must have had a reason other than a concern for your fellow prisoners' welfare and escape seemed the likeliest bet. I very much wanted to see what you'd do once you reached the outside world and you didn't disappoint. Just the opposite, in fact.'

'I had help.'

'Jenna Falstaff,' Royse said, nodding. 'A most impressive woman by all accounts, but then I'm sure you already know that.'

Bishop shrugged. 'I haven't tasted her chili yet.'

The LA Galaxy players began running out onto the pitch for the second half, clearly anxious for their hosts to join them. Spectators around the stadium were returning to their seats, the home crowd still bubbling with optimism at the Bulls' eight-match unbeaten run up to this point.

As Royse watched them he said, 'I'm still waiting for the question.'

'You mean the *why*?' When Royse nodded, Bishop said, 'Because Natalie was Brennan's daughter in name only.'

Royse closed his eyes and started tapping his feet against the ground. 'Yes.'

'It's the only answer that makes sense. It explains why he was so distant from her, why you both parted company not long after setting up RoyseCorp, and why you wanted the real killer found once you crossed me off the list.'

Just then, the Bulls jogged out onto the pitch to a roar of approval from the faithful, warming up as they assumed their position on the right end of the field.

Royse opened his eyes at the noise and said, 'Alicia bore us each a child while she was married to Randall. He never knew for sure and Alicia's power over him was such that he feared to probe further, but I think he knew instinctively Natalie wasn't his. For a start, she looked nothing like him and he wasn't a stupid man.'

And of course, if Brennan knew Natalie *wasn't* his biological daughter, it opened up the possibility that Cortiss's theory had been correct regarding their sexual history. But Bishop saw no advantage in mentioning this. Let the girl rest in peace. Bishop waited as the referee blew the whistle and the game started afresh. Then he said, 'I do have another question for you.'

'Yes?'

'Why are you here?'

Royse smiled for the first time and said, 'Marcus.'

Bishop turned at movement to his right. The quiet, nondescript man in the next seat along was holding a business card between his fingers. Bishop took it. It was for something called the Equal Aid Relief Organization. The logo showed two hands shaking and there was a toll-free number. That was all. On the back, there was another number scrawled in ballpoint. Bishop turned to Royse and waited for the rest.

'It may surprise you to learn that even I have a conscience,' Royse said, 'although it took the death of my daughter to bring it to the surface.' He jutted his chin at the business card. 'It's a non-profit enterprise I set up two and a half years ago to provide financial aid for people with certain problems. People who have gone through the proper channels without success and are unable to afford professional help.'

Bishop tapped the card against his knee. 'What kinds of problems?'

'The kind you're used to. Usually involving violence of some sort, or at least the threat of it. You and I both know the law's limitations in such cases, so Equal Aid gives them enough to relocate and escape their particular predicament if that's what's needed. However, there are occasions when a victim needs more than financial assistance.'

Bishop stared at him. 'You're kidding, right? You hang me out to dry and now you want me to work for you again? You got balls, I'll give you that.'

Royse lowered his eyes and said, 'It wouldn't be like that. Believe me, you'd be entirely independent. A man named Giordano makes the decisions and he's never met me. I provide finance from a distance, but other than recommending you I have nothing to do with the running of it. I've also provided him with a sizeable budget for outside referrals, such as yourself. That's his number on the back. You should call him. He's waiting and I'm sure he could tell you more than I can.'

Bishop turned his attention back to the field. He was tired of talking. And tired of listening. 'I'll think about it,' he said in a flat tone. 'Better warn him not to hold his breath.'

'Very well,' Royse said and got up from his seat. 'I'll warn him.' Marcus and the rest of the close protection team – one in the row ahead, one at Royse's left and two more in the row behind – immediately stood up, too.

Royse looked down at Bishop and said, 'I hope you make the right choice, Sergeant.' Then he turned and began walking towards the aisle fifteen feet away, surrounded at all times by his ten-legged shield.

Bishop watched them leave, then glanced down at the card again before dropping it into his shirt pocket. He'd think about it later. Maybe. Although the thought of having anything to do with Royse again left him cold. But right now there was a game on. He'd paid good money and waited a long time for this.

Leaning back in his seat, he watched as the visitors' number ten, a past-his-prime player from England called Jameson Wright, volleyed a through-ball from the centre line to the team's number nine running down the left flank. Wright kept running towards the goal mouth to await a cross. In it came, just as the Bulls' defender carelessly dived in and took the legs out from under the winger. The referee didn't blow for a foul and Wright leapt up past his two markers and twisted his head as the ball made contact, directing it past the goalkeeper's hands with the force of a bullet until it poked out the back of the net.

Five thousand voices screamed their delight as Wright was instantly smothered by his team-mates in front of goal. The home crowd showed their disapproval by remaining silent, some so annoyed they actually looked to be leaving their seats with most of the half still to go.

Bishop frowned and wondered how anyone could give up before the final whistle. There was still time yet. Lots of time.

Almost anything could happen.

Meet James Bishop again in

# BACKTRACK

Coming soon in 2013

# ONE

James Bishop put on his sunglasses and got out of the silver Toyota Camry. He didn't say anything to the driver. There was no need. He shut the door, adjusted his leather jacket and looked down at his watch. 09.12. He turned and headed north along Main Street at a steady stroll. Neither fast nor slow. As though he had some specific destination in mind, but wasn't in any rush to get there.

Which was true enough to a point.

It was a warm Tuesday. Warm for early May, anyway. The sun was out, but there was also a cool breeze to take the edge off. Good spring weather. Even better when you were experiencing it outside of a prison cell. Almost nine months since Bishop had gotten out and the novelty of walking around in fresh, pristine air still hadn't entirely worn off.

Parked vehicles already lined both sides of the street, but Bishop saw little actual traffic. Scratching his beard, he looked around as he walked and counted six other pedestrians. The town of Louisford, Eastern Pennsylvania, was still in the process of waking up. Most of the stores were either still closed or just opening. That was one of the things Bishop liked about small towns. That casual indifference towards scheduled hours.

But there were also plenty of places that opened on time, day in, day out. Banks. Post offices. Franchise stores. Especially the franchise stores. They took customer care a little more seriously. Like the small Starbucks over there. Bishop could already see a queue of people inside, waiting at the cash register for their morning caffeine fix.

But it was a franchise of a different kind that Bishop was heading towards. The one situated at the end of the street about two hundred yards away.

Bishop saw an elderly local coming his way, led by a black Labrador on a leash. The guy nodded a good morning to Bishop, who smiled and nodded back. Once they'd passed each other, Bishop immediately lost the smile and carried on walking until he reached his destination seventy-two seconds later.

The check-cashing store was one of hundreds operating under the Standard Star umbrella. Most offered cash advances too, but Bishop knew Pennsylvania was one of fifteen states that had either outlawed payday loans or capped the excessive interest rates to such an extent that there was no profit in it. Which probably made the banks happy, at least.

Bishop stood looking through the windows for two seconds before turning back to the street. Long enough for the interior to be imprinted on his mind in every detail.

It was still the same.

This branch had a row of four partitioned counters behind bullet-resistant glass and an ATM near the entrance. In the ceiling, closed circuit cameras covered each counter. A pair of customers – a bald, middle-aged guy and a young, blonde woman – were being served at two of the counters. Following a rash of check-cashing store robberies over the past six months, the owners had obviously felt the need for a uniformed security guard too. He'd been standing next to the ATM. Bishop figured late fifties. Overweight with a prominent potbelly. Probably a retired cop. Holstering an old service Walther 9mm and clearly bored beyond belief.

Bishop used a hand to brush his dark hair away from his eyes and checked the street. Empty of traffic now. He checked his watch again. 09.14. It was time to go to work.

He pocketed his sunglasses, pulled out a pair of thin leather gloves and slipped them on. As he reflected on how it had come down to this moment, he recalled a lesson that had been drilled into him more than once in the Marines: anybody's life can turn on a single event. It was true. He'd experienced one of those events already, and wondered if he was about to again. If he did, he'd have nobody to blame but himself.

*Well, too late to worry about it now. Besides, I've got no other choice.*

Then he walked over to the entrance, pulled the door open and stepped inside.

# TWO

Bishop paused just inside the door. The guard watched him and gave a welcoming nod. *Public relations at work. You can wear a gun, but be nice to potential customers or you're gone.*

Bishop walked over. He put a frown on his face as though he wanted to ask a question, but wasn't sure who to ask. The guard watched him approach. Once he'd closed the distance, Bishop turned so the cashiers couldn't see, leaned in and pulled the .357 Smith & Wesson from his waistband. Jamming the five-inch barrel into the guard's ample mid-section, he said, 'You know what this is, so don't do anything dumb. They don't pay you enough.' At the same time, he used his right hand to unlatch the guard's holster and pull out the Walther.

'Hey,' the guard said, wheezing. 'Are you crazy? You can't do this.'

'I am doing it,' Bishop said, sliding the magazine out one-handed and stuffing it in his pants pocket. He also ejected the chambered round and saw it drop to the carpeted floor. 'Relax and keep your voice down. A couple of minutes from now, this'll all be over.' After checking to make sure the guard carried no extra ammo, he placed the Walther back in the guy's holster and said, 'What's your name?'

'My name?'

'Yeah, your first name. What is it?'

The guard looked at him like he'd lost his mind, but Bishop noticed he'd stopped wheezing. 'Randolph,' he said.

'Is that Randolph or Randy?'

'It's Randy to my friends. To jerks like you, it's like Randolph.'

Bishop smiled. 'Okay, Randolph. Now, I figure you're the one holds the keys to the front door, right?' Bishop already knew this was so, but wanted Randolph to get in the habit of answering his questions. Simple psychology, but it made things easier in the long run.

'Yeah.'

'Good. What say we go over and lock it so nobody else walks in? Right now.'

Still keeping his back to the cashiers, Bishop slowly walked with Randolph to the entrance and watched him pull a keychain from his utility belt. He selected a key, inserted it into the lock and turned it a hundred and eighty degrees clockwise. 'It's locked,' he said.

'Not that I don't believe you,' Bishop said, 'but try pushing the door for me.'

Randolph pressed a hand against the frame. The door didn't move.

'Good,' Bishop said. He took the keys from the guard's hand while he studied the street outside. Still empty except for the occasional vehicle passing by. 'Okay, Randolph. Let's go over to the counters now.'

Randolph turned and Bishop stayed at his back as they walked towards the rear of the store. Bishop quickly stooped down to pick up the extra round he'd dropped as he passed. He didn't want Randolph getting any ideas. When they were a couple of feet away from the counters, Bishop said, 'Walk over to the first counter and just stand there.'

He waited as Randolph did as he was told, watching the two cashiers' faces. The woman serving the bald guy was the first to notice something was wrong. The eyes behind her glasses grew wide when she saw Bishop. She said something to her male colleague, who was in conversation with the woman customer. The man immediately stopped talking and stared at Bishop with his mouth open.

'Okay, everybody,' Bishop said. 'Hands where I can see them. I'm here for the company's money, not yours. So no heroics.'

The two customers jumped at his voice and turned round. The blonde woman saw the cannon in his hand and took a sharp intake of breath. The bald guy said, 'What? Hey, wait a minute. I ain't even . . .'

'Everybody relax,' Bishop said, cutting him off. 'This'll soon be over and then you can all go back to your normal lives. But right now, I want you and you,' he pointed the gun briefly at the two customers, 'to stand over there with Randolph and just be quiet. I'm calm right now, but if you play up I'll get angry and you really don't want that. And keep your cell phones in your pockets. They make me angry, too.'

Bishop watched the woman nudge the man. Then they both shuffled to the left and stood next to Randolph a few feet away.

'Don't worry,' Randolph said. 'Everything'll be fine. Just do what he says.'

The bald guy snorted and just looked at him. 'You kidding me?'

'No, he's not,' Bishop said. 'Now shut up.'

He stepped forward and faced the male cashier at the third window. Placing the revolver in plain sight on the counter, he glanced at his name badge and said, 'You stay right there, John. Don't move.' He turned to the bespectacled woman, checked her name and said, 'Leanne, I want every note in the place except singles. You'll place them in a bag fast as you can and when you're done you'll pass it through to me. Got that?'

Neither cashier moved. Neither of them said anything. Bishop knew they probably felt safe as houses behind the thick wall of glass. And that the only reason they weren't running out the back was because of the two customers on this side. He also knew one of them had already triggered a silent alarm somewhere, but he'd already planned for that.

Bishop tapped the gun barrel against the glass. 'Leanne, the only thing separating us right now is a three-quarter-inch thick layer of polycarbonate. You know why they call this glass bullet-resistant and not bullet-proof?'

Leanne's eyes were orbs. She swallowed and gave a small shake of her head.

'It's because they don't want to get sued for false advertising.' He tapped the glass with the barrel again. 'And this is a .357 Magnum loaded with light grain, one hundred and twenty-five-gram hollow-points. The main advantage of using a light-grain round is that it travels a lot faster than a normal bullet. Fast enough to zip right through this glass like it was rice paper. I've seen it happen. Which means there really isn't anything separating us at all. Randolph, I'm guessing you were a cop once. Convince Leanne I'm not making this up. I don't want to have to give John here an extra eye to prove my point.'

Randolph said, 'He's not making it up. Get the money.'

Neither cashier moved. They were probably still in shock. Bishop needed to get things moving. He tapped the barrel against the glass again. 'Three,' he said.

He paused. Tapped again. 'Two.'

Pause. Tap. 'One.'

John suddenly came out of his trance and said, 'No, wait. Please.' He turned to Leanne. 'Quick. Get him the money.'

Bishop watched Leanne jump off her stool and look around the room.

Then she knelt down and picked a small canvas sack off the floor. Then she started rummaging around under the counter and sorting through notes.

'When you finish here, Leanne, don't forget to get the rest from the manager's office out back. I'm sure he'll help once you fill him in.'

Leanne nodded as she worked and Bishop turned to look at the three people in the corner. He ignored their stares and checked his watch as it changed to 09.18. Then he heard the sound of sirens. Two vehicles, it sounded like. And not far away. Maybe three or four blocks at most.

'Faster, Leanne,' he said, and then heard the sound of a horn out front. He turned and saw the silver Toyota right outside where it was supposed to be, Sayles behind the wheel looking back at him, moving his head back and forth like a rooster. As the sirens got louder, Sayles beeped the horn once more. He looked at Bishop for a long moment. Then he shook his head, revved the engine and just took off.

Without expression, Bishop watched him disappear. He allowed a long breath to escape from his lips.

The sirens were getting much louder now. Probably already at the next block. Looked like from here on in, he was on his own. Bishop stared at a spot on the floor for a moment and then at the three people in the corner.

Well, not alone, exactly.

He focused on the woman. Early twenties. Very pretty, if pale. Five-six, slim, with straight blond hair down to her shoulders and large blue eyes. Wearing a long-sleeved baseball shirt and jeans. Gold band on the third finger of her left hand.

She must have felt his gaze on her. She turned her face from the direction of the sirens and stared at him. Bishop thought she looked plenty scared.

'What's your name?' he asked.

She paused. Swallowed. 'Sonja Addison.'

Bishop heard the screeching of tires in the street outside and then the sirens cut out entirely. He turned and saw flashing red lights in the reflections of the stores opposite, but that was all. Turning back to the girl, Bishop reached into his back pocket. He pulled out a set of nylon flex cuffs and said, 'Okay, Sonja. Step over here.'